They were their mother's children — passionate, willful, strong...

Aaron — The Eldest. The successful attorney. Riddled with the unrelenting grief of past tragedy, he finds solace in the arms of a beautiful Hungarian physicist — and finds new life as he joins her heroic struggle for freedom.

Michael — A child of the sixties. He translates his civil rights beliefs into action in a Mississippi freedom school — and finds himself torn between the love of two courageous women.

Rebecca — The youngest. An artist like her mother. She gave up her life of luxury to become the wife of an Israeli freedom fighter. And as she is forced to confront her own conflicts and desires, she discovers how much she really is her mother's daughter.

These are the lives of Leah's children. Their determination and passion. Their destinies...

LEAH'S CHILDREN

Books by Gloria Goldreich

LEAH'S JOURNEY
THIS BURNING HARVEST
THIS PROMISED LAND
LEAH'S CHILDREN

LEAH'S CHILDREN

GLORIA GOLDREICH

A JOVE BOOK

Grateful acknowledgment is made to Harper & Row, Publishers, Inc., for permission to reprint a line from "Howl!" by Allen Ginsberg, on page 156.

This Jove book contains the complete text of the original hardcover edition.

LEAH'S CHILDREN

A Jove Book / published by arrangement with Macmillan Publishing Company

PRINTING HISTORY
Macmillan Publishing Company edition published 1985
Jove edition / June 1986

For information address: Macmillan Publishing Company, 866 Third Avenue, New York, N.Y. 10022

ISBN: 0-515-08584-7

Jove Books are published by The Berkley Publishing Group, 200 Madison Avenue, New York, N.Y. 10016.

PRINTED IN THE UNITED STATES OF AMERICA

For my sisters
Cherie Kaplan, Kayla Silberberg, Esther Diament
Buba Leah's granddaughters

CONTENTS

LEAH'S CHILDREN

PROLOGUE

New York, 1974

THE YELLOW POLICE BARRIERS had been set up in front of the Ellenberg Institute early that spring morning, but it was not until late afternoon, when the television crews arrived, that small crowds formed and the wondering whispering began. "Some kind of conference," someone suggested. It was not unusual for the Institute to host a meeting of policymakers and social thinkers. A small Chinese boy wearing a bright red windbreaker insisted shrilly that a sequence for a television show was to be filmed.

"Maybe *Kojak*," he said hopefully.

The crowd considered the possibility. It was not unlikely. The neighborhood was often the setting for films and documentaries. Paul Newman himself had raced down Eldridge Street pursued by a gleaming black Trans-Am sports car. Dan Rather had leaned against the mailbox on the corner of Avenue A and sipped coffee from a paper cup during the shooting of a documentary on drugs. The narrow streets of the Lower East Side, with their graffiti-splashed buildings, bustling street vendors, and crowded shops offering Chinese vegetables, sacred Jewish books, discounted designer clothing, and corner trade controlled substances, pulsed with excitement and life. Producers and directors were drawn to the neighborhood, and oddly enough, the presence of the cameras and sound equipment seemed to soothe the junkies and the hoodlums. Films shot on the Lower East Side were usually completed on schedule.

"It's not a movie," a young mother said as she lifted her small daughter so that she could see the two mobile cameras, one labeled *ABC* and the other *NBC*, as they were wheeled up the ramps usually used by wheelchairs and baby carriages. "If it was a movie, *she* wouldn't be here."

She pointed to Kathryn Conyers, the anchorwoman, who stepped carefully down from the ABC van and walked briskly toward the white brick building. The Ellenberg Institute was a neighborhood phenomenon—during the five years of its existence no graffiti had defaced its tempting surface, and although the front doors were fashioned of glass and the rooms inside were girdled with wide windows, not a single pane had ever been shattered. The drug pushers and their clients, by tacit agreement, stayed clear of the Institute, and the homeless, who slept in the doorway, always left before dawn, carrying away with them the sad debris of their wandering lives.

Kathryn Conyers paused at the entrance of the building and read the simple bronze plaque. She turned and studied the crowd with the detached concentration of a surgeon preparing to operate. These people were the subjects of her cinematic scalpel. She would instruct the cameraman to pan from the milling crowd to the sober, sedate gathering that would assemble in the Institute auditorium. The street people stared back at her with a commingling of curiosity and hostility. She saw them, they knew, not as individuals but as the poor and the dispossessed, alien outsiders who conveniently provided the background for a good news story, a colorful show.

Briefly, the young mother, whose child had begun to whimper, resented the newscaster for her carefully combed and lacquered cap of dark hair, for her well-cut navy-blue suit and shapely legs, and for the calculating coldness of her gaze. But she would watch her program that night, after returning from her design class, and tell her husband, who would not care, how she had seen Kathryn Conyers walk up the steps of the Institute that afternoon.

"Don't cry," she said to her daughter. "Don't cry and I'll take you to the story hour at the Institute."

"There is no story hour today," a middle-aged Hispanic woman told her. "They said yesterday that all the Institute afternoon programs are canceled today because of the award."

"What award?" an old man asked querulously. He was stooped beneath the weight of books that he had planned to return to the Institute library. His eyes glittered with the irrational anger felt by the very old and the very young when their plans are interfered with.

"The Woman of Achievement Award. I heard it on television. They're giving it here today to Leah Goldfeder," the woman replied.

"Leah Goldfeder." The name traveled through the crowd, murmured with recognition, affection, repeated more loudly with admiration.

"Leah Goldfeder—you know, the artist who made that mural in the Institute auditorium."

"She comes sometimes still to teach a class. I seen her car."

"The judge's mother—yeah, I know who she is."

Some nodded vigorously, others shrugged. They knew her, they knew of her. She was not a celluloid personality to them. Some had watched as she painted the vast mural that spanned the eastern wall of the auditorium. The teenagers had vied for the privilege of holding the ladder steady as her brush flew to paint the windows of the tenements, the flapping laundry on the roofs, the small children concentrating on their street games.

"Hey, watch yourself, be careful," they had told each other roughly. They had feared for the safety of the aging woman in the bright purple smock who captured their world on the bright white walls. But the artist herself had not been fearful. She had hummed as she painted, and smiled at them, and occasionally she had sent out for Cokes and distributed Hershey bars—her children's favorite treats when they were younger.

"Aaron and Rebecca—my son and daughter—they would go to Librach's candy store after school. But I suppose Librach's is gone now," she had said musingly.

No one remembered anyone named Librach. The neighborhood had changed and was changing still, and it had taken them some minutes to establish that the Hernandez Bodega had once been a candy store where a man named Moshe Librach had mixed egg creams and sold chunk chocolate and candy bars. Still, some things had remained the same. They watched as she painted a woman standing at a window, staring wistfully down into the street. "That's Rosa Morales," someone said. "No. That's Lucy Chin." Many young women stood at tenement windows and looked yearningly down at the busy world below.

"Who is it, Mrs. Goldfeder?"

"It could be anyone," she had said softly. "It could be me."

The children had laughed. How could it be the artist? Her hair was white and she was old; the woman she had painted was young, and her long dark hair fell to her shoulders.

The mural had been completed, but Leah Goldfeder returned occasionally and held open studio classes. The young mother had attended a few sessions and watched the artist demonstrate brushwork techniques. Shyly she had offered her own portfolio for comment, and Leah Goldfeder had flipped through the drawings.

"You're talented," she had said at last. "But you need training. If you worked you could develop your talent—use it as a basis for a craft—perhaps fabric design. You have an eye—a good eye—and a flair."

"But how can I study?" The mother shifted her child from one arm to the other as though to demonstrate the reality of her encumbrance.

"I did it." The statement was matter-of-fact, unpitying, unrelenting.

"But I have the child." She would not mention her poverty to Leah Goldfeder, who fingered a necklace of pearls as she spoke.

"I had two small children. And I could barely speak English."

She had told the young woman then how she, a newly arrived immigrant, had taken art classes at the Irvington Settlement House. Charles Ferguson, who now owned a Madison Avenue gallery, had been her teacher. He had prodded and encouraged her, and she had worked and studied.

"Nothing happens by itself," she said. "Nothing happens unless you make it happen."

Her reply angered the young woman. Leah Goldfeder could talk. She had it made. A chauffeured car waited for her outside, and a diamond ring glittered on her finger. What did she know about stretching hamburger meat and waking up in the middle of the night in a cold apartment to comfort a crying child? Still, she had noticed that Leah Goldfeder's hands were work-roughened, and she had seen the flash of recognition in her eyes.

A week later she saw an ad for an evening course in design at Cooper Union. *Nothing happens unless you make it happen.* The remembered words spurred her to register. A small step, but she had taken it. If Leah Goldfeder had succeeded, she might have a chance—if she could get her head together, get her life together.

There were those in the crowd who had seen Leah Goldfeder when she visited the Institute with Joshua Ellenberg. Always, the elderly woman and the middle-aged man walked slowly down the corridors, glancing into rooms where classes and discussion groups were held. The work of the Institute was varied, almost eclectic. It offered classes and clinics, services for groups and for individuals. There were no rigid guidelines for Institute projects. It had been established, the directors of the Ellenberg Foundation patiently explained, for the betterment of the neighborhood where Mr. Ellenberg had grown up.

Leah Goldfeder and Joshua Ellenberg had once taken seats in the bright, airy day-care center and watched the resting children stir uneasily on their plastic kinder mats. Leah had whispered to him, and a week later small folding cots, easily stored in a corner, had been delivered. They had spent an afternoon in the library and listened to the volunteer librarian translate Help Wanted ads to an attentive Puerto Rican couple. The next day the library was authorized to subscribe to the daily Spanish and Chinese language newspapers.

"She sees everything," the librarian had observed wonderingly.

Leah Goldfeder's children were also familiar to neighborhood residents. Her son Aaron, the judge, got his picture in the paper often enough and there were those who remembered visiting the judge's office during a time of trouble. The other son, Michael, the college professor, lived in their midst, in the same house on Eldridge Street to which his parents had come as newly arrived immigrants from Russia. He gave lectures and ran a clinic for learning disabled children at the Institute. And the Goldfeder daughter, Rebecca—she lived far away but she, too, came to the Institute and had once given a joint session with her mother at the studio workshop. She also was an artist, but her work was very different from Leah's. Leah always worked in oils, but Rebecca experimented with medium and style, sometimes working in pastels and then dashing off graceful pen-and-ink drawings. The neighbors were prepared to concede that Rebecca was a fine artist, but nothing, they agreed, could compare with Leah's mural. She had captured their world and touched their hearts.

Suddenly, a new excitement swept the crowd. Two police department motorcycles careened down the street, their sirens screaming.

"The mayor's coming," someone yelled.

"You're kidding!"

"Oh yeah? Wait till you see him."

"I heard on the radio that the governor was coming also—or maybe it was a senator."

A cordon of police officers stood behind the barriers now, tall, smiling men who did not touch their nightsticks. They did not expect any trouble here this afternoon—not for an occasion like this and not for someone like Leah Goldfeder. They were there purely for crowd control. They grinned at the Chinese kids who came too close to the barrier and stood on tiptoe to read their badge numbers. They frowned at the overweight, dead-eyed Moonies who milled around selling flowers and fingering the municipal licenses pinned to their jackets. The young mother bought a bunch of daffodils, digging the money out of a tattered wallet. It was her milk money, but some days flowers were more important than milk.

A long, gray limousine pulled up, and Joshua Ellenberg and his family stepped out. The crowd cheered, and Joshua raised his black leather prosthetic hand in acknowledgment and flashed his familiar smile. Everyone knew the Ellenberg myth. His picture had even appeared on the cover of *Time* magazine. "A Jewish Horatio Alger," the caption read, "the man who turned rags into riches." They knew that he had grown up in the Eldridge Street apartment that his family had shared with the Goldfeders. He had been a peddler as a child, collecting fabric scraps from one sweatshop and selling them to another. He had gone off to fight in World War II, and a German bullet had smashed his hand on a French battlefield. He had returned to start a small business, which mushroomed into Ellenberg Industries, but he had never forgotten the neighborhood of his boyhood nor his allegiance to Leah Goldfeder and her family.

His wife was beautiful, the women agreed as Sherry Ellenberg hurried into the building, followed by the children. It was a shame about their daughter, though. "What happened to their daughter?" someone asked, but no one offered an answer.

Joshua Ellenberg, too, paused at the bronze tablet and briefly, gently, touched his fingers to the raised lettering. The crowd was silent. They all knew the legend on the tablet and why that particular plot of land, empty and weed-clogged for so many years, had been chosen as the site of the Ellenberg Institute.

Now the limousines arrived in rapid succession. The mayor and his entourage flashed obligatory smiles and hurried inside, glancing nervously at their watches. Andy Warhol came with Charles Ferguson, the gallery owner, who looked wistfully across the street to the Irvington Settlement House. He had taught painting classes there, and Leah Goldfeder had been his student. Now the building was a methadone center plastered with posters in Chinese and Spanish. The Lower East Side had changed since the days he had wandered it as a young man, sketching the new arrivals from eastern Europe, the bearded men, their bewigged wives, and the wide-eyed children who trailed behind them.

A steady parade of newcomers hurried into the building. State senators, the chairman of the President's Commission on Women's Rights, the youthful president of Columbia University. The entire ensemble of the Dance Theatre of Harlem emerged with heart-stopping grace from a sleek blue-and-silver minibus. Leah Goldfeder had painted the poster for their successful fund-raising effort; Joshua Ellenberg had underwritten their international tour.

"There's her son, the judge," someone shouted, and a small burst of applause greeted Aaron Goldfeder and his family.

Aaron waved, his cheeks burning with the fiery blush characteristic of redheads, although his hair was silver now and only his shaggy brows were copper-colored. Aaron's oldest daughter reminded some of the elderly retired garment workers in the crowd of Leah Goldfeder as a young woman. She had worked to organize a union in her own shop—the Rosenblatt Shirt Factory, and they still remembered that Friday afternoon when a fire had destroyed that factory. The old man, who stood clutching his books, had been a young pants presser then, and he had stood almost on the exact spot where he waited now, and had watched the young Leah, poised on a window ledge, her white blouse streaked with soot, her dark skirt scorched at the hem by the flames that leaped about her feet. She had jumped at last, and he had wept when she plunged to safety.

The judge's daughter walked with her grandmother Leah's grace and smiled her brilliant smile. She had inherited the family height, and someone said that she was a student at Harvard. The crowd marveled at that—the magic of America. Her grandfather, David Goldfeder, after all, had been a factory worker who had studied on the subway as he traveled to evening classes at the City College of New York. And now his granddaughter went to Harvard and one son was a judge and the other a college professor.

Michael Goldfeder and his family arrived next, and Leah's younger son squinted at the crowd with a scholar's myopia. His wife walked beside their children—startlingly beautiful youngsters, dusky-skinned and dark-eyed, with fanciful foreign names. Michael was the only one of the three Goldfeder children who had not grown up on the Lower East Side. He had been born when Leah's husband, David, had already completed medical school and qualified as a psychiatrist. Yet it was Michael who had chosen to live in the neighborhood. He had renovated the building to which his father had brought the pregnant Leah when they arrived from Europe. Aaron Goldfeder had been born in the room where Michael's own children slept, and Leah, when she visited, always avoided that room, as though she were haunted still by the conflict of that pregnancy, the violence of that birth.

Michael, too, glanced at the building's plaque as he entered, and a barely discernible shadow crossed his face.

"There she is! That's Leah Goldfeder!"

Excitement swept the crowd as the familiar black Lincoln Continental pulled up. The first to descend was a graceful woman in a bright red suit whose long dark hair, silver-streaked and curling, was coiled into a thick chignon. That was Rebecca, Leah's daughter. Wasn't she the one who had gone to Europe after the war and been involved in smuggling Jewish children into Palestine? They searched their memories but could not be certain. She was an artist, though—she had inherited her mother's talent, her mother's courage.

A tall man with iron-gray hair followed her—her husband, it was supposed, although no one knew his name—and then two boys who turned their faces away from the curiosity of the crowd and bent forward to assist the elderly woman who slowly eased her way out of the car.

Leah Goldfeder stood erect in the bright sunlight and smiled to acknowledge the spontaneous burst of applause that greeted her. Although the afternoon was warm, she wore a turquoise silk cape over the simple white wool dress, woven through with silver, that exactly matched her hair, which was plaited into an intricate coronet. Her weathered skin had a topaz glow, but the lines of age and loss were cruelly carved across her even-featured face. Still, a half dimple danced at the corner of her generous mouth, and golden shadows glinted in her large dark eyes. Her grandsons stood beside her, but although she smiled at them, she walked forward alone with a graceful dignity, slow-stepped but steady. As she passed the police barrier, the young mother, clutching her child, rushed forward and offered her the cluster of daffodils.

"How lovely," Leah said in the musical voice that still retained the trace of an accent. She accepted the sun-colored bouquet, removed a single flower, and gave it to the crying child, who pressed it to her tear-stained cheek and was quiet.

Leah studied the younger woman's face.

"You look so familiar."

"We spoke once." The reply was cautious, shy. Leah Goldfeder would not remember her.

"It will come to me." The sadness and courage in the young mother's face teased her memory. She balanced her child with tender strength, and Leah thought of herself, so many years ago, lifting the child Rebecca and straining to see the pastel streaks of an urban sunset. She smiled and the young woman smiled back. Again, recognition flashed between them.

She paused at the entry to the Institute and selected another daffodil. She placed the golden flower on the edge of the bronze plaque, with the care of a graveside mourner balancing a small stone on a slender marker. Only then did she hold her hands out to her grandsons and allow them to escort her into the building and down the blue-carpeted aisle of the auditorium. Thunderous applause swelled as the audience rose to cheer her in her slow walk to the stage.

The mayor was the keynote speaker. Briefly, he outlined the history of the Woman of Achievement Award, which was jointly sponsored by the municipality, the American Association of University Women, and the President's Commission on Women.

"This is one of the highest honors that can be paid to a woman in the United States," he said, and his eyes rested on the silver-haired woman who sat, tall and attentive, in the blue leather armchair. It occurred to him that he had not yet been born when Leah Goldfeder reached the shores of the great city that he now governed. Still, he came from a union family, and she had been part of the mythology of his boyhood. His mother and his aunt had worked as finishers at the Rosenblatt Shirt Factory, and once a year, on the anniversary of the fire, they journeyed to the cemetery in Queens and visited the graves of the girls who had not survived the fire. Always, they told him, they had met Leah Goldfeder there, sometimes alone, sometimes with her husband, David.

"It's like her to remember the dead," his aunt had said.

"And it's like her to care for the living," his mother had added.

The mayor's mother had died five years ago, and he winced now at the knowledge that he had visited her grave only once in all that time. Quite suddenly, he departed from his text and spoke of himself as a small boy, listening to the stories of Leah Goldfeder.

"I heard about her first as a woman of the people, a woman who honored the past and looked to the future. Later, I learned that she was a woman who could cause things to happen. During the war she mobilized the ready-to-wear industry and broke production records. She was responsible for the development of enterprises that provided jobs for thousands of citizens. Always, she remained first and foremost an artist." His eyes rested briefly on the mural, and then he continued. "She never considered it demeaning to use her art for the greater good of the world she lived in. She proved that a woman could be a loving wife, a nurturing mother, without abandoning personal fulfillment and communal responsibility. Her greatest achievement is the exciting life she has lived, which she continues to live with joy and dignity—a life that serves as example and inspiration."

Aaron Goldfeder was the next speaker: Judge Goldfeder, whose landmark decision on the rights of political refugees would soon be tested in the Supreme Court. He was familiar to most of the audience. He appeared regularly on public television panels, and although he spoke softly and slowly, viewers leaned forward to listen to him. Always his opinions were carefully considered and resonant with the authority of intellectual soundness and humane understanding. Now his voice was controlled, but those who sat in the front rows saw that his hands trembled and that his green eyes glinted with dangerous brilliance.

"I want to thank his honor, the mayor, for his tribute to my mother. I would like to take the liberty of adding to his remarks from a very personal perspective—that of a son, a firstborn child." He glanced at his mother, as though requesting her approval. She inclined her head, and he turned back to the audience, his voice imbued with a new strength.

"I ask you to think now, not of Leah Goldfeder, mother and grandmother, distinguished artist and designer. Rather, I ask you to think of a young Russian woman, a girl really, not yet out of her teens but already widowed and cruelly exposed to the brutality of irrational hatred. That girl, pregnant and married for a second time to a young man scarcely older than herself, undertook to cross a continent and an ocean, to begin a new life in a new land. A journey toward hope, an odyssey of optimism.

"She might have questioned that hope, that optimism, during her early years in this country—long, difficult years when my adoptive father, David Goldfeder, struggled as a sweatshop worker and our family shared a railroad flat on Eldridge Street with other immigrants as poor as ourselves. There are those who would romanticize poverty, but let us be honest. Poverty is interesting and dramatic only in retrospect, as the fodder of nostalgia. Poverty, in reality, is soul-destroying and, often, life-threatening. But Leah, my mother, would not allow it to destroy her soul, to threaten her life. She rose above it and seized control of her own destiny and the destiny of our family.

"She took my father's place in the sweatshop so that he could attend medical school and qualify as a psychiatrist. She studied design, and her talents became our salvation. She was, as the mayor said, a woman of the people who believed in social justice. She knew that hope must be coupled with perseverance, and she hoped and persevered and worked toward the formation of a labor union.

"That union was hard-won. Flames, blazing on this very spot, consumed the lives of those who fought for it, and my mother herself was saved by miraculous fortune." He paused. His voice broke and his eyes burned. Tears streaked Rebecca's cheeks, but Leah sat quietly, her face veiled in sadness. She had been saved by love, he knew. She had been saved because Eli Feinstein, with a lover's ruthlessness, had thrust her free of the flaming factory to the safety of the street below.

"I ask you to think of my mother," Aaron continued, "as a young woman who had at last savored some success, achieved some comfort. Still, she chose to leave the warmth of her home, her husband, and her children, in an effort to save the family she left behind in Europe. That effort was among her few failures. I never knew my grandparents. They are numbered in that grim census of the six million, and I do not know how or where they died. But I do know that I fought on their behalf, and my mother endured the uncertainty and the sorrow of that war without surrendering to despair.

"Leah and David Goldfeder fought their war in this country. He soothed the souls of the bereft, and she worked to clothe the warriors for freedom. Together they dreamed of peace, of our family safe and united. They could not have known how brief that peace would be for our people, or that the same irrational hatred that killed my natural father on an Odessa street would kill my adoptive father on a Negev kibbutz. Again, my mother was stricken with grief and loss, and again, she did not submit to despair." His voice was very low now, yet every word was clearly heard, and the audience did not stir when he wiped his eyes. There was dignity in his sorrow, and gentle acceptance. It occurred to some that he was his mother's son: he, too, would refuse to submit to despair.

Now his voice rose with new strength.

"I ask you, finally, to think of a mother who endowed her children with the greatest gift of all—the freedom to live their own lives, to forge their own destinies. My sister, my brother, and I myself—we three are heirs to a precious legacy, an inheritance of hope, a birthright of faith. We honor our mother, Leah Goldfeder, with our love, and we hope that our lives, our journeys, reflect her own."

There was a moment of silence, shattered by reverberant applause. The audience rose and continued to clap rhythmically, and the dignitaries on the stage also stood. Aaron, Michael, and Rebecca glanced at one another, and tears glinted in their eyes as remembered sorrow struggled with remembered joy. Aaron took Rebecca's hand, and she in turn reached for Michael's arm. Thus linked, they reclaimed their seats as their mother advanced to the podium. She turned first to them (always, they thought, she had turned first to them) and then to the audience. Her musical voice was very low, strained by emotion, weakened by age, but every word was clearly heard in that silent room.

"Your Honors"—she nodded to the mayor, to the state senators, and to the serious-eyed woman who was the president's personal representative—"my friends, and of course my children, I thank you for the honor that you pay me today. It is wonderful that we have gathered at the Ellenberg Institute, which my friend Joshua Ellenberg built as a gift of love to the community that nurtured him during his boyhood and that offered me and my family safe haven and opportunity during our early years in this great country. It is fitting that Joshua selected this site for a building that offers opportunity and promise to all who enter it. Perhaps you noticed the plaque on the entry; it is a memorial plaque for those who once came to this very location to earn their daily bread, for those whose lives were consumed in the flames that destroyed the building that once stood here—the Rosenblatt Shirt Factory."

The name stirred recognition in the audience. A susurrant murmur wafted through the auditorium, and then they were quiet again.

"That fire happened decades ago, but the creation of the Ellenberg Institute on this site proves that hope cannot be consumed, that creativity will fight destruction, that life will endure even where death has briefly triumphed. This belief has guided my own life. Through the darkness I looked toward light. During moments of despair I clutched at fragments of faith. Always, I sought to light my single candle."

She paused, and her children, hands still clasped, exchanged a secret glance. Was their mother remembering the war years when she had been consumed with worry about her parents in Europe, about Aaron, who had been taken prisoner in Ethiopia? Did she think of the risks Rebecca had confronted in Israel, of the dangerous roads Michael had traveled, of their father's tragic death? Aaron pressed Rebecca's fingers hard and teasingly; she scratched Michael's palm—the reassuring gestures of their childhood asserted themselves as they listened to their mother.

Leah turned to her sons and daughter. Her lined face was wreathed in the smile they knew so well. She was pleased because they were together and because their hands were linked in love. Her daughter's husband, her sons' wives, her grandchildren sat in the front row, their bright faces turned upward toward her. She trembled with gratitude for the gift of her long life, for generations spanned and generations promised.

"This is what I tried to teach my children," she continued. "To wrest hope from despair, to seize the moment, to recognize the strength of tenderness, the power of caring. I thank you for the award you give me today. I accept it on behalf of all those who know that flames leap skyward, yet are subdued, that although ashes cover dead land, green shoots press upward through scorched earth, and that a white building can rise on foundations of charred rubble. This I have learned from my life and from my children's lives. I thank you."

Again the audience rose, and now the applause was deafening. Men reached for their handkerchiefs and wept without embarrassment. Women turned to one another, muted secrets sealed in their eyes.

The ceremonies were concluded, and slowly the audience filed out of the white brick building, past the bronze plaque with its message of hope and survival, past the much-diminished crowd.

Leah Goldfeder remained on the stage in the cavernous room, her gnarled fingers caressing the golden medallion. The Ellenbergs and her own family clustered about her.

"You must be tired, Mama," Rebecca said.

"I'm tired. But they need some pictures for publicity still. And this reporter, Kathryn Conyers, wants a short interview—she's doing a story on the Institute, and it could be important for fund-raising—so a few more minutes. Could I say no?"

"We'll wait for you in the lounge, then."

The photographers' lights flashed. She followed their directions, leaning forward, settling back, turning her face in profile, smiling. They grinned at her, impressed by her composure, her quiescent compliance, and they thanked her with a gentleness atypical of their profession as they packed their equipment and left.

"I have only a few questions." Kathryn Conyers settled herself into the chair next to Leah's. She smiled with the radiant confidence of a woman who knows what she wants and is assured of getting it. The great statesmen of the world had been vulnerable to her smile, to her gentle, probing questions, her incisive conclusions.

"Mrs. Goldfeder, I came here today planning to do a brief spot on the Institute and on the Woman of Achievement Award. But I think there's a bigger story here—your story."

"I'm an old woman," Leah protested gently. "Old women don't have big stories."

"I don't mean a news story. Something more than that. I want to do a show on you and your children. You know, everyone is floundering for direction these days, yet you and your family steered a straight course. You seem to have always known exactly where you were going, and you were able to guide your children toward their own fulfillment. We'd like to share your secret compass with our viewers—do some in-depth interviews with your children." Kathryn Conyers's researchers had given her some background on the Goldfeder children. Aaron, the judge, had somehow been involved in the Hungarian revolution. Rebecca's name was recognized throughout the art world, and a profile on Michael Goldfeder, written at the time his sociological analysis of the sixties was published, recalled his own dramatic involvement in the civil rights movement.

"There is no secret compass, no blueprint." Leah's soft voice grew even fainter, as though drained by a sudden weariness. "Life happens to you. You start out with hope and dreams, with scraps of talent, shreds of ideas. David and I tried to give our children some direction, some impetus. We had known a great deal of sorrow before we came to America, and we spoke to our children about strength and belief, about courage and choice. But always we knew how chance balances choice. A man and a woman meet, and both their lives change. A child is born with a gift, a talent. There is possibility and promise, and then a car moves too swiftly down a city street, a man moves through the night toward an unfamiliar sound. In the space of a heartbeat, a life is changed. In all our lives—in all our journeys through the years—everything is possible and nothing is predictable. And my children's journeys were, perhaps, more unpredictable than most." In her mind's eye she saw Aaron walking alone down a Budapest street, Rebecca poised at her easel straining to capture a Negev sunset, Michael standing on the steps of a Mississippi courthouse. Such complicated journeys, undertaken without the aid of a steady compass, a reliable map.

Her voice had drifted into a dreamy whisper, and Kathryn Conyers understood that there would be no swift interview revealing the facile secret of parental success. The stories of Leah Goldfeder's children were entangled in memory and dream, in tales of summer days and autumn nights. They would not lend themselves to crisp, fast-paced cameo sequences, to the rapid crossfire of question and answer. She closed her notebook, picked up her tape recorder.

"Goodbye, Mrs. Goldfeder," she said. "I congratulate you and I thank you."

The newscaster left, but Leah sat on in the darkened auditorium. It was an old woman's prerogative, she thought, to sit quietly in the dim light of late afternoon, to unravel the skeins of memory and toy with discrete strands.

She looked at the mural, focusing on the portrait of the young woman at the tenement window. In the neighboring panel she had painted three children walking down a narrow street—two boys and a girl, moving through the sunlight beyond their mother's vigilant gaze.

How often she had watched her children move through shadow and light, together and alone. A sliver of memory pricked and teased; she saw her children's upturned faces brushed with amber light, heard her sons' deep voices, her daughter's gay young woman's laughter. Ah yes, she thought, untangling memories and grasping the moment at last—that first Labor Day party at the Ellenbergs', when they had laughed and talked beneath the loosely hung fairy lights. That night, after all, had marked a beginning, a new cycle of seasons in their lives.

Slowly, then, she went to join her children—Aaron, Rebecca, and Michael. She heard their soft voices, their children's laughter.

LABOR DAY

1956

LEAH GOLDFEDER stood at the window and studied the red-winged blackbird magically balanced on a slender branch of the maple tree that dominated her garden. Her first Labor Day without David, who always had a special fondness for the holiday that marked the end of summer. Still, she noted, with a pleasure that she had not thought to feel again, that the bird's scarlet flashings matched the tree's fiery crown of leaves. The brittle foliage, always the first to take on the bright mantle of autumn, rustled musically in a vagrant breeze, and a single leaf trembled and fell onto the thick green grass. She leaned forward, and her sudden movement frightened the blackbird. It soared southward, its brightly slatted wings scissoring their way through the azure summer sky.

The hallway clock tolled the hour with delicate chimes, and she turned from the window. Aaron and Michael would be arriving soon to take her to the Labor Day party at the Ellenbergs' Great Neck estate. Traditionally, the Goldfeders had hosted the festive reunion of family and friends that marked the changing season, but Leah had not protested when Sherry Ellenberg cautiously suggested that it be held at her home "this once." She had, in fact, been relieved. Her journey to Russia had exhausted her, and she was not yet ready to greet her guests alone in this garden, where once David's presence beside her had been so essential. She had known that it was best to have the party elsewhere, to mark a new beginning and acknowledge that there had been an ending.

Briskly, racing against a threatening melancholy, she went to her closet and selected a dress of topaz silk, shot through with intricate threads of silver that matched the moon-colored talons that wove their way through her long dark hair. She searched through her jewelry box for the smoky opal pendant and the small combs that matched it. She swept her hair back, sculpted the silvered plaits into a regal crest, and slid the combs into place. She studied herself in the long mirror and acknowledged with shy surprise, with an almost guilty pleasure, that her appearance pleased her. She felt a surge of excitement, of pleasurable anticipation.

It would be good to spend an evening with old friends, to laugh at mild jokes and stroll through Joshua's pleasant garden exchanging confidences with those who had shared her life. Tomorrow Michael would leave for Berkeley, but she would share this evening with her sons—a family together on this day when summer drifted into fall and leaves began to fall from laden trees. It was sad that Rebecca was so far away, but her last letter had hinted that she might be visiting New York very soon.

"Yehuda is involved in a project that may require a trip to New York," Rebecca had written guardedly. "Perhaps I will come with him."

Leah knew that Rebecca could not be more explicit. Her husband, Yehuda Arnon, was often called away from their desert kibbutz to undertake assignments abroad. Rebecca never described these "assignments," and her American family did not ask her questions.

Leah heard the car pull up and the front door open.

"Mom, are you almost ready? Joshua takes points off for lateness," Aaron called. Even in the brief, jocular admonition she discerned the melancholy in her son's voice. Sadness had adhered to Aaron since the death of his wife, Katie. He could not forget the fragile young woman whose life had ended beneath the wheels of a car. She had wasted her life and willed her death. Poor Katie, poor Aaron.

"I'll be right down," Leah replied and gathered up her gloves and evening bag. But before leaving the room, she went again to the window.

The flowers of early fall had blossomed and golden zinnias and tawny chrysanthemums blazed in bright profusion about the privet hedges. They were neighbored by the last of the roses, full-petaled in delicate tones of white and pink, breathing out their poignant, desperate fragrance. The seasons merged; endings and beginnings met in mysterious convection. Autumnal evening winds swept away the lingering warmth of the summer afternoon.

"Mom!" It was Michael who called her now, his voice as brash with impatience as once her own had been when she had called him in from play. So swiftly did the years pass and roles reverse themselves.

"I'm coming," she said again and descended the stairwell.

Her sons, lean and tanned in their dark blazers and pale linen slacks, looked up at her, and briefly, magically, she saw their fathers in the eyes that met her own—Yaakov, the husband of her girlhood, killed in an Odessa pogrom, in the emerald glint of Aaron's moody stare, and David, her life's partner, in the gold-flecked gray of Michael's gaze. A wave of loneliness swept over her, and she gripped the newel post with whitened knuckles, but when she spoke to her tall sons, her voice was, as ever, steady and controlled.

"I'm lucky to have such handsome escorts," she said.

"You look beautiful," Aaron said softly. He and Michael exchanged a swift, conspiratorial glance. They shared a secret and the temptation to reveal it to Leah was overwhelming, but they had pledged their silence and so they said nothing. They smiled in anticipation of the pleasure their complicity would bring their mother in only a few hours' time.

THE STONE WALL that rimmed Joshua Ellenberg's Great Neck estate was strung with glimmering lights that cast their drifting pastel hues across the dark-leafed trees and thick-boughed firs. Rainbowed prisms danced across the clear blue waters of the kidney-shaped inground pool. The bar had been set up near the cabana, and small white tables and chairs rimmed the pool. Uniformed maids circled the tiled area and offered the guests tiny frankfurters rolled into golden crusty blankets of dough, miniature knishes, small balls of gefilte fish balanced on brightly colored plastic toothpicks. Leah smiled as she dipped her fish into the sparkling red horseradish. Joshua might disguise the cuisine of his childhood, but he remained faithful to it.

"Exactly the sort of food Sarah used to cook," she said to Anna Ellenberg, Joshua's aunt, who sat beside her.

"What Sarah cooked you could see," Anna replied. "For this food you need a magnifying glass." Sarah Ellenberg, Joshua's mother, had died a year ago, and Anna kept house for her brother now, in the Brighton Beach red-brick house where the Goldfeders had lived after their move from Eldridge Street.

She shifted her bulk in the small white lawn chair and twirled a frankfurter around disconsolately. The green-and-white print dress her niece had ordered specially from Bergdorf's strained against her ample bosom, and her thin gray hair had straggled free of the beauty parlor's hair spray and hung in loose wisps about her florid face.

"I would have cooked for tonight," she said sadly, "but Joshua won't let me put a hand in cold water. 'Why should my aunt work when I can afford a caterer?' he says. He doesn't think that maybe I want to cook, that I enjoy it. *Ach*, children, do they ever know what we want?" She sighed heavily, and Leah touched her work-reddened hands in sympathy. Anna's fingers shook lightly, and she forced them into a fist as she struggled for control against the parkinsonian tremor.

And what do we want from the children? Leah wondered silently and leaned back because she knew the answer to her own question. She wanted them to be settled, to steer their lives according to a charted course; she wished them to be happy in their work, serene in their homes. But Michael was vague about a possible profession. The next day he would leave for Berkeley. She was skeptical about his plans for graduate work in sociology.

"Why sociology?" she had asked in the car as they sped toward Great Neck. Michael had explained before, but now, on the eve of his departure, she asked the question yet again, as though anticipating a different answer.

"I thought about different social patterns while I toured Israel. The collective. The kibbutz. The different ways we can live in the world. I want to understand more about people and how they manage their lives. I guess it sounds sophomoric, but more than anything else, especially since Dad died, I want to understand how we can change things, make them better."

"It doesn't sound silly," Leah had replied gently. He was David Goldfeder's son, and David Goldfeder had become a psychiatrist because he thought he might discover the origin of the bacillus of evil that had driven men to the excesses of hate he had witnessed during the pogroms of his young manhood in Russia. Michael, too, was a searcher after clues, a kindler of small candles that flickered valiantly against the encroaching darkness.

"And why Berkeley?" she had asked.

"I've never been to California," he had replied, apology and defense vying in his voice. She had understood then. California because it was so far away, across mountains and desert, at the edge of a sea she had never seen, distant from her and the life he had known. She, who had left her parents' village and traveled by herself to Odessa, understood that there came a time when children had to leave their parents, when distances had to be traversed and new pathways forged. It was Michael's turn now, to journey toward himself.

She watched him as he leaned languidly against the white-columned portico and chatted with a slender blond girl who kept her eyes fixed on Michael's face while her fingers toyed with the "Stevenson for President" button she wore on the collar of her pale blue button-down blouse.

"Leah!" Charles Ferguson strode toward her, his arms outstretched. "I've tried to call you but always missed you. I want to hear about your trip to Russia."

Her former art teacher would not ask about David's death, she knew, and she was grateful to him. He had written a tender letter of sympathy, but like many artists, committed to capturing life and movement in sketchbook and on canvas, he was uncomfortable confronting death and stillness.

He sat down beside her and, cocooned in the intimate, sharing silence of old friends, they watched as the long shadows of evening darkened the turquoise water of the swimming pool. Across the lawn, Lisa Ellenberg and a friend played badminton in the waning light. The girls' short felt skirts swirled about their bright bare thighs, and they pummeled the feathered bird as though fending off night itself. On the terrace a phonograph softly played "Que Sera, Sera." The languid song of a generation at peace, the accepting ballad of a country that believed its battles were over. World War II was in the past, and the Korean War was done with. The general who had engineered D day no longer wore a uniform. He sat in the White House, smiling benignly at his people, innocent Mamie in bangs at his side. And his people, in turn, whizzed down newly paved interstate highways in their pastel-colored large-finned cars. They rushed to lay claim to homes in new suburban developments. They filled their oversized trunks with shopping bags and cartons, television sets and Mixmasters, grills to be used on their flagstone patios, and portable radios to broadcast the happy music of peace and prosperity in finished basements painted to resemble knotty pine.

Joshua Ellenberg stood at the bar with Aaron and Michael.

"You didn't tell her, did you?" he asked.

"Held ourselves back," Aaron replied.

"Good. The car just left the airport. They'll be here in less than an hour."

The three men grinned at each other. Leah had prepared surprises for them during their childhoods. Joshua remembered still that the only birthday party he had ever had, Leah had made for him. A surprise party to which each of their Eldridge Street boarders had brought a small gift—a ball laboriously fashioned of rubber bands, a leather-bound account book, his first fountain pen. Rebecca had knitted a scarf for him, of bright yellow wool. Faded and frayed, he had it still and kept it in a secret corner of his armoire. It was his turn now, he thought, to startle Leah with joy, to confound her with pleasure.

The maids carried lamps over to the large buffet table and flooded it with light. The snowy white cloth was covered with platters laden with chicken and roast beef, bowls of potato salad and cole slaw, intricately cut sour pickles and tomatoes, bright red peppers and golden clusters of pickled cauliflower. Leah thought of the meal she had shared with Jewish activists on her last evening in Russia. Slices of cheese and hard-boiled eggs. Yellowing scraps of lettuce and pale slivers of tomato, all obtained after standing on food queues for hours. How could she explain the austerity of Russia, its stoic sadness, its wintry desperation, to these American friends and relations who surrounded her? They were so deeply tanned, so well fed and well clothed, so full of optimism as they argued amiably about the virtues of Stevenson over Eisenhower, of Long Island over Westchester, of the new large-screen television sets over the filtered magnifiers.

"When I think of Russia," Leah said softly, "I think only of darkness. Not of having but of wanting."

"What do you mean, Aunt Leah?" her nephew Jakie asked. He was, after all, Russian-born. Occasionally, in vagrant dream, he ran through the green forest of his boyhood, singing a song he could not recall in his waking hours.

"There was never enough light," she said. "In every room I visited we sat in shadows and strained to see each other's faces. There was talk only of what would be, not of what was. Someday there would be a refrigerator. Someday there would be a gas stove, a space heater, a new lamp for the corner where no light fell. In Odessa I visited my cousins. Three families shared one flat. The married couples had to make appointments to use the one bedroom that had a door that closed." She paused; she would not tell these guests of Joshua's how the others in the apartment could hear their gasps of delight, their moans of swift ecstasy as they hastily coupled. "They taught the children Hebrew from an old primer that they kept covered with a book jacket from a Russian text," she went on. "The pages were loose, and after each lesson they taped it carefully together. Like a love letter. I visited David's niece, who was about to be married. She did not want a wedding dress. She wanted a pair of boots. We tried to buy them in the government-run department stores. They showed us sandals from Bulgaria, canvas gym shoes from Poland. The Dollar store had no boots, and I bought her an electric samovar instead and left her my own boots. A strange wedding present. 'Never mind,' the bride said, 'I won't need them at all when we go to Israel.' But who knows when she will get to Israel? They say that the waiting list of applicants stretches the length of the Don." As she spoke, her voice grew softer, as though she struggled to contain a secret pain; her sentences became abrupt and complicated in syntax. She was again thinking in Russian and translating her thoughts into English. A quirk of age, she thought, annoyed with herself. Still, it had been pleasant to speak in Russian with Boris Zaslovsky, the middle-aged physician with whom she had felt such keen rapport.

Aaron stood on the fringe of the crowd and listened to his mother. She looked sad, he thought, yet there was a purposeful intensity in her tone, a determination in her movements. She was busy again, involved. Twice a week she went into the city to confer with officials who spoke of organizing a campaign for Soviet Jewry. She was designing a poster, wording a petition. Her absorption took her mind off David's death, absorbed the energy she might have diverted to wild grief. Vaguely, like a sick man who has despaired of finding a cure, he wished that a new passion had enveloped him at the time of Katie's death. Then or now. How wonderful to concentrate on agendas and committees, to work fiercely on position papers and memoranda, to exchange urgent phone calls and hold midnight meetings in dimly lit hotel rooms.

There would not be time, then, to remember the soft sobbing in the quiet of a springtime midnight, the random flares of irrational fury, the sad deceptions and the sadder truths. He had his work, of course, and he accomplished it competently but without the total immersion and involvement he had felt when he and his wife had practiced law together. *Together*. The word seemed a bitter mockery to him now. In truth, he and Katie had done nothing "together." Always, she had been sealed into a terrifying aloneness that excluded and deceived him. He had loved and had been unloved. He had wanted and had been unwanted. And, he thought, he had had the power of intervention and had not intervened. Harshly, he blamed Katie for the illness, the despair, that had swept her to her death, and even more harshly he blamed himself for his own weakness. He should have forced her to seek help. He was the son of a psychiatrist, and he had rejected David Goldfeder's gentle offers to help, to advise.

"Aaron, I'm going to fix a plate for myself. Shall I get one for you too?" the dark-haired young woman who stood beside him asked.

He was startled. Although he had walked across the lawn with her and had been aware of her hand lightly touching his arm, although she had been talking to him softly, almost intimately, her voice a breathless whisper, he had all but forgotten her presence as he lost himself again in memories of the past. His indifference to her saddened and shamed him. Laura. That was her name, he remembered now. She taught third grade at the Brearly School and took literature courses at Columbia University's School of General Studies. She loved Dylan Thomas. And she was pretty. Her long brown hair floated about her shoulders and was held in place by a headband that matched her turquoise peasant skirt. She had summered on Fire Island, and her white peasant blouse circled shoulders burnished to a rose-lit gold. She was the prettiest of the many pretty girls Sherry and Joshua Ellenberg had produced for him since Katie's death—the cousins of neighbors, the sisters of business associates, all of them attractive and single.

Laura wore a very good perfume that brushed the air with the drifting fragrance of wildflowers, and although her face was lean, impertinent dimples cleft her cheeks. Other young men had smiled at her as they passed, and Aaron's cousin Jakie Hart had, without asking, removed her empty cocktail glass from her hand and brought her another, newly filled with gin and tonic and the crescent of a lime. He had blushed when she smiled and thanked him. Clearly, she was a girl who was used to having her glass refilled without asking. And yet Aaron was indifferent to her soft voice, her teasing laughter, even to the glorious swell of breasts beneath the sheer white blouse. He felt no desire to touch the golden roundness of bare arm, nor did he wonder what her face would look like in shadow. Had all desire frozen within him, he wondered, when he stared down at Katie's lifeless, broken body, at the pallor of her skin and the rain-wet hair that clung so closely to her delicately molded skull?

"I'm not really hungry," he said and hoped that Laura would not see his words as a rejection, that Sherry Ellenberg (who watched them from the terrace with the wishful gaze of the matchmaker manqué) would not be disappointed.

She smiled, the indifferent grin of a good loser in a game that she had not particularly wanted to win. Aaron Goldfeder's sadness had briefly intrigued and challenged her, but he was too pale, too entangled in a web of grief. She made her way to the buffet table, where she stood beside Jake Hart and allowed him to select a tender piece of chicken for her plate, to spear a slice of roast beef and surround it with a snowy mound of cole slaw. Jakie Hart was not pale. His skin retained the ruddiness gained during long summer afternoons on the tennis courts. His father, Seymour, often reminded Jakie that he had worked eighteen hours a day to establish S. Hart, Inc. Jakie always smiled amiably and patted his father's arm.

"That was then, Pa. This is now."

They had come a long way from the crowded railroad flat on Eldridge Street where sewing machines hummed through the night in the living room while his aunt Leah bent, red-eyed, over designs and patterns at the oilcloth-covered kitchen table. Jakie Hart, in his plaid slacks and snowy white sport shirt (the inevitable hart that was the trademark of the family company sprinting across the pocket), radiated the optimism and prosperity of the times. Wars and want were done with. He was not sad. He was newly divorced and not displeased with his single status. He told jokes loudly and laughed at them before delivering the punch line. Now he held Laura's arm as they walked across the lawn and found seats beneath a giant elm.

Aaron remained alone on the fringe of the crowd, smiling politely at the friends and relatives who passed him, answering their questions with cordial restraint.

Sherry Ellenberg, newly elected to the presidency of her Hadassah chapter, asked him if he would speak at a meeting.

"On what topic?" Aaron asked

He liked Joshua's pretty English wife, who had always been considerate of his family, who touched Joshua's black leather prosthetic hand with unembarrassed tenderness.

"Something political. The election, perhaps. What's happening in Suez." Sherry's intentions were sincere, but her knowledge was vague. She giggled charmingly.

"They're closely related, actually," Aaron said. "Eisenhower speaks with Dulles's voice. President Charlie McCarthy to the Secretary's Edgar Bergen. And Dulles is so obsessed with containing communism in Asia that he reneged on the promise to help Nasser build the Aswan Dam because Nasser recognized Communist China. So last month Nasser paid him back. He nationalized the Suez Canal. Now our French and English allies are in trouble. That's going to be the major issue in this election—the direction of our foreign policy."

Michael Goldfeder had moved to his brother's side, and he listened carefully, fingering the Stevenson button that the blond girl who stood at his side had pinned on his jacket minutes before.

"What I can't figure out," he said, "is why Dulles is so hip on the SEATO pact. Why the hell are we involving ourselves in Southeast Asia? Damn it, he's committed us to the defense of a country that doesn't even exist—South Vietnam."

"I wouldn't even know where to find it on a map," Sherry said. "But if you could just concentrate on the impact of the Suez situation on Israel, that would be terrific."

"I'll try to work something up," Aaron promised. "Yehuda should be able to help me."

Sherry smiled knowingly.

"Isn't their timing fantastic? I couldn't believe it when Rebecca called from London last night and said they were on their way. It will make the party for Leah."

"Our sister, Rebecca, who lives in Israel, is arriving tonight," Michael explained to the blond girl. She smiled, pleased to be included in the secret.

Hand in hand, she and Michael walked over to the patio and began to dance to the music that blared from the phonograph. She laughed and whispered something into Michael's ear, but Aaron noticed that his brother did not return her smile, nor did his eyes change expression, although his arm encircled her slender waist and he commanded her body with the flexing of his wrist. Like himself, Michael was a victim of grief; they were, the two of them, fraternal invalids, slow to recover from the grievous malady of loss. Aaron went to the bar and asked for another drink, a double scotch, straight up.

Leah watched him down it in a single swallow and frowned. How long would Aaron linger on the edge of the crowd, restrained by grief and loss? She, too, had known overwhelming sorrow. She had been only eighteen years old and pregnant with Aaron when his father had been killed—but she had rebuilt her life, molded her own destiny. Her children would have to do the same. She could not shield them from the vagaries of life, the inevitable losses, the random wounds of rejection and misjudgment. They were solitary travelers now, embarked on their separate journeys.

Her thoughts were interrupted by the rush of a powerful motor grinding suddenly to a halt.

A late arrival, Leah thought—one of Joshua's business friends. She turned her attention to the dessert buffet and admired the huge pyramids of fresh fruit, cakes topped with swirls of cream, snowy caps of meringue, chocolate pools of mousse bordered with ivory-colored ladyfingers. This was always Rebecca's favorite time at any party, Leah remembered. Joshua and Rebecca shared the craving for sweets peculiar to those who had felt deprived of them as children.

She noticed now that the guests were not converging on the buffet table but were gathered still at the gate. The new arrivals were probably celebrities—television personalities involved in the shows Joshua had begun to sponsor. He had plunged heavily into television advertising.

"It's the wave of the future," he had told Leah. "Watch it. Television's going to elect presidents and market ready-to-wear."

He had watched the Kraft Television Theatre for three consecutive weeks and had called his advertising agency. A month later, *The Ellenberg Hour: Sixty Minutes of Fine Drama* was launched. Perhaps one of his stars had come to the party. Leah's own curiosity was piqued, and she moved toward the small crowd. They grew quiet and separated into two groups, leaving a path for the tall man and woman who rushed toward Leah, their arms outstretched, their faces sun-burnished.

"Mama!" Rebecca's voice was vibrant, joyous; her arms enveloped her mother and her lips brushed Leah's cheeks. She tasted the tears that streamed with joyous release from Leah's eyes.

"Becca, I didn't know, I never dreamed you'd be here." Leah was breathless, full of wonderment. How beautiful Rebecca looked, her dark hair caping her shoulders, her skin golden against the rich blue fabric of her dress. She had been traveling for hours, yet her strong, even-featured face betrayed no fatigue. Rebecca was energized, as she always had been, by joy and excitement. Michael and Aaron moved closer to their sister. She was still their golden girl, their brave and ebullient princess.

Yehuda, too, embraced Leah.

"Three days ago I was told that there was business for me to see to in New York. Luckily Rebecca could join me, and we were able to arrange flights that would bring us here in time for the party."

"Well, you made it in time for dessert," Joshua said. "When we knew you were coming, we doubled our mousse order, Rebecca. Do you remember how we used to lick the spoon when your aunt Mollie made chocolate pudding?"

"No mousse will ever taste as good as my mother's My-T-Fine," Jakie Hart said.

The family laughed, launched on the familiar tidal wave of reminiscence. Always, on Scarsdale verandas, on Long Island lawns, on the patio of Rebecca's small kibbutz bungalow, their conversation reeled back to their beginnings on the Lower East Side as, with practiced skill, they ignited each other's memories.

Yehuda Arnon watched his wife. Her eyes sparkled and her laughter was musical. Aaron's arm was around her shoulder; Michael's hand rested on her head. Yehuda looked about at the spacious garden. the sculpted bushes were patterned with the golden glow of the lights, and the glimmer of the dangling lanterns was refracted in the clear water of the swimming pool. All this warmth and luxury, these shared memories, this family closeness, Rebecca had given up to live with him on their stark border kibbutz.

"I don't regret it," she had retorted defiantly once when he spoke of it. "I don't think back to the past. The important thing is our future, the children, what we are building together."

Brave Rebecca, he thought, my radiant Rivka. He had thanked her silently then, for keeping silence, for not accusing him of too often lingering in the shadows of a time that had passed, of a love that had vanished. They were together. They had each other and the adventure of their lives.

"How are the children?" Leah asked Rebecca, the question tinged with grandmotherly anxiety.

"The baby, Yaakov, is fine," Rebecca replied. "He's such a happy baby. I sometimes keep him with me in the studio when I paint. And Noam and Danielle spoil him terribly."

"And Noam and Danielle?" Leah asked. She was fond of the children of Yehuda's first marriage. They had welcomed Rebecca into their lives with warmth and affection.

"They're fine. And my work is going well. The studio that the kibbutz built for me is marvelous. You can't imagine what it's like to paint in the light of the desert dawn. I brought some work to show to Charles Ferguson—just a few small canvases. There was no time to organize things properly. We had to leave in such a rush. . . ." Her voice trailed off. The haste and urgency of her departure cast a shadow across the bright picture she had painted of her life on the kibbutz—the happy children, the chortling baby, the involvement with work.

"Will you be able to stay long?" Leah asked.

"I don't think so. We need every working member. We have to mount a twenty-four-hour-a-day guard."

"Are things so bad, then?" Leah asked with sinking heart.

"Bad enough," Rebecca said, but there was no fear in her voice, no despair, and Leah remembered how calmly the Israelis assimilated the dangers of daily life in their beleaguered country. "A tourist bus was attacked near Beersheba about a month ago," Rebecca continued. "Nasser's actions on the Suez have made the fedayeen bold. Last week they attacked a team of surveyors on the Eilat highway and killed one man. Uri Cohen. We knew him well. He was a cellist and sometimes played with our kibbutz chamber music group. Noam is in the Scouts with his son." Her voice was tinged with accepting sorrow.

"But has anything happened on the kibbutz itself?" Leah persisted. Her question was laced with fear. David Goldfeder had been killed in front of the kibbutz children's house, during a nocturnal struggle with an Arab intruder. Sometimes Leah awakened in the night, remembering her husband's inert body sprawled across the ground, his blood petaling the ocher sand with a crimson rosette. She was seized with fear then, for Rebecca and her family. *The children are all right*, she would whisper to herself. Their grandfather's ghost protected them. Still, she trembled as she listened to the news, scanned the morning paper.

"We are very careful," Rebecca said. She touched her mother's hand reassuringly. She would not tell Leah about the harsh searchlight that illumined the kibbutz each night, nor would she describe the electrified fence they had built. "And besides, we will not allow things to continue this way." She spoke with firm determination, and Leah was gripped with a fierce pride in the brave, golden-skinned young woman who was her daughter.

Rebecca joined her brothers and Yehuda, who stood beneath a tall elm, its boughs threaded with tiny flickering bulbs. The amber glow of the lights lit their upturned faces, and their mother watched them, moved by their beauty, stirred by their strength and the sweetness of their laughter, as their memories converged onto a fragment of remembered joy.

Yehuda and Aaron walked together toward the small copse where Joshua Ellenberg had hung wooden swings for his children.

"It's wonderful that you and Rebecca could be in New York just now," Aaron said. "It means a great deal to my mother. Especially since Michael leaves tomorrow for Berkeley."

"I'm glad it worked out," Yehuda said. "A happy coincidence. It wasn't Michael we were thinking about when we undertook this journey, Aaron. It was you."

"Me?"

"Yes. I came because of you. I must speak with you about an important mission that I hope you will undertake."

"A mission?" Aaron repeated the word as though it had been plucked from a foreign language. "I'm not a secret agent, Yehuda. I'm a workaday lawyer and sometime law professor. I think you've come to the wrong address."

"I hope not," Yehuda replied gravely. "I pray not. Rebecca was sure you would help us."

Aaron looked at his sister, walking now beside the pool with Joshua Ellenberg. He supposed that he would always remain a hero to Rebecca. He was the older brother who had shepherded her through the streets of the Lower East Side, told her stories when their mother was delayed at a union meeting, their father absorbed in his studies. He had fended off the bullies who chased her across the Brighton Beach boardwalk, and he had struggled to answer the questions that had bewildered her during their shared childhood. "Are we still brother and sister even though we have different fathers?" "Of course." The brusque certainty of his reply reassured her as no explanation would have. "Do Mama and Papa love each other?" "I don't know," he had replied, whispering into the darkness of the Eldridge Street apartment. "Yes, they love each other," he had told her later, much later, after their move to Brighton Beach, after Michael's birth. The honesty of his earlier uncertainty affirmed the validity of his new assurance. She had believed him. "I'm glad," she had said, and she had pressed closer to his protecting shadow.

Rebecca still carried a snapshot of Aaron in his RAF uniform. She had never seen him behind the barbed wire of the Italian prisoner-of-war camp, nor had she seen him surrender to grief when Katie died. She did not understand that with the passing years their roles had been reversed. She, the younger sister, lived daily on the edge of danger, while he went each day to his law office, welcoming the predictability of his practice. It was Rebecca who now searched for answers, while he had all but stopped asking the questions.

Yehuda absently pushed a child's swing. It stirred the still air, moved with languid rhythm; moonlight whitened the slatted seat.

"This mission is very important. Important to both our countries," Yehuda continued.

"What is it about?" Aaron asked. His voice was steady, but he felt an odd surge of excitement.

"I cannot talk about it here. It involves other colleagues. Can we meet tomorrow morning—early?"

"My apartment. Seven o'clock," Aaron said.

"Good."

Abruptly, Yehuda turned and strode toward Joshua and Rebecca. Aaron watched them and wondered if Yehuda knew that once, so many years ago, Joshua had imagined himself in love with Rebecca. It no longer mattered, of course. They had each found new lives, new loves. Only he remained in limbo. Still, he was swept now, by the half-forgotten feverish excitement he had felt as a young soldier, just before a battle, that curious commingling of fear and fearlessness, of trembling trepidation and soaring courage. "An important mission," Yehuda had said. Aaron was eager suddenly for the night to drift into morning, for secrets to be revealed, mysteries divulged.

His mother touched his arm.

"I think we should leave. Michael has a long journey tomorrow. Rebecca will drive back with us, but Yehuda is staying in the city."

"I'm going to stay in the city also," Aaron said. "An early appointment I'd forgotten about."

"I see," Leah said. She had seen Yehuda and Aaron speaking earnestly, their heads bent close, in the darkness of the copse.

They thanked the Ellenbergs and made their farewells. The blond girl kissed Michael lightly on the cheek.

"Remember, you're for Adlai," she said. "I'll give you a call if I get to the Coast."

Aaron shook hands with his cousin Jakie and smiled at the woman named Laura, who looked absently at him. Would his cousin sleep with her tonight? Aaron wondered. Would she have slept with him, Aaron, if he had filled her plate, smiled into her violet eyes, and listened to her recite fragments of Dylan Thomas? It did not matter. He did not care. He wanted only to return to his empty apartment, to speculate briefly about Yehuda's "mission" before falling into heavy, nepenthean sleep on the wide bed he had once shared with sad-eyed Katie.

The family walked to the car together and stood with their arms linked. They inhaled the sweet night air, tinged with the melancholy fragrance of autumn, and looked up as a flock of gray geese sliced a swathe through the black velvet night sky. The birds soared above them in a smoke-colored streak, their wings softly beating against the resistant air.

"Dad loved the Canada geese," Michael said softly.

"I remember." Rebecca watched the birds, and thought that only a few days earlier she had stood beside the sand crater that shadowed their kibbutz bungalow and watched a flock of egrets wing their way to the Dead Sea. She was swept by the wondrous mystery of her life. It was exciting, after all, to belong to two different worlds. Tomorrow she would walk down Madison Avenue and show Charles Ferguson the canvases she had painted in the desert wilderness. Her father would have liked her new work, she knew, and she watched the wandering fowl that David Goldfeder had loved so well disappear into the darkness.

"Your father is dead," Leah said. She looked at her children. The steadiness of her gaze, the quiet of her voice, formed a command. "We must stop looking backward and see things through our own eyes now. We must make our own lives, our own new beginnings. That is what he would have wanted."

Aaron embraced his brother, kissed his mother and his sister, his lips brushing their cheeks. Rebecca's skin was petal-soft, Leah's as delicate as crepe.

He shook hands with Yehuda.

"In the morning," his brother-in-law said.

"In the morning," Aaron agreed, and he braced himself for the lonely trip, the long, dream-haunted night.

AARON

Budapest, 1956

AARON stirred uneasily in sleep, struggling against the dream, and then lay still, surrendering to it, enduring it. As always, in this nocturnal visitation, she lay motionless across the bed, her eyes wide and staring, the hint of a smile curling her lip. As always, he passed his hands across her naked body, surprised at the satin smoothness of her skin, at the delicacy of her bones beneath his probing fingers. He pressed his palm down hard on the jutting edge of her hip, moved to the twin columns of her sternum and then to her breasts; their soft fullness contrasted with the almost skeletal slimness of her body. His tongue licked at her nipples, as ripe and rosy as the first strawberries of spring. They tasted vaguely of milk, and he sucked wildly and felt her body move at last beneath his own. Her hands seized the great swell of his strength and moved across the taut, pulsing muscle, urging it to thrust, yet holding it back.

She pressed the heel of her palm against its smoothness and moaned softly as it trembled, straining and powerful, yet submissive to her touch. And then he was arched above her, glowing with a subdued radiance, and she allowed him to glide into the welcoming canyon of her body. Now his hands pressed against her shoulders and his body moved in desperate rhythm, but quite suddenly, as always, her skin lost its warmth. His hands fondled cool, unyielding marble; her arms rested at her side, palms upturned. Her body was motionless, as cold within as it was without.

Still, he would not surrender. He continued to ride her, pounding at her as sweat formed on his forehead, coursed down his body. Each thrust was a mighty blow, echoing resonantly, hammering at her resistance. Aaron whispered her name. "Katie." He shouted it. "Katie!" Her silence birthed his fury. He lifted himself high and descended with vicious thrust. She would awaken. Up and down again. She would live. His love would keep her alive. He pounded yet harder, battering at her with abandon. His love would keep her alive. He heard the sounds of his passion, the urgent beating of his body.

Exhausted, he lay still, yet a harsh tympany continued. It became a knocking, an insistent summons, punctuated now and again by the urgent ringing of a doorbell. His doorbell. The real world had invaded his dream.

Bewildered, disoriented, Aaron opened his eyes and sat up. He was, of course, alone in his bed amid tangled and sweat-stained sheets. The doorbell rang yet again, and he glanced at his clock. Seven-thirty. Of course. Yehuda and his colleagues were at the door. Lost in the punishing, familiar dream, he had overslept.

"I'm coming," he called. He pulled on his slacks and a shirt, found his loafers amid the clutter of bedside books and papers, and hurried to open the door.

Yehuda stood in the doorway flanked by two strangers, a tall, slender man who stood rigidly erect, the small dome of his balding head glowing pinkly in the dim light of the hallway, and a short, stocky man who trained a jovial smile on Aaron, although his eyes narrowed in a shrewd appraising glance.

"We are early?" Yehuda asked and looked at his watch.

"No. You're on time. My fault. I overslept."

The two strangers glanced warily at each other, and Aaron felt that he had failed a small test, disappointed them in an important way.

But Yehuda only smiled and preceded the others into the apartment. Clearly, he was the leader.

"I'm not surprised. I thought you looked very tired last night. I tried to call you this morning, but your line was busy."

"Damn," Aaron said bitterly. He had done it again, then. Always, he and Katie had taken the phone off the hook before they made love. Now, sleep-drugged, dream-bound, he made the same futile gesture as he pursued her illusory presence, her frozen, unresponding shade. "I must have knocked the receiver off. An accident."

"You are alone, then, Mr. Goldfeder?" the tall man asked.

"Apparently," Yehuda interjected, his tone at once protective and annoyed.

Still, he raised no objection as the tall man walked past Aaron into the bedroom, where he stared at the empty rumpled bed and replaced the receiver on the cradle. The assumption of proprietorship, the implied distrust, irritated Aaron, but he said nothing. It occurred to him that he did not like Yehuda's colleagues, and he wondered how Rebecca, who shared the familial sense of privacy, reacted to them. He shrugged and went into the kitchen, where he made four cups of instant coffee, congratulating himself on having milk and sugar and four clean teaspoons. He placed everything on a tray and carried it into the living room.

"Thank you, Aaron," Yehuda said. He nodded to the tall man. "I want you to meet Yoram Almogi."

Yoram Almogi held out his hand, and as Aaron shook it, he noticed that the Israeli's fingers were cruelly hard against his own and briefly unrelenting as Aaron withdrew. A brief and petty assertion of authority. There were lawyers who used that same disarming tactic before a trial, at a meeting.

"And this is Reuven Greenstein."

Reuven Greenstein nodded, ignored his coffee, and looked around the room. His eyes rested on Charles Ferguson's pen-and-ink sketches, drifted to an oil of brilliant anemones in Rebecca's defined primitive style, and finally concentrated on Leah's painting of the maple tree that dominated her garden. It depicted the tree in the autumn season, its leaves bloodied by impending death and drifting onto the lawn, dried and wearied by the seasons.

"Your mother is a wonderful artist," Reuven Greenstein said, and his voice was soft, almost reverent. A collector, Aaron decided, and the man corroborated his thought. "I know something about paintings. I run a small gallery in Tel Aviv—that is, when things are normal."

"And things are not normal?" Aaron asked as he shrugged into his jacket.

He sat down on the living room couch, indifferent to its careless bachelor disorder. Yehuda moved to the windows and carefully lowered each shade. He drew the drapes so that no light escaped and then went to the front door, where he fastened the chain and pulled the bolt on the double lock into place. The small, deliberate gestures transformed Aaron's apartment into a clandestine headquarters, darkened and secured.

"No, Aaron, things are decidedly not normal," he said. "Even for Israel, the situation is now extraordinary. The border incidents are no longer 'incidents.' They are acts of terror. Nasser's nationalization of the Suez Canal has made the fedayeen more daring. Rebecca does not want to alarm her American family, and so she has not written to tell you what has been happening only kilometers from the kibbutz—an attack on a tourist bus, a surveyor killed by snipers. We have grown accustomed to sleeping in shelters. But something must be done."

"But what *can* be done?" Aaron asked. "Short of marching on Suez itself?"

The three men looked at one another. At last Yehuda spoke, leaning forward, his voice low.

"Aaron, whatever we tell you must be held secret. I do not mean to be dramatic, but that is the reality of the situation. You remember that when I met Rebecca I was a Bericha agent?"

Aaron nodded. Yehuda had worked for Bericha, the organization that had rescued Jews from Europe and illegally transported them to Palestine in defiance of the British and their quota.

"Almogi and Greenstein worked with me. After the war the Mosad enlisted our services. The Mosad corresponds to your CIA, I suppose—it's an abbreviation for the Institution for Intelligence and Special Assignments. Perhaps it has never occurred to you, but intelligence is a natural resource for Israel." He paused, drained his coffee cup, and shook his head impatiently when Aaron reached for it. "Other nations have their gold and silver mines, even uranium or perhaps fertile soil. Our Arab neighbors harvest their black gold. We cannot compete with them. The Negev is barren, and there are no mineral deposits in the Galilee. The potash in the Dead Sea will not make us wealthy. But we do have our people, our ingathering of the exiles from every country in the world. They speak many languages, and they have intricate knowledge of many things."

Yoram Almogi laughed harshly.

"My garage mechanic in Tel Aviv can sketch the plans of the entire Moscow sewer system. There are kibbutzniks in the Sharon Valley who know about secret passes in the mountains of Afghanistan. I know an architect in Haifa who can reproduce blueprints for the airfield at Entebbe in Uganda. And what our people do not know, they can find out. We have the languages. We have the contacts."

"And of course you don't hesitate to use these contacts," Aaron said dryly. He was the cautious American, solicitous of privacy and privilege. He was the lawyer questioning men who had been forced too often to live beyond the law.

"We can't afford not to use them," Yehuda replied bluntly. "Information is international currency. The Americans want to know what our people can tell them about Belgrade—the climate of opinion, the leadership. Is the government stable? What are the rumblings within? We in turn want to know what is happening in the court of Saudi Arabia. Two items that we pass on to an American diplomat at a cultural reception in Athens may be worth one important clue for us. A rumor can have the value of a ten-page report. It's simple barter, Aaron. International trade with information as a variable commodity. Joshua Ellenberg would have no difficulty understanding it. Every connection is useful, vital."

"Of course, at different times, some connections are more important than others," Reuven Greenstein said. "Just now, the Hungarian connections are very important, which is why I am here. I was born in Budapest. My father owned a restaurant there. But that was a long time ago. My father died in Belsen. A curious irony. The best pastry chef in Budapest died of starvation. His restaurant was confiscated by the government. Today it is a processing plant for official photos for documents. I used to rush home from school, and as I reached our corner I would begin to smell the roasting chickens, the onions simmering in goose fat. Now all you smell on that street are chemical fixatives and stinking glue." Sadness fell across his face, covering his features like an ill-fitting mask. Tears glittered in his pale eyes. Was he mourning his father, Aaron wondered, or the vanished aroma of those days of peace and plenty? Both, he suspected, and turned away, shamed because the other man's grief embarrassed him and evoked his own sense of loss.

"Are you also Hungarian?" Aaron asked Yoram Almogi.

"If the nationality fits, I wear it," Almogi said. "For this week I am Hungarian. I speak the language well enough. I know the country well enough. But then I speak many languages and know many countries. This week I am Hungarian because it is about Hungary that we have come to speak to you."

"About Hungary?" Aaron asked in surprise. "But I don't know a damn thing about Hungary. And what interest does Israel have in Hungary?"

"There are Jews in Hungary," Yehuda replied. "Wherever there are Jews, Israel has an interest." There was no reproof in his voice, but he spoke slowly, as though he were a teacher instructing a student who had difficulty grasping a simple concept.

"Yes. I understand," Aaron said. "But I still don't see how I can help you."

"You are an expert in immigration law," Yoram Almogi observed. He opened his briefcase and removed a file, which he extended to Aaron. "These articles are all written by you."

Aaron glanced at them. Reprints from a review and an article he had written for the *Harvard Law Journal*, his précis for the *Compendium of Immigration Law*, an amicus brief he had written for the Department of Immigration and Nationalization, and a scholarly article analyzing Canada's policy of immigration for Jews during World War II—not much to analyze, considering that during that entire period the great Dominion of Canada had admitted fewer than five thousand Jews.

"Yes. They're my publications," Aaron acknowledged.

"We were interested in them because we need an American expert in immigration law. Who could serve us better than Rebecca Arnon's brother?" Reuven Greenstein said. "We are concerned about a Jewish scientist in Budapest. A Dr. Groszman. Groszman's work concentrates on radar research, aeronautical avoidance techniques. Such research would be invaluable for us in Israel, for reasons that we cannot discuss with you."

"I think the reasons are obvious," Aaron said dryly. "Your next war is going to be an aerial one, and you're going to have to develop techniques of evading radar perception. I may be an immigration expert now, but I was a soldier once. I understand a few things about war."

"It is not that we do not trust you," Reuven said carefully. "But it is safest that you know as little as possible. We have a saying in our military intelligence units: What is not known—"

"Cannot be revealed," Aaron finished the statement for him. "I heard that for the first time from Orde Wingate."

"As did I," Yoram Almogi said. "I trained with him at Hanita." He looked at Aaron with new respect. He stared at the emblem of the Jewish Brigade, the small gold menorah that Aaron wore in his lapel.

"And I fought with him in Ethiopia. In the Jewish Brigade."

"Yes. We know that, of course. And we are duly impressed. But it is your legal expertise and not your military background that interests us now. This Dr. Groszman of ours wants to leave Hungary."

"Surely that's not a problem. Under the Law of Return, any Jew is eligible for admission to Israel."

"The problem does not originate with Israel. Naturally, our doors are open to Dr. Groszman, but emigration from Hungary is not so easily accomplished. Hungary, like all the Communist bloc countries, has a special problem relating to Israel. When Israel was seeking its independence, the Communist world embraced it as an ally in the struggle against Western imperialism. They accorded it immediate recognition, even made noises about extending aid. But once we were established as an independent democratic state, suddenly we were foes of liberation, lackeys of imperialists. And so they mire Jewish emigration in bureaucracy and restrictions. An emigrating Jew must prove that he is totally free of debts and obligations. Some Jews have been told they must bring affidavits from every merchant in town. They must also prove that they are not leaving any dependents. A cousin of mine who has a senile great aunt whom he has not seen for twenty years has been denied the right to leave. And of course they do not want their scientific experts to leave." Yehuda sighed heavily and turned his palms upward. The gesture was a remnant of his past, half desperation and half supplication. Aaron was reminded of David Goldfeder, who had often ended an argument staring down at his upturned hands.

"Besides," Reuven Greenstein added, "it is not in Israel's best interest for it to be known that Dr. Groszman has involvement there. Groszman's work in radar technology might tip our hand—confirm what some of our Arab friends may already anticipate."

"That you have an immediate and urgent interest in radar evasion techniques."

"Exactly. However, if Dr. Groszman were to enter the United States, without any aid or interference from Israel, perhaps no suspicions would arise. There is a Groszman family here—a brother in Cleveland, I think."

"San Francisco," Almogi interjected. His forte, Aaron guessed, was accuracy. He was the guardian of the small detail, the essential minutiae that might betray an operation, jeopardize a life.

"All right. San Francisco." Yehuda was impatient. "It would be assumed to be quite natural that the United States would be the country of choice. Not an unexpected decision."

"Not unexpected," Aaron replied, "but probably not possible. This country's immigration laws are based on a quota, and the Hungarian quota is small and always well filled. I'm familiar with it because I have a client who is trying to secure a visa for a relative, and I know that the waiting list goes straight into the next decade. I don't think you want your Dr. Groszman to wait that long."

"Naturally not," Yehuda said. "But we have heard that when there are extraordinary circumstances, extraordinary intervention is possible."

Aaron marveled at how simple Yehuda made it sound. Perhaps

he imagined that Aaron could go into a courtroom and present a straightforward, uncomplicated plea. "Your Honor, my case is extraordinary and therefore I am sure that you will assign it special consideration. After all, we are all reasonable and decent men." Clearly, Yehuda had never confronted a black-robed federal judge, his shoulders stooped beneath the weight of constitutional responsibility. It seemed to Aaron that all the judges before whom he argued were round-shouldered and hard-eyed. He turned to the three men.

"There were extraordinary cases—millions of them during the course of World War Two, but very few of them were accorded this extraordinary intervention. There were a few, of course—Albert Einstein, Leo Szilard, various Rothschild connections—but even a personality like Thomas Mann's daughter had to go through the charade of a paper marriage to W. H. Auden to obtain a visa. I don't know that very much will be different in the case of Dr. Groszman." Aaron's voice was polite and regretful. Unfortunately, this was the law of his country.

He and other authorities on immigration procedures were working for change, but no change would come quickly enough to benefit Dr. Groszman. Hungary was a pressure cooker right now, ready to explode any minute. Only that morning the *Times* had carried a long article that again discussed the unrest in the Budapest intellectual community. There were clandestine student groups and simmering discontent. There seemed to be general anger against Gero, the premier, and the name of the discredited Imre Nagy was invoked with dangerous longing. The *Times* correspondent had attempted an interview with Yuri Andropov, the Soviet ambassador to Hungary, but the Russian had been mysteriously noncommittal. "He reminds me of a cautious, taciturn cook who watches a boiling pot, prepared to clamp a lid down just at the overflow point," the journalist had written in a burst of simile designed to substitute for hard news. Aaron supposed that it had been easier to write a news story during Stalin's regime. It was axiomatic then that the Russian reaction would be in favor of force and repression. Stalin's iron curtain had been impenetrable, and only perceptions of black and white had been permissible. Men like Khrushchev and Andropov were still less defined, and there were those who believed that they might see areas of gray, might countenance small pockets of dissidence.

"But of course special statutes can be introduced for special cases—is that not so? I have even heard of bills proposed by congressmen in the case of a particular individual which allowed for embassy hearings in the country of emigration," Reuven Greenstein persisted.

Aaron snapped his pencil in half. He was annoyed. Clearly, the Israelis had been well briefed on the intricacies of American immigration law. Why, then, were they playing this elaborate game of cat and mouse with him?

"Yehuda, perhaps we can discuss the purpose of your visit—of this so-called important mission. Surely we can be direct with each other."

"It's rather simple," Yehuda said. "We want you to go to Hungary. A special congressional bill has been introduced on behalf of Dr. Groszman, and a hearing will be held at the American embassy in Budapest. We want you to represent Dr. Groszman at that hearing."

"I really don't think that's necessary," Aaron said. "If you have a bill in progress, it's a rather straightforward situation. But I can give you a bit of added insurance. A former Harvard classmate of mine, Tom Hemmings, is at the American embassy in Budapest. I'll drop him a note and tell him of my special interest in the Groszman case." He did not want to appear unhelpful, and he and Tom *had* been close friends once. They had strolled through the streets of Cambridge together, with the girls who became their wives. They had danced at each other's weddings, and Betty Hemmings had written a kind note, postmarked Budapest, when Katie died. Kind, yet somehow unsurprised. She had known Katie well.

"That would not be sufficient." Almogi's tone was clipped, impatient. "Dr. Groszman's knowledge is vital to Israel's security. We cannot risk the slightest possibility of error. An attorney with your skill and reputation will guarantee the success of the hearing and safe entry into this country. It is very important that you go to Hungary."

"You really want me to go to Hungary?" Aaron said as though the import of their request was finally real to him. "Do you think I can just leave my obligations and take off?" He motioned vaguely toward his desk, which was littered with documents and correspondence. Reuven Greenstein shrugged.

"We know, of course, that you are a busy man, an important man. But surely one of your associates could assume the daily operation of your office for a short period," he said. "Just as someone manages my gallery, Almogi's business. Just as your brother-in-law's kibbutz manages without him."

The parallels were an unsubtle reminder of priorities, a nudge toward acquiescence. Surely, Aaron wanted to be counted among those who set aside their own petty professional interests for a larger good.

"But of course, you may be troubled by other aspects of this mission," Greenstein continued smoothly. "It is not an assignment without risks. That is one of the reasons for our haste. Budapest is an unsettled city just now. We all read the morning papers. It will grow more unsettled, perhaps even explosive. And an American will be especially vulnerable. Mr. Dulles and his talk of massive retaliation has not increased American popularity in Eastern Europe just now. You can be frank with us. Tell us if you feel it will be too dangerous."

"I'm not worried about the danger," Aaron replied curtly. There was no need for Greenstein to manipulate him with his tough-guy innuendos. Danger frightened only men who had something to lose.

"Then you will go, Aaron?" Yehuda leaned forward. He alone had not expected Aaron to refuse them. Aaron was Rebecca's brother. He shared her profound sense of responsibility, her spontaneous instinct to protect the vulnerable. Leah's legacy of courage and caring.

"Damn it, Yehuda. I can't give you a decision this minute. I have to think about it." He was angry suddenly. The bastards wake him up, pump him full of guilt, and put him on the spot. Who the hell did they think they were?

"Of course you need some time," Almogi said smoothly. "The problem is that we don't know how much time we have. Things are moving swiftly over there."

"Look," Aaron said reasonably, controlling his irritation, "I'll need a couple of days. Today is Tuesday. Let's talk again on Friday morning at my office. Fair enough?"

"All right," Yehuda said, deciding for all of them as Aaron had known he would. "We can gamble with two or three days."

They all shook hands with Aaron before leaving. Greenstein's features were frozen. He would be a formidable adversary in a poker game, Aaron thought. Yehuda spoke to him softly.

"I will be in contact with you, in Budapest," he said.

Aaron shrugged; his brother-in-law clearly presupposed his acquiescence. Yehuda was accustomed to recruiting volunteers. He had, after all, even recruited Rebecca.

Aaron made his bed, using fresh sheets. He took a hot shower and did twenty push-ups, aware that he felt electric with an excitement he had not known since before Katie's death.

He brewed real coffee for the first time in months, then took a cab downtown, and by the time Eileen Manning, his secretary, arrived, he had placed two calls to Washington, arranged a luncheon date with Joshua Ellenberg, and called a bookstore to order a history of Hungary, a guidebook to Budapest and its environs, and a Hungarian phrase book. He had also sent a clerk to the law library to take notes on all immigration cases during the past year that had relied on special congressional petitions.

Eileen, a thin blond girl who had worked for Aaron Goldfeder since her graduation from secretarial school, was pleased with the flurry of excitement. She had long felt that the best remedy for Aaron's lingering melancholy would be a new interest, an absorbing involvement. She had said as much to her fiancé, Kenneth White, the previous evening as they shared the specially priced dinner at Toffinetti's.

"I think he needs a girl," Kenneth had said.

"Oh no." Eileen did not want Aaron Goldfeder to have a girl, for reasons that were not entirely clear to her. "He just needs to get caught up in something."

Now she was pleased to think that in some mysterious way her theory had communicated itself to Aaron, who was dashing about the office checking files, making phone calls, and dictating letters to her rapid-fire, as though it were urgent that all outstanding correspondence be answered at once. They worked frantically all morning, and she was relieved when he left to meet Joshua Ellenberg. It gave her a chance to catch her breath, to restore order to his desk, and to make neat piles of his notes and papers. She unpacked the books that had been delivered by the bookstore and then went to the large atlas and studied a map of Eastern Europe. Hungary was a great blob of orange bordered by the blue mass of Czechoslovakia and the green expanse of Austria. Eileen concentrated on the names of the Hungarian cities, but only Budapest was at all familiar to her. There had been a story about Budapest in the newspaper that day, she remembered, and she was sorry now that she had given her newspaper to the elevator man. Still, it was probably not important. She went to the office strongbox, removed Aaron Goldfeder's passport as he had asked her to, and ascertained that it was up-to-date.

Aaron and Joshua had lunch in the private dining room at Ellenberg Industries, which overlooked the East River. They glanced southward, toward the street where they had grown up.

"I wonder if our house is still standing," Aaron said.

"It is," Joshua replied. "And somehow they still manage to get a minyan at the synagogue. Of course, most of the tenants are Puerto

Rican now, and Librach's candy store is a bodega. The Settlement House is in bad shape—used mainly as a drug rehabilitation center. Something is needed to replace it."

"How do you know?" Aaron asked, surprised.

"I go down there every so often." Joshua's answer was casual. He did not tell Aaron that he had bought the tenement building where he and his family had once shared an apartment with the Goldfeders. He had had the building gutted and rebuilt, had fitted it with a new oil burner and a fire alarm and sprinkler system. Once a year he took his children down to Eldridge Street and showed them the landmarks of his childhood, the corner where he had hawked his merchandise, the playground where he had once wiped Rebecca Goldfeder's tears and kissed her on the cheek (he remembered still that her skin had tasted of chocolate and Ivory soap), the empty lot, overgrown with weeds, strewn with debris, where once the Rosenblatt factory had stood. He had instructed his attorney to buy that neglected patch of land, although he was not clear about why he wanted it. The charred foundation of the building protruded from the earth like a blackened welt. He wondered if Aaron ever had the need to make such small pilgrimages to the past, to remember where it had all begun and how far they had come.

"Joshua, what do you know about Hungary?" Aaron asked abruptly now.

"Hungary?" Joshua shrugged. "A couple of bad jokes, maybe." He looked at Aaron curiously and noticed that his friend was eating with a gusto that he had not displayed since Katie's death. Aaron poured ketchup lavishly across his hamburger and asked the waitress to bring a second order of french fries. Joshua remembered now that Sherry had complained, after the Labor Day party, that Aaron ate, the way he did everything else, as though it were a chore.

"When is he going to rejoin the living?" Sherry had asked impatiently. She liked Aaron too much to see him still cloaked in an enervating grief, narcotized by his loss.

Well, Joshua thought, he seems to have done just that.

"Hungary," he repeated thoughtfully now. "We have very little contact. It's not one of our major markets, but we do sell there, just enough to keep a very small operation going. A salesman, a forwarder, a small staff. And we buy a little. They make a wonderful aquamarine dye, excellent rickrack. Their currency is stable enough now, thanks to the Russians. Florins. That's about all I can tell you, Aaron."

"That's about what I wanted," Aaron said. "Just a businessman's feel for the country. Would you say it's in a dangerous situation?"

"There are rumors," Joshua said. "The usual talk of political unrest, revolution. We're keeping very little capital there—transferring what we can to Austria. But with Stalin gone there's a softening of positions in Eastern Europe. Khrushchev is supposed to be more lenient—at least everyone thinks so except John Foster Dulles and your mother."

"But my mother, after all, is the only one of us who's been behind the iron curtain recently," Aaron said. "That is, so far."

"Ahh, Aaron," Joshua said quickly. "Are you planning a trip to the land of goulash?"

"I don't know," Aaron said. "Yes. Perhaps I am. Is your Budapest man Jewish?" It did not occur to him that he was betraying his mission by confiding in Joshua. He trusted his childhood friend as he trusted himself.

"Yes."

"What does he say about the Jews of Hungary?"

"You mean what's left of the Jews of Hungary?"

"Yes."

"They walk a thin line, like all the Jews who remain in Eastern Europe. They behave themselves and pay their taxes. They keep a kosher soup kitchen going, and they replace the bulbs in the memorial lights in the synagogue. They send their kids to Israel, and they try to get their money out of the country. That's what I've managed to pick up from him. What else do you want to know, Aaron?"

"Can you give me his name and address and a letter of credit drawn on your Budapest account?" This would be his insurance policy, he told himself, acknowledging for the first time that he might be entering a danger zone. Reliance on Joshua was, after all, a family habit. Aaron represented Joshua, and Joshua routinely did business in Hungary. A letter of credit would be standard procedure.

"Why not?" Joshua made a note in a pad that he drew from his breast pocket. "Is Rebecca enjoying her visit?" he asked.

It was Aaron's turn to be guarded, although of course Joshua had gotten over Rebecca long ago. They were both happily married. Still, he discerned a special edge in Joshua's voice when he mentioned her name.

"She's having a wonderful time," he said. "My mother took her and Yehuda to see *Look Back in Anger*, and Jakie sent them tickets to *Separate Tables*."

"What about *The Diary of Anne Frank*? Sherry loved it."

"Impossible to get tickets."

"I'll get a pair for Saturday night's performance and have them delivered to the house," Joshua said briskly. He had, he recognized, outgrown his love for Rebecca but not his proclivity to pamper her. And he liked Yehuda, her husband; he recognized him as a counterpart to Joshua himself—a man who knew how to get things done, a man who accomplished his objectives.

"I'll send you my agent's name and address and the letter of credit authorization tomorrow," Joshua said as he and Aaron shook hands at the elevator. "And by the way, welcome back."

"Welcome back?" Aaron was puzzled.

"Yeah. Welcome back to the land of the living. You've arrived, whether you know it or not."

And then Joshua disappeared down the corridor, and Aaron grinned as he walked back to his office, thinking that Joshua Ellenberg the international magnate retained the wily wisdom of Josh the urchin entrepreneur.

Aaron flew to Washington the next day and kept the appointments he had set up with a journalist friend and a law-school classmate who had a middle-echelon job in the State Department. His journalist friend introduced him to a Hungarian correspondent, a dapper, mustachioed man who drank too much in the bar of Aaron's hotel. Over dinner he talked expansively of the beauty of Budapest and the mists that veiled Lake Balaton in the fall. He had never heard of a scientist called Groszman, but then these Jews changed their names more often than their underwear. He caught his error and struggled to set it right. Some of his most treasured comrades were Jewish, he assured them, and he showed them a photo of his university debate society. The thin man on his right, his dearest friend, he confided, was half Jewish. And he remembered now that he had heard of a Groszman, after all. A radar scientist, he thought, but it seemed to him that the man was dead. He could look it up if they wanted.

"Not important," Aaron assured him.

Aaron's State Department friend did not think the situation in Hungary was particularly volatile.

"And even if there were trouble," he said confidently, "they wouldn't mess with an American tourist. I don't like Dulles much myself," he added, "but one thing is sure—he's got the Bolshies scared to death. Tom Hemmings thinks so, at least. He likes the Budapest posting, by the way, but Betty hates it. Poor Betty. She saw herself wearing a Balenciaga and holding her hand out to de Gaulle on a Paris embassy receiving line. Instead she's queuing up with a couple of shabby diplomatic biddies at the hard-currency store in old Buda."

"I always liked Betty Hemmings," Aaron said warningly. Betty had been Katie's good friend, which meant that Katie had often called her in the middle of the night and had sent her rambling, incoherent letters.

Back in New York, he had dinner with his mother.

"I may have to go to Europe," he said.

"I see," she said carefully. Like Joshua, she did not ask him the nature of his business.

"You'd be alone here, with Michael in California and Rebecca back in Israel."

"Hardly alone," Leah said and dismissed his worry with a smile. "I have my work, my friends." She gestured toward her desk, overflowing with folders and correspondence. Leah was involved in organizing an effort on behalf of Russian Jewry. She drafted letters, arranged parlor meetings, smiled brilliantly at congressmen and lobbyists. She did not ask him where he would travel to in Europe, nor did she discuss the purpose of his trip.

He was not surprised when a package arrived from Bloomingdale's charged to his mother. Three no-iron white shirts and a tan cashmere sleeveless sweater. He called her.

"Thanks," he said. "But why didn't you just come over and pack for me?"

"Be careful," she said. Not "Have fun," but "Be careful." That night he listened to a record by two young comedians named Mike Nichols and Elaine May and decided that whoever wrote the Jewish mother jokes had never met a woman like Leah Goldfeder.

He went over his calendar with Eileen. Pending cases were assigned to associates. All correspondence was up-to-date. The article he had promised to a law journal had been typed and delivered. It was a good thing he had declined to teach his Columbia seminar this semester.

"When will you be back, Mr. Goldfeder?" Eileen asked. She wanted to know so that she might begin counting the days.

"I don't know exactly," he said. "In a few weeks, perhaps. Hold the fort and drink a lot of milk shakes." He had noticed for the first time that she was too thin. Many such things were catching his attention now, as though he were emerging from a long hibernation.

He had seen that the fabric on his living room sofa was frayed and that his apartment needed painting. He would organize things when he returned.

Only Yehuda and Almogi came to his office on Friday. Yehuda looked tired, and Aaron noticed that Almogi's jacket was too small. When he went to the window, he saw Greenstein on the street below, watching the entry to the office building. Their conspiratorial vigilance amused him.

"I've made all my arrangements," Aaron said brusquely. "I will go to Budapest."

"Good." Yehuda opened his attaché case and withdrew a travel agent's packet. A first-class reservation on Air Hungary. A letter from the Grand Hotel on Margaret Island in Budapest confirming Aaron Goldfeder's reservation for a "suite with a scenic view." A map of Budapest and a road map of Hungary.

Almogi spoke rapidly, advising Aaron on the details of his contact meeting with Dr. Groszman. Aaron listened as he spread the literature out on his desk. His name on the airline ticket was spelled incorrectly—Aron instead of Aaron. Otherwise they had made no mistakes. He was perversely annoyed. The cocky bastards had assumed his acceptance and had arrived fully prepared to send him on his way. Still, he was surprised at the warmth in Almogi's handshake, the tension in Yehuda's arms when he embraced him.

"We shall perhaps be in touch, in Budapest," Yehuda said, and Aaron felt strangely reassured.

"Shalom," he said softly. "Shalom."

AARON stood on the heights of Budapest and looked down at the tiny crowns of foam that crested the wavelets of the Danube River as it hugged the hills on its winding descent. He shivered and wondered if they were flecked with ice. After the gentleness of the early New York autumn, he had been unprepared for the harsh, wintry cold and the icy rains that slashed their way across the helpless and dreary facade of Budapest. He focused his camera on the panorama of the city spread before him like the miniature towns that Joshua Ellenberg's children liked to build with intricately shaped blocks. He discerned the green canopies of the Grand Hotel on Margaret Island and the wide embankments on either side of the river. The somber Gothic buildings that lined the broad quays stared haughtily up at the frowning hills. Cars and buses moved slowly across the graceful bridges.

The acacia trees, their leafless branches straining skyward in a tangle of blackened veins, quivered against a fierce and sudden gust of wind. Aaron's hat was blown off his head. He scurried after it and found it nesting on a sheet of yellow mimeograph paper. The handbill was closely printed in Hungarian and decorated with a crude drawing of the Hungarian tricolor. The Soviet hammer and sickle at its heart had been angrily crossed out. A vagrant wind had blown the propaganda sheet up to this silent plateau, but Aaron had noticed others since his arrival in Budapest.

On his first night in the city, Tom Hemmings had dutifully taken him for a routine sightseeing tour to the Leopoldstadt Basilica, and he had watched a team of green-coated police officers confiscate a pile of leaflets from a group of young people, who rushed away. An overweight officer had halfheartedly given chase to an auburn-haired girl and then wearily returned to collect the papers, which were placed in a leather pouch.

"What do the sheets say?" Aaron had asked.

Tom, a tall, angular-faced man, had shrugged uneasily as though the unrest in the country of his posting was somehow his fault. Betty, his petulant blond wife, had kicked at one with her boot, smiling as the police officer scurried after it.

"Oh, the usual," she said. "*Ruszhik horza!* Russians go home!" She had been an apt language student at Vassar and had decided to marry Tom Hemmings when she discovered he wanted a career in the foreign service. She had envisioned herself in Paris and London, in Rome or Vienna. Almost anywhere but Budapest. Dull, shabby Budapest, where fashions were at least two years behind the times and discussions centered on when the next shipment of sugar would arrive. The opening of a new bakery sent embassy wives scurrying to the telephone to proclaim the exciting news. There was not much else they could discuss on the phones, which were of course tapped.

"Funny to use police to pick them up," Aaron observed. "More of a job for the sanitation department, isn't it?"

"This is Budapest, Aaron, not New York," Tom said impatiently. "In New York those leaflets would be so much annoying litter, but in Budapest they're sedition. Those officers are not ordinary police. They're AVO men—security, secret service. That propaganda will be on Yuri Andropov's desk within the hour. The Soviet ambassador takes a keen interest in the political climate of Budapest."

Aaron carefully folded the yellow sheet and put it in his pocket. Perhaps Dr. Groszman would translate it for him. He glanced at his watch. In another hour he was to meet the scientist at the coffeehouse near the zoological gardens. He hurried to the funicular railway and turned his head as it descended so that he could look up at the domed citadel and the royal palace. It was, he thought, despite Betty Hemmings's discontent, a beautiful city, and he felt oddly grateful to Dr. Groszman, whose predicament had brought him there.

How would he know Groszman? he worried as he strode up fashionable Andrássy Avenue to the municipal park. The Israeli agents had provided him with neither a photograph nor a dossier. Instead, there had been uncharacteristic mutterings about a delay in the transfer of papers, a foul-up in communications.

"You will not miss each other," Almogi had assured him. "Just be in the café at five o'clock on the appointed day. Hold up the financial section of the international edition of the *Herald Tribune*. Dr. Groszman will recognize you."

Stupid cops-and-robbers tactic, Aaron thought now, remembering his near-panic that morning when the last copy of the *Tribune* had been sold before he reached the Grand Hotel concierge. It was pure luck that a British banker, staying on Margaret Island for the mineral baths, had sourly offered him his copy. Much safer to have had a photo, a phone number, an address. The Israelis were not as smart as they thought they were. He felt a vengeful satisfaction. It would not be his fault if things went wrong.

He paused at a vendor's kiosk and bought a postcard of the archangel Gabriel on the millennium monument at the entrance to the park. Willfully, he turned away from the huge bronze colossus of Stalin that dominated the area. The sculptor may have conceived of the Russian leader as a benevolent figure, but the final effect was alien and threatening. Aaron had no doubt that his mother would prefer the winged angel. In fact, Leah would like Budapest. He imagined her walking across the suspension bridges that connected the banks of the Danube, perhaps sketching the river from the Franz Josef quay, where he had watched artists at work. Once Leah had concentrated on designs, on intricate geometric shapes that had been translated into the textiles and fabrics that had contributed to the success of both S. Hart, Inc., and Ellenberg Industries. But more recently she had been fascinated by landscapes and urban scenes. Her brushstrokes were broad and daring, her colors bright; she painted with a new optimism, a new strength.

Aaron bought additional cards for the Ellenbergs and for his brother, Michael, and as he shuffled through the assortment searching for a scenic view to send to Eileen Manning, he glimpsed a pile of the familiar mimeographed sheets. The kiosk keeper swiftly covered them with a stack of the afternoon edition of *Szabad Nép*, whose front page featured a candid shot of a smiling Premier Gero seated companionably on a park bench with Yuri Andropov, the Soviet ambassador.

Aaron walked at a steady pace and passed the terminus where the yellow streetcars stood in weary convoy, ready to maneuver the winding streets of the capital. The battered vehicles were the transport lifeline of the poor. On every corner, queues of weary men and women awaited the trundling streetcars. They were laden with clumsy bundles and swaddled in layers of clothing because no single shabby garment was heavy enough to ward off the damp, invasive cold. Yet they stood on line quietly, acquiescently. They accepted the inevitability of their wait with the pragmatic resignation of the poor and the powerless. Their lives were an endless series of queues. Perhaps they would have to wait in line for death itself.

On one such line, as he returned from the Hemmingses' flat, Aaron had seen a small redheaded boy who stood beside his mother holding a burlap sack of vegetables. Abruptly, he remembered himself as a youngster, standing beside his mother and his aunt Mollie as they waited for the Avenue B bus. They, too, had been poor and burdened with strangely wrapped packages, but Leah Goldfeder and her sister had been fiercely impatient during that wait. They had stamped their feet, peered anxiously into the street, muttering angrily to each other and complaining at last to the unfortunate bus driver. Anger was a powerful ingredient in the struggle for change, Aaron thought, but the only anger he had seen in Budapest was contained on the scrawled messages on the clandestine rainbow-colored sheets of mimeograph paper. He had been conscious of nervousness, of furtive backward glances, of a subtle, subdued tension.

Only yesterday he had seen police officers approach a small group standing on a street corner and disperse them. There had been no violence. One officer had raised his nightstick, and the other had opened a pad and searched for a pencil; that had been sufficient to send everyone hurrying away. A harmless enough group, Aaron had thought. Housewives holding plastic shopping bags and workingmen carrying small iron lunch pails. Still, they had been frightened, and their running footsteps had echoed down the wide boulevard.

And in the evening, as he returned from dinner at the Hemmingses'—a weary meal during which Betty had apologized endlessly for the toughness of the meat, the wilted salad greens, the overcooked compote—a young couple, walking ahead of him hand in hand on the Margaret Bridge, had been stopped by two men wearing raincoats and brimmed hats. Aaron had watched them produce their papers, heard the harshness of the questions they were asked, and as he passed, he noticed the pallor of the young woman's face, the glitter of fear in her eyes. What kind of a country was this, he had wondered, where lovers could not stroll peacefully across a moonlit bridge on an autumn evening?

He crossed the road now and entered the Budapest Wood, hurrying through the patterned pathways so reminiscent of an English park. The carefully pruned box hedges were covered with protective sacking, and the bound stalks of iris and chrysanthemum were bleached and brittle. Yet, even in this season of desuetude, lovers strolled through the park hand in hand and sat, shoulders delicately touching, on the bright green benches. An old woman carried a sack of crumbs, which she tossed to the ash-colored sparrows that winged their way down through the barren branched trees. There were few solitary strollers, but several meters ahead of him he noticed a woman following the path that led past the amusement park to the zoo.

He was arrested by her purposeful gait, the forward thrust of her shoulders beneath a scarlet cape. The courage of the color against the blanched landscape pleased him. Her hair was as black as once his mother's had been, and she wore it twisted into a neat yet luxuriant knot that rested in a swirl of ebony against her graceful neck. She carried an envelope, and as she walked it slipped to the ground, yet she made no effort to retrieve it, as though unaware of the loss.

Aaron hurried after her.

"Madame, vous avez perdu quelque chose." His French was rusty and his voice muffled as he struggled with the unfamiliar language.

She did not turn, and before he could reach the fallen envelope, a black Chaika, its fender dented and its left headlight smashed, paused for an instant. A door opened, and the fallen envelope was swiftly plucked up. Helpless and angered, Aaron watched the car speed away and then hurried after the woman, catching up with her before an ancient elm.

"Madame, you dropped an envelope. I meant to retrieve it for you, but a car stopped and someone took it and sped away. I hope it was not an important document."

She turned toward him. Her oval face, framed by the black wings of hair, was porcelain white, and her large turquoise-colored eyes were wide with surprise. He thought that she had not understood his English, and he struggled to formulate the sentence in French, but she interrupted him, speaking an excellent and charmingly accented English.

"So careless of me. But truly it was of no importance. I thank you for your concern," she said.

She smiled in dismissal and walked on, choosing a path that led to a distant copse. Confused and annoyed, he stared after her until her scarlet cape vanished in a cluster of evergreens. He shrugged then and cursed himself for his naiveté. He should have known better than to stop her. Yehuda Arnon would have ignored her, as he himself should have. This was Eastern Europe, he reminded himself, where telephones were routinely tapped and groups of housewives were dispersed by threatening police officers. He walked on, remembering the throaty quality of her voice, the lilting cadence of her English, in which she had so charmingly and gracefully lied to him.

The zoological gardens were deserted except for two small boys who stood aimlessly before a cage inhabited by a single sad mandrill. There was nothing in the animal's desultory antics to engage their interest, and they wandered over to the lake and studied the slate-gray sheet of water. In the summer they had perhaps boated here, and later, when true winter arrived, they would skate across its shimmering surface. But now they were trapped in this colorless season and could only wait for something to happen. It seemed to Aaron that all of Budapest was waiting for something to happen.

He glanced at his watch and saw that it was exactly five o'clock. Dr. Groszman had most probably already arrived at the small coffeehouse. Aaron had no doubt that the scientist would be on time, and he imagined him already consulting his watch, straightening his too-wide and somber tie, buttoning and unbuttoning the vest of his grim gray academic suit. Aaron's feelings toward this unknown client seesawed. Now, at the moment of meeting, he was briefly and irrationally annoyed with the man who had jolted him from the cocoon of his grief, from the narcotizing intellectual involvement of his work, into this shabby city with its dusty, decrepit buildings, its trundling yellow streetcars, and its threatening ambience of simmering danger.

The café was dimly lit and almost empty. The cashier held a sheet of paper, which she thrust beneath the counter when he entered. The waitress, a middle-aged woman in a shapeless black uniform, guided him to a table at the rear of the room. Glumly, he ordered a café au lait and a Sacher torte. He glanced at the photographs on the wall—

the Hungarian leaders Gero and Rákosi, the Soviet premier Khrushchev. One photograph, newly removed, had left the rectangular stain of its imprint on the patterned paper. Stalin, he supposed, and congratulated himself on living in a country where it was not the custom to adorn the walls of coffee shops with political portraiture.

A bell sounded as the café door swung open, and Aaron was surprised to see the woman in the scarlet cape hesitate in the entryway. She studied the room, her eyes resting briefly on his shadowed figure, but she chose a table close to the door. She did not look at him again, and he felt saddened, disappointed, as though he had been cursorily judged and found wanting.

When his coffee arrived, he stirred it carelessly, allowing the whipped cream to drip onto the tabletop in foaming tears. He opened his newspaper. The front page of the *Tribune* carried an article on the creation of a new Suez authority. Prime Minister Anthony Eden had announced the decision in the House of Commons.

Just like the British, Aaron thought, to lock the barn door after the horse has been stolen. There might have been a chance for such an authority before Nasser nationalized the canal, but now . . . He shrugged and turned to the financial page.

"Mr. Goldfeder, how very good to see you." The woman in the scarlet cape smiled at him as though they were old friends. She extended her hand. Her fingers were icy to his touch, yet her grip was firm. It was a conspiratorial clasp at once both monitory and reassuring.

"It is so dark in this café that I did not see you at first. May I join you?"

"Of course."

She slipped into the seat opposite him and gestured to the waitress, who brought her tea to Aaron's table. A small shaded lamp stood on the table, and she pulled at the dangling cord and lit it. In the new circlet of light, Aaron saw a pale crescent of a scar on his companion's wrist; a turquoise birthmark that matched her eyes was soft as velvet at the curve of her neck. The waitress brought a plate of croissants, a dish of strawberry confiture.

"*C'est assez*, Dr. Groszman?" She smiled deferentially, a dull silver tooth filling a gap between two missing molars.

"*C'est assez.*"

The woman withdrew and Aaron smiled.

"They didn't happen to mention that Dr. Groszman was a woman."

"Then let me introduce myself," she said. "I am Dr. Lydia Groszman. Would it have made a difference if you had known?"

"I'm not sure," he replied honestly.

"Then perhaps that is why they did not mention it."

"Possibly."

He wondered what else they had omitted to mention in view of the psychological profile they had drawn up on him. He imagined them meeting and talking about him in cautious, analytic tones: "This Goldfeder has been funny about women since the death of his wife . . . wants no closeness . . . perhaps it will be best not to make him apprehensive . . . once we've got him in Budapest he can hardly turn around and come home." Clever bastards. His own brother-in-law had felt no compunction about recruiting Rebecca, so young and naive then, totally untrained—yet Yehuda enlisted her as an agent in his rescue work. They were single-minded in their goal. Jewish survival took precedence over everything. Still, one had to admire them. Their techniques worked.

"Do you mind?" she asked.

"Not now," he replied and was surprised at the spontaneous truth of his answer. He was glad to be in Budapest, glad to be sitting opposite this beautiful woman in a deserted, tree-bound café.

"Good." She smiled. "I have my dossier with me."

"The very same dossier that mysteriously could not be found in New York."

"The same." She reached into her bag, pulled out a folder, and held it out to him.

"How fortunate that you did not drop this as you walked," he said.

She averted her eyes, and the camellia pallor of her skin was tinged with an underglow of rose color that petaled her cheeks with delicate blossoms of embarrassment.

"I'll explain that," she said softly.

"Of course you will." His tone was dry, impersonal. It was the voice of his private office, dispassionate and unrelenting. He had to know the truth of their situations, he always told his clients. The truth was his only weapon. Their honest answers became his arsenal of attack.

He sipped his coffee and read through the dossier with the detached preoccupation of his profession, searching out inconsistencies, lacunae that might raise questions, unexplained coincidences that would cause an immigration hearing officer to look up in puzzlement. One doubt begat others. It was his job to forestall that first hesitancy.

The facts were quite simple. Lydia Groszman, née Englander, had been born in Budapest in 1922 to Dr. Joseph Englander and his wife, Lotte. She was the third child and the only daughter in a family of four children. Her two older brothers had been killed in the massacre of Jews at Novi Sad during the Nazi occupation. A third brother lived in San Francisco, where he practiced public accountancy. An affidavit had been obtained in which he declared himself willing to sponsor his sister's immigration application and stating that he had the means to support her. Dr. and Mrs. Englander had both died in Budapest on the same date, March 20, 1944. Aaron penciled a light question mark on that line and read on. Lydia had spent the war years hidden by the nursing sisters of Saint Stephen's Hospital, where her father had served as chief surgeon. After the war she had enrolled at the University of Budapest as a student of theoretical physics. She had married her professor, Ferenc Groszman, and for some years they had worked together in the field of radar technology. Her husband had died in 1954, and his widow, now on the faculty of the Technical Institute, wished to join her only surviving relation, her brother, Alexander, in San Francisco. There was also a sworn statement from the chairman of her department that for the past two years Dr. Groszman had not been privy to classified information or involved in research that related to national security.

"I think everything is in order," she said, and he discerned a shade of defensiveness in her tone.

"Perhaps. Your parents died on the same day?"

"Yes." She stirred her tea and added a lump of sugar but did not raise the cup to her lips.

"What were the circumstances of their deaths?" His voice was steady, gentle but insistent. She answered in tones so soft that he had to lean forward to hear her.

"The date is important. On March 19, 1944, a German officer named Adolf Eichmann came to Budapest. His name is forgotten now, and they say he escaped to some South American country, but we have not forgotten him. It was the beginning of the German occupation, and he was the German authority on so-called Jewish affairs. He ordered the leaders of the Jewish community to appear at a conference at his office the next day. March 20. Do you know that on every March 20 since then it has snowed in Budapest? God's penitence, perhaps. A sign that He remembers. In any case, my father went to that conference. Before the Nazis came, before the Arrow Cross party began its campaign against the Jewish people, he had not had much to do with the Jewish community. But the war changed that. He was a man of standing in the community, and suddenly he was an active Jew, rushing off to meetings, organizing clinics. He knew, I think, what might happen, because he sent me into hiding very early and arranged for Alexander to go to America.

"In any case, he went to the conference in Eichmann's office, and he came to the hospital afterward. I met him in the visitors' room. I wore the costume of a novice in the nursing order; it included a wooden beaded rosary and a wooden cross. My father had never been a religious man. He considered himself, at most, a cultural Jew. When my brother Jan married a Gentile girl, he and my mother did not object. They went to the wedding, which was held in a church. Their friends were almost all Gentile—until the war, that is. Then, of course, their friends deserted them. A man with whom he had played in a string quartet for two decades passed him on the street without nodding.

"That afternoon, when he saw the cross I wore, he removed it form my neck and put it in the pocket of my apron. He told me then that Eichmann had told him he would have to become a member of the Judenrat, a council of Jews that would carry out German orders, inform on other Jews perhaps, draw up lists for deportations. 'I cannot do it,' he said. 'Impossible.' I nodded. I remember that my hand went into my apron pocket, and I began to move the beads of the rosary as though I might find some answer, some solution. The beads were so cool, so smooth. My father gave me the name of the Jewish organization that had taken my brother Alexander to America. When he left, he kissed me once on each cheek. That night, after dinner, he and my mother each drank a glass of plum brandy. They sat beside each other on our sofa holding hands. She wore her best maroon moiré dress with a lace frill at the collar, and he wore his black dinner suit with the satin lapels. He had perhaps played some music, because his violin was beside him when the neighbors found them the next day. Their hands were clasped, and her head rested on his shoulder. Our neighbors were very kind people, and they washed away the crystals of prussic acid that remained in the cordial glasses before they called the police."

"I'm sorry," Aaron said, "but I had to know. The American immigration authorities would have taken note just as I did, and they might draw unfortunate conclusions that would prejudice your application. A double suicide might indicate a background of mental instability in your family."

"Suicide was a rational act under the Nazis," she said. "But of course I understand that there is no room for those who are possibly unstable in your great country."

"Look," Aaron replied evenly, "I do not condone my country's laws and I do not justify them. I do work to change them, but until they are changed I must work carefully within them as competently as I can. I am here to help you, not to argue with you. And in order to help you, I must have the answers to any questions that I ask. Remember, I am acting for you, but there are those in authority who will be asking questions as adversaries."

"I know," she said. "I apologize. I suppose we live in this country in such an atmosphere of distrust that it is difficult to have faith in anyone."

"Tell me about your husband, about Ferenc Groszman," Aaron said.

Her voice grew very soft and he was reminded of the tenderness in his mother's voice when she spoke of David Goldfeder. Too often his own voice was harsh when he spoke of Katie.

"Ferenc was a wonderful man," she said. "Very kind. Very gentle. I was all alone after the war. I had no family, few friends. And Ferenc was also alone. His wife and his daughter had died during a forced march to Austria. Only he and his young son, Paul, had survived the war. I was a student in his lecture class, and he asked me to assist him in his laboratory. We met occasionally at the synagogue on Dohány Street, where we both went to say Kaddish. He would walk me to my hostel. We were companions in loss and sorrow. He was a father who had lost his daughter, and I was an orphan.

"Soon we began to meet and go to the synagogue together and share a meal afterward. It seemed only natural to have dinner together each evening, sometimes with Paul, sometimes just the two of us. Each Sunday we arranged to walk in the park together or to take Paul to the countryside. I made a cake for Paul's sixth birthday, and we felt like a family. Paul even laughed. The laughter of a sad child is a small miracle, a wonderful sound. And Paul was—is—a wonderful child. A handsome boy with the singing voice of an angel. He sang at our wedding. We were so happy, the three of us. And then Ferenc became ill. Chest pains, fatigue, a terrible racking cough. A result of his internment in a camp where the Jews worked in an asbestos factory, the doctors said.

"He knew he was dying. He asked me to take care of Paul. He did not have to ask. Paul is part of my life. He is my family, my son, my brother, my friend.

"Paul and I were with him when he died. And Paul sang the El Ma'ale Rachamim prayer at the funeral—'God Who is full of mercy.' And I thought to myself, Yes, God was merciful to my Ferenc. He let him die of disease and not by his own hand or the hand of others. He let him die in a bed. And He left me Paul, my sweet-singing son."

Her voice broke and tears slid down her cheeks. She made no move to wipe them away.

"I understand," Aaron said. All the deaths in his own life had also been violent. His natural father had been beaten to death during a pogrom in the streets of Odessa. His closest friend had died in his arms on an Ethiopian roadway. His wife had been crushed beneath the wheels of a taxi. David Goldfeder had been killed by a fedayeen's bullet. None of those he loved had retreated gently into the waiting night.

"Do you?" Her voice was harsh and laced with disbelief. The American lawyer came from a land that had never known the marching boots of a marauding army. The bridges that straddled the rivers of his land had never been destroyed, like the bridges of the Danube during the dark days of the war. American soldiers crossed the sea to do battle, but their homes were unscarred, their cities intact. Americans did not starve. They had never eaten soups cooked of wild grass and acorns. She had gone to the cinema and watched American women shop in brightly lit, wide-aisled stores where they plucked groceries and produce from laden shelves and hesitated between cuts of meat at a gleaming butcher's counter. No American could understand violence and loss, poverty and desperation.

He ignored her question. This was no time for revelations or a competition in misery. It was necessary for him to know her story, but his life, he acknowledged, was irrelevant to her.

"What were Ferenc Groszman's political affiliations?" he asked. The question was crucial. Lingering filaments of fear and distrust, the residue of the McCarthy years, still hovered over his country.

She hesitated.

"Let me explain," she said. "All during the war we were obsessed by our hatred for the Germans and our own Hungarian Fascist party, the Arrow Cross. It was the Arrow Cross that forced us to ally with Nazi Germany during the war, and it cooperated with the Germans in the deportations. The Soviet Army liberated us, and the Russians became our saviors. We were starving and they brought us food. Every bridge across the Danube had been destroyed, and they rebuilt them. There was inflation, and they introduced economic reforms. Slowly, we were seduced. The Communists formed alliances with the workers, with the peasants, and, of course, the intellectuals. Ferenc and his colleagues were ambivalent about the basic philosophy of communism. They were, after all, scientists, musicians, linguists, not political theoreticians. But they all saw the Communists as liberators and protectors. Ferenc was not a political person. He wanted only a benevolent and just government that would leave Jews alone. When he finally joined the party, it was with a certain amount of naive hope."

"Then he was a known advocate of Communism and the Soviet Union?" Aaron asked, frowning. The immigration authorities would love that, and the right-wing columnists would have a field day. He could see the headlines now: "Widow of Hungarian Communist Gains Entry to the United States! *How? Why?*"

"Yes. He was a Communist," she said impatiently. "But everyone was then. The Jewish intellectuals and artists, the concentration camp survivors, the true Hungarian nationalists—of course they flocked to a party that was totally opposed to the Arrow Cross, to the Nazis, to the killers. No one knew, then, that while the Soviets were courting the Jews and the liberals, they were also recruiting the Fascists. It is a classic Communist ploy. They work two ends against the middle, and in the end they had a very efficient, neatly balanced seesaw. Only then did they show their true aim—the creation of a totally Soviet-dominated state in Hungary. Ferenc was among the first of the intellectuals to recognize the truth. He wept the night Cardinal Mindszenty was arrested. People came to visit us at odd hours to tell us of sudden detentions, interrogations. A key laboratory assistant disappeared, and it became routine for mail to be opened and for phone wires to be tapped. The AVO—the security police—became more and more powerful. Ferenc signed letters of protest. He made an official complaint when a letter from my brother, Alexander, was opened. He raised objections and made inquiries on behalf of friends. At first the authorities disregarded him, but soon they could not afford such a luxury. They made notations on his *Kader Lopok*."

"His *Kader Lopok*?" Aaron asked, puzzled.

"Of course, you don't understand what that is. There is no such thing in your country. In Hungary the government keeps a complete record on each individual—occupation and personal history, political and religious views, family secrets, professional skeletons. That is the *Kader Lopok*. Ferenc's must have become suspect. He was denied an exit visa to attend an important conference on radar technology in Paris. The AVO visited us, asked questions. Twice we were certain that our flat had been searched in our absence, and once, at the beginning of Ferenc's illness, he was taken to AVO headquarters in the middle of the night. They threatened him and released him, but he ignored their warnings. He became a member of the Petofi Circle, a group of intellectuals who were convinced that Russian influence in Hungary had to end."

"Did the authorities try to stop him?" Aaron asked.

"They were reluctant to interfere with his work. Ferenc had been responsible for a major breakthrough in radar technology. He had an international reputation. It was more convenient for them, after a while, to ignore him; to allow him to continue his scientific research, even to display him to visiting foreign scientists at state functions. We would go together to a reception at Gero's home and then, still in our evening clothes, to a meeting where we discussed how Gero could be overthrown. Ferenc lived this double life until he died. And he died with the hope that we could win, that communism could be overthrown in Hungary. A few months later, Imre Nagy was removed from power. I have always been relieved that Ferenc died before that happened. He had loved Nagy and believed in him."

"Then in the end he was known as anti-Communist?" Aaron queried with relief. Nothing in that for Joe McCarthy's political and journalistic heirs to seize on. He rewrote his imagined headline. "Widow of Hungarian Resistance Leader Admitted to the United States!"

"Yes."

"And you?"

"I am a scientist. I continue Ferenc's research in radar technology."

"And do you continue his political work as well?"

She did not answer, but he persisted.

"That envelope which you dropped—is it relevant to our discussion? Madame, I remind you that I have come to Budapest to help you."

Delicately, with great care, she buttered a croissant and painted it with strawberry confiture, all the while studying his face. At last she sighed and wiped her fingers on a napkin.

"I suppose you must know about that envelope," she said. "It was, after all, important, as you guessed. It contained information that will be passed on to my comrades in an organization that is working toward the end of Russian domination of Hungary. I am continuing Ferenc's work, and so is Paul."

"I'm not sure I understand," Aaron said. "My Israeli contacts told me that you wish to leave Budapest and immigrate to the United States. They persuaded me to come here on your behalf. Now you tell me of your involvement in what I am sure must be an illegal organization. Isn't this a foolish undertaking if you plan to leave the country? It could jeopardize your position, endanger you." His voice was edged with professional impatience, reproof.

She toyed with the remnant of her croissant, arranging the golden crumbs in small piles on the brown-and-white pebbled marble table.

"It may be unwise, but in a way I feel I have no choice. I do want to emigrate. And I want to take Paul with me. Hungary is full of unhappy memories for me. But I promised Ferenc before he died that I would continue his work with the Petofi Circle, his efforts to see freedom and democracy restored to the country. I think now, at last, that it is possible. Stalin's death has changed many things. There are reforms in the Soviet Union. There have been many changes in Poland. We think that the same thing can happen in Hungary, and already we have seen a relaxation. We are moving toward new times. Only this past winter, the nine men who were on trial with Cardinal Mindszenty were released."

"But Mindszenty himself is still interned," Aaron reminded her.

"And in the spring some of our more liberal leaders were released from prison."

"And yet a man as important as Imre Nagy has still not been readmitted to the party."

"Our journalists are openly demanding freedom of the press."

"And their demands have been rewarded with expulsion from the party and the loss of their jobs."

They were caught up now in a fierce game of verbal Ping-Pong. She parried her claims of progress against his perception of political reality. Tom Hemmings had briefed him well. The Soviets would not so easily relinquish their dominion over Hungary. They would follow their established pattern; they would distribute a few crumbs and claim that they had granted a cake. They would give with one hand and take back with another.

At last she spread her hands out on the table as though acknowledging defeat.

"You may be right," she said. "There may be no hope of change. But how could I live with myself if I deserted my country when there was a possibility that my help might make a difference? I want to live in the West, but I can only go with a clear conscience if I know that I have fulfilled my obligation to my husband's memory. Can you understand that?"

He remembered suddenly a fierce exchange with Katie just before she died. They had been arguing furiously about vacation plans, and Katie had screamed that there was no time for vacations—there was too much for them to do. "We've got to make the world right!" she had shouted at him. Was that the obligation he paid to her memory, with his self-imposed crusade of endless work? The tyranny of the dead was a grim one. Corpses cannot be deposed; the dead cannot make rebuttal. Their victory is automatic.

"Why is your participation so important?" he asked gently. Rebecca had asked him a similar question so many years ago when he had enlisted in the RAF: *Why must you go? Why must it be you?*

"I just might make a difference," Lydia replied. "I might be in the right place at the right time." It was the same answer he had given Rebecca then. He could not argue with a logic that so closely matched his own.

"Paul is also involved. He is a leader of a small group of dissident students in his secondary school. He wants to see the struggle through to the end. And I am in a privileged position. I am an important scientist, and my own loyalty has never been questioned. After Ferenc's death, AVO ran a thorough security check on me, and no irregularity was found. I was cleared to work with classified information, although it has not been necessary and I was allowed to attend a scientific conference in London. Because of my status I can move freely throughout the city without arousing suspicion. I travel from the university center, where most of our group's decisions are made, into areas like Ulloi Avenue and Lenin Boulevard where our grass roots-leadership is centered. The envelope that I dropped contained a plan for a demonstration connected with the reinterment of Laszlo Rajk and the other victims of the purge trials of 1949. I was able to carry it from the university to the drop point. I carry propaganda leaflets and other documents in the same way."

"But how long can you continue to do this without attracting attention?" he asked. "I saw you today. How long will it be before an AVO agent spots you?"

"The revolution is imminent. It is only a question of a few weeks, a month. We have the momentum now and we can win. By the end of October, Hungary should be free. Paul and I can emigrate with the knowledge that I have been true to myself and true to Ferenc's memory. I will, of course, understand if you cannot wait that long for the hearing. Perhaps you feel now that your trip has been for nothing and your time has been wasted. If so, I am sorry." Her apology was tinged with gentle mockery. How could the schedule of any individual be as urgent as her revolution, as her involvement in Hungary's future?

"I was not told about Paul," Aaron observed mildly. "You realize, of course, that this complicates matters. We are now asking for two waivers, not one. And Paul, of course, would not receive the kind of preferential treatment that my government would award a scientist of your rank."

"But Paul is my son," she said fiercely. "According to Hungarian law I am his mother, just as if he had been born to me. Surely, if a mother is granted a visa she is not expected to leave a minor child behind."

"There may be complications," Aaron continued. "Perhaps you could leave without him. He could be enrolled in a boarding school, and we could arrange for his emigration when your own situation is more secure."

His calm voice masked the fury he felt. The damn incompetents. If he had known about Paul while he was in the States, he could have researched precedents, obtained opinions. He would have to rely on Tom Hemmings now and on Joshua Ellenberg's powerful congressional connections. Damn! Lydia stared at him, her blue eyes as hard as agates.

"You have no children, Mr. Goldfeder?" she asked.

"No," he replied shortly.

"Then I do not know if you can understand. When Ferenc and I were married, I told Paul, 'Your father is my husband and you are my son.' But for a long time he did not believe me. He worked very hard at being very good, very tidy, very quiet, because the woman on the farm where he had been hidden during the war had told him that she would not hide a noisy, untidy child. Then, one night, I went into his room. He was crying hard but without a sound. He had had a fearful nightmare and had stuffed a rag into his mouth to quiet his sobs. He did not want to be sent away. I was angry. I pulled it out and told him that this was his home and that children had a right to cry and to laugh and to scream in their homes. The day he left his crayons in the middle of the floor and ran out to play, slamming the door behind him, I knew he really belonged to us. That was almost ten years ago. Ten years is forever in a child's life. I nursed him through measles and chicken pox, and he helped me to nurse his father. He held my hand at the funeral. 'We won't be lonely,' he told me when we came home from the cemetery. "We have each other.'

"Sometimes I go with him to the singing teacher, and I sit outside during his lesson and listen to him. I think then that perhaps God had a special reason for saving Paul. He would not take a child with the voice of an angel.

"How could I go to America and leave my Paul?"

"You can't," Aaron said with a firmness that surprised himself. "We will find a way."

He stared out the window at the dying of the autumn day. The lingering light drifted into evening shadow, and he felt himself drift, just as unresistantly, into her perception, her consciousness. Briefly, he had hovered, like a spectator, at the periphery of her passion. Now, as though pulled by magnetic force, he felt himself drawn to its center. He would not try to dissuade her either from her work or from her determination to bring Paul Groszman out of the country with her. He would join her. His heart beat faster and he felt a rush of warmth, a surge of energy.

"I want you to let me help you," he said. "To let me help you and Paul."

"How?" she asked warily. "You will help us, of course, with the papers, the hearing. That is why you are here."

"Of course. That much is understood. But I want to help you with your work. I, too, can move with impunity through the streets of Budapest. I can visit certain places perhaps more easily than you can. I want to help you. If you will trust me, allow me."

"I trust you," she said softly. "I allow you. But we will have to devise a scenario for you."

"I will be your American uncle."

"No. You are too young."

"Then I will be your lover."

"I have never had a lover."

"It's time, then."

"All right." She smiled, and suddenly her face was alive with mischief and pleasure. Her eyes glittered with gemlike brilliance and a blush colored her skin. He thought he knew now what she must have looked like as a young girl; he imagined her laughing at a party, flirting with tentative timidity in a student café, before the war came to rob her of innocence and gaiety.

He leaned forward and with his fingertip traced the turquoise birthmark that flowered at her neck. It was velvet-soft, and he stroked it gently, rhythmically. The cashier dimmed the café lights, and the waitress removed their cups and piled them onto an enamel tray. He left too many florin notes on the table and slipped the scarlet cape over her shoulders. Outside they looked up and saw the first star of the evening clinging tenaciously to the violet-veined twilight sky.

DURING the days that followed their first meeting they worked diligently at the scenario they had so casually devised. Lydia came to the Grand Hotel each afternoon, and she and Aaron sat in the tea salon and ate elaborately sculpted pastries filled with tart berries from the woods of Buda. They toasted each other with glasses of tea laced with plum brandy. The other guests, mostly visiting businessmen and those who came to take the waters of Margaret Island's famous Palatinus Baths, looked at them with the wistfulness with which the ill consider the healthy and the unloved view the loved. All of them were bored in this dull and shabby East European capital. They had visited the Gypsy nightclubs too many times and eaten more than once at the barge restaurants along the Danube. Lydia and Aaron were an interesting diversion—such an attractive couple, the dignified redheaded American and the beautiful Hungarian woman. The Soviet diplomat who had come to the thermal waters to relieve his bursitic shoulder noted Aaron's name in his little black book, but his wife was intrigued by Lydia's clothing, by her swirling velvet skirts and the brilliantly hued blouses against which her skin shimmered like polished porcelain.

There were knowing, conspiratorial glances when Aaron and Lydia left the room and ascended, in the wrought-iron cage of the lift, to his third-floor suite. It did not escape the notice of these casual observers that the lovers (for surely only lovers shared wordless smiles and averted glances and sought aloneness at evening's edge) offered each other gifts—small boxes and elegantly wrapped parcels from the shops on the Grand Boulevard.

An elderly gentleman who always sat at a green velvet banquette in a shadowed corner, where he drank a single cup of black coffee followed by a small glass of golden brandy, walked past them one afternoon and dropped his gloves near their table. He bent to retrieve them and studied the box that rested beside Lydia on the floor, jostling it slightly. It was from an excellent haberdashery, and he smiled thinly, approvingly.

"He's an AVO agent," Lydia said. Her eyes followed him as he bowed charmingly to the wife of a British banker and nodded to the Soviet diplomat.

"How do you know?"

"I saw him once, outside Ferenc's office. And while they were verifying my clearance, I saw him follow me. He's gone now. Let's go upstairs."

In Aaron's room she opened the package and removed an elegant paisley dressing gown in rich tones of forest green and burgundy. Its sleeves had been padded with tissue paper, and within the folds of the tissue paper, documents had been concealed. She removed them carefully and explained them to him. An agenda for a secret meeting to be held by the electricians' union, a list of addresses of dissidents, a summation of student demands to be delivered to a printer.

Aaron hung the robe in his closet, where the chambermaid would see it in the morning. He looped the belt about the hanger.

"You have excellent taste," he said.

She shrugged.

"A colleague in Paris sent the robe to Ferenc. A student whose mother works in the shop obtained the box and wrappings for me."

He felt the sullen disappointment of a child who has been told that a supposedly new toy had once been owned by another youngster. He imagined the elderly Ferenc Groszman sitting opposite her at the breakfast table in the robe that had so briefly pleased him. Lydia would have adjusted the collar for him, her pale hands tender at his exposed neck.

"Ferenc never wore it," she said suddenly. She did not look at him but continued to slip the documents between the pages of the financial section of the *Herald Tribune*.

That night he carried the newspaper to a café in Old Buda, near the Vienna high road, where Gypsies played mournful melodies. A well-dressed businessman at a neighboring table politely asked if he had finished the paper.

"I am particularly interested in the new copper discoveries in South America."

"You will find that story on page nineteen," Aaron said politely, and it occurred to him that his prowess would have impressed those who had marched with him in demonstrations during his student days—the would-be revolutionaries of yesteryear, all comfortably settled now in Long Island or Westchester, doctors and dentists, lawyers and businessmen. Then they had all been members of the Young People's Socialist League, and at their meetings they had spoken feverishly of a new world in which social justice and equality prevailed. He and his closest friend, Gregory Liebowitz, had often talked through the night of projects they would undertake, arguing about food cooperatives and socialized medicine beneath the poster of Mother Bloor that hung in Aaron's cold-water flat. Gregory had enlisted with Aaron in the RAF and had died of dysentery in Ethiopia. *Poor Gregory.* Sorrow for his lost friend gripped Aaron, and he fought against it. Gregory was dead and he was in Budapest.

The businessman left the café, and two men followed him out. A coincidence, Aaron thought, but he felt a shaft of apprehension. He ordered a cognac, and the waiter who brought it gave him a folded slip of white paper.

"From that gentleman who is just leaving," he said.

Aaron looked up, startled at the sight of Yehuda Arnon tipping the girl at the checkroom. Yehuda's eyes met his without a flicker of recognition, and Aaron downed his cognac as his brother-in-law left the café. A phone number was scrawled on the half sheet. *Use only if necessary,* Yehuda had written in his unique cursive script. Aaron realized that Yehuda's presence had briefly unnerved him but had not really surprised him. He felt grimly reassured, and he tucked the slip of paper beneath the snapshot of Katie in his wallet and caught the last tram back to Margaret Island. As he hung his suit up, he noticed that the belt which he had draped on a hanger was now neatly looped about the paisley robe.

LYDIA invited him to dinner, and he met Paul Groszman. The tall blond boy was slender and moved with an easy grace. His narrow face glowed with the last of the summer tan gained at his music camp in the hill country. He had been the lead boy tenor in the choir—his last year in such a role, he said laughingly. His voice was changing.

"Perhaps you will sing for Mr. Goldfeder," Lydia suggested.

Paul blushed and threw her an embarrassed look.

"Perhaps later," he said, and Aaron liked him for his restraint, for the concealment of his annoyance.

Later, he saw Lydia talking softly to Paul in the kitchen. The boy bent and kissed her cheek. He supposed that he had apologized and they had made up. He liked Paul even more for being an adolescent who was not embarrassed to kiss his mother.

"What do you think of going to America with your mother, Paul?" he asked as they sat in the small, book-lined living room drinking cups of hot chocolate. He had been in Budapest long enough to know that Lydia must have stood on a food queue for hours to obtain the cream that floated like a snowy flower on the rich, dark drink.

"I'm not sure," Paul said. "Hungary is my country. My friends are here. But, of course, I will go with my mother if that is what she wants." He looked unhappily at Lydia.

"I would not do anything that made you unhappy," Lydia said quickly.

"No. Of course not. I am much interested in democracy," he added quickly, as though fearful that his answer might have offended Aaron. "And I know the American composers. Aaron Copland and Charles Ives. In the camp we sang songs by Leonard Bernstein. Do you know this?"

He went to the small upright piano and played "New York, New York" from *On the Town*.

Aaron joined him and together they sang the first verses of "I'll Take Manhattan." Paul's voice was vibrant, and he sang with a rare sense of joy. He was right. Within a few months it would reach its full depth, its ringing, soaring range.

They finished the song in a burst of their own laughter as their improvised lyrics tumbled into nonsense, and to Lydia's pleased applause. Paul left soon afterward. He was meeting friends, he said.

"Will Genia be there?" Lydia asked.

"Yes. Of course." He shook hands with Aaron. "I hope we will meet soon again."

"Who is Genia?" Aaron asked after Paul had gone.

"A special friend," Lydia said. "A nice little thing."

PAUL GROSZMAN AND GENIA LUCAS walked hand in hand down Saint Stephen's Square.

"What is he like, your mother's American friend?" she asked.

"I liked him," Paul said.

"Do you think they are lovers?" She grinned at him impishly, and he tousled her dark curls reprovingly.

"Don't be foolish," he said. "They've only just met. He's helping her in her work."

"Ah, is that what they call it?"

"Genia!"

He lifted his hand in mock threat, and she dashed away. He ran after her, and when he caught her, he held her tightly, his cheek touching hers. Sweet, foolish Genia. They had passed through childhood together into the sweetness of this new time. He dreamed of her at night and awakened to a mysterious moistness, a tender melancholy. They met in the afternoons at school and rehearsals; in the evenings they walked the streets of Budapest and sometimes pooled their money and had a coffee at a barge café. They studied the light-splattered waters of the Danube and smiled shyly at each other, mystified by their own happiness.

"Paul—you won't leave me."

"Ah, Genia." His reply was a soft moan, and later they each realized, separately, that he had said neither yes or no.

LYDIA AND AARON continued their pattern of daily meetings. They spoke very little during the time they spent in his room. She had warned him of the possibility of concealed listening devices. And, by unarticulated agreement, they did not touch at all; the concentrated lack of contact filled him with a nervous, almost pleasurable excitement. But always, as the afternoon light faded, they walked the patterned paths of Margaret Island. They followed the pebbled borders of the rock garden, winding their way through the Japanese dwarf trees and studying their twin reflections in the lily pond. They listened to the gentle chimes of the musical fountain and paused beneath the giant oaks that sheltered the bust of the Hungarian poet Janos Arany.

"Ferenc loved these oaks," Lydia said. "He felt a wonderful peace here. He used to quote Arany's poem about these trees. I remember the first lines: 'Under oak tree here, Would I find sweet quiet. . . .' Do you like poetry?"

"I did. Once." He sealed off the memory of himself and Katie, exhausted after lovemaking in his student flat in Cambridge, softly, lazily tossing favorite lines of poetry at each other until they drifted into sleep. But Katie would never have memorized a line like "sweet quiet." Not Katie, who feared sweetness and dreaded quiet.

He told her instead about his childhood in New York and about Leah, his mother, and her quiet courage and vibrant talent. He spoke of Michael, who had been so painfully bewildered since the death of David Goldfeder.

"But death is disorienting," she said. "When someone we love dies, we lose part of ourselves, and then we must go in search of it."

The days passed and light rains fell, but still Lydia and Aaron walked each afternoon. The fallen leaves crackled beneath their feet, and sere hedges rimmed the stripped and barren flower beds of the famous rose garden. The air was heavy with the rotting sweetness of decay, yet Margaret Island seemed beautiful to him. It was peaceful compared with the incipient unrest of Budapest. He noticed how pedestrians glanced nervously over their shoulders as they walked and how people in cafés huddled close to each other and spoke in hissing whispers. On Margaret Island they were at ease, unrestrained. One afternoon a mist rose from the Danube, and they walked through the silver web of its moisture. Droplets glittered like jewels in Lydia's dark hair. She talked that day of her hopes for Paul. She wanted him to live a good life, free of the sadness that had darkened his childhood. She wanted him to realize his gifts, to live in an ambience of freedom and joy. Aaron recognized that she wanted for Paul what Leah Goldfeder had wanted for her children.

He was growing up so quickly, she said, and spent so much time away from home. He had a girlfriend, she knew. Genia. A nice girl but a bit frivolous. They had gone to grade school together. But of course he would have many other girls. He was so young—they were both so young. Nothing at that age was serious.

"Sometimes such relationships are," Aaron said carefully. He had not been much older than Paul Groszman when he imagined himself in love with Lisa Crowley.

Lisa had been his sister Rebecca's classmate, and she and Aaron had come together in innocence and desperation. Children themselves (as Paul and Genia were), they had conceived a child. He had not known of Lisa's pregnancy and had gone off to war. Years later, he learned that the child had been born dead. He had never seen Lisa again. Poor Lisa. Her hair had turned milk-white in the summer sun and her laughter rang with careless joy. Perhaps Paul Groszman and his Genia laughed with such spontaneous gaiety. He pitied them and envied them as he pitied and envied all young lovers who walked hand in hand through the sunlight without anticipating the shadows.

"They will be all right," he said to Lydia, and that night he dreamed of Katie. There was neither terror nor passion in this dream in which Katie walked behind Lydia and himself in the Japanese rock garden. She sang as she trailed them, and wildflowers like those she had carried in her marriage bouquet were threaded through her hair. He awakened feeling strangely peaceful and oddly unworried. He glanced at his watch and saw that he had slept late, but he was not regretful. Like an invalid recuperating from an illness, he relished the quiet, empty hours that preceded Lydia's arrival at the hotel.

HE phoned Tom Hemmings to institute inquiries about Paul, and Tom invited him to a party.

"A *de rigueur* thing, actually," he said apologetically. "Betty hates them, and it would help to have a friendly face there. You might even find it interesting. Yuri Andropov is coming."

"The Soviet ambassador?"

"The same."

"Isn't that unusual?"

"Not really. We try to keep up appearances. You would be surprised at how the cold war heats up when there are good whiskey sours and hot canapés. And between sips and bites the ambassador might even pick up a scrap of information about Israel's scenario for the Suez. And if we're very lucky, we might learn something about developments in Poland. Bearing in mind, of course, that such scraps may be dropped because they are patently untrue. Still, even false leads may give us a clue to the truth. And the Russians are very nervous lately. They don't seem to know which way to go with Hungary. The Swiss chargé d'affaires gave a supper party after the Kodály concert last week, and one of the rumors I picked up there was that there are plans under way to reinter Rajk. I don't suppose you've ever heard of him. He was one of the victims of the purge trials of 1949."

"No, I haven't," Aaron said, although his bed at that moment was littered with leaflets urging the people of Budapest to assemble for a ceremonial reinterment of the martyred leader. He had spent the last two evenings helping Lydia distribute the leaflets at specified drop points. Did Yehuda know of his involvement? he wondered. Probably.

"Well, if the Soviets allow the reinterment, it might be a sign that they are softening their position toward more autonomy for Hungary. I plan to mention the Rajk situation casually to Andropov when he has a mouthful of deviled egg. He's very partial to deviled egg. He thinks it's an American specialty, and he's partial to a lot of things American. They say he never missed a broadcast of Radio Free Europe and he knows the words to every song in *Oklahoma*. Not that anyone has ever heard him sing anything in any language. Mysterious, unpredictable fellow, Andropov. No one knows much about him, although there are rumors of a dark lady in his past. A Muscovite Jewess, they say, but I don't believe it. He's got ice water in his veins, I think. Still, if he gets angry about the Rajk business, we'll assume that there'll be troops there. If he just nods and finishes his egg, we'll assume a softening. That's the world of diplomacy, Aaron—it revolves on the axis of good scotch and canapés."

"May I bring a friend?" Aaron asked.

Tom Hemmings's hesitation was almost imperceptible, and then he said, "Yes. Of course. The beautiful Dr. Groszman, I assume."

Aaron breathed deeply, but he did not know why he should be surprised. In Budapest, where everyone talked in whispers and glanced furtively over their shoulders, there were few secrets.

Aaron and Lydia arrived late at the party. A smiling maid, wearing a traditional embroidered Magyar blouse and a ruffled red skirt, escorted them into the Hemmingses' living room, which was crowded with members of the Budapest diplomatic community. The women wore their most elegant dresses. Taffeta rustled and silk skirts sighed as they moved about the room. Jewels glittered at their wrists and throats. They had worked hard to combat the sad, gray afternoon, the shabby, weary city.

They spoke of the new American film at the Corvin Cinema. *Bus Stop*, with Marilyn Monroe. Was it typical of small-town America? they asked Betty Hemmings, whose only experiences in American hamlets were confined to the villages in the Hamptons where her family summered. She smiled distractedly and nodded. She had not come to Europe to discuss Marilyn Monroe or small-town America. They talked about the new café on Museum Boulevard and the children's shop on Béla Bartók Avenue.

Their husbands spoke of the forthcoming election in the United States. They were all certain that Eisenhower would be reelected. They puzzled over the turn of events in the Middle East. There were rumors of an alliance among France, England, and Israel. They nodded sagely as they reached for the canapés, refused another drink. Nasser had gone too far when he nationalized the Suez Canal. The Belgian envoy confided that he had heard that Anthony Eden was very ill.

"Not true," the British vice-consul replied curtly.

They told harmless, bitter jokes. The French ambassador showed the Chilean military attaché a mock ledger sheet from Zahony, the Russian-Hungarian border post: Departed from Hungary for the USSR: 100 carloads of wheat, 200 carloads of corn, 5,000 barrels of wine, 250 trucks, 90 optical instruments. Arrived from the USSR: One Moiseyev folk-dance and -song group.

The two men laughed, but they did not share the joke with the Hungarian journalist who joined them.

They spoke of everything except the uneasiness that permeated the streets of Budapest. They did not mention the posters that were nailed into place at night and ripped to shreds by the morning, the handbills that were swept away by green-coated security officers, the small gatherings that so abruptly dispersed. All of them had seen AVO agents making swift, silent arrests. All of them had heard the dim buzzing on their phones, and some of them had heard police officers knocking harshly at their neighbors' doors. Imminent dangers shadowed this ancient city of their posting, but they remained silent. A danger unacknowledged might disappear.

"I'm so glad you came, Aaron." Betty Hemmings, trained from childhood to be a hostess, wore the white satin cocktail dress that an ambitious Bergdorf's designer had created for diplomatic receptions. Her eyelids drooped beneath blue shadowing. She had grown too thin, and the snowy fabric hung about her body like an elegant shroud. She wore too much makeup, to cover the tiny lines that crept insidiously about her eyes, and her powder was too white against the shadows that crested her cheekbones.

He kissed her. He had known her during her college days and always liked her. She had laid her plans well and envisaged a life of drama and excitement, but life had betrayed her, and she was relegated to supervising supplies of hors d'oeuvres and discussing new children's shops with overdressed women in a dull and desperate city.

He introduced her to Lydia, and she smiled thinly. Katie had been her friend, bridesmaid at her wedding.

Near the window that overlooked the Chain Bridge, a quartet of Gypsy violinists played love songs. Lydia hummed and swayed gently to the music. She looked especially beautiful, Aaron thought, in a dress of turquoise velvet, the color of her eyes. The small birthmark was a matching jewel that mysteriously adhered to her snow-white skin. A scene flashed back, across the years, to Aaron. He was again the small boy in the library on East Broadway, listening to the story of Snow White, whose skin had been as white as the flakes of winter and whose hair had been as black as charcoal. "Like my mother's," he had told the disbelieving librarian then. Like Lydia's, he thought now. He watched her move in her solitary dance—his secret princess who could not conceal her natural royalty.

"Do you know the song they are playing?" a man asked her. He spoke to her in heavily accented English, although Aaron had heard him converse in a Slavic language minutes before.

"Yes. When I was a child the Gypsies often played it. My father would sometimes take us to their encampments on the Buda hills when they held a festival. He was a doctor, and once they called him because their queen was in difficult labor. He saved her and the baby, but probably they were killed at Auschwitz." Her voice was dry, as though drained of anger and bitterness. Some men worked to preserve life and others practiced its destruction. She was simply stating fact, quoting from a ledger that could never be balanced.

Aaron stepped forward.

"Please. Let us introduce ourselves. I am Aaron Goldfeder and this is Dr. Lydia Groszman."

"I am very pleased to meet you. And I am Yuri Andropov."

Aaron restrained himself from staring hard at the Soviet ambassador. He had anticipated a much older man, a man of commanding girth, of dominating height. Yuri Andropov was slender and only a few years older than Aaron himself. He wore a steel-gray suit that exactly matched his eyes, which glinted with metallic sheen behind his rimless spectacles. He and Aaron shook hands, and his fingers remained rigid, unyielding rods within Aaron's grasp. His skin had the pallor of a man who seldom feels the touch of air and sunlight, and his finely chiseled features were trained to an absence of expression. When he spoke, he scarcely moved his thin, chalk-colored lips.

"I, too, remember the Gypsies," he said to Lydia. "They roamed through the Ukraine when I was a boy. I forget who it was who said that he could imagine a Europe without Jews but that he could never forgive Hitler for killing the Gypsies." He laughed, the thin, bloodless chuckle of a humorless man who has startled himself by saying something he considers to be amusing.

"Dr. Groszman and I are Jewish," Aaron said stiffly.

"I spoke without prejudice. Please understand that," the Russian said. "We have deep feelings for your people in my country, Mr. Goldfeder."

"My parents were born in your country. They emigrated from

Russia to America," Aaron replied. He was possessed of an irrational desire to unsettle and fluster this smooth, passionless man. "My mother visited her family only recently. Many of them would like to leave for Israel, and they cannot obtain visas."

"Can you blame Mother Russia for wanting her children to remain? All Russian citizens are vital to the country. There is no discrimination in Russia. There is no reason for Jews to leave." The Russian's voice was cool, controlled. He spoke with the conviction of a man who has repeated a lie so often that he has come to believe it to be the truth.

"My natural father was killed in a pogrom in 1919," Aaron continued. He struggled to keep his voice as controlled as that of the ambassador, to restrain himself from adding that his mother had been raped in the same pogrom and that his own childhood had been bitterly poisoned.

"There were no pogroms in 1919," the ambassador corrected him. He might have been a professor, patiently chiding an erring student. "There were, perhaps, misguided demonstrations against certain ethnic groups, triggered perhaps by perceived injustices. The proletariat is bound to resent a prosperous and parasitic aristocracy."

"Mr. Ambassador," Aaron protested. "My father was himself a revolutionary, an organizer. He and my mother were very young and newly married. They were as poor as their attackers."

"You have my sympathy, Mr. Goldfeder," the ambassador said. He studied the small gold pin in Aaron's lapel, the menorah insignia of the Jewish Brigade.

"An interesting design," he observed. He was a man with an eye for detail.

"I earned it when I fought with the Jewish Brigade in the British army." The tinge of boastfulness in his own voice embarrassed Aaron. He was impatient with men who told war stories and revealed their military pasts at peacetime cocktail parties. But the Russian had provoked him. He had stared too contemptuously at Aaron, too openly at Lydia. Now he plucked a deviled egg from the tray of a passing waitress and chewed it carefully. Tom Hemmings was right about his partiality to the delicacy, Aaron thought, and he watched the Russian methodically move his jaw as though operating a machine. He was not a man who spoke with food in his mouth. His manners were impeccable, and his words were carefully and deliberately calculated. Assertions masqueraded as denials, and denials were qualified with obscure promises. He wiped his mouth delicately.

"I know of the efforts of the Jewish Brigade. A courageous unit. Once I had a good friend, a Jewish woman. Her brother had migrated to Palestine and he fought with the Brigade. He was killed in Italy." Yuri Andropov's voice grew distant.

"I'm sorry," Aaron said.

"Yes. It was very sad. I admired him. I admire men who fight openly. I do not like secret cabals, nocturnal escapades. Only thieves move through the night. But come, let us not talk so seriously while we enjoy your friend Hemmings's hospitality."

He smiled thinly and deftly changed the topic before Aaron could reply. Surely, that was Andropov's technique when he met with activists and diplomats. He was a verbal acrobat, accomplishing great leaps with the skillful phrase, the swift diversionary compliment.

"Your dress is charming, Dr. Groszman. I admire your taste." He bowed elegantly and moved across the crowded room to join Tom and Betty Hemmings.

Aaron toyed with his lapel pin and wondered about the Jewish woman whose brother had died in Italy. Tom Hemmings had spoken of a dark Muscovite Jewess in Andropov's past. He thought suddenly of the carelessly replaced belt on the paisley dressing gown. Had Yuri Andropov's steel-colored eyes studied photographs of that robe, of his room? Impatiently, he dismissed the thought. He was growing paranoid in this country where elderly gentlemen were members of the secret police and well-dressed businessmen distributed clandestine propaganda. Still, he was not surprised to see Yehuda enter the room with a blond woman. Again, they did not speak.

That evening he walked Lydia back to her flat near the Kulsokorut, in an ancient quarter of the city.

"Tom Hemmings told me that he can schedule a hearing on your petition any time now. And he is optimistic about Paul. A special congressional bill has been introduced." Aaron reflected silently that Joshua Ellenberg's political IOUs were paid with unprecedented swiftness.

"Aaron, please be patient. Tomorrow they reinter Rajk. That will be the turning point. And then, very soon, we will be able to leave."

"Lydia, please be careful."

"There is nothing to worry about. The government even says that it approves the ceremony."

They had reached her block of flats, and instinctively they moved away from the circle of amber light cast by the weak bulb in the wrought-iron sconce of the concierge's portal. The concierge, like all the concierges of Budapest, was almost certainly an AVO agent.

"I worry about you."

He acknowledged now that he was consumed with concern for her. He worried about her as once he had worried about Katie. Was she all right? Would she be all right? He had claimed Lydia's cause as once he had claimed Katie's, yet he felt no disloyalty. She was so beautiful, so courageous. He ached with fear for her and for himself.

"Come with me to the demonstration." Her plea was shy, almost fearful. His acceptance would mean the crossing of a new border.

"If you want me to."

"I do."

His hand moved toward her neck, and again his fingers found the velvet surface of the birthmark. Again, with remembered touch, he stroked it, his fingers tender against the tiny neck pulse near it. Her lifeblood coursed beneath his touch; her lucent skin matched the white autumn moon. Gently, he pulled her toward him, tasted her lips. Even more gently, his lips moved against the petal softness of her face, the curve of her ear, until they brushed the downward slope of her cheek and pressed at last against the blue tear-shaped kiss of birth that flowered at her throat.

LASZLO RAJK. Aaron repeated the name aloud that morning as he shaved and wondered if he were pronouncing it correctly. He smiled wryly at himself in the mirror. A month ago he had never heard of Laszlo Rajk, and today he was preparing to go to a Budapest cemetery to witness the reinterment of the Hungarian patriot. And a month ago he had sat in Joshua Ellenberg's garden and watched the fairy lights splay prismatic paths of brightness across the night-dark lawn. That Labor Day evening had been warm, yet he had felt cold as death. His friends and family had surrounded him, yet he had felt isolated and alone. Now, a scarce few weeks later, he was a stranger in an unfamiliar city—a city besieged by fear and caught in the grip of unrelenting autumn rains and raw winds that coursed down from the frowning hills of Buda. But he felt warm and alive in the cafés of this foreign metropolis. He shivered as he ran through the streets, but he lifted his face to the falling rain and took a strange delight in the penumbral cloud formations that hovered over the city. He moved swiftly, startled by a verve that he had not expected to know again. His swiftness belonged to the young Aaron Goldfeder, the track star of Abraham Lincoln High School, but he had reclaimed it.

He was fired by a new energy, by an intense personal excitement. Lydia's battle had become his own. Her struggle for Paul had become his struggle. He had caught her fever, and by an effort of will, he had plunged himself into the history that was part of her life. He was tired this morning because he had stayed up half the night reading about the Budapest purge trials of 1949. He had been a student at Harvard Law School then, in love with Katie Reznikoff, the brightest and prettiest girl in his class. The shadowed courtrooms of Budapest had belonged to another world.

And yet, while he and Katie studied torts, edited a law journal, and made love before a fire, Laszlo Rajk, one dissenter among many, had been arrested, tortured, found guilty, and hanged. His body had been tossed into a pit dug on an empty lot just off the national highway, twelve miles out of Budapest. The body was to have been covered with slaked lime and rendered unidentifiable, but there had been a bureaucratic error and quicklime had been used. When Rajk's widow excavated the burial site, his corpse was found intact, although seven years had passed. Now the authorities, bewildered by the unrest of the people and influenced by the rumors of new liberalism at the Kremlin, had at last proclaimed the executed man "a martyr of the party." They had agreed to an official reinterment on the anniversary of the execution of the generals who had been the heroes of the 1848 War of Hungarian Independence. The secret operation that Lydia and her friends in the Petofi Circle had planned had been transformed into an official ceremony with government sanction.

"It's a trick," Lydia had told Aaron bitterly. "They want to deflate our efforts by legitimizing them. It's an old Soviet technique. They will come to the ceremony and find a pretext to turn on us."

"But perhaps they are sincere." He wanted them to be sincere. He had been raised by David Goldfeder, who sought out peaceful solutions, rational decisions.

"No. They are all like Andropov. Calculating. Bloodless. He spits in your face and wants you to believe that it is raining. They offer token concessions and would have us believe that they are offering freedom. I'll believe them when they release the political prisoners. I'll believe them when they allow new elections with secret ballots. I'll believe them when Russian troops leave Hungary." She had spoken quietly, yet her voice trembled and her shoulders quivered.

"If your group achieves its aims," he had asked, "would you and Paul want to stay in Hungary?"

"No." She was firm. "There are too many terrible memories for us here. But I want to leave a free Budapest. For my parents' sake. For Ferenc's sake. And especially for Paul. I do not want him to feel that he deserted his friends."

He had not pressed her further. His marriage had taught him that there were boundaries that could not be crossed and questions to which there were no certain answers.

They had arranged to meet on the Boulevard of Saint Stephen and to go to the reinterment ceremony together. Paul was going with a group of students. Aaron crossed the Margaret Bridge and braced himself against the harsh and unrelenting onslaught of the northern wind. Today he kept his face averted from the icy rain. He wondered if it had rained in Budapest on this same day in 1848. In point of fact, did the sun ever shine on this city of woodlands and bridges? Betty Hemmings thought not. "I should have forgotten about evening dresses and bought three raincoats," she said ruefully one afternoon.

Still, the weather had not deterred the people of Budapest from leaving their homes and offices, their factories and schools. Crowds of men and women thronged the bridges and streets with new groups surging forth on every avenue and boulevard. They wore the dark clothing of the bereaved, and black armbands were affixed to their sleeves. The government's insistence that work continue as usual had clearly been disregarded.

Children marched in solemn procession, holding torches fashioned of newspapers, which they shielded bravely from the falling rain. When the flames smoldered, they immediately rekindled the fire. The flames glowed against their faces, and they sang an ancient battle hymn as they marched, carefully protecting their blazing cornucopias.

Lydia rushed toward him from the shelter of the cathedral rectory. Her delicate white skin was striated by the lashings of the wind, and her hair swirled in damp waves of darkness about her shoulders. But her eyes glowed and her voice vibrated with excitement and pride.

"Look! We never anticipated such a turnout. The whole city of Budapest. Workers, students, housewives. Everyone. We were right, after all. We were right."

He did not answer her. He had glanced up and recognized the man who stood alone on the parapet of Liberty Bridge, studying the crowd. Yuri Andropov smiled grimly. It seemed to Aaron that his gaze focused briefly on Lydia. Then, as though sensing Aaron's recognition, the Soviet ambassador raised his hand in a tentative, warning salute and was lost in the swirling crowd.

A group of children passed them, singing in a rousing chorus. Lydia translated the song for him.

> Stand, Magyar, your country calls you.
> The moment has come. It is now or never.

"Do you believe that?" Aaron asked her.

"I believe it," she said, and he wished, with melancholy wistfulness, that he could share her faith.

They were caught up in the crowd then, and they walked with arms linked, to the Kerepesi Cemetery. As they approached the wrought-iron gates, the crowd grew silent. In single file, they made their way across avenues of gravemarkers and tombstones, so covered with twigs and bracken that they looked like stunted tree trunks in an abandoned forest. Someone passed Lydia a silver torch, and she held it high, as though the tongue of flame were a banner, a fiery proclamation.

Rajk's widow, Julia Foldi, a tall and statuesque woman, her face scarred by grief, stood beside her husband's coffin, her small son's hand clasped in her own. Members of the government and party leaders had assembled near her. They watched the crowd with the hooded, cautionary gaze of supervisory personnel, and they stood close together, huddling like visitors in a strange and unfamiliar city, uncertain and frightened.

Huge official wreaths, woven of roses and orchids, lavish gardenias and oversized gladioli, surrounded the coffins of Rajk and his three comrades, but each passing mourner dropped a single flower on the coffins, a small chrysanthemum in the muted, sorrowing hues of autumn. The small blossoms fell gently, silently; they blanketed the caskets and obscured the gaudy floral tributes of the government. A small and fragrant triumph.

Hundreds of thousands of people had crowded into the cemetery, and yet a heavy, threatening silence prevailed. The children marched past the open coffins with pale, frightened faces, but they did not avert their eyes from the corpses—a small act of bravery, a glance of tribute. The crowd was quiet, as though sorrow had frozen their songs, stilled their laughter. Immobile, they stood through the funeral oration, delivered by a man named Antal Apró.

"He is president of the Popular Front," Lydia whispered. "Ferenc knew him well."

Aaron shifted uneasily throughout the speech. Later, he knew, Lydia would explain the context, but for the moment he absorbed its passion, the sorrow of the orator's cadence, the mournful reaction of the audience. Men cried and women clutched the hands of small children. Had Ferenc Groszman also been so eloquent, so charismatic? he wondered, and felt ashamed because he begrudged a dead man his friendship with the leader who stood beside the open grave.

The crowd stood silent, and then the voice of a boy tenor pierced the grieving quiet. Paul Groszman sang a sweet and mournful requiem. He stood alone, his blond hair glistening wetly, a single white carnation in his hand, which he placed gently on Rajk's bier.

Julia Foldi burst into wild sobs. Her son, a solemn-faced, flaxen-haired boy, stood on his toes and gently wiped the tears that streaked his mother's cheeks with his blue cambric schoolboy handkerchief. A dark-suited man emerged from the crowd and embraced the weeping woman, who rested her head on his shoulder.

"Imre Nagy," Lydia said sadly. "How he has aged. Poor Uncle Imre. I wonder if he recognized Paul."

Slowly, now, the crowd dispersed and went their separate ways. Aaron saw two familiar figures turn a corner. Yehuda and Reuven Greenstein trailed a group of demonstrators. The newspaper torches were dropped to the ground, where they glowed briefly in flaming flowerets.

Aaron and Lydia made their way back to the Grand Hotel. Paul would be home late that night. He was spending the evening with Genia. Aaron was startled to see the businessmen calmly reading their newspapers in the lobby, their wives chatting over their bridge games. But of course the hotel guests were tourists. The Rajk funeral, the student unrest, the passion of the intellectuals—all were irrelevant to their careful itineraries. Probably tourists had played bridge in the lobbies of Berlin hotels during *Kristallnacht*, Aaron thought bitterly, as he guided Lydia into the elevator.

The phone was ringing as they entered his room. Struggling out of his sodden coat, he answered it.

"Aaron, it's Tom Hemmings. There's a new development in the Groszman case."

"Yes?" At once his voice became cautious.

"I've had a call from a friend with contacts at the Soviet embassy. Yuri Andropov has intimated that it would be wise for you and Dr.

Groszman to leave Budapest now. I can arrange that special hearing, and I think we can even manage to include the boy. Your friend Joshua moved quickly." Tom's voice was admiring.

"I'll talk to Dr. Groszman and let you know," Aaron said.

"Andropov doesn't fool around," Tom said softly.

"I know. Thanks."

He looked across the room to where Lydia sat on a green velvet armchair. She had removed her wet shoes and stockings, and her feet were pale and slender on the thick dark carpet.

"Who was that?" she asked.

"Tom Hemmings at the American embassy. He advises us to leave Budapest now. The Soviet ambassador suggests it. My friend Joshua Ellenberg has pulled some strings and made it possible."

"We can't leave now," she said. "Not when we are almost there." Her voice had the plaintive querulousness of a child who has worked on a project and is told that she cannot see its completion. "Besides, after today we don't have to be afraid of the Russians. What can Yuri Andropov do to me?"

He sat on the floor beside her chair and took her bare foot into his hand. No one would do anything to her. He would not allow it. And she was right. That afternoon, in that rain-swept cemetery, Russian power had been neutralized. The people of Hungary had asserted their will. He believed now, with absolute certainty, that freedom was just around the corner, and he wanted to be in Budapest when it arrived. If there was any danger, Yehuda would have warned him. He thought of the phone number and immediately decided against using it.

"Are you frightened?" she asked. Her hand rested lightly on his head.

"No," he said.

He turned and looked at her. Her eyes were closed and her lips were curved in an odd, childlike smile. She had surrendered herself to his care, his vigilance.

THE OPTIMISM AND CALM of that afternoon persisted for the next two weeks. Aaron and Lydia no longer conducted their elaborate charade at the Grand Hotel. The need for concealed documents and clandestine meetings had vanished. The furtive whispers, the nervous, hushed rumors, of his first days in the country, had become clearly articulated statements, ringing shouts.

The students who had once lurked in the darkness, secretly distributing their handbills and hanging posters, now openly handed out their material on broad avenues, in parks, and in busy squares.

Aaron saw Paul Groszman on a street corner, giving handbills to passersby. A pretty girl, whose dark curls clustered about her upturned cheerful face, stood beside him. Paul and Aaron smiled hesitantly at each other with the tacit restraint of men who share an acknowledged but undefined intimacy. *But Paul is only a boy*, Aaron reminded himself. On impulse he invited Lydia's stepson to a nearby café for a snack. Paul hesitated and glanced at his companion.

"This is Genia Lucas," Paul said, and Aaron gravely shook her hand.

"I am Aaron Goldfeder. I hope Genia can join us."

"Genia's English is not very good," Paul said swiftly. He spoke softly to her in Hungarian, and she nodded in assent.

"Yes. She would like to join us," Paul affirmed, although Aaron had known that Genia Lucas would follow Paul anywhere at any hour. Her hand clutched his and her eyes were riveted to his face. He wondered if they had slept together. Did teenage boys and girls sleep together in Budapest?

The café was crowded, but they found an empty table and Paul suggested that they all have blinis.

"This café makes them better than any other place in Budapest," he said.

Genia waved to friends at another table and flitted over to speak with them. Aaron and Paul looked warily at each other.

"I think you will miss Budapest," Aaron observed.

"It is my city. The only city I know."

"But you will be happy in America," Aaron persisted.

"My mother will be happy in America," Paul replied cryptically. "It is different for me. Here I have my music, my friends, my chance to work for a new Hungary." He watched Genia now as she bent to take a sip of someone's coffee and laughed. Relaxed, mirthful, her small face was like a flower bepetaled by the chestnut clusters of her curls.

"Genia's very pretty," Aaron said.

"She's beautiful." Paul blushed. He had both embarrassed and betrayed himself.

Aaron thought of all the sensible replies he might make. *You are seventeen and there will be many pretty girls, many beautiful women in your life. You are too young to be looking at a girl with such determined passion. America is full of girls as pretty as curly-haired Genia.*

Instead he stirred his coffee and told Paul that it seemed probable that the emigration process could now be swiftly accomplished.

"I must think about it more," Paul said. "So much has happened in such a short time. It is hard to leave when Hungary is on the edge of a new beginning."

"But Lydia is determined to leave," Aaron said.

"We will talk more, my mother and I," Paul answered, and then Genia joined them. Their blinis were served, and Aaron assured Paul that he was right—the small crepes were light as air and melted in buttery drops on his tongue.

They parted on the same corner where they had met. Genia shook Aaron's hand, but her eyes scarcely left Paul's face.

Aaron looked back at them. Paul's arm rested lightly on her shoulders; her hand touched his cheek. Would Lydia leave Budapest without Paul? Aaron wondered, and he walked slowly on.

LYDIA'S university colleagues now met openly. They spoke of their plans in cafés and wine taverns, where they met to drink raisin wine in the late afternoon. They held small dinner gatherings, and Aaron accompanied her. He, too, lifted his glass and drank to their extravagant, enthusiastic toasts.

"To peace!"

"Hungary for the Hungarians!"

"To freedom!"

"An end to the Warsaw Pact!"

The impromptu parties reminded him of the gatherings of his undergraduate days, of his friends in the Young People's Socialist League. They, too, had lifted their glasses to peace and freedom. A brief sadness swept over him, but he saw the flush on Lydia's cheek, the glint in her eyes, and struggled against it. He willed himself to believe in her beliefs.

"*Szabadságra és békéra!* To peace and freedom," he called, and they clapped because he had saluted them in their own language.

They made enthusiastic plans at those gatherings, which were held in faculty flats and in student apartments and studios along Museum Boulevard. Aaron thought their demands modest. He and his friends had worked for a universal campaign against hunger and illiteracy. They had dreamed of an egalitarian society. The Hungarians were more realistic. They wanted Russian removed as a compulsory language course from the university curriculum. They wanted freedom of expression for Hungarian writers and the release of political prisoners. They wanted freedom for Cardinal Mindszenty and guarantees that Hungarians would be allowed to worship as they pleased.

"Let the Angelus ring again," a bearded graduate student called.

"And let the people resume control of Radio Budapest."

"We might as well call it Radio Judapest. Gero and his Jew cronies control it," someone else said.

An embarrassed silence filled the room. Aaron moved closer to Lydia. He had not understood the speaker's words exactly, but their impact was clear.

"No offense, Lydia," their host apologized. "A joke. Unfortunate and in bad taste, but still just a joke."

Angry patches of red blotched Lydia's cheeks, but she nodded. They left the party early, and Aaron took with him the remainder of the bottle of vodka that he had brought.

"I suppose one can't escape it," she said wearily. "The anger. The hatred. The insidious mockery. One expected it from the Nazis, from the Arrow Cross. It is harder when it comes from friends, from comrades."

"I know."

"I suppose the only place a Jew is safe is in Israel."

"Israel is not the place to go for safety." He thought of his sister who slept with a rifle beside her bed; of Rebecca's husband, Yehuda, who haunted street corners and cafés in distant cities, scavenging scraps of intelligence; he thought of his sister's children, who slept underground in a fetid air-raid shelter; of David Goldfeder, killed by the bullet of an enemy who stole across the border to spread terror and hatred.

"At least the Israelis know who their enemies are." She was deeply hurt. The man who had made the remark was a colleague. She had helped him with his thesis and had been his advocate during his defense.

"And so do we," he replied gently.

HIS MOTHER called from New York. Eileen Manning, his secretary, phoned her daily, wanting to know when Aaron would return. He had been gone for weeks now, and he had dates approaching on court calendars.

"I left Eileen instructions about substitutes," he said. His New York practice belonged to another world. He was on leave from that life, and he felt a vague irritation that it impinged on his involvements in Budapest.

"The dean of the Law School called," Leah continued. "He wanted to know if you would be available to teach a course in the spring semester."

"I would think so." His voice was vague, and then he focused on her question and added firmly, "Of course."

Spring. His heart sang at the sound of the word, at the thought of winter's end, of Lydia walking beside him in the warm, sweet air of freedom. Warmth and liberty were only a season away.

Leah had had a phone call from Rebecca, who had returned to Israel.

"How did she sound?" Aaron asked.

"A bit worried, or perhaps just sad. Yehuda is still away, but she plans to join him in London shortly." Michael, on the other hand, she reported, seemed to be settling in well at Berkeley.

"Rebecca will be fine," Aaron assured her.

He had not seen Yehuda since the Rajk demonstration. Perhaps his brother-in-law had left the country. As he and Lydia would. Soon. Very soon.

"And Aaron—you're all right?" Leah asked cautiously.

He knew the effort it had cost her to refrain from asking what he was doing, was it safe, was he being careful? Once, during the sad, confused days of his boyhood, he would have thought her uncaring, indifferent. Now he knew that it was because she cared so much that she granted her children their freedom. Leah practiced the wisdom of David Goldfeder. "If you care about your children," David Goldfeder had said, "you must give them roots and teach them that they have wings." Leah had given her children roots, and she had allowed them to fly.

"I'm fine, Mama," he said. "I'm being careful."

REUVEN GREENSTEIN joined Aaron at breakfast one morning. "Such a surprise to find you in Budapest," he said as the waiter glanced at them curiously and took their orders. "Yehuda would have come himself," he said more softly but still smiling his unctuous grin of pleasure, "but he was afraid that they might make the connection. Their research is fairly thorough."

"I understand," Aaron said. If Yehuda was known to the AVO

as a Mosad agent, then all his family connections would also be known. A month ago he would have scoffed at such a conjecture. Now it seemed not only reasonable but obvious.

"We wonder how much longer it will be before you and the Groszmans leave. Yehuda asked me to tell you that there is some urgency."

Aaron stirred his coffee and pondered the question.

Much had happened in the two weeks since the Rajk reinterment. Imre Nagy had been readmitted to the party. The students had won some concessions. The university curriculum had been expanded. Russian university students had broken their ties to the Communist Youth Organization and founded their own political unit. Lydia was increasingly optimistic.

Lydia and Aaron had spent the previous evening at the Hemmingses', and Betty had told them that she was pregnant.

"It's funny," Betty had said, "I never thought that I wanted children, but now all I can think about is the baby."

It occurred to Aaron that it was the first time since his arrival in Budapest that he had seen Betty happy and relaxed. But then, he himself felt happy and relaxed. Like Betty, he was looking forward to new beginnings.

"I'm happy for them," Lydia observed as they walked through the deserted streets. "In a way I'm sort of sad that I won't be in Budapest when the baby is born. I've known them only a short time, yet I feel a closeness to them. I suppose the hardest thing about leaving will be the goodbyes."

They had paused on a small bridge, and Aaron tossed a pfennig into the water and watched the concentric moonlit wavelets dance on the ink-dark Danube.

"I spoke with Paul the other day," he said. "He does not seem enthusiastic about leaving."

"Ah, Paul, my Paul. Do you know he fancies himself in love?" She laughed lightly, but he remained serious.

"Genia is a beautiful girl," he said.

"Aaron, they are children—secondary school students."

He said nothing. He did not tell her that he, too, had been a student and had loved Lisa Crowley, gentle, sweet Lisa who had been as pretty as Genia, as vulnerable as Paul.

"For argument's sake," he asked cautiously, "would you leave Budapest without Paul?"

"I won't have to." Her reply had been firm.

He turned now to Reuven Greenstein.

"I think it is safe to say that I will leave Budapest with the Groszmans in a week's time."

Later, he would recall with wry satisfaction that he had erred only by a few days.

AARON AND LYDIA had decided not to meet on the afternoon of October 23. She had a great deal of work to do at her laboratory, and the demonstration planned for that day ensured a quiet work area. She wanted to validate and record the results of a recently completed experiment.

"I will have to leave all the corroborative data here," she told him. "And it will be a while before we can reconstruct the sonar equipment in the West. But at least I'll have the basic report to work with."

Lydia's work was a strangely exciting mystery to him. He did not understand it, nor did he ask for explanations. He took her statement as a sign that their departure was imminent and called Tom Hemmings to ask if he could work at the embassy library that day. He needed only to check a few more documents and await word from Washington on Paul's status. Joshua Ellenberg's Budapest agent had assured him that it would be forthcoming any day now.

"Everything going all right, Aaron?" Tom asked, and it occurred to Aaron that his friend had never again mentioned Yuri Andropov. One of those rumors that flew about Budapest, he supposed. It was just as well that he and Lydia had decided to ignore it.

"We're about ready to schedule the hearing," Aaron replied.

"Good, fine. I'll leave a pass for you at the front desk, but I won't be here. I'm taking Betty out to Lake Balaton. A sort of compensation prize. We were supposed to spend a couple of days in Paris. Mollet invited senior personnel from NATO countries to some sort of special briefing session, but it's been called off. Betty's in a funk about it. You know Betty—her last chance to wear her Bergdorf's designer specials before disappearing into maternity clothes."

"Too bad," Aaron said. He liked Betty Hemmings, but her social disappointments did not interest him.

"It seems that Mollet has unexpected visitors. Important ones." Tom paused significantly and cleared his throat.

"Oh?" Aaron remembered suddenly that that had been Tom's technique during their Harvard days. He beckoned with bits of information, teased and taunted with scraps of gossip: "I hear that a really big name is leaving the faculty." "Rumor has it that a certain fair-haired boy flunked Torts and is packing it in." There was no malice to his method. His knowledge and his companion's ignorance vested him with a brief and obscure power. He anticipated curious questions and would be annoyed if they were not forthcoming. Aaron was impatient, but Tom had been kind to him, and Aaron expected him to be kinder still.

"They must be very important visitors," he said, playing according to his friend's rules.

"As important as you can get. Key figures in the Middle East. Your boys."

"My boys?" Aaron was guarded and curious.

"Ben-Gurion. Moshe Dayan. Shimon Peres."

"Ah. *My* boys," Aaron said. His emphasis on the personal pronoun was lost on Tom, who was in a hurry to clear his desk and meet his wife. The students planned another demonstration today. That meant the roads would be blocked. He wanted to get out of the damn city early.

"Have a good time, Tom. My love to Betty." Aaron replaced the receiver and walked over to the window. Margaret Island was shrouded in a quivering mist, pierced here and there by shafts of sunlight. He thought he understood now why Greenstein had been sent to verify the Hungarian timetable. He and Lydia were barometers by which developments could be measured.

The attention of the world was focused on Eastern Europe and the anticipated crumbling of Soviet domination. Gomulka had glided quietly into power in Poland. Now Hungary was stage center on the international scene. There was room on the front pages of the *New York Times* and *Le Monde* for only one dominant headline, and if the screaming banner highlighted events in Budapest, the attention of the world's readers would be diverted from the Middle East. A publicized meeting of Marshal Tito and the Hungarian premier Gero was certainly of more interest than a secret encounter between David Ben-Gurion and Guy Mollet at an obscure safe house in France. A complicated game of chess was being played, and the international grand masters scurried about the world placing their key pieces into position.

"And which side am I on?" Aaron thought bitterly, resentful suddenly that he and Lydia were pawns, subject to remote control by invisible forces. But then, of course, there were no sides. The Israelis and the Hungarian liberals were fighting for the same cause—

the cause that had sent him across the border to Canada to join the British forces during the terrible fall of 1939. The strong must not be allowed to terrorize the weak. Then they had fought for Czechoslovakia and Poland and Ethiopia. And the Jews. Now they fought for Hungary and Poland and Israel. And the Jews. He fingered the menorah pin at his lapel and started out for the American embassy.

The streets of Budapest were even more crowded than they had been on the day of the Rajk reinterment. But of course it had rained that day, and today a perversely bright sun defied the season and beat down on milling throngs. Aaron felt warm enough for the first time since his arrival in Budapest.

There was a holiday atmosphere about the crowd. Young girls, their heads and shoulders covered with brilliantly patterned shawls, carried bouquets of brightly colored flowers. Beaming women offered candies and sweetmeats to excited children, who scurried about waving their red, white, and green Hungarian flags. Young men sporting tricolor pins smiled importantly as they distributed the inevitable mimeographed propaganda sheets. The rainbow-colored papers were passed from hand to hand. After his weeks of exposure, Aaron could discern the slogans. *Russians Go Home! Imre Nagy to Power! Hungary for the Hungarians!*

Middle-aged and elderly couples strolled leisurely through the crowd, dressed in their best. The day was warm and would grow warmer, but men in fur-collared coats and women in heavy wool suits trimmed with elaborate brocade smiled at each other. They nodded and bowed, perspiring profusely but unwilling to divest themselves of the splendid garments of another time. Now, perhaps, on this bright October day, they would see a return to a vanished era of elegance and grace.

Aaron entered the American embassy, went to the library, and worked steadily until he reached two forms that required Lydia's signature. Hesitantly, he phoned her at the laboratory and managed to get through.

"I'm so glad you called," she said. "It's impossible to work today. Most of the technicians have gone to the demonstration, and even the phone operators called in sick. Shall we meet in an hour at the Luxor Café on Saint Stephen's Square?"

"All right," he agreed. "But the streets are impossibly crowded."

He set out at once, but although the distance was short it took him an hour and a half to reach their meeting place. He saw her standing in front of the café, and he thrust himself through the surging crowd to reach her, struggling against the onslaught of shouting demonstrators.

"Isn't it exciting?" Her face was flushed and her blue eyes gleamed like polished lapis gems. Her scarlet cape had slipped about her shoulders, and he adjusted it, tied the grosgrain ribbons, and pinned her tricolored emblem firmly into place on the collar. His large freckled fingers were skillful with the supple, delicate fabric.

"How brotherly you are," she said teasingly. "Did you take good care of your small sister when you were a boy?"

"Yes," he said seriously. He had taken good care of Rebecca, his sister. He had tried to take good care of Katie, his wife, and he would, if given the chance, take excellent care of Lydia Groszman. Beautiful Lydia. His snow-white maiden. His sad-eyed princess.

He no longer deceived himself. The game of make-believe that he and Lydia had devised so that they might proceed with the propaganda campaign had evolved into reality. He was in love with her, he knew, and he trembled at the thought that she loved him.

They joined arms and followed the crowd to the Petofi Monument. As they passed the large apartment houses on Bajcsy Boulevard, windows were flung open and carpets and scarves were hung out.

"An old custom," Lydia explained. "This is the way the people of Budapest pay tribute to the passage of a sovereign." The people were sovereign in Budapest that afternoon, and they sang jubilantly as they marched.

National flags dangled on improvised broomstick poles and were nailed to window frames. The red, white, and green banners had been slashed down the center and the Soviet symbols removed. A small boy gave them little paper flags, and Lydia waved them as she walked.

"Look, there's Paul," she said. "Paul! Paul!" she called excitedly.

Paul Groszman broke out of the line of marching students but kept his arm around Genia's shoulders. The girl wore a pale blue dress and a matching scarf wrapped about her bright hair. She waved shyly, and Paul stepped forward into a circle of brilliant sunlight that transformed his golden hair into an aureole of brightness. His smile was radiant.

How wonderful to be seventeen and in love and in the vanguard of a successful revolution, Aaron thought.

Paul shouted something to Lydia in Hungarian and moved on. His friends were singing a soaring anthem, and even above the roar of the tumultuous crowd Aaron discerned the sweet clarity of Paul's voice.

"Could you make out what he said?" he asked Lydia.

"Yes. He probably won't be home tonight. His group is planning an all-night vigil at the radio station."

They drew closer to the monument and heard a great swell of voices, a mighty chorus. Lydia and the others paused and placed their right hands over their hearts as they, too, sang "God Save the Hungarians," the national anthem. Aaron stood silently beside her. How vulnerable they were, he thought, this passionate, singing crowd, with their paper flags and wilted carnations. In his mind's eye he saw Yuri Andropov, his steel-gray eyes metallic and unyielding, his stance rigid. Again he pondered the Soviet ambassador's oblique interest in Lydia. Did she perhaps remind him of another Jewish woman he had loved and betrayed? Would such feelings make him want to protect her—or punish her?

They had passed the Hotel Gellert, where most of the Russian diplomats resided. Heavy draperies had been drawn across the windows, but Aaron had seen those on the second floor part. Yuri Andropov had stood in a rib of sunlight looking down at the swarming street and smiling a bitter, patient smile.

At the monument, Imre Simkoviks, an actor with whom Aaron and Lydia had shared a bottle of plum wine after the Rajk demonstration, climbed onto the pedestal of the statue and recited a Petofi poem in resonant tones. The crowd thundered the refrain, and Lydia translated it for him.

> By the Hungarians' God
> We swear
> That we shall no longer be slaves!
> Never! We swear! Never!

"Never is a long time," Aaron murmured, but Lydia did not hear him. She was translating for him again as Simkoviks read the program of demands drafted by the students—the same program that had littered Aaron's bed at the Grand Hotel, that he had carried in the folded pages of the *Herald Tribune* to a Gypsy café in a distant quarter of the city. He felt a surge of pride, of self-satisfaction. He had, after all, been of service. Part of this bright, sunlit afternoon belonged to him and to the beautiful woman at his side. Lydia's finger pressed hard upon his own, a tactile acknowledgment that they were linked in song and flame, in common cause.

And then they were on the move again, following the crowd across the bridge to the Parliament Building. They were singing the Marseillaise now, and he lifted his voice and matched his deep tenor to Lydia's sweet alto.

A tranquil dusk dimmed the brightness of the day, and the marchers lit paper torches against the encroaching twilight. A gentle evening wind carried the dancing sparks skyward, and the faces of the crowd were bathed in the golden light of their brave, brief flames. At the Parliament the national tricolor, with the Soviet symbols excised from the center, was hoisted. The crowds roared in unison.

Restlessly, the assemblage listened to a speech delivered by a nervous and hesitant Imre Nagy. Aaron noticed that the popular leader's hands trembled and droplets of sweat rimmed his high, pale forehead. He looked about and felt a flicker of fear. Almost one hundred thousand people were assembled now. There was no way to control or organize such a crowd, and Imre Nagy was faltering; his voice was unsteady and his eyes were glazed.

"We should leave," Aaron whispered to Lydia.

He saw with relief that small groups were dispersing. Men and women were glancing at their watches. There were tasks to be accomplished, dinners to be prepared and eaten, children to be supervised. The day's objectives had been accomplished. The demonstration had been held and Imre Nagy had spoken.

"To the Stalin statue!" someone shouted, and the crowd answered with a tumultuous roar of approval. Others broke away and went in different directions, but Aaron and Lydia were swept along to the entrance of the great city park where they had first met. There, the huge bronze statue of the dead and discredited Russian dictator shimmered in the new moonlight.

Students circled the monument in a raucous, mocking dance. They pelted it with stones and with paper bags filled with dung, gathered on the bridle path. Globules of excrement trickled down the intricately sculpted mustaches, slithered onto the closed, unsmiling lips.

"He gave us shit. Now let him eat it," someone shouted, and the crowd laughed.

The task of toppling the statue began. Steel cables were thrown about the monument and attached to three trucks. The huge vehicles heaved and strained like mighty, impotent beasts. The air grew thick with the fumes of their laboring exhausts, but the statue remained immobile.

"That won't do it," Lydia said. "They haven't got anything near equal force. That statue is twenty-five feet of solid bronze. Even earth-moving equipment won't be enough."

Aaron looked down at her and smiled. He had forgotten, for the moment, that she was a physicist. The mysterious stores of her knowledge intrigued and fascinated him. He watched as she called a young man over—a physics student whom he had seen at gatherings and meetings. Lydia whispered urgently to him, and he nodded and minutes later rode off on a bicycle.

"One of my gradauate students," Lydia said. "I told him what must be done."

But the students, still struggling with their cables, were not discouraged. They formed a human ladder, and a few of them climbed to the head of the glaring colossus. One of them waved his hat imperiously, unbuttoned his pants, and urinated, aiming the stream of golden urine onto the statue's nose. Aaron smiled and wished that he could understand the orations being delivered from the demonstrators poised on the statue's shoulders. Still, he enjoyed the appreciative laughter of the crowd, the ribald gestures. And then Lydia's cycling student was back, triumphantly waving a flag. A sidecar trailed him filled with welders' oxygen masks and a welding gun. Swiftly, the instruments were seized by workers who trained the flame on the bronze knees, burning holes into the metal limbs. They climbed down and clambered back into the trucks. Once again the vehicles strained to pull the cables forward, and the statue swayed, wavered briefly, and fell at last. A deafening metallic crescendo thundered forth as it crashed to the concrete square. The two bronze boots, like neatly symmetrical roots, remained attached to the pedestal. Aaron read the inscription: TO THE GREAT STALIN FROM THE THANKFUL HUNGARIAN PEOPLE. The "thankful Hungarian people" were shouting ecstatically now, clapping wildly.

Aaron took Lydia's hand and they joined the crowd that trailed after the truck. The chained metal statue struck sparks as it dragged across the pavements; the fragments of light glittered like minuscule playful fireworks. At last at the intersection of the Grand Boulevard, the crowd fell upon the statue and pounded it to bits, seizing small bits of metal for souvenirs. Aaron, too, plucked up a piece of bronze. It was a portion of Stalin's pinky finger; the nail was sculpted into a crescent that curved cruelly upward.

As they made their way back to Margaret Island, they passed groups of young people, all singing the same song.

"What do the words mean?" he asked Lydia. He had heard it sung at other parties and gatherings.

"It means, 'We'll turn the whole world upside down overnight,' " Lydia translated for him. "And we will," she added fiercely. "We will."

Her voice rose in song again, high and sweet and painfully tender.

"Overnight," he repeated.

She turned and stared at him uneasily. There was a strange harshness in his voice, a grim set to his mouth. He was remembering his friend, Gregory Liebowitz, who had said to him, so many years ago, "You'll see, Aaron, we'll turn the whole world upside down." The same words. Poor Gregory. Poor dead Gregory. Each year Aaron vowed that he would visit the sloping Ethiopian hillside where Gregory was buried, but he had never gone. He shivered now, in memory and in apprehension. Slogans were too easily mouthed, and too often they claimed the lives of the young. Stalin's statue had taken too long to topple, and Lydia's eyes were so dangerously bright that he feared for her, feared for both of them and for golden-haired Paul, so vulnerable in his youth and beauty.

He noticed, suddenly, that a new mood had overtaken the crowd. The wild excitement was quenched. All about them people were talking in hushed tones. Cyclists wove their way through small groups, shouting out information. Clusters of men and women rushed toward the city, trampling flowers and paper torches as they ran. A man shouted with fury and a woman screamed in desperation. Somewhere in the madding crowd a child wept in fear. The singing stopped, defeated by the new thunder of angry voices, the rush of pounding feet.

Lydia's fingers dug into Aaron's arm, and her breath came in gasps. He feared that she might faint, and thrust his arm about her in support. Her body collapsed against him.

"What is it, for God's sake?" he asked.

"They say that there's been a riot at the radio station. The AVO fired on the students. They don't know how many are dead. Aaron, Paul is at the radio station. Paul!" She shouted his name. "Paul." She whispered it now, almost in prayer.

"Come." He took her by the hand as though she were a small child. "We'll go to the station."

They followed the crowd and ran through the teeming streets. Their hearts beat arrhythmically, and fear coursed through their veins. Their linked fingers were cold as ice, and when they spoke, their voices rasped out of raw and aching throats.

PAUL AND GENIA clutched each other's hands. They had become separated from their student group on Kossuth Square, and now they were desperately afraid that they would lose each other in the frenzied crowd that milled about outside the headquarters of the radio station.

"Genia, we must go home," Paul said, but she shook her head.

"I don't want to go home, Paul. I want to stay here where everything is happening. I don't want to miss anything."

He did not argue. Genia had the fierce tenacity of the soft-spoken. When she set her mind to something, she would not be dissuaded. He had known that since the summer evening when they had wandered away from their music camp and found themselves alone in a small fir forest. He had wanted to return to the camp, but Genia's soft voice had controverted him; her sweet breath on his face, in his ear, against his neck, had subdued him.

"Stay," she had said softly then, and she had pulled him down beside her on a bed of fragrant pine needles. They glistened in the darkness, against her hair and her rose-gold skin. Afterward, he had scooped up a handful and threaded them across her shoulders and the blue-veined rise of her breasts.

"Stay," she said with matching softness now, and he marveled that her gentle voice was audible above the shouting of the crowd, the wild songs, the choruses of slogans and poetry.

"Rise for the motherland—now or never!" The shout came from a man standing on the pedestal of a statue.

"Now or never!" the crowd roared back in unison.

A student leader leaped up to the parapet, unfurled the white scroll he carried, and shook it at the crowd.

"What are we doing here at the broadcasting station?" he shouted, and immediately answered his own question: "We are here to demand that they allow us to read this list of reforms on the radio. Is this the people's broadcasting system? Then let the people speak!"

"Yes. Let the people speak!" they shouted after him.

"Why are they afraid of the people?" the speaker asked. A bright red light, a reflection of the neon-lit star atop the building, glowed crimson on his face, turned his eyes into angry specks of flame. Irritated, he stopped, plucked up a stone, and tossed it at the star. "Extinguish the red lights over Budapest," he bellowed. "Let the lights of freedom shine instead!"

"Kill the red star," the crowd chanted. "Light the lamps of freedom."

Another stone was hurled at the star and then another. Someone tossed a brick, and then a group of students formed a Jacob's ladder and began the climb to the roof. It seemed suddenly that all the fury in Budapest was focused on the red star, which continued to throw its fiery light across the upturned faces of those assembled beneath it.

The soldiers, standing guard at the gates, stared uneasily at the crowd. They lifted their rifles, but they did not shoot. The air trembled with the sounds of breaking glass as the stones aimed at the star shattered window panes. Slivers of jagged glass rained onto the street, and within minutes, canisters of tear gas were thrown through the broken windows.

"People of Budapest, disperse!" a voice warned harshly over the amplifier.

"Never!"

Smoke filled the small square now, and people were crying and coughing. Children vomited, and a woman who had fainted was carried to a waiting ambulance. Still, the crowd surged forward and the climbers continued their ascent to the star.

Genia tore off her blue head scarf and covered her face with it to mask the gas. Still, she pressed forward. She was at once frightened and exhilarated. Paul kept his hand on her shoulder.

Genia loved the movies, the theater. Only last week they had seen *For Whom the Bell Tolls*, and she had wept in the darkened theater, her tears dripping hot upon his hands. Now, on this darkened street, she imagined herself starring in her own film. She had written herself into the scenario of the liberation of Budapest. Pretty Genia. Foolish Genia. He had to take care of her, protect her.

"Please, Genia, let me take you home," Paul said, but she moved forward, pulling him with her to the outermost fringe of the crowd.

"Citizens of Budapest, disperse or we will shoot!" the authoritative voice shouted again through the amplifier.

Fire trucks screeched to a halt and enormous hoses were trained on the crowd. Those who turned were lashed by whips of water that soaked and immobilized them. An old woman fell to the ground, shivering and sputtering.

"For God's sake, stop!" Paul shouted. "No one here is armed." But his voice was lost in the tumult. A tear-gas canister hurtled near him, was caught by a demonstrator, and thrown back into the station.

"Take aim and fire!"

Marksmen appeared at the windows, but now the soldiers standing guard outside the building suddenly broke ranks. They passed into the crowd and distributed arms to the demonstrators. Soldiers and insurgents mingled; uniformed men and civilians stood side by side. An arms cache had been broken into, and weapons were being distributed at random.

The crowd surged forward, and Paul was separated from Genia. Frantically, he searched for her, his eyes tearing and his throat dry. Bullets whirled past him, but he moved on until at last he glimpsed her blue scarf.

"Genia!"

She whirled and he saw the fear in her eyes. He reached her at last and thrust her behind him, shielding her from gleaming steel ovoids of death. A small blond boy stood near them, his face contorted with fear.

"Mama, mama," he cried plaintively.

Instinctively Paul lifted the child and placed him a few yards back.

"Stay down!" he shouted to the boy, but his command was caught in his throat as one bullet pierced his neck and another plunged into his body. He fell and heard Genia's shriek, felt her hand on his face. His fingers flew to his chest, but he could not comprehend that the thick, dark moisture that poured out of his body was his own blood. Now he was on fire and now he was turning to ice. The world was exploding about him and the world was frozen in tableau. He drifted through darkness into fiery light and then back again into darkness.

"Genia!" Why was his voice so faint? He found her hand and tried to grasp it.

"Paul. I'm right here, Paul."

Lydia's voice, so strangely muffled. What was she doing here and why was her skin blanched to such a deathly pallor? Why was she crying? He could not remember her crying since his father's death. And why was Genia crying? She should be happy and singing. Suddenly he wanted to sing. *We've turned the whole world upside down.* The lyric spun crazily in his mind, but his voice froze in his throat. He noticed now that Genia's blue head scarf was ribboned with streaks of scarlet. Perhaps that was why she was crying. He opened his eyes, felt the searing pain again, and closed them. And then he smiled, because all pain had ceased and, blissfully, he was neither too hot nor too cold.

It was Aaron Goldfeder who moved forward through the frenzied crowd and took Paul's limp wrist in his hand. There was no pulse. A woman offered him a small mirror, and he held it up to the boy's mouth. No mist formed. There was no breath. He touched Paul's hair and pulled his eyelids down.

"No!" Lydia's scream froze them into silence. "It can't be!"

She knelt beside Paul and lifted his hand, pressing it to her mouth.

"No!" She pressed her head against his heart, as though she might command it to beat again.

"No!" She tried to lift the inert form; she cradled him in her arms, tears streaking her face.

"Paul. Paul." Her voice was pleading, cracked with grief. She willed him to life, and knew that he was dead.

Gently, Aaron Goldfeder separated her from the boy and led her away so that she would not see the strangers who covered Paul Groszman's slender body with a coarse gray blanket.

PAUL GROSZMAN was buried the next day, beside his father, in the Martyrs' Cemetery of the Dohány Street Synagogue. Aaron averted his eyes from the mass graves that bore the single date 1945. At least Paul's grave would be marked with his name and the date of his death. Sweet-voiced Genia sang the Kaddish for Paul. The young people who had been Paul's friends and were now his mourners, stood in a circle, their faces frozen into the masks of incredulity peculiar to the newly bereaved. Today, youth itself had abandoned them. Their lithe bodies were stiff with sorrow and their bright eyes faded with grief. One girl fainted. Her body fell lightly onto a pile of leaves.

Genia, her face pale and her eyes red-rimmed, trembled uncontrollably. She bit her lips until they bled and pounded at her chest with her fists. She was an initiate into the rite of death, the terrible reality of loss. Her parents spoke softly to her, but Lydia moved toward her and encircled the weeping girl in her arms.

"It was my fault," Genia sobbed. "He wanted to leave and I wouldn't go."

"You mustn't think that," Lydia said. "Things happen and we cannot control them." Her voice was fierce, and she remembered all the sadnesses and losses of her own life. "You must not blame yourself, Genia."

She held the girl close. Her own tears coursed down her cheeks in a flow that would not cease; the source of her sorrow could not be sealed. *Paul. Paul. Paul.* Soundlessly, she mouthed the dead boy's name, but Genia, who had at last stopped trembling, uttered it softly, tenderly. "Paul . . . Paul . . . Paul." They would both remember him always, Lydia who had been mother to him and Genia who had loved him. Always, for them, he would be the sweet-singing boy whose idealized tomorrows had never been shadowed by reality.

The service was over and Paul's friends moved forward. They had marched beside Paul Groszman and lifted their voices with his. They were the sharers of his dream, the gentle companions of his brief life. A boy who had been wounded the previous night, his arm cradled in a black sling, dropped the first handful of earth in the open grave, and the others followed him. Genia placed the bough of a fir tree gently on the raw pine coffin. How happy they had been beneath the evergreens that summer evening. She would never be happy again, she thought. Lydia moved forward and dropped a white carnation, the color of snow and sorrow, into the grave. The flower fell soundlessly, and the mourners turned and parted on the corner of Dohány Street.

LYDIA could not face the return to the small apartment she had shared with Paul. A friend packed a small bag for her and brought it to the Grand Hotel. Exhausted by her grief, she slept for two days, waking only to nibble at the food Aaron had sent up to the suite. She drank small glasses of plum brandy, gazed disconsolately out the window, wept again and slept again. Genia called to say goodbye. Her parents were sending her to relatives in Austria. Lydia's colleagues and friends called and sent messages of condolence. Her concierge told them where she was staying. The conservatory where Paul had studied sent a basket of flowers, and Aaron carried them to Saint Stephen's Hospital. A small floral offering arrived—blood-red chinaberries entwined with ribbons of black and scarlet. There was no card, but the hall porter told Aaron that Russians sent such gifts to one another as condolence gifts. Andropov, Aaron thought, and he imagined the steely-eyed ambassador arranging for the gift, delegating the errand at last to an aide, pondering whether or not to include a card. What lingering dybbuk did the Russian hope to exorcise by his peripheral involvement with Lydia? Aaron was certain that they would never know. Always there were stories of high-ranking Soviet officials who had betrayed lovers and wives for obscure crimes of origin and aspiration.

Aaron slept uneasily on the brocaded chaise longue in the dressing room while Lydia tossed and turned beneath the huge feather-stuffed comforter in the bedroom. She moaned. He thought he heard her call her husband's name, but he could not be sure.

"Paul," she called clearly, and then her voice trembled and broke.

Aaron himself dreamed again of Katie—a weeping Katie in a gossamer shroud. Poor, restless, death-dressed Katie, wandered through narrow streets, past blazing buildings, carrying a single white carnation and a paper flag.

In the morning he and Lydia stared at each other through darkly circled eyes. Only they had slept in the ornate suite, but the spectral wraiths of Paul and Ferenc Groszman and Katie Goldfeder had shared the uneasy darkness. They decided to breakfast in the brightly lit dining room because they could no longer bear the silence and the shadows.

Their waiter, a slight young man, treated them with extreme courtesy. He knew who they were. The story of Paul Groszman had spread through Budapest. His name was spoken softly, reverently. A small bonfire had been lit on the spot where he had died, and passersby kept it alive by adding twigs and papers to the low-burning brave flame.

The fighting continued, the waiter told them as he poured Aaron's coffee, Lydia's tea. He himself had decided to resign his position at the hotel and join his friends, who had formed a fighting unit at the Corvin Cinema. He waved away the tip that Aaron offered him. He had been a comrade-in-arms to Paul Groszman. There could be no question of an exchange of money between like-minded men, warriors for freedom.

"We must make plans," Aaron said when they were alone. "Now is the time to leave. There is nothing more that you and I can do to help, and the situation is so uncertain."

"But in the end we will win." Her voice was as timorous as that of a child asking for reassurance. *Will everything be all right? Paul must not have died in vain. Please tell me that there was reason to his death.* The unspoken questions glittered in the unnatural brightness of her blue eyes.

"I don't know what will happen," he said honestly. "Everything depends on what the Russians do. If they make a show of force, how will the Americans react? It's a question of timing. If all this had happened after the American elections, everything might be different. But Eisenhower and Stevenson are both caught up in their campaigns, and neither has outlined a scenario for Hungary."

"But things are not as they were under Stalin. There is a softening. Khrushchev and Andropov are different. There were no Soviet tanks at the radio station." Her voice was insistent and vaguely querulous. He welcomed her argument. It marked an emergence from the first stage of mourning. And she was not entirely wrong. A Hungarian bullet had killed Paul Groszman, not a Russian grenade. Even in death there were gradations. They had lost Paul and were comforted because his death had been swift. He was dead, but his death was the result of a demonstration gone berserk, not of a Soviet onslaught. Tragedy was ameliorated and rationalized until it became bearable.

"What you say is true," Aaron conceded. "But men like Andropov take their time. They wait to see which way the wind is blowing. They wait until the songs are silenced and the paper flags are ripped and the carnations are wilted. And while they are waiting they say 'yes' and 'maybe,' while all the time, perhaps, they mean 'no, never.' "

"You are so cynical," she said bitterly. Anger froze her voice, sorrow dulled her eyes. "Paul died full of hope. Ferenc never despaired."

Paul and Ferenc Groszman formed a shadowy but impenetrable barrier between them. Aaron competed with the shades and beliefs of the dead. If he slept with Lydia, would she whisper Ferenc's name into the darkness? If they had a son, would she compare him with Paul? And would he call out for Katie? They were ghost-haunted, the two of them, bereft but entangled. And yet it was possible to break free of the past—his mother had done it and so had David Goldfeder. He felt a brief surge of courage, a new tenacity.

"It is not cynical to confront the truth." He kept his voice hard. "We must make a decision. We must leave Budapest as soon as possible."

"Yes." She looked down at the table, her slender fingers again constructing a roadway of bread crumbs—the remembered gesture of their first meeting. He was right, she knew. She was too well trained in the assessment of problems, of alternatives, not to see that.

"I'll call Tom Hemmings. Your papers are in order. He'll arrange for an immediate hearing."

He left to phone the embassy. Lydia stared into her teacup as though she might read the future in the blackened, muddied dregs. Soon it would all be over. They would leave Budapest. Efficient Tom Hemmings would arrange everything. She looked up as Aaron returned to the table and saw that his face was ashen, his eyes clouded with sorrow.

"What happened?" she asked.

"There was an accident. Tom and Betty drove to the Lake Balaton district, and at the Bickskel intersection their car was rammed by a truck. Betty was killed, Tom is badly hurt. He's in the hospital."

"Betty is dead?" Lydia asked, and her voice was shrill with disbelief. She pressed her fisted hands to her eyes. Another death. When would they receive news of life?

Aaron nodded wordlessly.

He thought of slender Betty Hemmings, who had only wanted to have a good time, to live an exciting life, to entertain others and be entertained herself. She would never be a mother. She would never be posted to Paris or to London. She would never laugh again with her Vassar classmates or walk the Hampton beach at the end of a summer's day. He remembered now that Betty had caught Katie's bouquet of wildflowers at their wedding. He imagined Betty lying on the concrete highway, like a fragile broken doll, and again he saw Katie's lifeless body, a ribbon of blood trailing from her pale lips. Nausea swept over him, and he fought desperately for control as Lydia watched him. She understood instinctively, he knew. She did not speak but filled a water glass and gave it to him. He drained it thirstily, as though the water were a secret elixir that would restore his balance, lessen his pain.

"Look," he said finally, "Tom's assistant is going to try to get things moving. It will take a little longer, of course, but it will give you a chance to get things in order. What do you have to do?"

"Just some packing. My papers are in order, and I've already disposed of most of my things. But I want to get to the laboratory and collect my data. I should have kept copies."

"You couldn't have known," he said.

"Known what?"

"That today the whole world would be turned upside down."

They laughed bitterly together then, declaring a truce, a respite against new grief and lingering sorrow.

THEY never reached the university. The Russians had at last come to a decision, made their move. They would not relinquish their hold on Hungary. They had never planned to. Aaron understood now that Andropov's message had been a warning and they had ignored it. He cursed himself for his stupidity, his optimism.

The ancient city of bridges and boulevards had become a battlefield. Soviet tanks rolled through the streets, and small children dashed after them, hurling bottles of gasoline. The church bells, stilled for so many years, chimed in melodic threnody and clashed with the staccato tympany of automatic rifle fire. Rumors abounded. The Russians controlled the university. The revolutionaries occupied the newspaper offices. It was dangerous to walk in the old quarter. The Corvin Cinema and the Killian Barracks were held by the insurgents, the freedom fighters.

Aaron and Lydia walked slowly, cautiously, pressing their bodies against buildings, keeping their heads down. Twice, when the sounds of automatic weapons were dangerously close, he thrust her to the ground, shielding her body with his own.

"We can't go on," he said finally. "It's too dangerous. How important is it that you have that data?"

"I can rerun the experiments," she said. "It would have been helpful, but it isn't vital."

Her voice was weary. Her revolution of songs and flowers, of paper torches and passionate poetry, had turned into a nightmare of tanks and explosives, blood and fire. Her shoes were sticky because she had walked through a puddle of blood. Whose blood? she wondered. They had seen no body. She was weighted with sorrow. The sonar experiments on which she had worked for so many months seemed unimportant now.

"All right, then. If we can, we'll make it back to the Grand Hotel. If not, we'll go straight to the American embassy," Aaron said decisively.

"All right." She was too exhausted to argue with him, to suggest an alternative plan. Most probably he was right. She was grateful to him now for his forceful direction, his ability to make a swift decision.

They crossed Museum Boulevard and paused at the small bonfire that burned still on the spot where Paul had died. She bent and added a twig to the flames. She thought to say a prayer, but instead she murmured a farewell.

"Goodbye, Paul. My friend. My son." No tears came. They had been dried by a terrible, absorbing sadness. Her grief was as heavy as stone; it did not require the moisture of tears.

Aaron's hand came down heavily on her shoulder.

"Close your eyes," he said harshly. "Don't look."

Reflexively, she obeyed him, and he guided her past the street lamp where a dead AVO man was suspended by the neck. The bulb was still lit, and its orange glow illuminated the face of the corpse, which grinned at them like a grotesque jack-o'-lantern. He hurried her off the tumultuous main thoroughfare and onto a small side street that seemed peaceful and deserted. Like many Budapest byways, the small street curved intriguingly, and it was only after they had walked several paces that he saw that a Soviet tank blocked the exit.

"Just remain calm," he told Lydia. "I don't think they'll stop us."

But the click of her heels alerted the Russian who sat astride the tank. He wheeled around, his carbine lifted in readiness.

Odd that he should be alone, Aaron thought. The tank was a TX 34, made in a single weld and impervious to the Molotov cocktails. It was always manned by a crew of two or more. But of course the Russian was probably waiting for his partner, who had gone off to answer nature's call. Even during a revolution men had to empty their bladders.

The Russian lowered himself to the ground, drew his gun, and approached them. He barked a question at them in Russian.

"Say nothing," Aaron cautioned Lydia, whose fingernails dug deeply into his wrists. He felt the skin break and was dimly grateful for the pain.

"I don't understand Russian," he said, and began to reach into his pocket for his passport.

The Russian's arm shot out and restrained him. Aaron stood patiently while his body was frisked and his passport removed and closely studied. The Russian glanced at him and then at his picture. He passed his hand across the green cover, fingered the paper. When he returned to Moscow he would authoritatively describe the American's passport, embellishing the incident. Aaron did not begrudge him his moment of power.

"I am an American tourist," he said firmly. "And this is my fiancée." He drew a protective arm about Lydia.

"Tourist," the Russian repeated. *"Americanski touristka."* He smiled proudly. He had understood the word. Now he approached Lydia.

"Also *touristka*," Aaron said.

But the Russian frowned.

"*Nyet*," he said. *"Nyet touristka."*

Aaron followed his eyes. The man was staring at the small Hungarian tricolor, the symbol of the revolution, that was pinned to the collar of her scarlet cape. He cursed himself mentally. He had secured it there himself, damn fool that he was, to have been deceived by sunlight and songs, by laughter and flowers.

The Russian grabbed her arm, and she pulled away. She pummeled him and shouted angrily, and her eyes glinted with fury. The soldier's eyes narrowed. His teeth clenched. Again he clutched Lydia's arm, and she spat in his face. Her spittle rested in a foaming globule on the man's cheek; his skin was rage-mottled, his fists brutal. Lydia broke away from his grasp yet again, and the Russian steadied his carbine, took aim. Swiftly Aaron thrust himself between them, seized the Russian's wrist, and dug his knee into the man's groin. Forgotten secrets of combat flooded back, poured strength into his limbs. He wrestled the man to the ground and smelled the sourness of his breath commingled with the stink of the flatulence that came with fear.

"Zhid," the Russian hissed scornfully, clawing at the menorah pin in Aaron's lapel.

Aaron's fist smashed against his mouth. The man screamed in pain, spitting out blood and splinters of enamel, but still he kept his grip on the weapon. Lydia screamed, and Aaron twisted the man's wrist. Fury ruled his body now; an unloosed rage possessed him. He was claiming vengeance at last—vengeance for his unknown father, the redheaded youth in the blue cambric shirt beaten to death on an Odessa street. His father's murderers had also shouted *"Zhid"* and brandished deadly weapons. He avenged his mother—the young Leah, stripped and raped beneath the lombardy tree by a Russian who hissed obscenities into her ear and poured his seed into the uterine cove that sheltered the fetus that had been Aaron.

All the angers of his life, the loneliness of his childhood, the betrayals of his youth, and the bereavements of his young manhood were concentrated now on this adversary who battled him on a narrow street in a city that was not his own. He struck another blow—this one for sweet-voiced Paul, who would never sing again.

The Russian strained to reach the weapon that had clattered to the ground, but Aaron reached for his throat. With thumb and forefinger he pressed down on the carotid artery, pushing with all his weight against the leathery neck. The Russian ripped at his body, clawed at his face, until at last his fingers weakened. His body slumped and he fell to the ground, moving heavily from the death grasp of Aaron's fingers. Foam rimmed his lips and his face was the color of ashes. Aaron heard Lydia's scream, then a strangled sob and an unfamiliar rasping rattle. He looked down at the lifeless body and understood that he had killed a man.

"Come." He urged Lydia forward. The Russian had a partner who would return any minute. They ran onto a connecting square, mingled with the crowd, and turned down one side street and then another until at last Aaron found a phone kiosk. He removed the slip of paper with the phone number from his wallet. *Use only if necessary*, Yehuda had written. Well, it was necessary, damn necessary. Miraculously, Yehuda answered the phone after the first ring.

"We must make arrangements to leave at once," Aaron said. "There has been trouble."

Yehuda's reply was calm, unsurprised. He did not ask what kind of trouble.

"Go back to the hotel. I'll contact you there," he said and rang off.

Aaron took Lydia's arm. She leaned against him as though devoid of will, and slowly they made their way back to the Grand Hotel.

The lobby was crowded. Departing guests and those who were frantically making arrangements for departure milled about. Liveried page boys marched about with their signboards indicating messages and phone calls. A large radio had been placed on the head porter's counter, and a small group clustered about it, listening to the dispassionate tones of the Voice of America announcer.

"Tension continues high today in Budapest, but the forces of freedom are gaining power. Student groups control the national radio. The Soviet-controlled newspapers have suspended publication. There is sporadic fighting, and a spirit of unrest prevails."

"We have to listen to transmissions from London to find out what is happening on the other side of the Danube," a British businessman said bitterly. Just a few nights ago he had explained to Aaron that he and his wife had chosen to vacation at the Grand Hotel because Margaret Island was so peaceful and British sterling bought good value in Budapest. Now his fingers trembled as he lit his pipe, and he repeatedly checked his breast pocket as though to reassure himself that his British passport was in place.

"You were in the city today, Mr. Goldfeder?" his wife asked.

"Yes."

"What was happening?" Her voice was curious but dispassionate. She might be asking if he had been at the races and which horse had won.

"It was not pleasant," he replied. What would she say, he wondered, if he described the AVO officer he had seen hanging from the lamppost? *And by the way*, he would add, *an hour ago I strangled a man—a Russian. I wonder what his name was.* (Had his father's murderer known his victim's name? Were the scales somehow balanced then?)

"The Russians are getting their comeuppance in any case," her husband added. "The concierge says that the student radio reports that a couple of their tanks were hit by Molotov cocktails. And they found the body of one of their Ivans in an alley next to his tank. Strangled, they say."

Aaron saw Lydia sway, and he slipped his arm about her waist.

"If you'll forgive us," he said. "My fiancée is not feeling well."

Gently, he guided her to the iron cage of the lift. Once in his room, she stretched out on the bed, and he took a long, hot shower, soaping himself again and again.

He studied his arms, his hands, the long freckled fingers from which tendrils of russet hair sprouted. He had killed a man with those fingers. And he had wanted to kill him. The remembered ferocity of his rage frightened him, yet he knew that he had had no choice. He allowed the water to rain down on his body in searing, cleansing torrents, and then he emerged from the shower and vomited into the high white sink. Mechanically he cleaned up the mess, then washed his face with very cold water and studied himself in the mirror. A jagged scratch scarred his cheek, and tiny pockets of flesh had been gouged from his chin. A light purple bruise rimmed his right eye, and he was vaguely surprised to discover that it was painful and tender to the touch.

Lydia was asleep when he returned to the bedroom, but the phone in the living room was ringing.

"Aaron Goldfeder here," he said, and his own name sounded strange to him. He had read that there were societies where men who killed took on new names. But such men were murderers. He was not a murderer, he reminded himself. He had killed in self-defense. And no one would ever know that Aaron Goldfeder had killed a Russian soldier on a Budapest street. He wondered now at his own urgency in the call to Yehuda. He had not been thinking clearly. He was safe. Nothing connected him to the murder.

"Yuri Andropov speaks." The Russian's voice was clipped, pedantic. There were those who said he practiced his accent and repeated the intonation of the announcers on Voice of America and Radio Free Europe.

"Good evening, Mr. Ambassador," Aaron said calmly, although a wave of panic swept over him and he felt unfamiliar tremors in his fingers. The telephone receiver trembled in his hand. "What can I do for you this evening?"

"I think it is I who can do something for you," the Russian replied.

"Oh?"

"I believe you lost something of great sentimental value to you today."

"I cannot think of anything," Aaron said.

"You recall the pin that I admired when we spoke at the Hemmings'? I especially remembered it because, if you will recall, I explained that the brother of a dear friend of mine also had such an insignia. She was a lovely woman, my friend. In any case, just such a pin has been brought to my attention. As there cannot be many such insignia in Budapest, I thought it might be yours. If you have lost it, you will perhaps remember where."

"It is very kind of you, but I am certain that I have my pin," Aaron replied. His throat was dry, and he fumbled wildly at the clothing he had worn that day. He picked up the jacket, fingered the lapel, and, with a sinking heart, felt the rip of the fabric. The pin was gone. Sickened, he remembered the frantic clutch of the Russian's fingers, the clawing at his face, his clothing. Had they found the small gold pin in the dead man's fist or beside his lifeless body? It did not matter. It was in Yuri Andropov's hands and he had recognized it, had surely read the initials that Leah Goldfeder had had engraved on its back: A.G. There would be no doubt. The pin was enough evidence to warrant his arrest, and yet Yuri Andropov had sent no officers to detain him. Instead there was his strangely polite phone call.

"If you have your pin, there is nothing more to be said," the Russian countered. "We are grieved at my embassy over the death of young Mrs. Hemmings."

"Yes. It was very tragic," Aaron said.

"Such times as these create many tragedies, Mr. Goldfeder. But of course, tragedies can often be avoided. One can turn one's back, leave. Budapest must be a sad city for your friend, Dr. Groszman, just now." The Russian's voice was careful, controlled, and Aaron tried to match its tenor.

"I think it is."

"There are other cities. Vienna is lovely this time of year. My friend, the woman whom Dr. Groszman resembles so closely, loved Vienna."

"Vienna," Aaron repeated. "We will consider it, Mr. Ambassador."

"I hope you will do more than that, Mr. Goldfeder." There was a new edge in Andropov's voice, a veiled urgency. "Good night."

"Good night, Mr. Ambassador."

Had the Russian been threatening him or warning him? Aaron wondered. It was also possible that he had been setting a trap for him. But it did not matter. His intent was irrelevant. The same decision applied no matter what the case. They had to leave Budapest at once. There was no time for a special hearing. There was no time to wait until American travel documents were issued. There was no longer time for the luxury of hesitation, for the assimilation of grief.

A sharp knock sounded at the door. The stacatto summons was repeated.

"Who is it?" His voice was casual but his heart pounded.

"Yehuda."

He opened the door, and Yehuda Arnon slid into the room and bolted the door behind him.

"Aaron."

They clasped hands, embraced. They were linked by more than family ties now. They had common cause, fled common danger.

"What happened?" Yehuda asked. He looked tired. An urban pallor had erased the bronze glow of his skin, and his gray eyes were bloodshot, as though he had spent too many sleepless nights in too many smoke-filled rooms. The sleeves of his suit jacket were too short for him and his tie was awkwardly looped, yet he moved with lithe certainty, drawing the drapes closed, turning the radio on, lighting all the lamps.

Aaron told him. He was ashamed because his voice trembled, because doubt shadowed his mind.

"I shouldn't have killed him. I should have knocked him out, grabbed Lydia, run like hell."

"You did what you had to do," Yehuda said. "There was no time for judgments, for careful assessments. You weren't sitting behind your desk in your law office. You were in a Budapest alley and the bastard had a gun." A reminiscent melancholy tinged Yehuda's voice. "You know, Aaron, the mother of my children, of Noam and Danielle, was named Miriam. Mia, I called her. Mia. My own. We grew up together on the kibbutz and were married when we were in our teens. Mia was only twenty when Noam was born. During the war we worked as Mosad agents in Czechoslovakia. We would meet, sometimes, in the woodlands outside of Prague. One day a German officer followed her. She struggled with him, and I rushed from my hiding place to protect her. I was too young, too much in love, to be cautious. The German drew his gun, and Miriam, who was also too young and too much in love, ran between us. She was killed with the bullet meant for me.

"I strangled the German, Aaron, just as today you strangled that Russian soldier. Still, sometimes, I can feel my bare hands against his neck, the muscle tendons cutting into my fingers. There are no choices at such times. Our instincts make the choices. We strike to survive, and we know that we must survive because our lives extend beyond ourselves. Others wait for us, rely on us.

"I remember now, and I am ashamed, but I did not weep as I hid Miriam's body in a cave covered with bramble bushes. I thought only of how I would get away, how I would complete my mission. And that is what you must concentrate on now, Aaron—how you will get away and how you will get Lydia Groszman out of Hungary. Andropov may have given you a head start. We'll have to gamble on it."

Yehuda lit a cigarette, and it occurred to Aaron that he had never seen his sister's husband smoke before. But then, there was much that he had not known about Yehuda Arnon, who had always been strangely silent with his wife's American family.

"Not quite the simple mission of representing Dr. Groszman at an immigration hearing," Aaron said.

Yehuda shrugged.

"We didn't foresee the imminence of the revolution. We didn't know how deeply Lydia was involved. And most important of all, we couldn't predict the Russian reaction. Do you want an apology, Aaron?"

"No. Probably I owe you a debt of gratitude." He glanced at the door to the bedroom where Lydia slept. "But I do want to get the hell out of Hungary and to get Lydia out with me."

"Good."

Yehuda flipped open his attaché case.

"We have a new identity card for Lydia. Not a bad job." He showed Aaron the document, which had been creased and stressed. Clearly, he had had it in readiness—an insurance policy if the regular immigration proceeding failed. "A Jewish printer on Dohány Street. A master engraver. During the war he manufactured birth certificates for the children we smuggled into Palestine. His revenge on Hitler, he said then. Now he calls it his revenge on Stalin. It seems that only the names change."

"A terrific job," Aaron said. "Congratulate him for me."

"Here is a road map with your route marked. A list of addresses of safe houses on the route."

"Safe houses?"

"Mostly Jewish families or friends who have helped us before. This is not our first time along this route," Yehuda said wearily.

"We've arranged for a car. A black Chaika. Greenstein will be driving. He'll leave it in the hotel parking lot and lean against it. Then, when he sees you, he'll walk away. The keys will be under the mat on the driver's side."

"When?"

Yehuda checked his watch.

"In an hour's time. Can you manage?"

"We can manage."

"Do you need cash?"

"I cashed a check against Joshua's letter of credit this morning."

"Ah. Your sister would be proud of you." Yehuda flashed him a conspiratorial grin and shut his case.

"Is she proud of you?" Aaron asked, curious suddenly about his sister's marriage. Rebecca had married into Yehuda's world. She had plummeted from the tennis courts of Scarsdale, from the tree-shaded paths of Bennington, into life with a man who lived at the edge of a desert yet negotiated the cities of the world with clandestine ease. It was possible, after all, for two people from different worlds to build a life together. Rebecca and Yehuda had done it. He, too, could do it.

"I don't know," Yehuda said, and his voice was strained. "We don't speak of such things. Aaron, you'll cross the border at Sarfolld. Go straight to Vienna, to the American embassy. They'll be expecting you. Rebecca and I will meet you in London."

"London?"

"Yes. You will understand why."

Aaron asked no further questions. Yehuda stood.

"Shalom, Aaron. Good luck."

"Goodbye, Yehuda."

Again they clasped hands, embraced. A new bond had been forged between them. They had shared secrets, uncertainties. They smiled in parting, offering each other the comfort of optimism, the gentleness of friendship.

Aaron went into the bedroom where Lydia still slept, so exhausted that she had not heard Yehuda enter or leave. Her long black hair fanned out against the white pillow slip. Her pale skin was almost translucent and her mouth turned upward, as though brushed by a brief, happy dream.

"Lydia, wake up."

She stirred and stretched luxuriously.

"Ferenc?" Her voice was drowsy, dream-bound, and he felt irrationally betrayed. It was her husband who had caused her to smile as she slept.

"Lydia." He told her about Andropov's call, Yehuda's visit.

Fear darkened her eyes and she pressed his hands, her nails carving small arcs into his skin.

"It will be all right," he said.

"Of course," she said. They could not afford to believe otherwise.

She dressed quickly and helped him to pack, placing the paisley dressing gown in the largest case. He called the desk and asked them to have his bill ready.

"Rather a sudden departure," the desk clerk said.

"Not really." He kept his tone casual, indifferent. Yehuda had taught him to ration his words. Words left unsaid cannot be regretted.

Greenstein was in the parking lot. He left the car without acknowledging them, and they waited until he had turned the corner before getting into it, stowing their luggage, and driving away.

As they drove out of Budapest, Lydia turned and looked back at the city of her birth. She did not face front until the last of the city lights had disappeared; she sat quietly then, her hands clasped in her lap, like a mourner resigned to an irrevocable loss.

IT took them two days to reach the small town of Sopron. There they bought tickets for a small commuter train, which moved slowly and laboriously toward the border town of Sarfolld. The railway guard pointed to a small wooded area.

"There is a bridge just beyond the copse," he said softly. "When you cross it, you will be in Austria."

He asked them no questions. Indeed, no one had asked them any questions along the way. They were two more marchers in the parade that was wending its way through the country. Everywhere in Hungary, people were on the move, carrying their possessions in flimsy suitcases, showing snapshots of their children and their aging parents to strangers briefly encountered at inns and safe houses. The optimists among them moved toward Budapest. They believed still that the

Soviets would capitulate, that the Hungarian people would triumph. The pessimists rushed toward the border.

We are in the company of the disenchanted, Aaron thought as he and Lydia paused, with the small group that had disembarked. A child began to weep suddenly and was lifted into the arms of a tall man. A woman stared across the rolling hills and crossed herself, and a sad-eyed youth stooped and scooped up a handful of earth, which he placed in his pocket. And then, moving swiftly, they turned to the border.

Aaron walked rapidly, and Lydia kept pace with him although gray circles of fatigue rimmed her eyes and her breathing was shallow. It had rained, and the ground was sodden beneath their feet, the sky mantled in gray. They were almost at the bridge. He tried to estimate the number of steps they would have to take to reach it. It was only meters away. He grasped Lydia's hand.

"Can you run?" he asked.

She nodded, but before they could sprint forward a shout rang out.

"Hey. Hey, you there! Halt! Stop, I say!"

Aaron turned. The mild-mannered railway guard was racing after them, brandishing his club.

"Stop, Aaron. He has a gun. I saw it at his belt."

"But he seemed so friendly. So sympathetic."

"Perhaps he received a telegram. If we stop, perhaps we can bluff our way out. If we keep going, he may shoot us in the back." She spoke with the professional tone of a scientist who has weighed two possibilities and come to a decision. She paused and turned to their pursuer, smiling inquiringly.

Puffing and panting, he came up to them, put his club away, and reached into his pocket.

"You are American?" he asked Aaron.

"Yes."

"Please. When you reach your country, mail this for me. It is a letter to my brother. In the city of Chicago. In the state of Illinois. Here is a florin for the stamps."

"That's all right," Aaron said. He waved away the money, took the envelope. "I'll mail it."

"Good luck." The guard shook his hand, and Aaron read the envy and despair in the man's eyes. The fear and weakness he had felt only seconds ago left him. He and Lydia were among the fortunate, the chosen. They had been selected for survival, for freedom.

They walked on, hands linked. As they crossed the bridge the clouds parted. They walked through a vale of silver sunlight into a woodland of evergreens and saw a small Austrian flag planted on the velvet bed of moss that grew between the borders.

AARON AND LYDIA remained in Austria just long enough to obtain a temporary visa for Lydia at the American embassy in Vienna. The vice-consul handed Aaron a manila envelope that contained their airline tickets to London. Tom Hemmings was recovering, he told them, and would be reassigned to the States.

Rebecca met them at Gatwick. She had been in London for only a day.

"I planned to come in a month's time to confer with a gallery here," she said. "But Yehuda cabled me and asked if I could meet him now, and so I juggled things and here I am. Marvelous, isn't it?"

She flashed him a smile, but Aaron saw the lines of worry about her eyes, the tiny nerve that throbbed at her neck.

"How are things at home?" he asked.

"Not good," she replied tersely. "We are not at war, but there is no peace. Yehuda is here for a conference at Whitehall. I always think that Yehuda's conferences increase in direct proportion to the dangers in Israel—not that I ever know what they are about." She laughed with rueful acceptance, but her eyes were shadowed, and she nervously twisted the bright green scarf that matched her dress.

"That must be difficult," Lydia said gently. Ferenc, too, had been involved in secret meetings, clandestine conferences, but always he had shared his experiences with her. It took a special kind of courage to accept exclusion, to anticipate danger without knowing where it lurked, how it might present itself. Aaron had told her that Rebecca sometimes did not know where Yehuda was and never did she know what he was doing. She was anxious, suddenly, to meet Yehuda Arnon, the architect of her escape, of her safe passage into freedom.

But he did not join them for dinner. He had phoned to say that he would be delayed, and Rebecca, Aaron, and Lydia decided to have coffee in the sitting room of the Arnons' small suite. The BBC had announced a program of Mahler's "Song of the Earth," and Lydia wanted to listen to it. Aaron remembered that Paul had been rehearsing for a Mahler concert just the week before his death. He covered Lydia's hand with his own. Her fingers were icy cold to his touch, but she did not withdraw her hand. She was leaning back, almost hypnotized by the lyric beauty of the first cycle of songs, when the news broadcaster suddenly interrupted.

"An emergency news bulletin," he said in his clipped accent, and they leaned forward in their seats as he continued. Israeli Defense Forces had penetrated Ras el Naqb and Kuntilla and engaged fedayeen forces. They had also seized positions west of the Nakhl crossroads in the vicinity of the Suez Canal.

"It's war," Rebecca said. "It had to come. I knew it. We could not go on living in fear, but still I'm frightened, Aaron. I wish Yehuda were here. I wish we were both in Israel."

Rebecca knew now that it was unlikely that Yehuda would return to the hotel that evening. She glanced worriedly at the clock and tried to imagine what was happening in Israel. Their children would be huddled together in the kibbutz bomb shelter, and Danielle would cradle the baby, Yaakov, who would whimper piteously as he always did when he was plucked from his crib in the bright children's house and carried into the subterranean canyon of safety. Danielle and Noam might shiver with fear, but they were native-born Israelis and would not cry. It was Mindell who caused Rebecca the most worry. Mindell had lived with the Arnons since Rebecca had spirited her out of Europe. Always, she grew short of breath in an enclosed space, and only recently she had stopped dreaming of the malodorous tunnel in which she had been hidden in Auschwitz. Now she again sought refuge beneath the earth. Would there ever come a time when Jewish children would walk freely, without fear, beneath an open sky? Surely, it was not so much to ask, Rebecca thought, and soundlessly, she began to cry.

"Don't, Becca. It will be all right." Aaron's voice was soft, tender. He patted his sister's shoulder, stroked her hair. He noticed for the first time that its darkness was flecked with silver, and he was newly saddened. Rebecca, his little sister, was a woman whose hair was graying too early. Once again, they were Leah's children, brother and sister united in a mysterious conspiracy of blood and memory, reassuring each other, protecting each other, whispering small lies, fictive talismans that would protect them from danger, shield them from loneliness.

Lydia watched them and realized suddenly the depth of her own exhaustion. She excused herself and went to bed in the room assigned to her, but through the closed door she heard the brother and sister continue their conversation. In hushed voices, they scattered names and memories, exchanged information.

"I had a letter from Michael," she heard Rebecca say.

Michael. He was their younger brother in California, who was bent on changing the world. ("I'll turn the whole world upside down overnight.") She wondered if he was redheaded like Aaron or dark-haired like Rebecca. Did he, too, walk with that confident determination she had noticed in both Aaron and Rebecca?

Joshua. That would be their childhood friend, the poor boy who had become a millionaire. *Joshua.* The repeated name soothed her, and she fell asleep at last when Yehuda, Rebecca's husband, joined them. His voice was husky, and Lydia imagined him to be a tall, wide-shouldered man, possessed of great strength and great gentleness.

LYDIA awakened the next morning to a city shrouded in mist. Automatically, she switched on the radio. Once she had been indifferent to international news; now it possessed her. The BBC newscaster read with dispassionate clarity. In Budapest, Cardinal Mindszenty had been released from prison. Crowds had cheered him in the street. Men and women had wept and asked for his blessing. Lydia felt a surge of pride, a stir of longing. Like Rebecca Arnon, she wanted to be with her people, in her homeland, in this hour of crisis. But Rebecca had a home and she had none. Rebecca had a family and she was alone. Rebecca would return to Israel, but Lydia would never see Hungary again. She would never lay a small stone on Ferenc's grave or on Paul's. She had seen the Dohány Street Synagogue for the last time.

She fought back an unfamiliar wave of self-pity, commanded herself to wash and dress. The announcer's voice trailed her as she moved through the room. In the Middle East, the Israeli Seventh Armored Brigade was moving across the central axis of the Sinai. Scattered uprisings continued in Hungary. Yuri Andropov, the Soviet ambassador, deplored random acts of violence. There had been no arrests for the murders of at least three Soviet soldiers. In the United States, on the eve of the presidential election, both Adlai Stevenson and Dwight Eisenhower had issued cautious statements. Both the incumbent president and the challenger regretted the violence in the Middle East. Both men regretted the violence in Hungary. Both implored all Americans to go to the polls to demonstrate their commitment to democracy.

"Who will win your election—Eisenhower or Stevenson?" she

asked. She could not ask him if Budapest would go up in flames or if Israel would be destroyed.

"Eisenhower, I think," Aaron said. "But it will make no difference. Neither of them will do anything."

They left the hotel and walked through Kensington Gardens, pausing to watch a small boy, swaddled in layers of brightly colored sweaters, chase after a flock of pigeons. They sat on the top deck of a bright red London bus and rode to Hyde Park, where they listened to an intense, bespectacled young woman rant against the sale of liquor. They wandered to another soapbox, on which an elderly gentleman in an elegant velvet-collared topcoat called for an end to national welfare. Free speech was new to her, and she stared in wonder at the speakers and the clusters of listeners.

Aaron took her to a department store off the Tottenham Court Road. Lydia had fled Budapest without even a change of clothing, and they had bought only a few essentials during their few days in Vienna. She wandered through the large, brightly lit emporium, marveling at the towering hillocks of merchandise; she stared down long aisles crowded with racks of dresses and suits, children's clothing, and rainwear. The array of clothing was a miracle. In Budapest, shoppers stood in queues for hours only to confront bare shelves, sullen salespeople.

She bought a black wool suit and two sweaters, one gray and the other black. She had selected the clothing of a mourner, Aaron thought, but he said nothing, although he remembered the satin blouse that matched her eyes which she had worn to the Hemmings's party.

"You'll need a dress," he said, and he took her to Fenwicks because he had seen one of turquoise silk in the window as they passed.

He left her in the dress department and went to the lingerie boutique, where he bought her a simple white nightdress of fine batiste. He fingered the delicate fabric. He imagined it falling gracefully about her body, swirling at her slender ankles.

"For your wife?" the saleswoman asked pleasantly as she wrapped it.

The question startled and flustered him. He did not answer but busied himself with the bill, counting out the unfamiliar currency. Lydia was not his wife. Katie had been his wife and Katie was dead. Lydia was his snow-white princess, with hair as black as coal and skin as white as snow. Only the fairy tale had been reversed. It was she who had awakened him from the apathy he had felt since Katie's death; she had rescued him from the long sleep of despair, the numbness of uncaring. And he, in turn, had rescued her from danger, slain her attacker, and carried her across the border into freedom. In the fairy tale, the knight always married the princess. But in the fairy tale, unvanquished ghosts did not haunt the enchanted lovers; a single kiss sealed their destiny and decreed the happiness of their "forever after." He had kissed Lydia in the glow of a Budapest street lamp; he had held her close in shadowed forests and gently stroked her neck in a dimly lit café. But still, their own "forever after" remained shrouded in mist, draped in silence.

They had dinner with Rebecca and Yehuda that night. Rebecca was more relaxed. The news was good. Nasser had ordered a complete withdrawal from the Sinai, and Israeli armor had captured Gaza.

"The war will be over in a few days," Yehuda said. He spoke with calm authority.

Aaron stared at his brother-in-law. The battles in the Sinai held no mystery for Yehuda Arnon. The object of the war was not obscure for him. It had been carefully predetermined in smoke-filled Jerusalem conference rooms, in Guy Mollet's safe house in Sèvres, in Patrick Dean's austere suite in Whitehall. He and Lydia Groszman had been tossed by the winds of history, but men like Yehuda Arnon built windmills to harness dangerous currents. Briefly, he envied his sister and her husband.

"The war will be over but the killing will go on," Rebecca added. Aaron was startled by the bitterness in his sister's voice. It did not relate entirely to the desert war, he thought. Even as children, he and Rebecca had been acutely sensitive to each other's moods. He discerned her sadness now and pondered its source. There was an odd tension between Rebecca and Yehuda, a strange, elusive uneasiness.

Music played, and Yehuda politely asked Lydia to dance. Aaron and Rebecca watched them move across the polished dance floor. The dress Lydia had finally chosen was a navy-blue silk with a high collar that accentuated her pallor.

"She's very lovely," Rebecca said. "I'm sorry about her son."

"He was her husband's son," Aaron interposed.

"But she raised him. As we have raised Mindell. Mindell is my daughter."

"As your father raised me," he said.

"Our father," she reminded him. David Goldfeder had loved them equally.

"Yes." He played with his silverware, pleated the linen napkin. "Are you happy, Rebecca?" The abruptness of his own question startled him.

"Happy?" She repeated the word as though it were somehow foreign to her. "I don't think about it anymore," she said at last. "At Bennington I once wrote an essay. 'On the Nature of Personal Happiness,' it was called. I couldn't write such an essay now. I suppose I'm happy. I have the children, my painting, the feeling that what we are doing in Israel is important."

"And Yehuda."

"And Yehuda. Whom I love. Who loves me. But he also loved his first wife, Miriam, and in some complicated way, her memory has become part of our lives, shadowing us. Sometimes I awaken in the night. Yehuda is beside me in the darkness, yet I feel so alone that I know he is with Miriam. If he were to speak, he would say her name. And I am jealous. Crazy, isn't it—to be jealous of a dead woman?"

"No," Aaron said gently. "It's not crazy." Lydia had murmured her husband's name that night in the Grand Hotel, and he, who was neither husband nor lover, had been jealous of the dead man.

Yehuda and Lydia returned to the table, flushed and exhilarated. They were both unused to dancing, to gaiety, to normality.

"What will you do now, Lydia?" Yehuda asked. He liked the beautiful Hungarian woman. Aaron would be a fool to let her go.

"I will go to the United States. My brother and his family are living there. And it will be the best place for me to work. American scientists have a sophisticated approach to radar technology."

"We had hoped, when we first learned about you, that you might decide to come to Israel eventually," Yehuda said.

"There has always been a close exchange of information between Israeli radar experts and Americans," Lydia said. "I know this from my participation at international conferences. I would like to visit Israel, of course, but now I will go to the United States."

She did not meet Yehuda's eyes. She was ashamed to tell him that she trembled at the thought of living in a country that faced the constant threat of war. She had lived her life in fear and hiding. She had suffered too many losses, seen the flames of too many fires. The faces of the mourners in the Great Synagogue in Dohány Street haunted her dreams. Her parents had taken their own lives; her husband had died beleaguered and embittered. The soil of the cemetery where Paul Groszman had been buried only days ago still clung to her shoes.

She wanted a new life, an end to fear. She wanted to hike along trailways that had never known the march of soldiers' boots, the rumble of tanks' thunderous treads. Others might choose renewed danger; her own courage was depleted. She was too tired, exhausted by the effort of her life. She felt Aaron's eyes upon her. His sympathetic gaze caressed her face, and she turned away.

"I must go upstairs," she said.

He rose, too, and they left Yehuda and Rebecca at the table. But as they left the dining room, they both looked back and saw Rebecca gently lift Yehuda's hand and press it to her lips, against her cheek.

He and Lydia looked away from each other, as though the observed intimacy had somehow wounded them. When they reached their own corridor, they slipped wordlessly into their separate bedrooms. Minutes later, he knocked at their connecting door.

"I have something for you." He handed her the large white box that the saleswoman in the Fenwicks lingerie department had so carefully wrapped with blue satin ribbon.

"For me?" Her eyes were awash with liquid brilliance. Had she been crying? Why did her hands tremble as she took the package from him? A deep blush rose from her neck and blossomed in her cheeks. She touched his face. "Thank you." The words were a whisper. She closed the door as he stood there, shutting him out.

He sat on the edge of his bed, not bothering to light the lamp. A desperate fatigue overwhelmed him. He yearned for sleep, but he feared the dreams that sleep would bring. Weariness gritted his eyes, but he dared not close them. She had closed the door behind him and confirmed her loss and his aloneness. Before Paul's death, perhaps, there might have been a chance for them. But now she was benumbed by grief, bound by ghosts.

"Aaron."

Lost in his melancholy, he had not heard the door open, yet she stood beside him. Her blue-black hair caped her shoulders; it matched and surpassed the darkness. Her skin was tallow-white beneath the sheer cotton folds of the nightdress. The golden aureoles of her breasts were small and gentle flames. If he touched them they would surely burn his fingers. His arms moved toward her; his hands traced the curve of her arms, the slope of her back. Her lips were soft and gentle on his face. She kissed his eyes; her lashes brushed his cheeks, light as the wings of a butterfly.

Gently, he eased her down onto the bed and pressed his hands across her body. Her skin ignited his, but he was not seared. They were aflame; their shared fires, so long subdued, mingled and burst in a mighty and mysterious conflagration. Their separate worlds, their separate sorrows, came together and were transformed into joy, blazing, fiery joy that convulsed their bodies and melted at last into exhausted contentment.

"Aaron." She celebrated his name. "Aaron, I could not let you go."

"And I would not have let you go."

He stroked her hair and studied the translucence of her skin. The turquoise mark on her neck shimmered in the darkness. She was very beautiful, his snow-white princess, his gentle love. He closed his eyes and fell easily into dreamless sleep.

THEY walked the patterned paths of Kensington Gardens the next morning, their fingers loosely linked. They had things to say to each other that could only be uttered in the clear, cold air of the November day. The sky was gray, yet streaked with lingering ribs of pale sunlight, uneasily balanced between fall and winter. Brittle leaves fell to the ground; in a few days' time they might be covered with snow. They, too, hovered at season's edge, aware of their entry into a new length of days. Aaron fed the crumbs he had brought from the breakfast table to a flock of greedy pigeons and told her at last about Katie.

"I loved her," he said simply, "even though I knew from the beginning that there was something wrong. She was not like other people. She fell into moods of such despair, of such darkness, that I could not reach her. Still, I married her. I was young and full of wonder at what I felt for her. When you are young, I suppose, you think you can do anything. I had survived a childhood of strange secrets, of mysterious loneliness. I had survived a war. I was strong. The world was mine, and I was sure I could help Katie and share it with her. But I couldn't, of course. She shut me out, told me lies, and lied to herself. She became pregnant and did not tell me. Instead, she flew to Puerto Rico and had an abortion."

He fell silent. The aborted fetus had assumed a reality for him. He grieved for the child it had not become; he grieved for the loss he had unknowingly, unwillingly sustained. Only yesterday he had looked at a toddler in Regent Park, so brightly bundled in scarlet suiting against the encroaching cold; and wondered whether the small bit of detritus sucked from Katie's womb had been male or female, a son or a daughter, blond like Katie or copper-curled as he himself had been as a boy.

Lydia leaned against him as though the pressure of her weight might ease his sorrow. When she spoke of Ferenc her voice was soft.

"For a while, after I was married, I did not think about having children," Lydia said. "I suppose I thought of myself as a child still, because the war had stolen my childhood. I was the daughter-wife and Ferenc was my father-husband. And Ferenc was so weary, so frightened. He could not bear the thought of bringing another child into such an uncertain world. And, after all, we had Paul. It was Paul who made me think about myself as a mother—a woman who nurtured and protected a child." Her voice broke, and Aaron held her close.

"Who can protect their children?" he said softly. He thought of the Arnon children, huddling in a bomb shelter. He remembered that Sherry and Joshua Ellenberg's daughter, Lisa, had miraculously escaped death when she fell beneath the wheels of a speeding car on a quiet Great Neck street. Children were hostages to danger and mischance, fortune's playthings.

"Once, I thought I was pregnant," she continued. "It was such a sweet secret. I smiled when I thought about it, and Paul asked me why I smiled. Children always want to share a secret. I thought, I am smiling because you may have a brother or sister and we will be a family again, looking forward instead of remembering back. I decided that no matter what Ferenc said, I would have the baby. I thought of how I would tell him. I would wait for an evening when Paul had a late rehearsal. I would prepare a good dinner and later, while we drank plum wine and the candles burned low, I would tell him. When he saw my happiness he would abandon his sorrow. But in the end there was no need to tell him. One night I awakened and my body was twisted with cramps and my bed stained with blood. The pregnancy was over. The hope was gone."

"For then," he said firmly. *"Only for then."* They would have to draw boundaries carefully and define the *then* and the *now* of their lives. They would learn to distinguish between apparition and reality. In this quiet London park, they shared their sadness, lifted the shadows.

"Katie died in a traffic accident," he said. "She was hit by a taxi, but she had walked directly into its path. She died because she wanted to die, because she could not control her life. And I could not help her. Sometimes I awaken in the night, and I am confused and desperate because I cannot think of what I must do to help her. And then I remember that she is dead and I cannot help her."

"I know." Lydia's voice was so soft, he bent close to hear her. "I watched Ferenc die. Week after week I sat by his bed and saw him grow thinner and thinner. The pain weakened him and the morphine brought him memories. He wept like a small child. There was nothing I could do. I held his hand and I wiped his tears, but I could not help him."

Her helplessness had matched his own. He had been powerless to help Katie and she could not help Ferenc. And together they had watched Paul Groszman's lifeblood stain a Budapest plaza. Their sorrows were unevenly balanced, their memories weighted and exposed. She closed her eyes and lifted her face to the pale autumn sun. She was thinking of Ferenc and Paul Groszman, he knew, but he felt no fear, no threat. They had laid their ghosts to rest.

THAT SUNDAY, they drove to Gatwick Air Terminal with Yehuda and Rebecca. Their flight to New York was scheduled to leave only a half hour after the Arnons' plane to Lydda. It was a clear, crisp day, and they stared out the windows of their taxi at small family groups walking home from church. Young couples pushed gleaming prams and middle-aged men diligently washed their cars. Small boys in striped jerseys played rugby on the bald lawns of council flats while their mothers leisurely walked the high streets and peered into the dimly lit windows of clothing shops. Suburban England was enjoying its day of rest. The *London Times* was spread open on Yehuda's lap. In the Middle East the Sinai Campaign was over. There was a front-page photograph of a troop of Israeli soldiers at Sharm el Sheikh. In Budapest, Soviet tanks rolled imperiously through the streets. Russian soldiers fought Hungarian high school students. An exclusive dispatch from Reuters described a fierce battle fought on Ulloi Avenue, close to the bypass where Aaron had killed the Russian soldier and blocks from the spot where Paul Groszman had so swiftly died. The bonfire would be extinguished by now, Aaron thought sadly. He wondered suddenly what Yuri Andropov had done with the small gold lapel pin.

At the El Al departure gate, Rebecca and Aaron embraced, Leah's children meeting again at a moment of separation.

"Tell Michael to write," Rebecca said. "I worry about him." Only Michael now, of the three of them, was alone and unanchored.

"I will," Aaron said. He had found his way, and Michael, in his turn, would find his own.

"And tell Mama that I'm fine, happy." Her voice was oddly monotonic, and dark circles shadowed her eyes. She was tired, he told himself, worried about her children, upset by the war.

He nodded obediently. He would not share his apprehensions about Rebecca with their mother. Leah had been the guardian of their childhoods. It was only fair that they protect her now from their secret sorrows.

"Shalom."

"Goodbye."

"*Viszonlátásra.*"

They embraced and kissed. Their farewells were promises of reunion. Their tears were droplets of love.

LYDIA AND AARON were married two months later, on a wintry afternoon. Leah filled her living room with white tulips, and the dancing flames of the fire that Michael had so carefully nurtured burnished the delicate flowers with an amber glow. The small gold emblem of the Jewish Brigade glinted in the lapel of Aaron's dark suit. It had been delivered to his office by special messenger.

Leah, in jade velvet, nodded her approval of Lydia's simple dress of turquoise silk. Leah had designed it, and she and Lydia had shopped for hours to find the fabric that exactly matched Lydia's eyes. There had been instant rapport between Aaron's mother and his bride. They had recognized each other at once; they were survivors who had witnessed death and who had chosen life. They were journeyers who crossed borders and forged new pathways. They had laughed as they shopped for the silk, and shared small secrets, gentle memories.

"She looks very beautiful, your Lydia," Boris Zaslovsky, Leah's Russian friend said to her. He was newly arrived from Moscow, where Leah had first met him—a gray-bearded man who looked sad even when laughter creased his face.

"She is beautiful," Leah replied. She was suffused with contentment. Aaron was happy at last—Aaron, her firstborn son, the child of her sadness and her uncertainty, the son of Yaakov, her first husband, murdered on an Odessa street. She listened as he sang the bridegroom's pledge, and again she heard the voice of his father, Yaakov, the youthful groom who had stood beside her beneath the marriage canopy that distant day in Odessa.

"Behold with this ring you are consecrated unto me according to the laws of Moses and of Israel."

Tears spangled Lydia's eyes, but her hand was steady as Aaron slipped the plain gold ring on her finger—his pledge of love, his symbol of claim.

Michael moved closer to his mother. They both felt an almost palpable sadness at the absence of Rebecca and Yehuda. But Rebecca was pregnant again, and Yehuda was needed on the kibbutz to help in the harvest of the winter melons. They had phoned earlier in the day, their voices vibrant with warmth; Rebecca's tone was lightly tinged with wistfulness. "We miss you."

"I command you to live happily ever after," Yehuda had boomed into the phone, and they heard the laughter of the child Yaakov.

"They will have a good life together, Michael," Leah said.

"I know."

He felt the strength in his mother's fingers entwined about his own and followed her gaze to the window. The barren branches of the maple tree arched achingly upward, and the first snowflakes of winter swirled in dizzying dance. Leah smiled, moved anew by the mystery of changing seasons, altered lives.

Aaron's heel smashed the white-wrapped glass, and the room resonated with shouts of "*Mazel tov!*" Sherry Ellenberg wept and her children clapped. Joshua whirled Lisa, his elder daughter, in an impromptu hora. Boris Zaslovsky joined them, and Leah thought that it was the first time she had seen her Russian friend's face free of its mask of sadness.

"May you, too, find your happiness, Michael, my Michael," she said softly. Her younger son took her hand in his own, and together they moved forward to embrace Aaron and Lydia, his bride.

RHODES

1960

THE STREET OF THE KNIGHTS on the island of Rhodes is a perfectly straight thoroughfare, carved with precision and determination into the undulating seabound hills. Yehuda Arnon proceeded down it slowly, as though with each step he continued a mysterious journey into the past. The ancient houses were decorated with the insignia and armorial bearings of those noble houses of Europe who had sent their Crusader sons to claim the island so many centuries ago. Yehuda paused and studied the facade of a building on which crossed swords had been carved. The Latin inscription had long since faded into the rose-colored stone, but the weapons, drawn with unerring symmetry, had endured.

He wondered now what had possessed the Knights of Saint John to journey eastward from the capitals of Europe and build their homes on the ancient island. Perhaps they had been intrigued by its proximity to both Greece and Jerusalem. Once he and Rebecca had stood on Mount Atairo and looked out at Mount Ida in Crete. A brief sea journey would carry them back to Haifa. Rhodes had offered the Crusaders a window on both worlds and a small island kingdom of their own. They had left their mark on the island, and even now its medieval ambience prevailed. The great stone fortifications they had erected at both the northern and southern harbors stared warningly out across the azure waters of the Aegean. The lighthouse at the Fort of Saint Elmo still radiated a monitory beam, a faint splinter of light, unaltered in intensity through the years.

Lydia Goldfeder, who would deliver the closing address to the International Conference on the Peacetime Uses of Radar, had remarked on the irony of convening the scientific assembly on Rhodes.

"It seems strange to come to an island that looks as though it still belongs to the Middle Ages for a conference on modern technology," she said.

"I suppose it was a convenient and neutral location for most of the delegates," Yehuda replied. "That was why it was selected in 1949."

It was then that he and Rebecca had traveled to Rhodes with the delegation that drew up the armistice agreement among Israel, Lebanon, and Syria that terminated Israel's war for independence. He had worn his Haganah uniform to that peace conference, but he had packed it away when they returned to Israel.

"No more uniforms," he had told Rebecca then. "The war is over."

He should have said, he realized now, that only *that* war was over, but he had been younger then and full of hope. And papers had been signed, terms agreed upon; there had been hesitant talk of a permanent peace treaty. Ralph Bunche had scurried from one conference table to another, a skillful, optimistic negotiator, an American Negro sent by the United Nations to mediate between Jew and Arab. Yehuda remembered still the party that Dr. Bunche had given for the delegates at the conclusion of the negotiations. The Egyptians had flown in a special plane from Cairo loaded with delicacies from Groppi's. The Israelis had provided wine from the cellars of Rishon le-Zion, oranges from the orchards of Jaffa. Yehuda had tasted caviar at that party for the first time as he studied photographs of his Egyptian counterpart's smiling dark-eyed son. In turn, he had shown the Egyptian a snapshot of Noam and Danielle. The two men had smiled happily at each other, proud fathers whose young sons might just manage to live in peace. Their smiles, their hopes, had been premature. Only seven years later their countries had been at war again, and the Sinai Campaign had not brought peace. In two years' time Noam, too, would don a uniform, and now Yehuda himself was back on Rhodes, wearing civilian clothes but practicing the vigilance of the warrior.

"You're listed as an adviser to the Israeli delegation," Lydia had said that first evening on the island as they drank thick Greek coffee on the terrace of the Hotel des Roses. She added a drop of anisette and smiled, remembering that Yehuda had also had "adviser" status in Budapest.

"A wonderful term," Yehuda said. "So all-encompassing. I did think of calling myself an 'observer,' but I'm getting tired of that title. I was an 'observer' at the NATO war games and during the Helsinki conference. I thought I'd be an 'adviser' for a change. Besides, it brought us good luck in Budapest."

Still, he had laughed bitterly, recalling all the dining rooms and lounges where he had lingered over lukewarm coffee and melting ices as he carefully noted which delegates conferred too frequently, who drank too much, who passed documents to whom. Always, his reports were economical and concise, his observations insightful, and occasionally he happened to be in the right place at the right time. As he had been in Budapest. His assignment to Rhodes had not displeased him. It had at least given him the opportunity to spend some time with his sister-in-law, Lydia.

A woman opened the window of one of the ancient houses and shook out a dust cloth. The white fabric fanned the soft air like a banner of submission, and the woman remained at the open casement, listening as the muezzin of the mosque summoned the faithful to prayer.

Damn it, I'll be late, Yehuda thought, and he walked rapidly now toward the hotel. Lydia was to deliver the concluding paper, and he did not want to miss it. Besides, he had noted an unlikely friendship between a Swiss physicist and a graduate student at the American University in Beirut. It would be interesting to see if they lingered again after the closing session. If they did, Israeli agents in Zurich and Beirut would be apprised.

Lydia was already at the podium when he entered the conference room. She stood, as always, unselfconsciously erect, a tall woman proud of her height. Her long black hair was swept back into a silken coil, and the whiteness of her skin was emphasized by her navy-blue coat dress. She had changed since their first meeting. There was color in her cheeks now, and her turquoise eyes flashed with warmth. The few short years in America, her marriage to Aaron Goldfeder, and the birth of their daughter, Paulette, had softened and relaxed her. She laughed more easily, and she no longer started at a sudden sound or grew rigid when a stranger spoke to her. Her voice, well modulated, lightly accented, was oddly musical as she spoke to her colleagues in the mysterious terminology of their profession. Her paper was entitled "New Methods of Scanning in Microwave Radar" and was based on her research in the New York State University laboratories on Long Island.

"Her appointment at the university is ideal for Lydia," Aaron had told Yehuda. "It's an easy commute, she has her research, access to the finest equipment, and she works closely with graduate students. That was important to her. She feels that she is continuing Ferenc's work, teaching Paul's generation."

Aaron spoke sadly but easily of Lydia's first husband and her stepson now. He had assimilated his own grief and was no longer threatened by his wife's past. If only Rebecca and I could do the same, Yehuda thought wearily. Sometimes it seemed to him that their marriage was frayed by too many separations; always it had been shadowed by their divergent pasts. He turned his attention back to Lydia, who was describing the work she had done in developing a new receiver.

"The ideal receiver must amplify and measure an extremely weak signal at an extremely high frequency," she said. "Originally we assumed that such a receiver should be stable but my laboratory experiments have led me to conclude that a mobile amplifier might solve many of our problems."

Deftly she produced charts and drawings, and the delegates leaned forward, taking rapid notes, following her pointer as it danced across the carefully marked oak-tag sheets, illustrating her explanations. She opened the floor to questions. The size of the wavelength band? Less than one centimeter. She agreed that they would have to employ a sophisticated microsound technology. They had already had some success using very small acoustic devices that substituted for electromagnetic counterparts.

The Bulgarian delegate, a short, goateed man who chewed gum incessantly, rose.

"I congratulate you, Dr. Goldfeder. Clearly, your amplifier is the most sophisticated approach we have discussed at this conference. It is exceedingly generous of your government to share this information with us. That generosity might even give rise to suspicion." He smiled with wily insouciance and unwrapped a fresh piece of gum.

Lydia turned to him and smiled. A man would have frowned, Yehuda thought, but Lydia's intuitive reactions were always exactly right. He himself would have responded angrily, but Lydia spoke in her soft, level voice.

"The government of my adopted country, the United States of America, is pleased to share unclassified information with the international scientific community. It is stated policy. We believe that scientific information should be shared and that all advances in our field should be directed toward peaceful purposes. Surely, there is nothing suspicious in this. Radar was developed for military purposes, but we are in a new decade now—a new decade and, we hope, a new era. Perhaps the sixties will see us harness radar and utilize it to make the world a better place to live in. My government is pleased to contribute any information that will help to control air traffic and prevent tragedy, any information that will help to detect weather patterns and monitor the health of unborn children. It is true that war coerced us into our discovery, but now we must work to confound the forces of darkness and use our knowledge for the good of man and for the survival of mankind." Her voice rang with passion and conviction.

She sat down to a burst of applause, to the resonance of murmurs of approval, shouts of agreement.

Yehuda waited until the last of her colleagues had congratulated her before he joined her. He noticed that the Lebanese delegate and the Swiss physicist left the room together, although they did not speak.

"Your speech was worth my trip to Rhodes," he told Lydia.

She smiled at him gratefully. "It was a successful conference."

"I didn't understand most of the technical material, of course," he acknowledged ruefully. "But I did notice that there was no discussion of radar evasion techniques."

"This was a conference on peacetime usage," she pointed out.

"But is progress being made?"

"We are optimistic," she said cautiously. "It may be as important for the United States in Southeast Asia as it is for Israel. It is not being ignored."

"Work fast," he said. "A day is a long time in the Middle East. The next time around, radar will decide the outcome of the war." His voice was grim. The next time round, his son Noam would be a combatant—gentle Noam who loved to watch things grow, who drew diagrams of irrigation systems and experimented with hybrid melon vines.

Lydia touched his arm lightly, reassuringly.

"Enough serious talk, Yehuda. Let's enjoy this afternoon together."

She had a special fondness for her Israeli brother-in-law. This was not the first time they had met at an international conference; always such meetings became an occasion for catching up on family news, comparing their reactions, sharing their feelings. Always they felt the special intimacy peculiar to those who meet in a city not their own, who look out across unfamiliar landscapes and listen to strangers speak in mysterious foreign cadences. They recognized that they were linked by ties more complex than those of blood. Yehuda had married Leah's daughter, and Lydia was wife to Leah's son. They spoke with each other of the secrets and mysteries of the family that had become their own. They shared perceptions and insights as they struggled to understand those vanished distant years when Aaron and Rebecca had been strangers to them, children of America, safe and secure while Lydia confronted the perils of an embattled Europe and Yehuda experienced an endangered Palestine.

They offered each other pieces of the complicated puzzle that formed the Goldfeder past. It had been Lydia who told Yehuda that Joshua Ellenberg had once thought himself in love with Rebecca. And it had been Yehuda who told Lydia of the long and anguished silence that had stretched between Aaron and Leah for so many years.

Always, during the days of his boyhood, Leah had seemed at a remove from her son, studying him as though searching out a clue that might solve an elusive mystery for her. It was not until Aaron was a grown man, returned from the war, that she had shared the truth with him, had told him that she had been the victim of a rape in Russia and that for years she had tortured herself with uncertainty as to who had fathered redheaded Aaron—Yaakov, her first husband, or the copper-haired peasant who had forced her to submit to him. Leah had waited long years before confiding her secret to Aaron, and Aaron, in turn, had not shared it with Lydia, his wife.

Lydia had understood then Aaron's constant need for reassurance, his sudden bouts of insomnia when he seized her in the darkness and whispered earnestly. "Do you love me? Do you really love me?" She had wondered how he could doubt her love, but Yehuda's words had explained those doubts to her. Aaron had spent his childhood never certain that his mother loved him.

They ate lunch on the patio of a taverna on Platia Martyron Evreon—the Square of the Martyred Hebrews—staring out at the fountain crowned by three bronze seahorses. Lydia wondered if the sun had shone so brightly on that July day in 1944 when the eighteen hundred Jews of Rhodes had paraded past that fountain on their way to the cattle boat that began their journey to Auschwitz. She could not finish her coffee and thrust the tiny gold-rimmed cup away. Yehuda's hand covered her own.

"Don't think about it," he said. Their pulses throbbed and their hearts raced. Memories of death spurred them to life.

They drove to the archaeological ruins of Lindos and wandered through a grove of carob trees and studied the fragments of metal said to be the only remnants of the great Colossus of Rhodes. They climbed the ancient acropolis and photographed each other against the background of the medieval castle that the diligent Knights of

Saint John had built there. An orange tree grew wild, and they inhaled its melancholy fragrance. He thought of the orchards of his childhood; she remembered her mother's cologne. And then, at last, they sat in the shade of a fig tree and spoke of the Goldfeder family.

"How is Leah?" Yehuda asked.

"Unbelievable. Paulette is staying with her now because Aaron is arguing a case in Washington. I think Leah has more energy and patience than I have. She tells Paulette stories, teaches her songs; she even bought her a sketch pad, although all Paulette can do is scribble."

"I suppose being a grandparent must be something like being given another chance," Yehuda speculated. "When Aaron and Rebecca and Michael were small children, Leah had no time to tell them stories, sing them songs, draw pictures with them. She was too busy working to keep bread on the table. And when Michael was little, there was the war. So all that she could not give to them, she gives to Paulette."

He picked up a carob pod and ate it, spitting the seeds out. He, too, spent little enough time with his own children. For much of Noam and Danielle's childhood he had been involved in the rescue of the remnant of European Jews, and later he had been away working for the Haganah. Now, during Yaakov and Amnon's childhood, he traveled constantly on intelligence missions. Like Leah, in order to protect his children's futures, he was forced to miss their present.

"And Leah sees a great deal of her Russian friend, Boris Zaslovsky," Lydia continued. "They're both involved in working for Soviet Jewry. Leah is forever going to a protest or a lecture, a congressional hearing or some sort of demonstration."

"I've never met this Zaslovsky," Yehuda said. "We seem always to miss each other. What is he like?"

"Very kind. Very gentle. Intelligent. Introspective. Distinctive-looking. Tall with a white goatee and fine dark eyes. He has a wry sense of humor, but somehow, even when he laughs, I sense a terrible sadness, a kind of weary resignation."

"You never knew David Goldfeder," Yehuda said, "but except for the goatee, you have given a very good description of him. Do you think they will marry, our Leah and her Boris?"

"I think it's a very distinct possibility," Lydia said. It occurred to her that she had never discussed the possibility of Leah's remarrying with Aaron. Oddly, there were things that she and Yehuda discussed openly that neither of them would speak of with Rebecca and Aaron.

"It would be good if she remarried," Yehuda said. "They worry too much about her—Aaron and Rebecca and Michael."

"Ah yes. Michael," Lydia repeated and sighed.

"How is he?"

"I saw him when I lectured at Berkeley a few months ago. He is almost through with his doctorate. All that remains is the defense of his dissertation, and he will receive his degree in June. He loves teaching and seems to have a talent for it. And he has many friends, but he seems always so lost, so lonely. As though he is searching for something, for someone." Lydia's voice was soft. Her young brother-in-law troubled her, reminded her somehow of Paul. "He seems always so alone. So vulnerable."

"I hope Michael finds what he is looking for soon," Yehuda said. "It is not easy to be always alone."

He himself felt invaded, suddenly, by an aching loneliness. He would not be returning to Israel from Rhodes. An international conference on terrorism was convening in Brussels, and he was to deliver a paper. Again, he would be in a strange city when evening fell. Again, he would return to an empty hotel room and eat a solitary dinner ordered in a language not his own.

The sun was setting now, and mauve shadows veiled the crenellated arches of the castle. Lydia stood and brushed twigs and heart-shaped young fig leaves from her dark skirt. She lifted her arms to the dying light; a golden glaze settled on her pale skin. Her hair had escaped its neat coil and draped her shoulders. Yehuda plucked an orange blossom and held it out to her. She accepted it, her fingers touching his own, and he was strangely pleased when she braided the fragile flower through her thick dark hair.

"Lydia." He recognized the plea of desire in his voice and was shamed and astonished by it.

She turned to him, her face radiant.

"But I haven't told you the most important news," she said and moved toward him, brushed a shard of bark from his jacket.

He stood quite still and felt the gentle westerly island wind brush across his face. (*If only I could paint the wind*, Rebecca had said all those years ago when they stood on this same spot.)

"What is your news?" he asked.

"We're going to have another child. The baby will be born in the spring."

"Lydia. That's wonderful. I'm so glad."

He took her hands in his own and kissed her cheek. The spontaneity of his gladness reassured him and extinguished the vagrant spark of desire that had at once invigorated and saddened him. Yes, he acknowledged, there was an attraction between them, woven perhaps of their shared brushes with danger, knowledge of death, the brief and fleeting solitude that thrust them together in cities far from their homes. She was Aaron's wife, and thus sister to Rebecca and to himself. The orange blossom fell from her hair and he did not stoop to pick it up but allowed it to lie there amid the detritus of moss and twigs.

"A new baby for a new decade," he said.

"I hadn't thought of that. But yes. My child of the sixties." Her hand passed protectively over her abdomen, and he saw that although the navy-blue coat dress had obscured it, her body had already begun to gently swell as the new life grew within it.

"It should be an interesting decade for our family," Yehuda said. He felt the press of new events—envisaged the newborn infant in swaddling clothes, Michael in academic cap and gown, Noam in uniform. Perhaps his Rebecca would even learn to paint the wind.

"I think so."

Lydia held her hand out to him and they walked, fingers linked, to the car. They drove slowly then back to the city of Rhodes that rose from the sea like an amphitheater, encircled by wall and towers, starkly silhouetted now against the bloodied sky of sunset.

MICHAEL

The Sixties

MICHAEL GOLDFEDER, his arms laden with empty cartons, heard the ringing of the telephone as he entered his apartment building and knew at once that it came from his fourth-floor flat. He cursed softly to himself as he loped up the stairwell, and on the second landing (and the third ring) he slowed his pace. There was no point in breaking his neck to catch a call that would surely be for one of his roommates, summoning them to a victory celebration. Both Jeremy Cohen and Les Anderson had been Kennedy supporters since the Massachusetts senator had announced his candidacy, and they had returned jubilantly from Los Angeles the previous evening. John Fitzgerald Kennedy had won the Democratic nomination for the presidency—admittedly by a narrow margin, but nevertheless he had won. Now the parties would begin—not that the Berkeley community ever needed much of an excuse for a party. During his four years at the university, Michael had attended celebrations of the new moon, of tenure granted and tenure denied, of marriages and divorces. A presidential primary was the ideal focus for Berkeley celebrants, a party with a purpose. There would be no dearth of purposes in the summer of 1960 with a presidential campaign revving into gear.

The Stevenson supporters would congregate in candlelit rooms and hold good-natured wakes while they drank the very good scotch that had made Kennedy's victory possible. They would be philosophic and resigned, and by the end of the evening they would join the Kennedy parties and become boisterous and argumentative. Naturally, there would be more exuberance in the Kennedy camp. He envisaged kegs of beer, wine from gallon jugs, music blaring from the newly popular amplifiers, competing amiably with the inevitable guitarists. Jeremy and Les were welcome to the scene, Michael decided as he shifted his cartons. He would pack. He was too old for Berkeley and Berkeley parties.

The phone was still ringing when he reached the third landing.

A wrong number or a breather, he decided, but remembered suddenly that Melanie Reznikoff had promised to call him that afternoon. He took the steps two at a time then and reached his door just as the phone fell silent.

"Damn," he muttered and tossed the cartons down on the worn sleeper sofa, which Melanie had covered with a bright madras spread. He noticed now that the spread was ripped and stained with coffee spilled while he had proofread his dissertation. The same stain marred the straw mat that covered the floor—another decorating effort by Melanie. It could be cleaned, he supposed, but it was hardly worth bothering about now. The next tenant would probably throw everything out. He might have done something about the apartment if his mother had come west for commencement, but in the end Leah had succumbed to his arguments and decided to remain in New York.

"Why do you want to bother, Mom?" he had asked. "I'm not even sure I'll go myself. It's going to be a mob scene. This isn't a university, it's a factory. There'll be thousands of us getting degrees. You won't even be able to tell who I am."

He had heard stories of other Berkeley commencements where parents had been unable to locate their own graduate son or daughter and had wandered disconsolately about, their cameras dangling uselessly from leather straps.

"But a commencement is important, it's a milestone," Leah had protested. "I remember so clearly the day your father graduated from medical school. Aunt Mollie cried, but me—I couldn't stop smiling. And don't you remember how we all went to Cambridge for Aaron's law school graduation?" All of them. They had been an intact family then, and David had stood beside her and wept unashamedly, as strong men weep.

"Those commencements were different." Michael's voice was strangely harsh, his tone unyielding.

"I don't see how, but we'll talk about it more when I call next week." As always, Leah hung up without saying goodbye. A persistent aversion to farewells, Michael supposed, because so many arbitrary partings had been thrust upon her.

Michael had stared sadly at the phone then and reflected that this commencement was, in fact, different from those of his father and his brother. Like everything else in his life, it had been too easily earned and had involved him too little.

David Goldfeder's graduation from medical school had been the realization of an impossible dream. His father, the immigrant factory worker, had confronted every economic and cultural adversary—a new language, the strain of poverty, the demands of a family, the rigors of night school—and earned a medical degree, confounding all odds. A mighty battle had been fought, and David Goldfeder's commencement (captured in sepia-print photos proudly displayed in his mother's Scarsdale living room) was a celebration of perseverance, a vindication of ideal. His father's achievement had been awesome, Michael knew, and he cowered in its shadow. Could I have done it? he wondered. Would I have had the courage, the tenacity? He had teased himself with the question during his undergraduate years at Princeton and later at Berkeley, but the truth was that he did not know and would never know. It was impossible to confront a challenge that did not present itself.

Aaron's love of law derived from his agonizing confrontation with the lawlessness of war. He had begun reading law in a prisoner-of-war camp in Trieste—an unlikely student in prison stripes, thin and anemic but charged with a fiery intellectual energy. He had completed those law studies at Harvard, and his commencement had been more than the earning of a degree—it had been an affirmation of the freedom of the mind, the power of the intellect.

Michael contrasted his own pallid and passive academic career with those of his father and his brother. He had not struggled toward success. He had slid into it, effortlessly, carelessly. He was the child of privilege, the heir to his parents' late and hard-earned prosperity. His birth had presaged the end of poverty and struggle. "We already lived in a house when you were born," his aunt Mollie had said proudly. A house! The culmination of the American dream. The acquisition of property and land by those who had been denied ownership, forced into the impermanence of tenancy.

He had drifted from an enchanted childhood into a relaxed suburban adolescence. His memories of growing up in Westchester were a mosaic of sunlit playing fields (always he had been chosen as pitcher, always he had been first up at bat), tree-shaded bicycle paths, snowmen grinning beneath the maple tree in winter and barbecues at the end of long hot summer days. In dreams he smelled the delicious aroma of charred meat, heard the laughter of his parents' friends, the clink of ice cubes in tall glasses; he felt the muscular embrace of strong-armed men, the light kisses of sweet-smelling women. "How are you, Michael? Still growing? Are you going to be as tall as your brother? As smart as your father?" And why had such questions bothered him? he wondered. He had grown taller than his brother and had taken every scholastic prize at school. They had not, after all, asked him if he would be as daring as his brother, as determined as his father.

There were, of course, dark tiles on that mosaic—the tension and anxiety of the war years, the melancholy desolation of a suburban street in the midafternoon, the echoing loneliness of a large house after school. The phone rang and his mother told him that she would be home late—there was a design problem, a production problem. His father called. He, too, would be late. An emergency. A very sick patient. A conference. Michael would turn on the television set and watch the shadow of Howdy Doody glide across the screen. The puppet's voice fought the loneliness, the silence, and he would turn the volume up as he pondered his trigonometry. But suburban loneliness did not qualify as tragedy. He never traded stories in the dormitory marketplace of unhappy childhoods. His own childhood had been happy, perhaps too happy.

There had been no loneliness at Princeton. He had rushed through his four years with ease and acceptable success, and then suddenly he was wearing a cap and gown, marching in solemn academic procession, smiling shyly at his mother and father as he passed them. Their faces glowed with pride and his father's eyes were bright with unshed tears. Their joy bewildered Michael. He had, after all, only done what had been expected of him, unlike his father, who had achieved what had been thought unachievable, and his brother and sister, who forged their own history—Aaron in Europe and Rebecca in Israel. "My brother and sister are a tough act to follow," Michael would tell his Princeton friends.

His classmates were not interested in following tough acts. They were interested in split-level houses, station wagons, and good corporate jobs with solid pension plans. Security was the watchword of their generation, although insecurity hovered dangerously over them. The Bomb haunted their dreams, and they fled from its malevolent threat by conforming to straight and narrow paths. They had been dubbed the "silent generation," but they knew that they did not speak because their words would reveal their fears. They did not trust Michael Goldfeder's restlessness, but they assumed that he would settle down. A job at IBM or General Electric would pull him into the safety of their own silent and steady orbits.

It had been assumed that he would go on to MIT. Hadn't he built intricate models with his expensive erector sets as a child and written a paper on suspension bridges as an undergraduate project?

His framed physics citation hung in David Goldfeder's wood-paneled study. But when his father was killed in Israel, he changed course suddenly. He wanted to learn more about the social forces that had led to David Goldfeder's murder on the sands of the Negev (just as David had studied psychology to learn more about the dynamic of hatred—a generational pattern, Leah had thought, but said nothing). Michael was drawn to sociology—the science of the origin, history, and constitution of human society. There was a good department at the University of California at Berkeley.

Leah had raised no objection. Sociology? Good. Berkeley? Fine. The maternal skepticism she felt was not articulated. Her life of chance had given her son the luxury of choice. The arguments he had developed to defend his position were unnecessary and thus stillborn. They congealed within him. He had wanted to argue, to justify himself, but his mother was understanding, his brother accepting, and his sister, far away in Israel, supportive. "It is wonderful that you have this opportunity," she wrote. She lived in a country where young men wore uniforms and lived on the edge of danger. Rebecca had gone to too many funerals. She visited the children's house in the still hours of the night and studied the faces of the sleeping youngsters. She wrote to her brother and urged him to take advantage of his life, to live it fully.

Leah paid the tuition and gave him a generous allowance. He returned half of it. He was not a child but a man in his twenties. He found a half-time job teaching at a small community center. Evening classes, like those his father had attended at City College. But his students were not immigrant Jews. They were Chicanos and blacks and the sons and daughters of farm and factory workers. Michael discovered that he loved teaching. He relished the development of a lesson, of charming his restless students into a sudden expectant silence. He thrilled when a previously silent student suddenly raised a hand and asked a question that betrayed a new and unsuspected curiosity. Warm pleasure flooded him when Jared Parks, a lean black youth who had registered for every class he taught, told him that he was going on to the university.

"On account of you, Mr. Goldfeder. On account of you said it could be done."

He had realized then that sociology was his discipline but teaching was his vocation.

It took him four years to earn his doctorate. He attended seminars while Eisenhower sat benignly in the White House and the Korean

War veterans filled the lecture halls. He formulated the thesis statement of his dissertation on the afternoon that federal troops integrated Little Rock. He sent a one-hundred-dollar money order to help cover Rosa Parks's court costs and voted against a congressman who wanted to establish funding for shelters designed to be impervious to radioactivity. He sat in smoke-filled rooms and listened to earnest appeals for a sane nuclear policy.

"There can't be a sane nuclear policy. It's a contradiction in terms," argued pretty Melanie Reznikoff, but Michael continued to solicit signatures for petitions. He had inherited his parents' penchant for lighting small candles against the encroaching darkness. He silenced Melanie by putting on a record, and they danced to the strains of Elvis Presley's throaty desperation.

He had met Melanie on a registration line his first week at Berkeley. They had looked familiar to each other, and within minutes they each had remembered their first meeting. Katie, Aaron's first wife, had been Melanie's cousin, and she and Michael had spent time together in New Orleans during the week of the wedding. They had been teenagers then, had kissed gently, shyly, beneath the fig tree in the garden of the Reznikoff house on Corondolet Street. Now, years later at Berkeley, they were young adults, and they made love gently, shyly, in Melanie's studio apartment. Twice, during their four years together, Melanie had told him that she had fallen in love with someone else—once with a married history professor who, in the end, would not leave his wife, and once with a graduate student of literature whose incessant recitations of Yeats had finally bored her to distraction. Each time she had returned to Michael, and he had dutifully comforted her and thought that it was a shame they were not in love with each other.

Despite the distance between them, Michael had remained in close touch with the family. Aaron occasionally came to California on business, and Lydia had visited Berkeley for academic conferences. Michael was fond of his sister-in-law and proud of her. He enjoyed introducing her to his friends, who recognized her stately beauty and acknowledged her accomplishments. He admired the life that Aaron and Lydia had built together, the careful balance they sustained between career and family. It seemed to Michael that they sensed each other's moods, predicted actions and reactions. Once he had visited them and watched as they sat together on the terrace of their home. Lydia's pale hand covered Aaron's fingers and then caressed them. Aaron lifted the long dark sheaves of her hair and pressed them to his lips. Michael watched them wonderingly, like a viewer at an exhibition, bemused by the elusive beauty of a painting. He had been in New York when Paulette, their daughter, was born, and he had seen the tears glitter in Aaron's eyes as he held the baby.

Rebecca had been visiting then, and they had stood together and watched their brother with his newborn daughter.

"Daddy cried when you were born," Rebecca said. "I remember that."

Her voice had been wistful, as though she wondered still whether their father had cried at her birth as well.

Rebecca's skin had been bronzed by the constant impact of the desert sun, and strands of silver glittered in her curly dark hair. She had brought several new paintings with her for Charles Ferguson's appraisal, and Michael saw that she no longer painted in bright primary colors but now used more muted tones. She gave Lydia a landscape for the nursery—the desert at the sunset hour, haunted by long, strangely shaped shadows. Lydia, however, had hung it in Aaron's study. It was too sad a painting for a baby's room.

"Tell me about Berkeley," Rebecca had said wistfully. "I've never been to California."

Michael had wondered at the melancholy that trailed his sister, whose life, unlike his own, was so directed, so clearly defined. There had been no time for at trip west, although he had suggested it. Her visit to America had been brief, made possible by Yehuda's participation in a conference at Harvard on civil resistance movements. Yehuda's paper dealt with terrorism. The reception of his arguments had saddened and discouraged him.

"It's strange," he said ruefully. "Even with all that is happening in Algeria, the explosion of plastiques, the random kidnappings—there is still no recognition that terror is going to be the primary enemy of democracies in this decade."

"Perhaps it's because in this country we've been relatively free of any such threat," Michael countered.

"Michael, the Ku Klux Klan is a terrorist organization," Yehuda said. "Until now it's confined itself to scattered cross-burnings, to lynchings. But once the Klan realize that Martin Luther King and his followers are not going to be frightened away, they'll expand their activities. There will be a wave of terror in the South."

"You don't understand this country. It can't happen here," Leah said firmly.

Yehuda did not argue with her. Leah's belief in American democracy was unshakable. She had the reverence of the immigrant for her adopted country. There were no pogroms here, no government-endorsed acts of violence. Of course there were injustices, but in time they would be rectified; Martin Luther King would prevail. This was, after all, the United States.

Deftly, Yehuda changed the subject.

"I should like to hear more about Berkeley," he said to Michael. "Are there many Arab students there? From what countries do they come? Do you know many of them?" His questions were casual, but Michael knew that his answers would find their way into the small green notebook Yehuda always carried.

"Oh, stop, Yehuda," Rebecca had said. "This is a family gathering, not an interrogation."

She knew that Yehuda was always on the alert, always scavenging for scraps of information that might somehow, sometime, prove useful. She shot him a warning glance and showed her family snapshots of the children. Admiringly, they studied the color prints of Yaakov playing in front of the kibbutz children's house (not far from the spot where David Goldfeder had been killed, Aaron thought as he passed the picture to Lydia); of Amnon, the baby, asleep beneath the avocado tree, his rounded face dappled by the slender leaves; of Noam pruning a vine, and of Danielle and Mindell in leotards. Michael observed that Mindell, who had lived with the Arnons since her arrival in Israel, had grown into a startling beauty. Her honey-colored hair hung to her waist, and her full lips curved into a warm and wondrous smile. Only a vague sadness in her eyes revealed her as the frightened, skeletal child whom Yehuda and Rebecca had rescued from Europe and smuggled into Palestine. She was a medical student now, at the Hebrew University, Rebecca told them proudly.

Back at Berkeley he told Melanie about Rebecca and her life in Israel.

"Too parochial," Melanie said decisively. "I want to do something for humanity, not just for the Jewish people."

"They're not mutually exclusive," Michael retorted dryly.

He and Melanie traveled to San Francisco and sat on uncomfortable stools in the Six Gallery, drinking warm red wine and listening to a bearded poet from New York named Allen Ginsberg read a long poem called "Howl." Michael emptied his glass as Ginsberg mourned ". . . the best minds of my generation destroyed by madness, starving hysterical naked . . ."

Ginsberg and his disciples frightened Michael. "Beats," they called themselves, but he judged them beaten. He shied away from their threatening anger, the visceral contempt they heaped upon the world. He believed, still, that he could make a difference. (*On account of you, Mr. Goldfeder*, Jared Parks had said. *On account of you said it could be done.*) Vigorously, impatiently, he worked on his thesis: "The Integration Patterns of Eastern European Jewish Immigrants into American Society: Circa 1920." It did not occur to him until he was deep into his research that he had selected the year of his family's arrival in the United States. He was chronicling his own history. He completed his writing in record time.

The examiners at his defense had been impressed. A distinguished emeritus observed that he had written with both accuracy and passion—rare qualities in doctoral dissertations.

"I suppose I had a peculiar involvement," Michael had explained. "The immigrant experience is part of my personal history."

The assembled academics glanced quizzically at each other. What had the immigrant experience to do with this tall, personable young man in his J. Press suit, button-down shirt, and the striped orange-and-black tie of his Ivy League alma mater? Still, they knew that young people romanticized obscure and dramatic origins. They smiled and passed on his dissertation with enough superlatives to earn him a teaching appointment at Hutchinson College, a small but prestigious woman's school in southern Westchester. He relaxed and waited for commencement. He had decided to attend, although in the end Leah did not come to Berkeley.

"If you don't want me to come, there is no point to it," she said reluctantly in a final phone call. "I'm designing a new line for Joshua, and Lydia is due to give birth any day. Perhaps you're right. It's just as well that I stay in New York."

"I think that's best." His tone was even, and he found himself unable to account for the profound disappointment that stole over him. He realized then that he had, after all, wanted his mother to be in the audience when he rose in cap and gown to become Dr. Michael Goldfeder. The second Dr. Goldfeder.

Melanie had come instead, and there had, after all, been a euphoric quality to that commencement day. How different this class of 1960 was from the sober, silent men who had stood beside him at Princeton. His California classmates radiated energy and determination. Bright buttons jeweled their academic gowns, advertising their beliefs, their priorities. They were for free speech, civil rights, John Kennedy, and Adlai Stevenson. They advocated the banning of the bomb and open universities. The women graduates wore garlands of flowers. Several were pregnant, and at least one carried a baby in her arms. The new decade, the sixties, belonged to them. The future was theirs, and they would make it work. Another generation had created the bomb; they would control and harness it. Another generation had perpetuated racial injustice; they would reverse it. Their battle lines were generational and clearly drawn.

They were full of joy and optimism that commencement morning. Les Anderson had concealed a magnum of champagne within the voluminous folds of his academic gown, and they had toasted one another exuberantly, waving the thin leather portfolios that contained their new degrees. Melanie had taken them all back to her apartment afterward for a celebration meal of chicken cooked in wine and spinach salad. They all drank too much wine and discussed their plans for the coming year. Melanie was uncertain. She wanted to *do* something that would be meaningful, she told them plaintively. "I'm tired of taking. I want to give."

Les laughed, but Michael understood her. She articulated his own yearnings, his misgivings about accepting the job at Hutchinson. It was an academic plum, he knew, but he, too, wanted to do something beyond teaching the daughters of privilege on a well-manicured campus. Again, foolishly, irrationally, he envied his brother and sister.

Jeremy Cohen, a native Californian (the only one in all of California, he said jokingly), was to intern at a municipal hospital in New York, and Les had landed a job at a national magazine as an investigative reporter.

"What the hell is an investigative reporter?" Michael had asked when Les told him about the job and suggested that they all room together in New York.

"Probably a glorified copy boy," Les acknowledged. "But it's going to get me to New York."

Tall, blond Les had spent years running away from the Kentucky mining town of his childhood. New York was his Emerald City, and the Berkeley degree was the last stop on the yellow brick road that led there. He had grown up in a dingy apartment behind the company store that his parents ran. The Sears catalogue and the Bible had been the companions of his childhood and Thomas Wolfe's novels the lexicons of his adolescence. New York meant an escape from ignorance and bigotry, from poverty and narrowness. Once he had asked his mother why the Negro women who bought their dresses in the store could not try them on. She had looked at him in amazement. "They got this funny stuff on their skin. You can't see it, but it's there." He had not argued with her. Instinctively, he had known that any argument was pointless. Once he had asked his father if they could spend a day in Cincinnati. There were museums there, a university, a great library. "So what?" the shopkeeper had replied indifferently. Les had not persisted. His father's limitations had been revealed, and Les had never again suggested a trip, initiated a conversation. He went to Cincinnati alone at last, having earned a scholarship to the university. And then there were journalism prizes, a Berkeley fellowship, and now, at last, the job in New York. The Kentucky hick was about to conquer the world's greatest metropolis. And he was one step ahead of Thomas Wolfe. He had no desire ever to go home again. Sometimes, he could not clearly remember what his parents looked like.

Melanie had baked a chocolate cake in the shape of a mortarboard.

"The New Orleans touch," she had said. "My heritage."

Michael heard the bitterness in her voice. Melanie, too, would not go home again. They were all on the fringe of new lives then, all wanderers in search of a cause.

It had been very late when he left, and that night, too, the phone had been ringing as he entered his apartment building, but he had bounded up the steps and caught the call. It had been his mother.

"Lydia had a little boy," she said breathlessly. "A beautiful baby. Aaron is so excited. Isn't that marvelous, Michael?"

"Wonderful," he said, but he felt no joy. "How did Paulette react?"

Michael adored impish Paulette, whose hair nestled in dark ringlets about her delicately molded head. Her turquoise eyes were like small jewels, and her ruddy complexion matched Michael's own coloring.

"Oh, Paulette's as pleased as Rebecca was when you were born. She thinks David is a doll that she will be able to play with."

"David?" he repeated heavily.

"Yes. They named the baby for your father. I thought you'd be pleased."

"I am," he said, but a quiver of disappointment ran through him. His own father's name had been claimed by his half-brother's child. Swiftly, his disappointment was replaced by shame. Aaron had been through so much, and David Goldfeder had been the only father he had ever known. Michael could not (*and would not*, he vowed silently) begrudge his brother his late-found happiness.

"Listen, Mom," he had said. "Tell Lydia and Aaron that I'm happy for them and that I can't wait to hug my new nephew."

"I'll tell them."

Leah hung up then, and he realized that she had not asked him about the commencement or congratulated him on receiving his degree. The birth of Aaron's child had eclipsed his own achievement.

Now, days later, as he sat on the worn couch and stared at the empty cartons, the phone rang again. He placed a single book into a carton, congratulated himself on having made a beginning, and answered it. It was Melanie, and as always, her voice bubbled with excitement.

"Michael, did you just come in? I've been trying you for hours."

"I had things to do." (Why, he wondered, was he so curt with Melanie lately and why did she tolerate it? Jeremy Cohen had noticed it. He had seen his friend frown at the abrupt tone he used and rush in to comfort Melanie and speak gently to her.) Immediately he felt apologetic. "Anything special?"

"I'm having a party tonight to celebrate the Kennedy victory."

"It was just the primary," Michael said. "Which, by the way, he barely won."

"Oh, come on, Michael." When Melanie wanted something her southern accent grew thicker and her voice became cajoling. He imagined her pouting, sucking on a strand of her light brown hair. She was a cute girl, a good girl. He wished that he loved her and wondered occasionally if he would have been drawn to Melanie at all if she had not been Katie's cousin. Would he always trail after Aaron, seeking the elusive drama of his brother's life?

He wondered, sometimes, if he subconsciously sought a lover whose past was as dramatic as Lydia's. He had attended Lydia's Berkeley lectures, and while he had not understood the material, he had recognized the admiration and respect she received from the audience. She was a regal presence on the podium; the pointer she waved majestically across her charts and drawings was a scepter. She accepted questions with the patience of a benevolent regent. Yet, back in his student apartment, she relaxed and laughed with Michael and his friends, charming everyone with her warmth, the musical cadence of her voice.

"Berkeley is wonderful," she told Michael. "The warmth, the

intellectual excitement, the parties." She admired all that had been denied her during her own troubled student years in Budapest. "You must take every opportunity, Michael. These are the years of your youth. They will not come again." She was thinking of Paul, he knew, and he touched her hand with understanding, with unarticulated sympathy.

It occurred to him now that Lydia would want him to accept Melanie's invitation.

"All right, Melanie. I'll come to the party."

"Nine o'clock, and bring some beer."

"I think JFK's more of a champagne man," he said, "but if you want beer, I'll bring beer."

"Thanks, Michael. And listen, I invited this girl I met when I worked at the child-care center. Be nice to her. She won't know anyone there."

"I'm nice to everyone," Michael said easily. "But I'll be especially nice to her. What's her name and what does she look like?"

"Her name's Kemala Jackson. She's very beautiful. Tall and sort of ballerina-thin. She wears her hair in a long braid down her back." Melanie hesitated. "And she's black."

Had he imagined it, or had Melanie raised her voice in a decibel of defiance when she said "black"? Melanie, he knew, was self-conscious about the civil rights struggle as only a southern liberal could be. She was burdened with shame and guilt (as Katie had been, he remembered) and determined to reverse the tide. A picture of Martin Luther King hung over her desk and a canister for King's new Southern Christian Leadership Conference stood on her kitchen counter. Her name appeared on every civil rights petition that circulated on campus, and she could always be counted on to attend a rally, to buy a block of tickets for a benefit performance. But still, she felt a strange uneasiness when a black sat beside her in class or approached her at a party. A southerner's uneasiness. Once, Melanie had confessed to Michael, a black girl had borrowed her comb and she had thrown it away afterward. Good, generous Melanie, Michael thought, to seek out Kemala Jackson and invite her to a party. Maybe Kennedy and the sixties did mean a new beginning, a turnaround. Maybe his infant nephew David Goldfeder would grow up in a world in which blacks and whites talked and shared easily with each other. A modest enough goal.

"I'll watch for Kemala," he promised and went out to buy a case of Miller's for the party and a split of champagne for afterward.

HE arrived late and wove his way through Melanie's crowded living room to the small kitchenette, where she was filling enormous straw baskets with potato chips. She wore a bright red peasant skirt and a white blouse. Her light brown hair was pulled back, and the golden crumb of a potato chip nestled at the corner of her mouth.

"Slob," he said and licked it off.

"Don't be disgusting, Michael." She wiped her mouth. "Did you bring the beer?"

"Right there." He had set the beer down beside the trays of canapés that crowded the counter. "Pretty fancy," he said. Caviar perched on slices of cucumber, small slivers of salmon were wrapped in scallions, chopped egg dotted squares of black bread.

"A donation from Jeremy," she said. "Does it look like a good party?" Her voice was anxious.

Michael smiled. "It looks like a terrific party," he said, amused at her question. Like her New Orleans mother, she was a nervous hostess. She might reject her background, but it clung to her in small, significant ways.

And it was a good party, he thought as he circled the room. Pretty, long-haired girls in brightly colored Indian skirts smiled and talked earnestly to young men wearing sandals and faded jeans. A joint was passed from hand to hand. Wisps of blue smoke wreathed the air, which smelled of incense and orange blossom. Three guitarists had stationed themselves in different parts of the apartment, and each strummed happily and sang to a separate circle of disciples. A girl with very short blond hair squatted in front of Melanie's bookshelves and read aloud from Pasternak's poems. Tears coursed down her cheeks, yet she did not look unhappy. A dark-haired girl plucked at a mandolin and sang a song Michael had not heard before, "What Have They Done to the Rain?" Her voice was piercingly sweet, and the song was melancholy and tender. Someone said she had written it herself.

"Who is she?" he asked a research assistant whose name he could not remember.

"Joan Baez. Good, isn't she?"

"Very good," he agreed and went to the piano, where Les Anderson was pecking out "Itsy Bitsy Teenie Weenie Yellow Polka Dot Bikini."

"More your speed?" Jeremy Cohen asked him.

"I'm not feeling too political tonight," Michael replied. "I'll worry about the rain tomorrow."

"Then you're at the wrong party," he said. "Melanie's got a tape of the Kennedy acceptance speech, and she's going to play it later. Listening is the price of admission."

Jeremy's cynicism was homegrown. He was the son of a husband-and-wife team of Hollywood writers who were rumored to be the cleverest and most expensive in a field of very clever and very expensive professionals.

"We don't talk in my house," Jeremy had told Michael once. "We trade dialogue. When I told my mother why I wanted to go to medical school—and I was being very serious—she stopped me in midsentence and said, 'Hey, that's good, that's very good,' and wrote down what I was saying in her goddamn notebook. Sometimes I think that I wasn't really born—maybe they wrote me and I crawled out of their typewriters like a character in one of their scenarios. 'Enter the socially conscious, introspective son of the brilliant, iconoclastic extrovert couple. . . .' "

"Come on, Jeremy, you don't mean that," Michael had protested. Criticism of parents made him uneasy, opened emotional floodgates he preferred to keep closed. He did not tell Jeremy that he sometimes thought he himself had been conceived to confirm his parents' happiness, to stand as a living imprimatur to their success. Such thoughts, disloyal and irrational, frightened him.

"Sure I do," Jeremy affirmed. "My family's not like yours, Michael."

Jeremy had visited the Goldfeder family in Scarsdale and had been impressed by their warmth and closeness. Since David Goldfeder's death, Leah lit candles every Friday evening, and the family gathered for the Sabbath meal. Always, in a strong voice, Leah added a prayer for the safety of Rebecca and Yehuda and their children, for the freedom of Russian Jews.

"It is our responsibility to care—to work and to care," she had said once, and Aaron and Michael had exchanged glances and smiled.

Their mother's zeal and energy bemused them. But then, she had always been a warrior. She had fought for the rights of workers to organize; she had worked tirelessly for the war effort, and now, during her later years, while her contemporaries joined golf clubs and wintered in Florida, she battled vigorously for the remnant of her people. Across the table, Boris Zaslovsky, a frequent guest, smiled at Leah, before he intoned the kiddush.

Watching them, Jeremy felt a sense of loss. Although both his parents were Jewish, he had never celebrated his own bar mitzvah.

"Not our scene," Janet Cohen had said when he pointed out that other Jewish boys at Hollywood High were having synagogue services and parties. "We're sort of what you might call 'white Jews.' " She had laughed charmingly, and his father had picked up the trail of her metaphor with the skill that made their partnership so successful.

"Yes, white Jews—fully laundered, the religion bleached out of us, the customs and superstitions discreetly faded."

His parents did not object when Jeremy studied medicine, but they were bewildered by his decision to intern at a municipal hospital in New York. California was the last frontier, the end of the rainbow. Screen credits in blazing Technicolor were the pot of gold. There were wonderful hospitals in California, and their connections could get Jeremy any job he wanted. Still, they understood that this was a generation that stood on its own, that turned its back on parental influence. Jeremy's life was his own. They had a film to complete in London, locations to check out in France. They had, in fact, left for Europe that very afternoon, and the lavish canapés on Melanie's kitchen counter were the remnants of the catered leave-taking lunch they had ordered for themselves and the contingent of Berkeley friends they had invited to share in their goodbye to their only son.

Melanie circled the room, offering canapés to a cluster of guests sprawled on a rya rug.

"You are what you eat," a bearded man in overalls said as he reached for an hors d'oeuvre.

"There's mayonnaise in that," a girl cautioned him.

"I'm feeling suicidal," he retorted and popped it whole into his mouth.

Across the room a group newly returned from Los Angeles argued the Democratic Convention's decisions.

"Maybe Stevenson was the better man, but you can imagine what Nixon would do with him—he'd chew him up and spit him out."

"Listen, Stevenson couldn't get his act together in fifty-six. He'd be a disaster in sixty," one of the young political science instructors said. They waited for him to elaborate—his doctorate had been a learned treatise on dissident American political parties—but he had wandered over to the blond girl, who was still reading from Pasternak, although her tears had stopped and she had refreshed her makeup. In another corner Joan Baez continued to pluck her mandolin and sing softly to herself.

"Yes, but Stevenson's a man of principle. He doesn't make political concessions," a bespectacled young woman insisted.

"Everyone makes political concessions," someone said softly from a darkened corner. The musical tone of the woman's voice intrigued Michael and he turned.

Kemala Jackson wore a yellow dress and sat on a bright green butterfly chair. She was, as Melanie had said, ballerina-thin. Her long arms were sinuous, and her long glossy hair was woven into a single braid that flowed down her back. Her features were narrow and finely chiseled. She sat with her legs tucked beneath her, her head held high. Her legs would be long and shapely, Michael knew, and he waited for her to speak again, but she was silent. The conversation whirred on, concentrating now on the concessions made in L.A.

"Why the hell did they select Johnson for the vice-presidential slot? A southerner, for God's sake!"

"Because they needed a southerner to balance the civil rights plank."

"Did Martin Luther King endorse Kennedy?"

"No, but Arthur Goldberg did. If you've got one minority, you've got them all."

Anger and laughter mingled. They spoke the language of the disenchanted. They laughed with the bitterness of the spiritually discontent. And yet, despite their veneer of sophistication, they were not without optimism. Theirs was the generation that would make the difference. They would find a new enchantment. Dreamers spoke to them. Martin Luther King, Jr., had visited Berkeley, and the mellifluous cadence of his voice lingered in their memories. They would forge a new tomorrow. Stevenson had disappointed, but they had recognized Kennedy as a new claimant to a Camelot lost in shadow. They acknowledged that it was not his fervor that moved them but his youth. The auburn-haired senator had an ageless quality. They could not envisage his ever growing old. His youth ensured their own.

They drank more beer and dimmed the lights. Joan Baez took her mandolin and wandered out into the night. Someone put a Brothers Four record on the phonograph. The party had thinned, and there was room for everyone to sprawl out as they listened to "Green Fields."

Michael made his way across the room to Kemala Jackson.

"My name is Michael Goldfeder," he said.

She nodded; her elegant head rose and fell in regal acknowledgment. He was reminded of a frieze he had seen, a pharaonic princess accepting an emissary's credentials.

"I'm Kemala Jackson. Not hard to remember. Just think of the town in Mississippi."

"You're not from Mississippi." He tried to place her accent, to isolate it from the musical cadence of her voice.

"No. But I'm going there."

"Why?"

"Don't you read the newspapers, Michael Goldfeder? There's a war going on in Mississippi."

"There are wars going on everywhere," he replied, impatient suddenly with verbal teasing. "Wars on poverty, wars on ignorance, wars against littering. Not counting, of course, wars in Southeast Asia, in Israel, cold wars, hot wars."

"And yet you're not in active combat," she retorted. "You don't look as if you ever fought for anything in your life."

"How kind of you to say so," he said easily, although her words hurt him. She had, with lilting voice and deft and mocking thrust, exposed a vulnerability he concealed even from himself. "You're right. I apologize for my lack of battle ribbons. I was too young for World War Two, still in school during Korea. No war on poverty because I was born rich. No war on values because my family understands me. I'm the poor little rich boy, the perennial rebel without a cause."

"Oh, there are causes all around," she said. "Shall I offer you a few?"

"What did you have in mind?"

But she did not answer because just then Melanie called for quiet. She wanted to play the tape of Kennedy's speech accepting the nomination.

They glanced uneasily at one another as Les Anderson set up the tape recorder. Across the room a girl giggled, and Melanie frowned. The strangely reverberant voice of the senator from Massachusetts filled the room. Within minutes he caught their attention. They recognized that he spoke the unarticulated language of their hearts. Candlelight flickered on their upturned faces as they listened. John Kennedy shared their disappointment with the world of their inheritance—but not of their making.

"The world is changing. The old era is ending. The old ways will not do. . . ."

The Democratic candidiate for the presidency of the United States echoed the arguments they had with their parents in dining rooms in Shaker Heights, in the finished basements of Long Island homes, in the sprawling mansions of Beverly Hills. John Kennedy, in his Massachusetts twang, was calling for "a peaceful revolution for human rights . . . demanding an end to racial discrimination in all parts of our community life. . . ."

The black students among them leaned forward. A Chinese intern, diminutive in his white lab jacket, took the hand of a tall girl wearing a black leotard and a paisley skirt. Melanie turned the volume up, and Jeremy Cohen moved to her side.

"It is time . . . for a new generation of leadership . . . we stand today on the edge of a new frontier, the frontier of the nineteen-sixties, a frontier of unknown opportunities and paths, a frontier of unlimited hopes and threats. . . . I am asking each of you to be new pioneers on that new frontier."

They glanced at each other proudly, happily. The cynical ideas they had voiced only minutes before had been forgotten and replaced by a new and soaring hope. The disembodied voice flowing from the tape recorder spoke to each of them individually. They were the new generation of leaders, they were the pioneers and inheritors of the new frontier. They would build the bridge between past and future.

"I'm going to campaign for him full time," Melanie said. "The hell with my trip to Europe. It's important to get Kennedy into the White House."

There were murmurs of approval. Les Anderson whipped out his pad and took rapid notes. He saw a projected headline: "Kennedy Captures Students' Secret Hearts. A New Generation Has a Cause." He crossed it out. "Kennedy Offers Youth New Answers to Old Questions." He underlined it.

Melanie produced a sign-on sheet for campaign volunteers. Michael wondered if she had held it in readiness throughout the evening. Was the celebration party actually a draft? Signatures were being added rapidly. Kemala Jackson remained in the green butterfly chair, watchful, almost amused, her hands still cupped beneath her chin.

"Do you want to sign up, Kemala?" Melanie asked, extending the sheet to her.

"Now, Melanie, isn't a political campaign a kind of a luxury?" Kemala asked in a slow, controlled tone. She might have been a patient lecturer, instructing a student who could not grasp a concept, an amused older relative confronting the whim of a naive youngster. "If you want someone elected, you need people to vote for them.

They don't let people vote in Mississippi unless they can pass what they call a literacy test. So I'm going to work on helping people to pass that test. I won't have time to ring doorbells for Mr. Kennedy."

Melanie blushed, and Kemala Jackson rose languidly from the seat she had not left all evening.

"I'll be saying good night now," she said. "It was a nice party, Melanie. Thanks."

"You're welcome," Melanie said, tight-lipped and tense. She continued to circulate her sign-up sheet, but the magic was gone, the momentum lost. There were desultory murmurs about academic obligations, prior plans.

"That was a bitchy thing to do," Michael said to Kemala.

"Oh, I'm a bitch all right," she agreed amiably, softly. "And would you like to take this bitch home?"

"One minute," Michael said harshly. She both angered and intrigued him.

He went into the kitchen, removed the split of champagne from its hiding place behind the wilted lettuce, and put it into a brown paper bag with two plastic cups. Melanie, her lips pursed, was brewing coffee.

"Good night," he said and kissed her lightly on the forehead. He had never kissed her on the forehead before.

On the darkened stairwell Kemala Jackson slipped her hand into his. Her palm was satin-smooth against his own, and he stroked it gently as they walked to his car, noting that he had been right—her legs were long and shapely.

"Let's move on, then, to a new frontier," he said, and their laughter mingled and echoed in the darkened street.

THEY drove to Golden Gate Park and looked down on the ink-black waters of the Bay. A cool breeze blew and the soft air was suffused with the melancholy fragrance of the blossoming citrus trees. They wandered across a grassy embankment, and Kemala paused.

"Wild strawberries near here. I can smell them."

"Are you a country girl?" he asked.

"I'm from the country and from the city," she said, and smiled at his skeptical glance. "No. I'm not trying to be mysterious. We moved a lot, an awful lot. My father was kind of a combination teacher and preacher. He was born in the South, but somehow he got himself north for his schooling. He was Columbia University's black boy, plucked out of Morehouse College and given all sorts of scholarships—the Urban League Grant, the Booker T. Washington Living—that sort of thing. My daddy studied history and philosophy, and he got good grades, but he wasn't that smart—he believed what he read. One of his professors gave him a leather-bound copy of John Stuart Mill's *On Liberty*, and he carried it everywhere. He thought if he got enough people to read and understand it, everything would be all right. They'd take down the 'Colored Only' signs in front of the drinking fountains and the bathrooms.

"My mother knew better. She was a southerner, after all, who had gone north to do her nurse's training at Harlem Hospital. She knew what things were like back in Dixie. But he had a dream, and she wasn't about to stand in his way."

"She went back to the South with him?" Michael asked. (As Leah, his mother, would have followed her husband, given a similar set of circumstances. Leah, who had taken a factory job so that she could support her husband through medical school and not stand in his way.)

"Yes. They went back down South and I was born and my daddy with his fancy Columbia degree taught in a lot of different schools—some in the city and some in the country. Some were in towns so small the school was in a corner of the church and some so far out in the bayou country that the school was an abandoned sharecropper's cottage. You see, he was preaching civil rights twenty years ago, and that wasn't what the black elders of the community wanted to hear. They didn't want a wise-guy nigger stirring the people up—if Mr. Charley got to hear about it, they'd be the ones to pay. My father never had a contract that went beyond a year. We kept moving, and my mother kept getting wearier and wearier. Finally, she went north for tests. Anemia, they said, but it wasn't anemia. It was some rare kind of blood deficiency, but they didn't find out until one afternoon she began hemorrhaging from the mouth. The blood came spurting out, and we rushed her to the nearest hospital for coloreds, twenty miles away. The doctors there said she needed a transfusion, but they didn't have enough blood. The white hospital wouldn't send their blood for a black woman, even though the doctor pleaded in an oh-so-respectful voice. I counted five 'pleases' and five 'sirs' in one call. He should have saved his breath. Three hours later my mother died. The doctor wrote 'blood deficiency' on the death certificate, but I knew better. 'Bigotry,' he should have written. 'Hatred.' My mother died because she was a black woman in the state of Mississippi."

She was silent, and they watched the lights of the bay. The lights of a low-flying plane were reflected in the dark waters, blinking upward like a star. Michael touched Kemala's hand. She did not pull away.

"Can you understand?" she asked.

He nodded. He did not tell her that his mother's first husband, his brother Aaron's father, had died because he was a Jew in Odessa.

"Go on," he said gently.

"My father took her death hard, but he didn't stop his teaching and preaching, and then, six years ago, the civil rights movement finally caught up with him. 'We only had to be patient,' he said, oh so proudly. But I was done being patient with the South, and I came west to Berkeley. California wasn't north and wasn't south, I thought. Freedomland at the edge of the Pacific. My father joined the Fellowship of Reconciliation. He wrote me long letters quoting Gandhi and Jesus. But I was busy earning good grades to keep my scholarship and working two jobs to earn my board. I didn't care about Gandhi or Jesus or the rights of black people. I cared about Kemala Jackson. And then last February, the same day I got his last letter, I got a telegram from North Carolina. My daddy's body had been found in some woods just out of Greenville. The authorities said he had been killed by a hunter. An accident. The hunter probably didn't even know he had shot anyone because he hadn't come forward.

"The black community knew better. My father had been at a lunch-counter sit-in that afternoon, and a couple of rednecks had followed him out. They wrote 'accidental homicide' on my daddy's death certificate, but I knew that he and my mother had been killed by the same thing. Bigotry. You don't know what it's like when someone you love is killed because of plain, ugly, unadulterated hatred." She fell silent now and her breath came in gasps, as though the long narrative had exhausted her.

"But I do know," he said, and he told her about David Goldfeder's death. Again he heard the shot ring out across the silent desert. Again he saw his father's blood, carmine streaks across the pale sands. They shared that much, he and Kemala. Both their fathers had been shot because of irrational hatred. A strange and improbable linkage.

"That was different." Her voice was unyielding. She was impatient with his tragedy, absorbed in her own grief.

He did not argue. He remembered the paralyzing misery he had felt during those first months after David Goldfeder's death. He had been abandoned and stood alone. He spoke to a voice that would not answer. He had thought then that he would never recover. He knew now that grief was neither negated nor obviated but eventually it was muted and soothed. He remembered, suddenly, a conversation he had with Yehuda Arnon one evening as they sat in Leah's garden. Always Yehuda moved and spoke with forceful energy, but that night a strange, almost sorrowful lassitude had overtaken him.

"Is something wrong, Yehuda?" Michael had asked hesitantly.

"I lit a candle tonight. It is the anniversary of the death of my first wife. Miriam's *yahrtzeit*."

He had told Michael then how Miriam, the mother of Danielle and Noam, had died. His voice had broken as he spoke, and tears had streaked his face. His grief had not shamed him; he had allowed himself to weep. And then, newly calmed, he had shown Michael photographs of his younger sons, of Yaakov and Amnon. His sorrow was contained. He had kept faith with the past but he would not surrender the future.

Lydia had named her first child, Paulette, for Ferenc's son, whose grave she could never visit. Michael had understood her choice. New lives comforted and consoled, filled lesions and linked generations. His own father, David Goldfeder, was dead, but there was a child to carry his name, to claim his dream. Michael was eager now to see his nephew, to hold that soft new bundle of life who validated his father's promise and presence. But he could not explain all this to the beautiful black girl who sat beside him, her face frozen in grief.

Beside him, Kemala Jackson, whose loss was still new, looked up at the star-streaked sky, and tears forged silvery paths down her dusky cheeks. He opened the champagne then and filled the two plastic glasses with the bubbly liquid. They made no toast but drank quietly, luxuriating in the wine and the silence.

"Why are you going to Mississippi?" he asked.

"I want to do what he would have wanted me to do. The time for change in the South is here. My father would have worked for it if he had lived, and so that's what I'm going to work for."

"You want to change the world in his memory?" Michael asked.

"I want to try."

"I know." Naively, he, too, had thought he could penetrate the mystery of the forces that molded human society, that perhaps he, too, could be responsible for change. Small changes, he knew now. Jared Parks. Single candles flickering against a terrible darkness.

"There's so much to be done," she said. "You're a teacher."

"I'm a teacher. A spoiled, rich Jewish boy, but still a teacher."

"Come with me."

"I've got a job waiting for me in the fall."

"Come for the rest of the summer, then."

He considered. The summer stretched emptily before him.

"Where to?" he asked.

"There's a small town in Mississippi called Troy. The blacks there are small landowners, and they've managed to build their own school. It's a good school. The kids there learn to read and write. They built the building themselves and maintain it themselves. They know it's good, and they want to make it better. They want to get a library started and hold summer classes for adults. To prepare them for the literacy test. It's a small-scale project. They're away from most of the bigger towns where a white working with blacks would set people talking, start trouble. We had a volunteer all lined up to go, but he backed out at the last minute. Not that we were surprised." Her lips set in a thin line of contempt, and bitterness coarsened her voice.

"Why did he back out?" Michael asked.

"He thought it might be dangerous."

"And will it be?" (Had Rebecca asked if it would be dangerous to guide that small group of children across the Mediterranean into Palestine? Had Aaron asked if it would be dangerous to join the RAF, to venture into a besieged Hungary?) Suddenly he told Kemala about his brother and sister—about their courage and their achievements.

"Troy won't be dangerous," she said. "No Budapest. No war-torn Jerusalem. It's pretty isolated. The white volunteer would stay with a black family and keep out of sight mostly. The blacks in Troy have a reputation for being peaceable. It's the perfect place to start. For now, that is. In a couple of years we'll have armies of teachers coming down to set up freedom schools, freedom libraries. But we'll need federal protection for that—troops and marshals. For now we've got to be content with one little place at a time. Troy's a little place."

"Troy, Mississippi," he said. "I wouldn't mind spending the summer in a place called Troy. Where will you be, Kemala?"

"A couple of miles away. I'll be working with one of the national organizers. Matt Williams."

"Will I see you?"

"Occasionally."

"Occasionally in Troy. A good title for a movie. I'll pass it on to my friend Jeremy's parents."

"Jeremy's the medical student?"

"No. He stopped being a medical student last week. He's a doctor now."

"We always need doctors," she said.

"You always need teachers. You always need doctors. Hey, my brother's a lawyer. Do you always need lawyers?"

"Michael." Her voice was grave now. "Don't make fun of me."

"I wouldn't make fun of you, Kemala." He opened her hand and traced his name across her palm with his finger. "I wrote my name across your lifeline," he said. "And I'm coming to Mississippi. You're a terrific recruiter. Much better than Melanie."

They drank the last of the champagne. A barge drifted up the bay. They saw its lights, heard the soft, mournful bleat of its horn. He drove her home then, and in the dim light of her entry hall he touched her cheek with his open palm. Her hand flew up and her fingers lit briefly, gently, on his lips—a butterfly gesture of farewell, a fleeting touch of welcome.

He flew to New York the next day, leaving Jeremy and Les to pack up and sublet the apartment. He was spurred by a new and welcome sense of urgency. He went to dinner at the new fieldstone-and-wood home his brother had built not far from Leah's house. Michael tossed small Paulette into the air, listened to her happy laughter, and held the infant David in his arms as he told his family about his summer plans.

"I'm not sure I understand," Leah said worriedly. "Mississippi." She could not even envisage it on a map. "Will you be welcome there? Will you be able to help?"

"Was Charles Ferguson welcome at the Irvington Settlement House?" he asked. "Was he able to help?"

It struck him, for the first time, that by going to Mississippi he had involved himself in a reciprocal arrangement. He was, in part, paying America back for all it had given him and his family. Charles Ferguson had come east to help educate immigrant Jews. He was going south to help educate southern blacks.

Leah smiled. Michael's parallel was not irrelevant. Without Charles she would never have been able to establish herself as a designer, an artist. Michael would play a similar role in other lives. She looked up at her youngest child. Understanding and love flashed between them.

"I think that it is a wonderful thing that you are going," Lydia said. "It is important to feel that you can make a difference, that you confront an opportunity. You may not succeed as you would wish, but you will never have to blame yourself for not trying."

She had not succeeded in her efforts in Budapest, but she had tried. She closed her eyes briefly, surrendering to memory. Ferenc. Paul. Vanished lives; untended graves.

"I agree with Lydia," Boris Zaslovsky said. "It is not the victory that counts, but that we keep faith with the struggle." He had fought in Moscow and had carried the struggle with him to his new life.

"But we *can* succeed," Michael said. "This is America."

There was no NKVD, no secret police here to harass and threaten him, as Lydia had been harassed, as Boris had been threatened. He had been born into freedom, and he believed in his birthright. One nation, indivisible, with liberty and justice for all. All. He might have to work hard for its realization, but he would prevail. He was, he supposed, not unlike Kemala's father, and he found himself telling his family about her. Lydia and Leah exchanged a swift and knowing glance, and Boris drummed his long fingers on the table as he listened.

"This girl you mentioned, Kemala Jackson," Aaron said cautiously as he drove his brother to the airport, "are you involved with her? Is that why you're going?"

"She's not even going to be in the town I'm going to," Michael replied.

"You didn't answer me," Aaron persisted. He was a lawyer, and he knew when a question was being evaded.

"I'm not involved with her," Michael said. "I hardly know her." The brush of her fingers across his lips was not an involvement. The touch of her cheek against his palm was not an involvement.

ALTHOUGH they kept the window shades pulled down and a ceiling fan created a small breeze, the Troy schoolroom was stifling hot. Michael's fingers were damp as he gripped the chalk, and his chambray shirt was blotted with patches of dark sweat. He wrote the word *King* on the blackboard, underlined it, circled the *K*, and turned to his class.

"Who can read this word?" he asked. "Remember, we begin by sounding out the first letter."

A tiny white-haired woman leaned forward and said, in a quavering voice, "K-ing. King." She looked up into his approving smile, pleased with herself. "Like Martin Luther King, who's going to make a new world for us. Amen."

"Amen," the other students echoed, and Michael nodded.

They were an odd lot, this class that came to the Troy schoolhouse each afternoon. The woman who had read the word correctly was the wife of an elderly sharecropper. The elderly couple walked two miles to attend his class, although Michael insisted on driving them home. Two giggling teenage girls sat in the rear of the room—Lizzie, her hair plaited in corn rows, pregnant with her second child, and Norma Anne, a mill worker who had left school when she was eight. "I didn't leave," she said. "The teacher left and there was no more school that year, and the next year my mama was sick so I didn't go back." Two middle-aged women in white uniforms who worked as cooks in the large, white-pillared mansions that rimmed the nearby town of Lynnewood wrote everything down in new black-and-white-speckled copybooks. They hid their notebooks beneath the ironing they carried home each night. If their "ladies" discovered them, they would lose their jobs, they told Michael. An unlikely class, but within two weeks they had all learned their letters and were recognizing words, constructing sentences.

"They say you're a real good teacher," Mrs. Mason told him.

Michael lived in the Masons' house because it was set well back from the road, and his car could be parked in an unused outbuilding. He slept in a tiny room, and he had lived there for three days before he discovered that the room belonged to the Masons' youngest son, Rodney.

"I didn't mean to displace him," he had protested, but Mrs. Mason waved her hands disparagingly.

"You ain't displacing him. It's only right," she said. Michael was white and Rodney was black. It was only right that the white stranger who had come to help them should get the best bed, privacy, the choicest bits of meat from the fragrant stews she cooked, the heel of the bread she baked each night after coming home from work. The Masons' hospitality both touched and embarrassed him.

He turned back to the blackboard now and wrote the word *FREEDOM*.

"Sound it out," he told the class.

Their mouths twisted into tortuous knots. Norma Anne pursed her lips, worked her way through the first syllable.

"F-R-EE," she said hesitantly, and then her voice rose as she forged the letters together into a word.

"Free—I see it now—free. D-OM. Freedom! You wrote *freedom* on the blackboard, and I can read it."

The others were nodding. They, too, studied the word, mouthed it silently, whispered it tentatively and slowly, gave it voice. At last they all repeated it in unison.

"Freedom! Freedom! Freedom!" Their mingled voices became a shared shout of triumph, and he added his voice to theirs. "Freedom!" He was suffused with a strange and unfamiliar happiness, a newly discovered sense of pride, of elation.

"Amen," Lizzie said in her high, squeaky voice.

"Amen," a soft musical voice echoed.

"Kemala."

He had seen her infrequently since his arrival in Troy, but a few nights ago they had had dinner together in the tiny apartment she shared with two other civil rights volunteers, who were not home that evening. They had smiled at each other across the small bridge table cluttered with unmatched crockery and the chipped jelly jars that served as glasses for the red wine he had brought. They had spoken rapidly, as though fearful that there would not be time to complete their thoughts, to share their feelings. The wine had warmed and relaxed them, and again he felt the electric rapport that had shimmered between them on the incline above the San Francisco Bay.

Tired at evening's end, he had stretched out on the floor and listened to her singing softly as she washed the few plates and utensils. When she sat down beside him her hands were damp and smelled of soap suds. He pressed them to his forehead and was instantly cooled. When he left he kissed her, and her lips were petal-soft against his own. She was like a flower, he thought, a delicate blossom; she had to be gently treated lest she bruise and wither. The sudden tears in her eyes were as luminous as morning dew.

"What's the matter?"

"I don't know. I guess I'm just tired and confused. It's so hard to sort things out."

"Of course it is," he had replied. Her work, after all, was in the beginning stage, and Matt Williams, with whom she worked, was insistent and demanding. Her fatigue and confusion were natural. He felt himself imbued with an obscure wisdom that could tolerate and assimilate her ambivalences. Her tears vested him with the power of the comforter, and he encircled her with his arms and wound her long dark braid about his wrist.

But now her eyes were calm as she leaned easily, comfortably, against the whitewashed wall of the small classroom.

His class turned to look at her, but they did not smile when they turned back to him. When he dismissed them, they filed quickly out of the room and averted their eyes as they passed Kemala.

She looked after them regretfully.

"It was a mistake to come," she said. "Matt Williams was right. He told me to stay away."

"Why was it a mistake?"

"Because you're white and I'm black. It may come as a shock to you but blacks aren't any crazier over black girls being with white men than whites are. In fact they hate it even more, I think."

"Why more?"

"It's a reminder, I suppose, of all the times they haven't had any choice—all the times when their women were forced to go off with the whites—all the yellow-skinned babies with straight hair."

"We're different," he said harshly. "You and me. Kemala and Michael."

"All right, we're different." Her voice was oddly despondent. "Let's take a walk," she said. "It's suffocating in here."

"Well, this year we got the Britannica. Next year we'll think about air conditioning," he said. "Come. Let's walk."

He guided her down a ribbon of shade formed by a brace of persimmon trees. The thin-skinned fruit dangled in silken, sun-colored bulbs on the slender, dark-leafed branches. They looked down on waves of white cotton plants—an endless sea of growth, but the fields were deserted. The workers of Troy, who had risen at dawn to avoid the day's fierce heat, were asleep in their homes, protected against the invasion of light by the closely drawn black window shades. They passed two small children, a barefoot coffee-colored boy and a little girl whose skin shone like ebony, asleep in an envelope of shade formed by the branches of a tupelo tree. The children had drawn very close to each other, in pursuit of the soothing shadow.

"They both come to my reading readiness class," Michael said. "Their first-grade teacher is in for a surprise."

"We'll need a lot of surprises to make any difference in this state," she said bitterly.

"Hey. You're the one who sings a different song. Remember? One step at a time. This summer a couple of classes in a safe place like Troy. Next year or the year after a network of freedom schools, a freedom library." he reminded her. "What happened?"

"A couple of weeks in Mississippi happened," she said. "You're cloistered here in Troy, but I see what's going on. Last week they arrested a whole load of freedom riders. I saw it. The cops were beating down on the kids with hoses and clubs, and the kids were doing all the things they'd been taught. They covered their heads and curled themselves up as though they were about to be born, not about to die."

"They won't die," he said.

"Not this time. Although there was a lot of blood and one Harvard kid got a broken arm. But how long do you think it will be before one of them gets killed? Matt says it's only a matter of time."

"Matt?" It was the second time she had mentioned his name.

"Matt Williams. You know, the organizer I'm working with. You've got to read the manifesto he wrote for *The New Leader*. He says we've got to be ready to break down all the barriers—to organize in such strength that we'll force the whites back."

"Not all whites are against you."

She did not answer.

"I'm white," he added.

"You're different."

"And so are a lot of other whites. The freedom riders. The Harvard boy who broke his arm. People you don't know." He thought of his mother, who had sent him a generous check to be used to buy supplies for the Troy school; of Charles Ferguson, who had sent a package of art materials; of Les Anderson, who was covering a freedom ride for his magazine. Melanie had written him a jubilant letter from the Kennedy campaign trail: "Everyone knows that he will make a difference. We can feel the changes already." Melanie had enclosed a snapshot of her fellow campaign workers at a barbecue—a smiling crew of black and white young people wearing Kennedy buttons and waving ears of corn. Changes were coming. The promise of the new decade would not be betrayed.

"We've got to stop talking about breaking down and start talking about building up," he said.

"Oh, you talk like a child," she retorted impatiently. "You remind me of my father. Read John Stuart Mill's *On Liberty* every night. Study the Bill of Rights. Remain patiently at a lunch counter during a sit-in. Teach a couple of classes, touch a couple of hearts, and get shot down in a Carolina meadow."

"Do I talk like a child?" he asked angrily. He was speaking as she had spoken to him as they sat in Golden Gate Park and watched the lights on the bay, only a few short weeks ago. His words echoed her own. Her denial of them was a betrayal, a repudiation. He could not believe she had changed so much in so short a time. Who was this Matt Williams, who had exerted such power over her? A sudden jealousy suffused him.

Kemala did not answer him but kicked a flat stone out before her and shoved her hands deep into the pockets of her jeans. They had reached a stripped cottonwood field and stood beneath a magnolia tree on which a few mournful blossoms lingered.

"Like a child?" he repeated. Her accusation was translated into a taunting question that fed his new fury.

He took her into his arms and felt her body tremble, heard her whispers of protest. He tightened his hold and pressed her lips into silence against his own. A new determination ripped through him. He would still her bitterness, vanquish her sorrow and his own new uneasiness.

"Kemala." He crooned her name, he loved her name. "Kemala."

He cradled her gently, took the silken braid of her hair and wrapped it about his wrist. She was his prisoner, yet he was her captive—they were bound in mysterious symbiosis. Her fingers flashed across the buttons of his shirt, her satin-smooth hands slid across his chest, his back. They came together on a litter of decaying magnolia petals. Afterward, lying amid the fragrant debris, he looked up and saw a wide-winged crow scissor its way blackly across the heat-streaked sky. A mockingbird sang softly into the glare. He closed his eyes against the mingled omens. Kemala lay still beside him; her hand reached up to brush away a heart-shaped leaf that had drifted onto his shoulder.

A TALL WEST INDIAN MAN waited for her at the Troy schoolhouse. Sweat glittered in diamond droplets on his dark skin. His face was very narrow, cruelly beautiful. Kemala introduced them.

"Matt Williams," she said. "Michael Goldfeder."

A smile carved its way across Matt Williams's face.

"Nice to meet you," he said but did not extend his hand. "Your school's pretty well outfitted."

"My mother helped," Michael said and wondered why he should feel defensive rather than proud.

"Nice to have a rich mama. I had a poor mama. Is it your mama who owns S. Hart, Inc.?"

"My mother does some work for them. My uncle and cousin own it," Michael said stiffly.

"Your mama's got an interest. You surprised that I know that?"

Matt asked. "Why shouldn't I know that? I didn't go to the Harvard School of Business Administration for nothing. I read my *Business Week* regularly. We do our research, you know."

"I'm sure you do," Michael said heavily.

"We have to go, Kemala. It's a long ride back."

"Yes. I know. Goodbye, Michael."

"Goodbye, Kemala." He tried to read the message in her golden eyes. A plea for silence? For understanding? Fear? He could not tell.

He wrote long letters that night to his mother, to Aaron, to Rebecca in Israel. He told them about his small school, the library he was trying to build, the Mason family, who shared their home and their lives with him. He described the strange, cool stillness of the Mississippi dawn and how he had seen a white-tailed deer glide across the cotton fields at dusk. But he did not mention Kemala—Kemala, who danced through his dreams that night, a circlet of magnolia blossoms aglow on her dark, slender wrist.

KEMALA came to Troy once a week after that initial visit. She looked forward to those afternoons with Michael, although she knew that Matt, in his silent, brooding way, disapproved of them. She spent more and more time with Matt at work, following his directions, coordinating his efforts. He was a daring, innovative planner, and she had a talent for detail, for meticulous follow-up. Matt conceived of a meeting of southern academics who were sympathetic to voter registration reforms. He journeyed from campus to campus to meet with them. His strong, insistent voice subdued their doubts, his anger negated their hesitancy. But it was Kemala who arranged for meeting rooms, for travel arrangements, for the distribution of agendas and press releases. It was Kemala who reminded him of his appointments, maintained his calendar, brought him cups of black coffee when he worked on a speech or a proposal. His energy fascinated her, his intellectual verve excited her.

"This is wonderful, Matt," she said as she edited a speech.

"And what do you think of this?" He flashed a newly completed article at her and paced the room restlessly as she read it. He worked at a frenetic pace and was impatient with those who lingered behind him. The white volunteers cowered beneath his sarcastic tongue-lashings. Black students exaggerated their militancy in a desire for his approval. But Kemala was always honest with him, considered in her assessments, deliberate in her decisions. She read his article carefully.

"I'm not sure about it."

Her uncertainty angered him.

"Why? Why aren't you sure?" He mimicked her tone, gripped her shoulder as she explained her doubts. Here he had expressed himself too strongly, and in the following paragraph he had failed to clarify salient points. The pressure of his fingers on her skin intensified; he countered her arguments with a strident defense, yet in the end he made the changes and smiled brilliantly at her—the white flash of his teeth a grimace of gratitude.

He grew increasingly demanding of her, and she made no effort to evade the dark orbit of his authority. She admired, even envied, his anger. It counterposed her father's acquiescence and passivity. Matt Williams would not wait for change—he would cause it to happen.

Still, his fierce abrasiveness wearied her. She took refuge against Matt's driving fury in thoughts of Michael's gentleness, his reasoned earnestness. She did not speak of Michael to Matt, but she occasionally allowed him to drive her to Troy. She turned her face from him when she greeted Michael so that he would not see the gladness in her eyes. Matt would count that as a betrayal, she knew, and she did not want to wound him. She was at once frightened of him and fearful for him.

She was more at ease when she came to Troy alone and she and Michael spent the long, hot afternoons together. Once they drove to the Bienville National Forest and walked through the dark velvet paths of patterned shade cast by the giant pines. There, in the tree-shadowed cool, they linked fingers and almost forgot that they were in Mississippi. They did not think of the harsh epithets a white motorist had shouted at them from a passing car:

"You like dark meat, you commie bastard!"

Kemala had not turned her head, but her hands, clasped on her lap, had trembled. Michael burned with rage and gripped the steering wheel tightly. Would Aaron have challenged the man? he wondered. No. Aaron, too, would have driven on. They talked a great deal that afternoon, in the forest. Again, Kemala told him of her father. Again, he spoke of his brother and sister, of his own self-doubts. Yet this summer he had learned that he, too, possessed secret sources of strength. He, too, had a cause and was prepared to fight for it. Kemala told him of her work with Matt, of their efforts to establish grass-roots leadership in Mississippi.

"In the end it's the people who live in the state who will have to change things. There is a limit to the participation of white volunteers."

"Isn't that a kind of racism in reverse?" he asked.

"We don't think so," she replied. By "we," he knew she meant herself and Matt Williams, although by tacit agreement, they did not mention him by name.

Michael, of course, had learned something about the slender West Indian. Stories traveled swiftly through the ranks of the movement. Legend was soft currency, and the authentically minted and the counterfeit were passed with equal ease. A single incident created a reputation. The briefest retreat into fear destroyed one. Matt Williams's reputation had preceded his arrival in Mississippi.

His parents had come to New York from the West Indies, determined to succeed. His father had been a skilled garage mechanic and his mother a restaurant cook. Matt was targeted early by observant teachers as a gifted student. He was in the top ten percent of his class at Stuyvesant High School and won a scholarship to Columbia University.

"You see," his father told a reporter at his graduation, "hard work is the answer in this country." A picture of the smiling parents, flanking the shyly smiling undergraduate, appeared in the afternoon edition of the *New York Post.* "Proud Dad Says Hard Work Is the Answer."

The garage mechanic himself worked two shifts, and his wife clocked as many overtime hours as she could manage. Their dream was in sight. On a spring day during Matt's junior year at Columbia, his father put on his only suit, a white shirt and a tie, and traveled to St. Albans, a small residential neighborhood in the borough of Queens. There he made the down payment on a small frame house. He was warned that he would be the first black to move onto that street. He was unperturbed. He believed, as he had always told his only son, that hard work and pleasant manners triumphed. He wept when he signed the contract. He was the first person in his family to own property. The family moved in on the last day of June. On the first day of July a cross was burned on the neatly mowed tiny square of lawn.

Neighbors saw teenagers running from the scene. An adolescent prank, they said. Summer mischief. One man even crossed the street to express his sympathy. Matt's father smiled, raked the lawn up, and planted new grass where the ugly burn had seared the soil itself. Two nights later a stone was thrown through an upstairs window.

This time no one offered sympathy. He replaced the windowpane. He smiled at the grim-faced neighbors, who did not smile back.

In August, he painted the trim on the neat little house. The bright green paint was barely dry when rags soaked in kerosene were set afire and tossed through the living room windows. Matt's mother, asleep on the couch, died almost at once, the pathologist said. The torch had consumed the synthetic fibers within minutes. The street smelled for hours of charred flesh, simmering human fat. His father was burned over ninety percent of his body and died weeks later, whimpering like a baby. The president of the St. Albans Civic Association sent Matt a letter of regret, which he did not acknowledge. He did answer the phone.

"Move, nigger," one caller said.

"We'll be back," another caller warned.

Matt sold the house to a white family, completed his Columbia degree, and took advantage of the scholarship he had won to the Harvard Business School. Major corporations offered him jobs. His credentials were impeccable, his organizational abilities formidable. But Matt decided to become a professional organizer for the civil rights movement. He no longer believed in hard work and pleasant manners. He believed in direct action, fierce confrontation. He was not popular in the Southern Christian Leadership Conference. He was not moderate. Sarcasm had replaced the courtesy so prized by his father (who had died whimpering, apologetic even about his pain). He made no effort to get along with white volunteers. He sounded a call for grass-roots leadership, for black power. There were rumors that he planned a more militant breakaway organization. But he was a brilliant organizer, a dynamic speaker. He was promoted to positions of leadership where he was more visible and thus more easily watched.

When Michael drove Kemala back from the Bienville Forest, Matt was waiting in the doorway of the schoolhouse. Michael noticed that she stiffened and that her face grew grave, her manner distant. He wondered at the power that Matt exerted over her.

Still, she was in Troy on the day Lizzie read her first complete sentence, and she was there the day the elderly sharecropper bravely made his way to the courthouse, took the literacy test, and passed. And Kemala was there the day Norma Anne failed.

"You'll pass the next time," she assured the weeping girl.

"I ain't gonna try no more," Norma Anne protested.

"Yes, you are." Michael was firm. "I'll be back next summer, and we'll start earlier." His students' challenge had become his own. He designed new materials, new exercises. Kemala had ignited his interest, his enthusiasm, but it blazed independent of her now.

Kemala was in Troy the day Yehuda Arnon visited the school. Michael had known that Yehuda was in the South at a conference, but he had been surprised when his brother-in-law walked into his classroom, touched that Yehuda would drive miles out of his way through the torpid heat to visit him. He introduced him to his class.

"Mr. Arnon is here from Israel," he said and saw the bewilderment on their faces. An ideal opportunity for a geography lesson had presented itself. He unfurled the map and showed them where Israel was situated.

"What's it like over there in Israel land?" the elderly sharecropper asked.

"As hot as it is here," Yehuda said, and they all laughed. Briefly, then, he told them about Israel's history, about the displaced persons who had been smuggled into the country, and of the battles that had been fought for the independence of the new Jewish state.

"Those who had been slaves in the concentration camps became warriors determined to protect their freedom, their right to live and survive as other free peoples in the world live and survive."

"Amen," Norma Anne shouted, and the others turned to one another and nodded vigorously.

They had listened carefully to the man with earth-colored hair whose hands were as callused as their own. They recognized his story. They understood the need to fight for survival, to do battle for equality. They had recognized their own history in Yehuda Arnon's words—the passage from slavery to freedom, from trauma to normality. They, too, would live as others lived. There would not always be black shades on their windows.

Lizzie's rich contralto led the sudden burst of song:

"Go down Moses, way down to Egypt land. Tell old Pharaoh to let my people go."

Kemala stood in the rear of the room and joined her voice softly to theirs. She was sorry that Matt had not been there to listen to Yehuda Arnon. They would have understood each other, she knew. They were both men who were not content to accept the decrees of history but would forge their own destinies and those of their people.

Michael was a teacher (as her father had been, she thought, surprised that the parallel had for so long eluded her), but Matt and Yehuda were warriors. She loved Michael's gentleness, but the vibrancy of Yehuda's voice had excited her that afternoon, had reminded her of Matt's ringing tones as he read the speech he would deliver at a rally in a few weeks' time.

Michael spoke gently to his students and to her. Matt exhorted his listeners, issued imperious and impatient demands to her. Michael's touch was tender against her skin. Matt gripped her wrists, dug his fingers into her flesh. She wondered if Yehuda Arnon was forceful with Michael's sister, his wife, or if he spoke to her quietly in the darkness.

"I liked your brother-in-law," she told Michael that night. "I can see that he has courage—that he can stand up and fight."

"There are different ways to do battle," Michael said mildly and turned away. He felt a foolish jealousy, as though Kemala had compared him with Rebecca's husband and had found him wanting.

Always, when she visited Troy, they walked together to the isolated cottonwood field. Always, he wondered at her initial resistance and her swift submission. But she grew thinner, and she seldom laughed.

"Kemala, what's wrong?" he asked.

"How do you know anything's wrong? You don't know anything about me—nothing at all," she lashed out bitterly.

He did not answer. Their relationship was so fragile that a misplaced word might shatter it. He knew only that she had changed, that she was hurt and grieving, and that she had translated her grief into a bitterness he recognized but could not comprehend. Matt Williams exercised a strange control over her, but he knew, too, that it was dangerous to speak of it.

She came to the school on the day he was to leave. The Mason family shyly shook hands with him.

"We hope you'll come back next year," Mrs. Mason said. "Rodney learned real good with you. I'll be piecing a new quilt for your bed."

"I'll be back," he said.

Norma Anne baked a chocolate cake, and they ate thick slices from paper plates and drank cherry Kool-Aid from plastic cups. He brought a drink to Kemala.

"Do you remember the Golden Gate Park?" he asked. "The champagne?"

"I remember." Again he touched her cheek with his open palm. Again her fingers flew up and lit gently on his lips. "I'm staying on in Neshoba," she said. "As Matt's assistant."

A cold streak of sweat ran down his back.

"Will you come to New York Thanksgiving?" he asked.

"If you still want me to."

"I'll want you to."

"We'll write." He had not yet parted from her, but already a letter took shape in his mind. *My darling Kemala . . . my heart's own flower . . .*

"We'll call," she assured him. She imagined his voice on the phone, the caring questions, the urgent concern. "Are you getting enough sleep? Are you eating well? Please, please, don't work too hard." No one had ever worried about her the way Michael did. No one had ever cared for her as Michael did. He had bought her a light blue cashmere cardigan as a parting gift.

"It gets cold in Mississippi in the winter," he had said. She had pressed the wool against her cheek. Never had she felt anything so soft.

"Kemala—it's time to start back." Matt Williams leaned against the doorjamb. He would not accept a piece of cake, a drink of juice. He kept himself separate from the small party, the small celebration of gratitude and affection. "You going back to your real life, Goldfeder?"

"I'll be back next summer," Michael replied evenly.

"Sure you will," the West Indian said smoothly, contemptuously. "If it doesn't interfere with your career."

He turned. Kemala pressed Michael's hand and trailed obediently after Matt. Michael watched her, suffused by an apprehensive sadness.

He turned to the blackboard and wrote a single word. They read it aloud in unison. "Freedom."

"Freedom! Freedom!" They circled the room, repeating it aloud. They embraced each other and then moved shyly to Michael, who shook hands with each of them.

"Come back next year, Mr. Michael," Lizzie said.

"I'll be here," he promised.

The sun was setting as he drove away from Troy. He watched it slowly disappear into banks of blood-rimmed clouds, and he pressed fiercely down on the accelerator, saddened and angered and sweetly proud.

LEAH GOLDFEDER rose early on Thanksgiving morning and hurried to the kitchen to put the turkey, which she had seasoned the previous evening, into the oven. The size of the fowl pleased her, as much as it had astonished Boris Zaslovsky, who still could not accustom himself to American abundance.

"In Russia you would wait on line three, even four hours for a skinny chicken—a pound of meat full of gristle," he said and watched admiringly as Leah skillfully filled the turkey's yawning cavity with wild rice and chestnuts. He was like all who have known real hunger; food remained a minor miracle to him. Leah was glad that he was spending the holiday with her, content that he and Michael, who had stayed the night, were still asleep upstairs. She was pleased to be cooking for a lot of people again, and she watched the winter sunlight streak its way through the barren branches of the maple tree, full of happy anticipation. The years of sadness had passed, and once again there would be the laughter and talk, the music and gaiety of a holiday afternoon shared by family and friends.

Always, the generations mingled cheerfully at Goldfeder celebrations. Joshua Ellenberg's teenagers would happily play with Aaron and Lydia's children, small Paulette and the baby David. Lydia was pregnant again. Too soon after David's birth, Leah thought worriedly, but she said nothing. Seymour Hart, her aging brother-in-law, would trade reminiscences of Russia with Boris Zaslovsky. Their memories were a litany of vanished communities, of forests become burial grounds and burial grounds become playgrounds. And yet again and again, they invoked the place names of their younger years. Kattowitz. Kiev. Odessa. Kharkov. The winding streets of the towns of the Pale. The tart blueberries in the woodlands beyond Babi Yar. Boris closed his eyes when Babi Yar was mentioned. His wife and children had been killed there.

Jeremy Cohen and Les Anderson, Michael's roommates, always listened closely to the talk of the older men. Les had the journalist's curiosity, but Jeremy was seeking after a past that had been denied him. He spoke restlessly of visiting Russia, of working in Israel.

Leah liked Michael's friends. They were sharp-tongued and witty, yet they shared a gentleness and a sense of compassion that she recognized intuitively. It was a rare quality among men, but David Goldfeder had had it and his sons had inherited it. It was not surprising that Michael should seek out friends who shared it.

It startled Leah, occasionally, to realize how similar Michael was to his father. He had a natural and immediate sympathy for the downtrodden, an instinctive indignation at social injustice. Like David he was possessed of powerful passions and intense, almost selfless compassion. David would have understood Michael's involvement in the civil rights movement, his commitment to that small school in Mississippi. But David's experiences in Russia, the harshness and poverty of his immigrant life in New York, had provided him with a wariness, a swift system of emotional and intellectual defense, which was alien to Michael's background. Michael was, after all, the child of their happiness and prosperity, their fortunate inheritor. Of her three children only Michael had been carried with love and raised without the tension of poverty and conflict. It was ironic, then, that it was Michael who sought out the world they had worked so hard to leave. Michael and his friends even lived in the Eldridge Street apartment that had been the Goldfeders' first home in America. Of course, he had not known that when he called her excitedly to tell her that Joshua Ellenberg had found them a terrific apartment and he wanted her to see it at once.

"You'll love it, Mama," he had said enthusiastically (and she reflected that it had been years since he had called her Mama). "Lots of rooms and all off a long corridor. We can use the corridor as a kind of a gallery, hang our friends' paintings there. A big kitchen. The bathroom's small, but I guess we'll manage."

Aaron drove them to the apartment, and as they drew closer, following Michael's instructions through the warren of Lower East Side streets, she and her elder son exchanged glances of recognition. Aaron slowed the car as they passed the public library on East Broadway, the Irvington Settlement House.

"Do you remember, Mama?"

"I remember."

There was no need to further articulate the question. (*Do you remember a sad-eyed, redheaded boy? A tall, lonely woman who wore her black hair in a regal coronet?*) As they passed the Eldridge Street Synagogue, Leah closed her eyes, but she could not block the memory of herself limping past the sanctuary on the evening of the Rosenblatt fire as the mourners' Kaddish was recited. She, too, had been in mourning that distant day—in mourning for her friends and for her lover, whose lives had ended in the fire that still haunted her memory decades later. She wondered if Kaddish was still recited at the Eldridge Street Synagogue, but she supposed not. The stained-glass windows were shattered and nailed over with boards, and even the great brass railings had been ripped from their concrete cornices.

"Here it is." Michael's voice was jubilant.

They stood in front of the building where she had begun her life in America, and she knew at once as they climbed the narrow stairs that the door which Michael would open with the key he held so proudly would be the door to the apartment where they had lived for so many years. She was only surprised, when they entered it, that she felt no sadness, although she reeled beneath an onrush of powerful memory, of renewed wonder, that so much had happened to all of them, that they had journeyed so far and yet were connected still to their beginnings.

"We lived here before you were born," she told Michael (while Aaron went at once to the bedroom that he had shared with Rebecca, to seek out the window where he had sat night after night, waiting for his mother, waiting for David, waiting for the revelation of a mystery, for the beginning of a love).

She went into the kitchen, newly fitted now with a gleaming refrigerator, a gas stove, a washing machine and a drier. Joshua Ellenberg had renovated with a vengeance, tearing out the coal-fed cookstove, the icebox that did not close properly, the wide sink for laundry—symbols all of his mother's unrelenting labors, their shared poverty, and the desperate fear that they might never move beyond it.

She walked slowly down the hallway, where Jeremy had hung three Museum of Modern Art prints from Picasso's Blue Period. During her own tenancy, they had strung a clothesline down that hallway in winter and walked carefully to avoid the dripping of the wet wash.

"Sometimes," she told her sons, "a whole family would arrive from Europe and stay with us. We would set up cots and pallets in this hallway. Always we found room for the stranger."

"Like the Masons," Michael said. "The black family I stayed with in Mississippi." They had found room for him, the stranger. His mother would like Mrs. Mason, would understand her determination to make things better for her children.

"Didn't Joshua tell you that we once lived here?" Aaron asked his brother.

"I'm not sure he knew. One of his agents told us about it."

Leah had helped Michael and his friends furnish the apartment and transform it into a comfortable, casual bachelor realm with tweed couches, burlap drapes, and bright rya rugs on the newly scraped wooden floors that had been covered with scarred linoleum so long ago. It had been an accident and Joshua Ellenberg's caprice, perhaps, that had brought Michael to that apartment, she knew, and yet there was a chimeric quality to the coincidence. Michael was always looking backward, seeking out something that had been mysteriously and inadvertently denied him. He had spent part of the previous evening looking at family photographs.

"You're up early, Mom." Michael stood in the doorway, watching her as she sliced apples for the pie. He had stayed up late talking with Boris Zaslovsky. Now he rubbed his eyes with curled-up fists, reminding Leah of the sleepy-eyed small boy he had been.

"There's a lot to do," she said. "And I told Sophie I wanted to do most of the cooking myself. I love Thanksgiving. I always did. But I thought you'd want to sleep late."

"I wanted to talk to you before anyone got here," he said. "I guess Lydia will be over early to help."

"Yes." Leah smiled in pleasurable anticipation. It was wonderful that Aaron and Lydia lived so close by and even more wonderful that she and Lydia had become close and loving friends. Paulette often spent the night with her, and the baby David had a special corner in her studio for his toys. Leah reveled in the hours she spent with her grandchildren. She told Paulette stories of Aaron's childhood on the Lower East Side and her own girlhood in Russia. She walked with the children across the frosted trails of the Rye Nature Preserve, on wintry days, and in the spring she took them to the botanic gardens. Boris often joined them, and then they walked more slowly because Boris limped slightly.

Leah was happy also in the quiet companionship she and Boris shared. He was comfortable with her children and her grandchildren, and she relied more and more on his advice. She wondered now if they could share more than friendship. Sometimes, in the evening, alone in her bedroom, she thought of him and felt a slow stirring of desire. His fingers were slender, his touch light against her skin. His eyes were sad and gentle, and though his steps were slow, he was a strong man still; muscles rippled at his arms, and his shoulders were straight and broad.

The children loved Boris. Joshua Ellenberg's youngsters trailed after him, and they begged again and again for a retelling of the story of Babi Yaga, of the beautiful young tsarina, of the Jews who had lived in the comical town called Chelm.

"Could Boris be our grandfather?" Paulette asked one day, and Leah was surprised at the hot blush that swept her face.

When Lydia had an out-of-town meeting, Aaron and the children stayed at Leah's house. It was compensation for Rebecca's being so far away and for the loss of real intimacy with her Israeli grandchildren. There was talk now of Mindell coming to America after she completed medical school, but Mindell was not Rebecca's child, although the family felt a great closeness to her.

"I wanted to talk to you about this friend I invited," Michael said. "Kemala. She'll be coming with Jeremy and Les later."

He wondered now, why, after months of not seeing Kemala, he had not waited for her arrival in the city. Was it because he wanted to observe her as she entered his mother's house, to filter their reunion with the presence of others? Her infrequent letters had disturbed him. Tersely, bitterly, she described the slowness of their organizational work. When they spoke on the phone her voice was weary, and he wondered if Matt Williams stood nearby. Still, she had written and had returned his calls, and today she was coming to this house where he had grown up.

"Kemala," Leah repeated. She liked the name. It rolled musically about the tongue. "What sort of a name is Kemala?"

"I'm not sure," he replied slowly. "I never asked her, but I think it's African. Kemala is black."

Leah began to knead the dough for the piecrust.

"This is what you got up so early to tell me, Michael?" Her voice was neutral. Her face did not change expression.

"You don't mind?"

"Should I mind?"

She slipped the dough into the greased pans, fluted the edges with swift clamps of her fingers. It was natural for her to execute a design, to form pattern on pastry. She was used to controlling the tools of her craft, her brushes and canvas, her stencils and molds. Wistfully, and not for the first time, she thought of how it might be to exercise similar control over the lives of those she loved—to create the pattern that would result in happiness, to conceive the design that would be at once coherent and meaningful. But her children's lives, of course, were not as malleable as clay, as submissive to her will as paint and canvas.

"Your father and I never chose our friends because of the color of their skin or because of their religion," she said calmly. "We have never caused any friend of yours to feel unwelcome here."

"I know that," Michael said. He felt an odd resentment. It might have been easier, he thought, if barriers were more clearly defined, if his family had not always been so carefully civilized, so fair. Les Anderson had told him that he could never invite Michael to his home.

"My parents hate Jews," Les had said with bitter honesty. "It makes me mad. I argue with them. But they say it and they mean it, and I know for sure that I'm never going to change them. Of course that means I don't go home too often. But don't feel too special, Michael. They also hate Californians, New Yorkers, Orientals, intellectuals, and Democrats, not to mention blacks. Since I'm now a New Yorker who studied in California and I earn my living by my intellect, I'd qualify for a couple of enemies lists except that I happen to be their son."

"But at least you know where you stand," Jeremy Cohen had said. "Their position stinks, but it's defined and even honest. My parents, on the other hand, are the quintessential liberals. One cultured Negro at least at every big party. Two or three if they're lucky. They sign their names to every civil rights petition that circulates in Hollywood, but they're the biggest secret bigots I know—the whole bit—jokes, shoddy comments."

"Could you invite Kemala home?" Michael asked him.

"As a token black, sure. As my friend, maybe. As my date, my girl—never. See what I mean? What about you, Michael? How would your family react to Kemala as in 'Michael and Kemala'?"

"I don't know," he had replied. Today, this morning, he would find out.

Leah went to the stove and poured them both coffee in the large milk-white ceramic mugs she had crafted herself.

"Sit down, Michael," she said.

They sat opposite each other at the kitchen table, their hands curled about the steaming mugs; the fragrance of roasting turkey and baking fruit pies filled the large, pleasant room.

"I don't tell you lies, Michael. It's true that anyone is welcome in our home. Your father and I were refugees from hate, from prejudice. We tried hard to fight in ourselves what we had seen in others. We worked, both of us, with Jews and non-Jews, with whites and blacks. Some became our friends. We laughed with them, shared with them, wept with them. With Jews and non-Jews. With blacks and whites."

"What are you trying to say, Mama?" Michael asked.

"I'm trying to tell you that it does not bother me that your friend Kemala is a Negro."

"And if she were more than a friend?"

"I don't lie to you. It would bother me." Her voice was flat, low. Her words were twisted around the armature of hated truth. She did not want to say what she said, but she was too honest to deny her feelings or to remain silent. "It would bother me very much. I want for you what every mother wants for her children—what Aaron and Rebecca have. A shared life. Continuity. Acceptance. Acceptance and happiness for your children, my grandchildren. Can you have that with this Kemala?"

"We're not up to marriage," he said.

"I see." He was not up to marriage, but he had reached love, she knew. She could tell it by his voice, by the softness in his eyes, when he spoke the girl's name. Kemala.

Her fingers found a sliver of dough, and she fretted it into a tiny ball. What would David have said? she wondered, and thought back to a distant Thanksgiving when Rebecca had brought Joe Stevenson to their home. They had read a letter that day from Leah's brother Moshe in Palestine, a letter written in Yiddish and describing rescue operations for Jewish children in Europe threatened by the Nazi specter. David had turned to his daughter and her Gentile lover that afternoon and said something about the irony of Jews like Moshe risking their lives for Jewish survival while in America it was treated so lightly. She struggled now to remember his exact words, but could not. Still, his feelings had been clear—clear enough to anger Rebecca, to touch a nerve of truth.

"Your father," she said to Michael now, "believed in Jewish survival. Intermarriage means assimilation, and assimilation means Jewish disappearance."

"My father did not believe in racism," Michael retorted harshly. He was on safe ground now. He was no longer battling the ghosts of his mother's unarticulated objections, her vague generalities that in the end did not mask her rejection of his relationship with Kemala. Kemala was welcome as his friend. She would be less welcome as his lover. She would not be welcome at all as his wife.

"Wanting you to marry a Jewish girl does not make me a racist," Leah replied quietly.

"This is all a little sudden, isn't it?" he said bitterly. "Suddenly it's important that we're Jewish. Was it so important when I was growing up? No one objected when I stopped going to Hebrew school right after bar mitzvah. You didn't keep kosher until the war. Sometimes you lit candles on Friday night and sometimes you didn't. And now I'm supposed to be looking for a Jewish girl!"

Leah bit her lips. Everything he said was true, and yet even during those years when her observance was minimal, her Jewishness had been like a second skin. She and David had grown to maturity in the total Jewish environment of their *shtetl* village. They dreamed in Yiddish, knew the Sabbath service by heart. Their faith had been as integral to their natures as the color of their hair, the texture of their skin. But in the rush to Americanize their lives, to realize themselves professionally, they had not realized that what had been true for them would not be true for their children. Scarsdale was worlds away from Makover. Yet their Jewishness, until Rebecca's marriage, had been largely economic and gastronomic: checks dutifully written to the United Jewish Appeal and the synagogue; chicken soup and stuffed cabbage. Perhaps it was not surprising that Michael could fall in love with a black girl. Perhaps the real accident was that both Aaron and Rebecca had chosen partners with deep Jewish commitment.

Michael stood at the kitchen window, flushed, angry, yet oddly satisfied. They were arguing. They were disagreeing. Emotional blood, at last, was being drawn.

"All right. Maybe 'racist' is too strong a word," he said. "But we both know what you mean."

"Let us say, then, that you know what I mean. Does it matter to you?"

"Matter?"

"Yes. Would you go ahead and do what you pleased, no matter how I felt about it?"

She stood opposite him now, and he noticed, for the first time, that where once her hair had been black and streaked with silver, now it was silver threaded with random black strands. Small lines of weariness wreathed her fine dark eyes, formed a delicate network about her generous mouth. Often, as a small boy, he had coaxed forth her laughter so that he might see the dimple that blossomed magically at the corner of her lips. Once he had pressed his small hand against a newly finished painting, still shimmering with wetness. The effort of weeks had been ruined. "Never mind," she had said. Once he had broken a delicate teacup. She prized it because she had brought it with her from Russia. "Never mind," she had said. He wanted to be a small boy again, to coax forth his mother's dimpled gaiety, her unequivocal, unhampered love.

"Mama," he said, and his voice was heavy with regret, uncertainty.

"I asked you a question."

"I know." He loved her but he would battle her.

"And?"

"I can't answer you. I just don't know."

For them both his doubt was a defeat.

"Uncle Mikey. Uncle Mike!" Paulette hurtled into the room and he tossed her, laughing and squealing, into the air. His niece's laughter stifled his mother's deep sigh. Her merriment obscured the sadness that lingered in the bright and fragrant kitchen.

In the doorway Boris Zaslovsky studied his friend, Leah Goldfeder, with a worried gaze. She was a strong woman, but he knew that too often, the strong were cruelly vulnerable. He moved to her side, and it was Lydia who noticed how the morning sunlight that streamed through the window formed an aureole of light about their bent heads.

KEMALA shivered in the northern cold as she exited from the plane at Idlewild Airport. Briefly, she was sorry that she had not stayed in Mississippi. The Mason family had invited her for Thanksgiving, and Matt had even accepted an invitation for the both of them to attend a dinner at the home of a professor at Ole Miss who was determined to demonstrate his liberalism by sharing the meal with a Negro couple.

"I told you I was going to New York," she had said.

"But I promised you would be there."

"You had no right."

It was one of the few occasions when she had resisted Matt, and she wondered if she had won the battle because she was fighting for Michael and not for herself.

"Whatever you want." Matt's voice had been curt, his body rigid.

She did not know what she wanted, she acknowledged, as he left, slamming the door behind him. As always, she straddled two worlds, powerless to choose either. Michael drew her toward him with his gentle protectiveness, his caring concern. Matt enticed her with his fury, his febrile energy. She sensed the sorrow that birthed that energy, although he did not speak of it.

She had stood beside him on an autumn evening, shortly after Michael's departure, when the lightning of a gulf storm ripped the sky and pellets of rain battered their window. A stone, tossed by a White Citizens Council vigilante had shattered the pane, and they had fitted a sheet of cardboard in its place. It provided no defense against the impact of the rain, and they grew wet as they watched the downpour. Matt stepped back at last and she followed him. He wiped her face and arms with a towel.

"We're so damn alone," he had said bitterly. They were exposed, vulnerable to hatred, to the elements.

"Not so alone." She drew him to her then, felt his body relax against her own. She was moved that she had the power to soothe this man whose moods controlled her, whose vision commanded her.

The storm subsided and they made love on the battered leather office couch. With swift passion, he reasserted his authority over her. He pinioned her arms, hammered his way into her deepest being.

She lay awake long after he slept and thought of how Michael's hands had passed over her body in slow caress, how he had loosened the plait of her braid and threaded his fingers through its dark tendrils. *Michael . . . Matt.* She whispered their names. How different they were, yet both of them caused her to moan with yearning, to cry out with joy. Oddly, she felt no disloyalty. Neither man was betrayed because she cared for both of them, she told herself. Each answered different needs for her. *Gentle Michael. Fervent Matt.*

She had remained in Neshoba with Matt. It was only fair then that she travel north, as she had promised, and spend Thanksgiving with Michael. Meticulously, she balanced the scales, distributed the months of her years, the hours of her days. One day she would be forced to make a choice, she knew, but there was time.

She tried not to think of the dream that wakened her more and more often in the darkness of the night, although its details were clear to her. Dressed in a harlequin costume, half black, half white, she stood at a crossroads, and two figures danced toward her through a shimmering mist. One was dressed in black, the other in white. The man in white beckoned her, danced ahead of her, his hand outstretched to lead her, but his adversary gripped her wrist. A willing prisoner, she followed him into the mist and looked back at the man in white who waved sadly to her and whistled an intricate tune.

A foolish dream, she thought, yet she wept when she awakened from it. She would not tell Matt about it. He would be impatient with her, annoyed. And she could not tell Michael about it.

Matt drove her to the airport.

"Do you know what you're doing, Kemala?" he asked harshly.

"No," she replied. "No, I don't. How can I know?"

She had no guides. Her parents were dead, her friends dispersed. They lived in new times, and no manuals had yet been written for them, no examples set.

Michael's roommates, Jeremy and Les, met her at the airport and drove her to Scarsdale.

"A Berkeley reunion," Les said. "Melanie's here, too. The victorious campaigner. Without Melanie, Kennedy would have lost the election."

"Oh, Melanie's all right," Kemala replied.

Michael had shown her the letter Melanie had written him in response to his own long letter explaining his friendship with Kemala, his decision to go to Mississippi.

"Kemala is a wonderful girl," Melanie had written, "and I can understand that you should care for her. We live in new times, Michael, and I guess I envy you because you have the courage to meet their challenge. We had our fun, but it was never more than that—was it? I know that we shall always be friends—you and I, Kemala and I, and of course, the three of us together."

Kemala had sensed the relief that Melanie concealed between the lines. Michael had cut her loose, and she could travel on her own. After the Kennedy campaign trail, new vistas would open and Melanie, eager and unhampered, would explore them each in turn. She was glad that Melanie would be at the Goldfeders'. She counted her as a friend, a confederate.

The car pulled up in the circular driveway, and Michael came down to meet them. His heart beat rapidly and his eyes stung. He had not realized, until this moment of seeing her, how much he had missed her. She was even thinner than she had been when he left her in Mississippi, but she looked very beautiful in a suit of burgundy wool, her glossy black hair caught back into a smooth chignon.

"Kemala," he said, and his hand touched her cheek.

"Michael." Her fingers lightly brushed his lips. He wondered if they would remember this code of touch after much else had been forgotten. Would it endure past their memories of the scent of the last magnolia, the whorls of trillium, the rich blue of the gentian that grew wild in the field behind the Troy schoolhouse and in the Masons' kitchen garden?

He saw that her hand trembled slightly when she held it out to his mother, but Leah was warm and welcoming. She greeted Kemala as openly as she had greeted Melanie an hour earlier.

Had Kemala had a good trip? Was she tired? Did she have family in the area? Kemala's answers were careful and polite. Her trip had been pleasant because she had flown north. She was tired, but this weekend was the first vacation she had taken since leaving Berkeley, although she had meetings scheduled in New York, so the trip would not be all holiday. She had no family in the area, only friends, very good friends. She smiled at Michael.

"All you young people work too hard," Sherry Ellenberg said. "Causes. Campaigns. Meetings. You ought to have more fun."

"Oh, come now, Sherry," Joshua Ellenberg said in the teasing tone he reserved for his English wife. "What were you doing at their age?"

"That was different," Sherry said. "There was a war on. We had no choice."

Sherry had been a nurse in Bournemouth when the war began. Her parents had been born in Warsaw, and the day that Hitler invaded Poland, Sherry had joined the British Nursing Corps. She had met Joshua in an Allied army hospital. He had been a skinny infantryman who stared disconsolately down at the tautly wrapped bandages that covered the severed stump where once his hand had been. Now he maneuvered his black leather prosthetic hand with skill, and he had grown portly. Too often, he released his belt a notch after a meal, causing his children to laugh.

The Ellenberg children—the twins, Scott and Lisa, and Joanna and Stevie—lived in a different world than the one their parents had known. War and poverty were banished, spoken about in whispers. Peace and plenty formed the parameters of their lives. They ate red meat every night, took vitamins, and plundered refrigerators amply stocked with fruits of the season, juices that gleamed in rainbow colors, any delicacy for which they expressed a preference. Laughter ruled their lives—the canned laughter of the half-hour comedy programs on television, the insistent gaiety of the professional clown hired to entertain at their birthday parties, the comedians hired for their bar mitzvahs and sweet-sixteens. Only one demand had been made of them during their brief, golden lives. "Be happy!" That was what Sherry and Joshua Ellenberg, who had seen war and death, smelled singed bodies and putrefying limbs, wanted for their children.

"Did you have a good time? Did you have fun?" Their questions were urgent and fearful.

"We had fun. It was great."

Their children did not disappoint them. They dared not.

"There's a war on now," Kemala said. Michael was catapulted back to the party in Melanie's Berkeley apartment. She had said the same thing then, and in the background the girl called Joan Baez had plucked her mandolin and softly sung of peace.

"Oh, come on, Kemala." In Berkeley Melanie had been sympathetic, now she was impatient. "Things are getting better. You've already seen what Kennedy could do when he was only a candidate. Now he's president. He'll turn everything around. The whole world."

Melanie had already volunteered to serve in the new Peace Corps Kennedy had proposed. She had been with the group of volunteers who had met with Kennedy early in October at the University of Michigan at two in the morning and had heard him advocate the daring new program. His words whirled in her memory. "I want to demonstrate to Mr. Khrushchev . . . that a new generation of Americans has taken over this country . . . young Americans who will serve the cause of freedom as servants of peace around the world. . . ." The new president had turned them from a generation of takers to a generation of givers. Melanie saw herself working at a schoolhouse in Ghana, at a clinic in an Asian outpost.

"Exactly what did Kennedy do?" Kemala asked, and again her tone was reminiscent of the control she had displayed at Berkeley. "He phoned Coretta King and told her that he was really sorry that her husband was in jail. I don't call that an act of heroism."

"Oh, be fair, Kemala. He did more than that," Les Anderson protested. "Bobby Kennedy called Georgia and insisted that King be given bail."

Les had been in Detroit that day, covering the campaign. The sustained fury of the Kennedy brothers over the black leader's plight had impressed him. They had called in a lot of important IOUs with that call, he knew.

"It was all a political ploy," Kemala retorted calmly. "A friend of mine who really knows what's going on told me that if the election hadn't been so close, neither of those calls would have been made. Those two calls delivered the black vote and put Kennedy over the top."

"I didn't think Matt Williams attended Kennedy's kitchen cabinet meetings," Michael observed mildly. "How can he be sure?" Immediately he was ashamed. It was the first time he had mentioned Matt Williams directly to Kemala. It struck him as an act of cowardice that he should do so at a festive holiday dinner surrounded by his family and friends.

Leah, as though sensing unease, served the turkey just then. Aaron carved expertly, never faltering, although Paulette's hand rested on his wrist. Four years of marriage had added weight to Aaron's solid frame and contentment to his features. Like many redheads, his hair had lost its color early, and Aaron's silver-gray hair reminded Michael that his brother was no longer a young man, nor was he himself growing younger. It would be nice to have children of his own, to feel a child's trusting touch on his own wrist. He shook the thought away and turned to the Ellenberg children, who were happily singing a new jingle for Ellenberg Industries that Joshua's advertising agency had composed for television.

"Not a work of art," Joshua said, "but it sells jeans. That's the wave of the future—merchandising with television."

"Ellenberg Industries has a factory over in Fayette, Mississippi, doesn't it?" Kemala asked. "I noticed a sign there."

"Jakie Hart and I operated a plant together there for a while, but we closed it down."

"Why?" Les Anderson, ever the investigative reporter, asked. He wanted to do a couple of labor relations features now that the election was over—there could be a tie-in with the Judy Bond story. The boycott of blouses manufactured by the plant that resisted ILGWU organization was spreading.

"We closed it down because the powers that be in Fayette resisted a union and I only operate a union shop."

"I'm going to have to close down the uptown outlet for another reason, Joshua," Jakie Hart said. "I can't get insurance. Three fires on that block in the last three weeks."

"Accidents?" Joshua asked.

"Arson. Caught two of them. Local kids. No rhyme or reason to it. Just malicious mischief."

Michael, helping his mother carry the pies in, watched Kemala carefully. He saw the anger that flashed across her face, watched her struggle for control. He was not surprised when she turned to Jakie Hart.

"But there is rhyme and reason to those fires," she said. "Were the kids who were caught black? I assume that 'uptown' is Harlem."

The others looked uncomfortably at each other. Great attention was paid to Leah's apple pie, to the glass of juice that Paulette had spilled across the cloth. There was nervous laughter, much scurrying with napkins.

"The kids were black and uptown is Harlem," Jakie said calmly. "So what?"

"The black kids are letting you know that they're tired of being exploited, that they're reclaiming their own territory. I'm not saying that it's right or that it's constructive. But there is reason behind it. Not all reasons are reasonable, unfortunately."

"I think you've got your facts a little mixed,'" Jakie said harshly. His wife raised a warning finger, but he ignored her. What was Michael doing with this bitter, black bitch? Was this the *naches* he had brought home with his fancy Berkeley Ph.D.? His aunt Leah deserved better. "I never exploited anyone. I pay good wages and charge fair prices."

"You have to understand," Kemala objected, and now her voice was at once more heated and more confident, "you're confronting the culmination of generations of resentment. These kids are the children of men and women who have endured an economic and social slavery. They're turning their anger about that on you because they perceive you as responsible for their situation. Those fires are retribution of a kind. They're paying you back because people like you lived on their misery. It's too bad about your insurance premiums, but the dynamics are complex."

Les Anderson glanced at Michael. He recognized the rhetoric. It echoed an article by Matt Williams in a recent liberal quarterly, "Why Will Your Cities Burn?" Michael, however, moved closer to Kemala. Her hands were trembling, and when she set her coffee cup down it clattered noisily against the saucer.

Leah turned to Kemala but did not pause in her careful pouring of the coffee. The silver carafe was steady in her hand.

"Not people like *us*," she said evenly. "Not my people. When your people were being enslaved, my people were fleeing from one country in Europe to another. When your people were being persecuted, my people were being clubbed and whipped by cossacks. And killed. Murdered. Whole villages burned to the ground. The Jews of Europe, our parents, our grandparents—what did they know of blacks and slavery and exploitation? They were on another continent fighting for their lives. And when we came to America, what did we know about the Ku Klux Klan? We read about them in the paper and called them American cossacks. Whom did I exploit when I worked fourteen, fifteen hours a day in a sweatshop to pay my husband's tuition? Terrible things happened to your people. I don't say no. My heart breaks for them. I'm proud of what Michael is doing. But the guilt is not mine—not ours. And I will not be burdened with it."

Leah's color was high, and Lydia placed a warning hand on her arm.

"I don't think that Kemala was speaking personally," she said, but Kemala turned to Joshua Ellenberg.

"Did you open an outlet in Harlem to lose money?" she asked.

"I never do anything to lose money," Joshua replied. "But there's a difference between making a decent profit and exploitation. Look, I don't think this is the time for a seminar on economics. It's Thanksgiving, and we always have a little music here on Thanksgiving. Scott, get your guitar. I spend enough for lessons that you should show off a little."

Scott produced his guitar, and the children sang in uneasy chorus. Their voices were too shrill at first, as though they felt the responsibility for breaking the tension, the uncomfortable silence that had overtaken the holiday meal. They sang traditional favorites: "Over the River and Through the Woods," "We Gather Together." Then, as the others slowly joined in, their voices softened to a natural, unhurried sweetness, and they sang "He's Got the Whole World in His Hands" and "Tom Dooley." Les and Jeremy parodied "The Sound of Music," and Seymour Hart, his voice quivering with age, sang an old Yiddish song about a rabbi and his obedient Hasidim. Melanie and Jeremy danced to "High Hopes." Lydia borrowed a guitar and strummed a Gypsy love song. Aaron lifted Paulette into his arms and waltzed about the room with her. Lydia's voice broke as she sang. She was remembering Budapest, he knew, and the sweet-singing youth for whom his daughter was named. He danced on, and when he sat beside Lydia again, she was calm. The baby, David, rested on her lap and she leaned her head on Aaron's shoulder.

The contentment of the afternoon was restored. They gathered about the fireplace in the living room and talked easily with each other. Only Kemala and Michael remained alone at the far end of the room, untouched by the glow of the firelight. They were the first to leave. Leah kissed her younger son and shook hands politely with Kemala. Kemala's hand was cold and rigid in her own, and she did not smile when she said goodbye. The door slammed heavily behind them when they finally left, shattering the ease and mood of the afternoon.

"I shouldn't have said anything," Leah said worriedly.

"You said what you had to say," Aaron replied.

Paulette slept against his shoulder, and David played contentedly on the floor. David was beginning to crawl, and next year he would be walking. It occurred to Aaron, for the first time, that the raising of children was an awesome thing. He threaded his fingers through his daughter's dark hair and studied his son's upturned face.

Lydia watched him.

"They'll be all right—we'll keep them safe, " she said, as though reading his thoughts. Somehow, accounts had to be balanced. The loss side of her ledger was heavily weighted. Her parents, her brothers, Ferenc, Paul. Her children had to be kept safe, secure. Her lips moved in silent prayer and her hands rested protectively on her abdomen. She turned her thoughts to all that would have to be completed before the birth of this third child. She wanted to finish the model of the mobile amplifier, and edit one more research paper.

Aaron's hand encased her own. She marveled again at the miracle of their lives together and frowned as she thought of Michael and Kemala.

Later that night Leah and Boris Zaslovsky sat alone before the fire that was slowly dying. Small, valiant tongues of flame splashed showers of glittering sparks, and the embers glowed with fiery tenacity.

"Don't be sorry," Boris said. "Parents say what they think is right and children do what they think is right. So it has always been—so it will always be. It is his life, Leah. You cannot live it for him."

"I only want him to be happy," Leah said.

"He will have to make his own way." The Russian's voice was weary. "He is lucky to have the opportunity to find his way." Boris's own children had not been so lucky. His two sons and a daughter had been mowed down by German *Einsatzgruppen* at the place called Babi Yar. His wife had died soon after. Heart failure, the doctor said. But Boris Zaslovsky, a doctor himself, knew better. Heartbreak. There had been tears in her eyes when he found her lifeless body. When he pressed his face against hers, to search for breath, the tears had rolled down her cheeks and moistened his own. The dead woman had wept. Boris had held her hand and thought that he could never be happy again. Always grief and memory would stalk him.

Grief and memory had not left him, but he had found solace in his work. And he had found community with the Jews whose consciousness had been aroused after the war. He became their healer and their advocate, and on a magic afternoon, when clouds encircled Moscow and a wind rustled the leaves of the lombardy trees, he had met Leah Goldfeder, the Russian-born woman from America. She was newly bereaved; he was a veteran of loss and sorrow. They spoke easily to each other and sometimes found it peaceful not to talk at all. They wrote to each other, and through her efforts he was at last granted permission to emigrate. Now he sat beside her and watched the patterns of light that formed on her outstretched hands. Wonderful hands—graceful and capable, with a small, pale callus flowering at her forefinger, because often she held her paintbrush with fierce intensity.

"Michael will be fine, Leah," he said. "And we—you and I—we have our own lives to live. Can we be together now, Leah? There are years before us still."

"I don't know." The last of the small twigs burned out and fell onto the embers. "I'm sorry."

"Don't be sorry. I will wait."

His voice was gentle, as ever David Goldfeder's had been. His hand was light and comforting on her shoulder. She reached up and touched it. His skin was age-roughened, almost brittle, and she traced the network of veins with her fingertips.

"Michael will be fine," she repeated, and she closed her eyes and prayed that Boris Zaslovsky, her wise and tender friend, was right.

HUTCHINSON COLLEGE was nestled in the gentle hill country of southern Westchester. Its many-windowed Gothic buildings were constructed of the wondrously textured fieldstone carved out of the cliffs on which Mohican warriors had stood to survey their vast and verdant holdings. Once the college had been the estate of an industrial baron who had dreamed that his many children would live on its grounds. He had built mansions for each of them, communal buildings for their children. But they had quarreled with one another in his lifetime and sued his estate at his death. The victorious heir, in order to demonstrate to his siblings that his suit was not motivated by greed, had donated the grounds and the buildings to the Hutchinson Academy, a small progressive institution "for ladies of breeding." By the turn of the century, progressive "ladies of breeding" were interested in obtaining bachelor of arts degrees, and the Hutchinson Academy became the select and prestigious Hutchinson College, with a unique and highly specialized program in arts and sciences.

Modern buildings were added to the original structures, and the gleaming edifices of glass and steel, many of them boldly topping the gentle hillocks, somehow did not violate the sylvan ambience. In the fall, the campus was brilliant with autumnal foliage; leaves of scarlet and gold, pale yellow and somber ocher, blanketed the lawns and meadows. Michael Goldfeder, returning to Hutchinson for his second year, was surprised at how pleased he was to be back on the campus. He studied his course list with pleasure and worked carefully on his curriculum.

His second summer in Mississippi had exhausted him. The programs at the Troy schoolhouse had intensified. He had added evening classes and taught special tutorials for promising students like Rodney Mason. He had been disturbed because there was little continuity from summer to summer, and he worked out a program that his students might follow during the winter months. Again, Kemala had drifted in and out of Troy, and again they had spent solitary afternoons together. But too often he had sensed her restlessness, her impatience. A mild remark stirred a bitter reaction. Once, after they had made love, she wept uncontrollably in his arms.

"You work too hard," he had said soothingly.

"There's work to be done," she retorted harshly. "This isn't a summer adventure for me—it's my life."

The unfairness of her reply wounded him. He did not counter it, and an unbridged silence stretched between them. She came less frequently after that day. Matt Williams was away—at conferences, at meetings, negotiating funding—and her work load was heavy. He felt lost and empty, yet pleased that Matt was away. Michael saw him only twice that summer, and again the antagonism between them surfaced.

It was his mother who visited Michael that summer. Leah arrived with Boris one August afternoon, and Michael returned to the Mason home after his noon class to find his mother sitting at the scrubbed pine kitchen table with Cora Mason. The two women sat over large ceramic mugs of fragrant coffee, engrossed in an earnest conversation, which they continued after Michael greeted them.

"I know how you feel," Leah told Cora Mason. "It used to seem to me that I would never stop being tired. I worked all day in the factory and came home to the children, to caring for the house. But I was lucky. My sister came over from Russia, and she and her family lived with us and helped us during those early years. And my friend Sarah Ellenberg did a lot of the cooking." She sat in the small Mississippi house and remembered the frantic activity in the Eldridge Street apartment—tired women shouting at small children, rushing from sink to counter. Their poverty had energized them, spurred them to work and hope. She had recognized that energy in Cora Mason.

"It's like that, here in Troy," the black woman said. "We're like family to each other. My neighbors help me out and I help them. Still, it's wearying and worrying. Some days more than others." A frown of fatigue creased her forehead, and her shoulders were rounded by years of labor.

"Yes. The worrying. The children. Are they all right? Will things go well for them? Will they be safe, healthy? Will life be good to them?" Leah's voice quivered.

She went to the window and looked toward the cotton fields, where Rodney Mason and his sisters tossed a red ball to each other. Cora Mason stood beside her, and Michael studied the two women: his mother elegant in a pale green suit, mysteriously uncreased by her hours of travel, her long hair concealed beneath a matching cloche, and Cora in a housedress, starched and ironed but faded from its original brown to an ocher hue that almost matched her skin. Yet their life-worn faces were not unlike; they were carved with lines of strength and caring and their eyes were similarly soft as they watched the children. They were sisters in the fierce sorority of motherhood; always they would struggle so that their children would not accept less than their due.

"I want things to be better for them," Cora Mason said softly. "I want them to have learning. I want them to sleep in the night without being afraid of rocks comin' through windows, of crosses burnin' up the lawn."

"I know," Leah said. She thought that she would like to paint the black children as they tossed their red ball amid the serried rows of white cotton plants. She, too, had fled the fires of hatred, the forces of terror, and her children had found a better life. She had vowed when she left Russia never to be a victim again, and she sensed that same determination in Cora Mason.

Leah taught a class in Michael's one-room schoolhouse that afternoon, a simple drawing lesson. She showed Michael's students, with a few deft strokes, how she created a soaring bird, a fleet-footed hart, a full-petaled rose. And before she left, she painted a rainbow, straddled by a dove, on the eastern corner of the wall. Always, Michael would see it as he taught. The bright symbols of peace and hope were his mother's gift to him, her blessing, just as her own battle for social justice was his heritage.

"She's a fine woman, your mama," Cora Mason said as Leah and Boris drove away. "Full of strength. Full of caring. You're like her, you know."

Michael thought about her words that night as he walked alone to the stripped cotton field where the bare magnolia tree stretched its stark branches skyward. It comforted him that his mother had so briefly shared in his life. It neutralized her confrontation with Kemala on Thanksgiving. He would show Kemala Leah's rainbow, her gentle dove of peace.

The day before Michael left Troy to return to Hutchinson College for the fall semester, he and Kemala drove again to the Bienville Forest. They looked up at the giant firs, whose crowns converged to form a verdant citadel across the pale blue, cloud-strewn sky. Sunlight embroidered golden paths across the fallen pine needles.

"It was not a good summer," she said. "I'm sorry."

"I'm sorry too."

"Will you come back?"

"I'll come back." His students would draw him back, and the unfinished Troy library. Rodney Mason, who would be ready by next year to take the scholarship examination for the New York preparatory school, would draw him back. And she would draw him back—her slender arms, her throaty voice, her sadness and her wistful laughter.

"Kemala, I think we should talk—about us—about what is happening between us." His voice was hesitant. The words he searched for eluded him, and he feared to articulate those that came to him. The question unasked required no answer.

"We are as we were before," she said evasively.

"And how were we before?" he asked. That much he could risk.

She whirled and faced him, her fists clenched, her golden eyes glinting with anger.

"Does everything need to be said, Michael? Do we need to tie our feelings up in neat little packages with words and explanations? Are we so terribly important that we need to analyze and examine our relationship? There's so much going on in the world, Michael. Kids take their lives in their hands and travel down lonely Mississippi roads. We're fighting to turn the world around, and you want to talk about how we feel about each other."

He flinched against the impact of her words, the flood of accusations that avoided his intent. Anger welled up in him, bilious and hot, but before he could answer her, he saw that she was crying. She leaned against a slender pine tree, her hands outstretched, tears streaking her cheeks. He understood, then, that she had surrendered to rage because she could not, would not, confront the truth. He had pitied her then and pitied himself as well. They were lovers who dared not speak of love.

"Everything will be all right," he said, and because he recognized the doubt and grief in his own voice, he held her very close, as though he might weld her body to his own.

His heart had splintered at leaving her again, and yet he was glad to return to Hutchinson, to the cool of fall afternoons and the sound of his own voice talking calmly, steadily, to young women who listened to him with upturned faces and took copious, competent notes.

He plotted his next lecture for his class in the sociology of religion, as he strode across the campus, so absorbed in his thoughts that he did not hear the hurrying footsteps of the young woman behind him.

"Dr. Goldfeder, may I speak to you for a moment?" Her voice was breathless, and when he turned he saw that she was familiar. He had perhaps met her, and certainly he had seen her before. She was a pretty woman whose pale brown hair fell to her shoulders in a careful pageboy and whose green eyes matched her linen shirtdress.

"I know we've met," he said, "but I just can't seem to remember where or how."

"Of course you can't," she said, smiling. "We met at the opening tea for the faculty, and you were probably introduced to about twenty new people. I'm Elaine Handler, and I'll be teaching the introductory courses in sociology."

"Oh yes, I remember now. University of Chicago. You did your dissertation on Weber, I think."

"Actually on Weber's influence on C. Wright Mills," she said, and a blush colored her cheeks. Immediately, he liked her for that blush.

"Yes, I remember now," he said. "I'd like to read it sometime if I may."

"I'll leave a copy at the library for you. But actually, I wanted to ask you about my classes. I know you taught one of them last year, and I wondered if I could show you my outline."

"Of course. How about tonight, over dinner?"

The invitation surprised him almost as much as it seemed to surprise her. He had planned to have dinner with Les and Jeremy and to spend the evening writing a long letter to Kemala. And yet, suddenly, he was pleased at the thought of sitting opposite Elaine Handler in the small Chinese restaurant on East Broadway. He would introduce her to cold sesame noodles, to broccoli in hot garlic sauce, and they would talk of C. Wright Mills and of Max Weber and of Hans Gerth, the translator of one and the friend of the other. It had been a long time since he had spent an evening with a colleague, and Elaine Handler was a very pretty colleague.

"All right," she said, after the briefest hesitation.

It developed that evening that she already knew about cold sesame noodles. She shared his passion for Chinese food and also his passion for chamber music and Humphrey Bogart. It was so late when they began discussing her syllabus that they immediately made a date for a weekend evening. She lived in SoHo, and he walked back to his Eldridge Street flat, whistling happily, after seeing her home. He did not write to Kemala that night.

He saw Elaine frequently during the weeks that followed. He was not surprised that her background was not too dissimilar to his own. Her grandparents had been Polish Jews who settled in the Midwest, and her father still ran the shoe factory founded by her grandfather. His dream had been to see his children achieve academic success. Her two older brothers had dutifully gone off to medical school and become doctors, and she, less dutifully, had been drawn to sociology for reasons that matched Michael's own.

"Social structure fascinates me," she said. "The way society organizes itself, establishes its traditions, its priorities. The more we understand, the more we can reverse injustices. It's happening already—the woman's movement, the civil rights movement."

"I know." Her understanding exhilarated him. "Your father must be proud of you," he said.

"Not as proud as he would be if I would just settle down and get married," she replied.

"Oh, does he have anyone in particular in mind?"

"A nice Jewish boy like you," she said, laughing.

"And my mother wouldn't mind a nice Jewish girl like you," he admitted.

"What are we waiting for?" she asked.

"We're too young," he said wryly, and they burst into spontaneous laughter. They were having dinner that evening at a Chinese restaurant in celebration of Michael's twenty-eighth birthday. As they walked to her apartment, through the deserted streets of lower Manhattan, he told her about Kemala.

"I'm not surprised," she said quietly. "I knew there had to be someone." She had seen Michael start uneasily when the phone in his apartment rang. She had noticed how a filter of sadness slid across his face, how he distanced himself from her suddenly and inexplicably.

"Does it make a difference?" he asked.

"Not for now. No." She had a quiet faith in her own powers, in the ease and attraction they shared. Kemala was in Mississippi—a breathless, conflicted voice on the telephone. Elaine saw Michael each day at Hutchinson, spent evenings with him. When he kissed her that night, her body was soft and yielding against his own. He remembered, with a pang of disloyalty, that Kemala had always been wiry with tension in his arms.

Aaron gave a party, and Michael brought Elaine. His family liked her. She helped Lydia in the kitchen, played with the children, talked with Leah and Boris about the acculturation of the Russian Jews who were arriving in America.

Aaron told them about the legal clinic he had visited that week. Lawyers were joining together to protect young men who were resisting the draft because they opposed the war in Vietnam.

"Did you volunteer your time?" Elaine asked.

"Not yet," he replied. "I'm not sure where I stand. I'm opposed to the war, but then there were Americans who were opposed to World War Two. What if there had been substantial draft resistance then? There's an excruciatingly fine line between conscience and national responsibility." He held his hands out as though weighing the alternatives. Always Aaron struggled for fairness and equity, and, in the end, always his decisions were based on hard-earned clarity and consideration. Such qualities had not gone unrecognized. It was rumored that he would soon be proposed for a judgeship.

"My hesitations come from a different discipline," Elaine volunteered. "As a sociologist I think we have to be very careful about undermining a basic social structure."

"But that might be what German soldiers said when they did not resist service in the forces of the Reich," Lydia protested. "Of course I speak subjectively because I was involved in the undermining of such a social structure. Sometimes one has no choice."

"But that's just the point," Michael said. "In this country there is a choice."

The discussion was considered and probing, without the passion and anger that a similar discussion with Kemala would have engendered, Michael thought. He felt vaguely disloyal and tried to call her in Mississippi that night, but she was not home.

Elaine moved among Michael's family and friends as though she had known them forever. They liked her and were comfortable with her.

"Michael's friend Elaine is just lovely," Michael overheard his mother tell Rebecca on the phone, and he knew that his sister and Yehuda would like her.

How easy it would be, he thought, to marry her and live with her calmly, peacefully, as Aaron lived with Lydia. Shared lives, shared work. How pretty she looked tonight in the jade-colored dress that matched her eyes, her light brown hair sweeping her shoulder.

"I like her," Leah said to him, her mother-eyes raking his face for secrets, pleading for him to be happy.

"I do too."

He and Elaine left early that night, and Leah and Boris stood in the doorway and watched them drive off.

"I told you Michael would be all right," Boris said.

"Do you think so?"

"They're so well matched."

"Yes. Yes, they are." She had watched her son and Elaine laugh together, had seen them engaged in earnest discussion over an academic point, their heads bent close, their fingers touching.

"And we—we, too, are well matched," Boris said.

Leah looked at him, this gentle aging man who had endured so much and who understood her so well. She held her hands out to him, and he pressed them gently to his lips.

LEAH AND BORIS scheduled their wedding for the following month—a quiet ceremony at Leah's home. Michael, Aaron, and Lydia were pleased by the news, and Rebecca, whom they phoned in Israel, promised that she and Yehuda would arrange to be there.

"A holiday this time," Rebecca said firmly. "This visit will not include one of those damn conferences or fact-finding missions."

But two weeks before the wedding, Noam Arnon, whose hair was the color of winter wheat and whose eyes were silken gray, like those of Yehuda, his father, took a walk in the upper Galilee with his friend Yair. He had received a leather-covered watch as a gift to mark both his eighteenth birthday and his induction into the army, and it was not running well. He was studying it as he walked, and he did not notice the odd movement in the roadside overgrowth and thus did not move swiftly enough to avoid the bullet that pierced his right temple. He was killed instantly, his face frozen in an expression of comprehension, as though at the moment of his death he had at last solved the problem of his timepiece.

Rebecca phoned Leah. Her voice was strangled with grief. She wept softly into the phone. Noam had been like a son to her; she had nurtured him from boyhood to young manhood.

"He only wanted to make things grow," she said, and her voice broke. "He loved flowers," she added, as though somehow a reverence for blossoms, for delicate growing things, should have kept him safe from violence, protected him from death.

Leah held the phone and wept because eighteen-year-old Noam was dead and because Rebecca was in pain, and she was powerless to comfort her.

"You must be strong, Rebecca," she said with all the firmness she could muster, although tears streaked her cheeks, "for Yehuda and for the other children."

"I'll try," Rebecca said. "Oh, I'll try."

She came to America alone for the wedding, her face ravaged with grief and loss. Yehuda remained in Israel. He lay awake for hours each night, and during the day she was frightened because he walked alone in the desert. Fear shadowed her eyes, slowed her steps. Her eyes filled suddenly, inexplicably, when she saw Aaron walking in the garden with his children.

"Listen to me," Leah said to her, one night as they sat together before the dying fire, "you must grieve, but you must not surrender to grief. You must go on. As I went on."

She held Rebecca's hands tightly, as though to infuse her with new strength.

The next day Rebecca visited Charles Ferguson's gallery. She studied his new acquisitions, talked of the possibility of an exhibition of her own work. Her mother was right. Noam was dead, but their lives would go on. Each day brought her new strength, new courage.

On the morning of the wedding day, Rebecca wakened in her girlhood room and was filled with gladness because the sun shone brightly and a cardinal perched impudently on a branch of the maple tree. She wished, with febrile urgency, that Yehuda could have been with her so that she might somehow infuse him with the new hope she had so mysteriously discovered.

Leah and Boris were married at the twilight hour. Leah's children watched Boris Zaslovsky slip a plain gold ring on their mother's finger. The ring that David Goldfeder had purchased from an Odessa goldsmith so long ago was passed on to Rebecca, who would give it to the first of her children to marry—or perhaps to Mindell, who had been bereft of all legacy.

Boris stepped on the glass wrapped in white linen, crushing it with a vigorous stamp. The room echoed with happiness. Lisa Ellenberg clapped her hands and whirled small Paulette in celebratory dance. Aaron and Michael hugged each other. Lydia and Sherry clutched Leah's hands, kissed her. Leah felt herself a young woman again, a radiant bride poised at the edge of a new life. She linked arms with Boris, who stared at her as though dazed by the mystery of his own good fortune.

Joshua Ellenberg, ever sensitive to Rebecca, moved to stand beside her and gently kissed her on the forehead.

"*Mazel tov,* Becca," he said.

Elaine, moving across the room toward Michael, saw that tears filled Rebecca Arnon's eyes even as she hurried to join the rest of the family in the traditional wedding hora.

Michael told Kemala about the wedding on the phone. She did not come to New York, although fall had drifted into winter and it was months since he had seen her. There was too much work to do. Her voice was weary and irritable and then tearful and apologetic. Her letters were brief, yet he opened each with trembling fingers, and always, after he spoke with her, his throat was dry and his body ached with longing. He avoided Elaine after such calls, and she asked him no questions, did not press him.

He took Elaine to a Miriam Makeba concert at Town Hall. The audience, black and white, young and old, was enthusiastic. They linked hands as they sang the hymns. They laughed as they tried to sing "The Click Song." The lights went on at intermission, and he stared into the well of the orchestra. Matt Williams, strangely elegant in a camel's hair jacket and a blue shirt, studied his program. Kemala, to whom Michael had spoken only two nights before ("I can't stay on the phone too long . . . we're so swamped here I can't breathe . . . how can I even think of coming to New York?"—her voice strained, annoyed), sat beside him. Elaine noticed Michael's swift intake of breath, followed his eyes.

"That's Kemala?" she asked.

"Yes."

"She's very beautiful."

Kemala's glossy silken braid was wound about her head to form a graceful coronet. She wore a brightly patterned orange-and-green African dress that hugged her narrow body. He waited for them at the aisle, his heart pounding.

"Michael!" Fear (or sadness? or apology?) flashed in her golden eyes. "The idea of coming north was all so last-minute that I didn't call you. And besides, there wouldn't have been time to see you—meetings, planning sessions. Matt's speaking to Miriam about a nationwide television show—all sorts of things."

"All sorts of things," Matt Williams echoed sardonically. He seemed more amused than perturbed by the meeting.

Kemala laughed nervously, turned her hands up in mock despair. Michael looked down at the curve of her lifeline where once he had written his name, and introduced Elaine. And then Matt and Kemala were rushed out in a flurry of apologies. They could not even stay for the second half of the concert. There was a press conference, an organizational meeting, an anticipated phone call from Martin Luther King—she would call him, write him. He saw the bright fabric of her dress disappear into the crowd and felt his heart grow heavy with bewilderment. Elaine's hand on his arm was gentle; her touch was tentative and cognitive of his pain.

He slept with her that night. She was sweet and soothing, and carefully avoided the parameters of his sadness. She kissed his eyes and slept with her head upon his chest, her long hair silken on his arms. She did not mention Kemala.

Kemala called him twice that week. Her voice quivered with anguish.

"You're not angry, Michael? It couldn't be helped. I didn't know I was coming myself."

He did not believe her, but the misery in her voice compelled his forgiveness. Her fear of his disbelief mitigated his sense of betrayal. He reminded himself that she had suffered so much and that always he himself had been so sheltered. With agonizing delicacy he arranged and rearranged emotional scales. She sent him a letter enclosing dried gentians and trillium. Carefully, he put them in his wallet, concealing them behind her picture.

Les Anderson rented a ski house in Vermont, and Elaine and Michael spent weekends there. After a day on the slopes Elaine's cheeks were bright and her eyes blazed emerald-green. During the evenings they worked. He wrote a monograph, and she made small but vital corrections. Often he did not think of Kemala for days at a time, but he dreamed of her. With Elaine lying beside him, he dreamed of walking with Kemala through a forest dark with danger, carpeted with flowers that had lost both color and fragrance.

Elaine called to tell him that her parents were coming to New York. She wanted Michael to meet them, to have dinner with them.

"It's important to me," she said shyly.

"But I want to meet them," he assured her. "When?"

"Saturday night. At seven."

"Fine."

He bought a bottle of good wine and wrapped a batik wall hanging of his mother's design as a gift. At five o'clock on that Saturday afternoon the phone rang. Kemala. She was at LaGuardia Airport. Someone from the coordinating committee had been scheduled to meet her but had not shown up. She had cartons of mimeographed material and no money, and she felt sick. Her voice was laced with weariness, and she whispered into the phone.

"Can you come and get me, Michael?"

He heard the desperation in her voice. She was so alone. She had been so often abandoned. Love and pity swept over him, tinged by anger. He recognized and ignored the anger.

"I'll be there, Kemala."

He called Elaine.

"Michael!" His name uttered with gladness, without demand. In the background her parents talked softly. He heard the clink of china. Her mother was setting the table.

"I can't come."

She was silent. He heard her breathe hard as though recoiling from the impact of his words.

"Is it Kemala?" she asked at last.

"Yes."

"Goodbye, Michael. Don't call me again."

"Elaine—"

But she had hung up, and he did not call back. Instead he hurried because Kemala was waiting at the airport, alone and ill. Beautiful, sad-eyed Kemala who inhabited his heart like an adhering shadow.

Elaine did not return to Hutchinson for the next semester. She went to London University to do research and then to a small midwestern university. More than a year later he received a marriage announcement in the mail. Her husband was a Dr. Martin Levenson. Michael studied the stiff white card and ran his fingers across the raised lettering. He hoped that Martin Levenson deserved Elaine Handler. He was suffused with sadness and regret, gripped by an almost palpable sense of loss. The monograph Elaine had helped him with was on his desk. Her corrections were lightly written in pencil.

He wrote her a polite note of congratulation and remembered, as he sealed the envelope, how lovely she had looked in her green silk dress, how light her head had been upon his chest as she slept.

Lydia and Aaron gave a dinner party to celebrate Leah and Boris's first wedding anniversary. Michael attended alone and remembered how Elaine had stood beside him at his mother's wedding. It occurred to him that the year had whirled by with astounding speed and that at its end he was still alone, watching for letters from Mississippi, answering too quickly when the phone rang. He was marking time while the lives of others surged forward. In a few months' time he would return to Mississippi, but this summer would be different, he decided. He and Kemala would confront the future. The thought filled him with a blend of fear and hope. He drank deeply when Aaron called for a toast to Boris and Leah.

"L'chaim," Aaron said loudly. "To life."

"L'chaim," Michael murmured softly and felt his mother's hand cover his own.

MINDELL KRASNOW glanced uncertainly about the Neshoba bus station and loosened the straps of her knapsack. If Michael was going to be much later, she supposed she should take it off. It was very heavy, and the fierce heat of the Mississippi afternoon adhered to the nylon fabric and seared her skin. It was her own fault, she acknowledged ruefully. She had grown up on the desert and certainly knew enough to use a canvas knapsack. She had, in fact, taken her army knapsack with her to America, but Joshua Ellenberg, who had recently begun manufacturing camping equipment, had pressed this one on her as a gift.

He had presented it with her initials carefully worked into the shiny royal-blue fabric and proudly showed her the intricate compartments for storing bedroll, toilet articles, cooking gear, and clothing.

"Wonderful for your camping trip around America," he had said enthusiastically.

Mindell could not resist his gift. She had a passion for the new, for the touch and feel of pristine items, for sweaters and blouses still nestled in tissue-paper wrappings, for dresses with tags still swinging from uncrushed sleeves. Since leaving the kibbutz, she had taken special joy in the purchases she made for her student room, for her sparse but carefully chosen wardrobe. Often she kept a new garment in its original box, as though to assure herself of its newness. An outgrowth of her childhood years, she supposed, when she had been kept hidden in the concealed tunnel of a concentration camp barrack and had worn whatever clothing the women prisoners who were her protectors and providers could scavenge to cover her nakedness. Once they had fashioned a garment for her from a uniform torn from the body of a newly dead prisoner. The scent of death and despair, of the dead woman's mingled sweat and vomit, had clung to the worn striped cloth, which they had sewn into double lengths to fit Mindell's tiny, emaciated body.

She had loved the crisp touch of Joshua's gift, the scent of its newness, and she had been touched by Joshua's kindness in traveling from Great Neck to Leah's house just to give it to her. But then Rebecca's family and friends had all been so kind. She wondered why it was she still thought of them as "Rebecca's family" when she had been assured and reassured, through the years, that they were her family as well.

"We think of you as our daughter," Rebecca had said more than once. "We want you to have our name, to share our lives."

Yehuda's arm, gentle about Mindell's shoulders, had affirmed Rebecca's words. Mindell was saddened now as she thought of Yehuda Arnon. A full year had passed since Noam's death, but Yehuda seldom spoke the name of his firstborn son, although he often visited his grave. He slept poorly and he walked alone, in the desert darkness, the ember of his cigarette glowing, his steps slowed by the weight of his memories. He traveled more than ever, and when he was on the kibbutz he seemed withdrawn, insulated and isolated by his sadness. Once Mindell had heard Rebecca protest his frequent absences. He had turned to her, his features contorted, his voice harsh.

"Do you think I want to be away? But I must go where I am sent. Maybe what I am doing will make life safer for other children."

She had not replied. More and more often silence ended their discussions, and more and more often they averted their eyes from each other as they spoke.

Mindell was troubled. She loved Rebecca and Yehuda Arnon and had thought of them as surrogate parents since she had journeyed with them to Haifa harbor. But for reasons that she could neither articulate nor understand, she had kept her parents' name, which matched that of the small village of her birth. She was human testimony to the fact that once Krasnoye had existed, that once ten thousand Jews had lived peacefully in a quiet Polish village bordered by cherry trees. And the name, too, was all that remained of the gray-faced man and woman, the village apothecary and his wife, who had been her parents. She remembered only their colorlessness, the sour breath of their fear against her face—which meant, perhaps, that they had carried her very close to their bodies, concealed her against their skin, until the very last minute when her mother had been selected for death and had thrust her into the arms of a strange woman. Her life had been saved because a guard had turned away for a split second, because a strange woman had been both brave and kind. Always, Mindell thought, her life had depended on the tenuous solicitude of strangers—the women in the camp; Signora Sarfadi, who had hidden her in the basement of her Bari home; Rebecca and Yehuda Arnon, who had guided her to freedom and taken her to share their lives. Even now, in this hot and fly-infested bus station, she quiescently awaited the kindness of a near-stranger. She did not really know Michael Goldfeder. It had been years since his visit to Israel—that terrible summer when Rebecca's father had died and Yaakov had been born—life and death entwined, a man buried and a child named.

She and Michael had belonged to separate worlds then. She was a young adolescent, but she ran and played with the children, tenaciously clinging to a childhood that had been denied her. She had perceived Michael as an adult. He was a university graduate who talked soberly with the men of the kibbutz about the irrigation system, discussed politics with Yehuda and Rebecca, and asked invasive questions of the kibbutz members. Did they find fulfillment at Sha'arei ha-Negev? What were their personal goals? Did they feel that communal living in a rural setting was more satisfying than conventional urban life? His questions had become more intense, more urgent, after his father's death, and Mindell had been glad that Michael did not know how the kibbutz members laughed and mocked his questions.

"Like all the Americans," one of them had said scornfully, "he thinks he's in a laboratory and we are the guinea pigs."

No, he's not like that, Mindell had wanted to say. *He's searching for something—can't you see?* But she had, of course, said nothing. What had she known of Michael, after all, except that he was Rebecca's brother and thus a kind of surrogate uncle to her? She had been surprised to realize some years later that Michael was only six or seven years her senior—not her age but of her generation.

Jeremy Cohen, his friend and roommate, had spoken a great deal of Michael during his visit to Israel. It had been Jeremy who encouraged Mindell to apply for a fellowship at the New York hospital where he was on the pediatric staff.

"The medical training you've gotten in Israel is terrific, but we have important new techniques, and besides, a girl like you should see the world—and the world should certainly see you."

Mindell had laughed, but weeks after Jeremy's return to America he sent her an application for the fellowship, and she had filled it out. He had been with Leah at the airport when she arrived.

"Jeremy is standing in for Michael," Leah had explained. "Michael spends the summers at a small school in Mississippi, and he is there already."

It was Jeremy, then, who guided her through bureaucratic intricacies at the hospital and introduced her to New York. Her fellowship would not formally begin until the fall, and it was Jeremy who suggested the detour to Mississippi when she told him that she had decided to tour the States.

"You haven't seen America until you've seen Dixieland," he had said. "And you'd better see it now because it's disappearing fast."

"The sooner the better," Les Anderson added.

Jeremy had written to Michael, and arrangements had been made for Michael to meet her bus in Neshoba. *But where was he?* She was hot and tired now and vaguely annoyed that she had decided not to join a group of Israeli students who were traveling together to California.

Glumly, she walked over to a bench, undid the straps of her knapsack, and allowed it to slide down and rest against the wall. It was good to be free of the oppressive weight, and she breathed deeply with relief and glanced around the room, aware suddenly that everyone was staring at her—not with curiosity but with open, unmasked hostility. Across the room two women in faded flowered cotton housedresses glared at her. Their lips were tightly set, their pale eyes hard. Small flecks of angry color mottled their skin. A man who sat beside them in faded dungarees and a dirty blue workshirt spat a wad of tobacco toward Mindell and smiled evilly, displaying yellow teeth interspersed with gaps.

"Don't pay her no mind," he said, and Mindell realized, with surprise, that he was pointing to her. "I expect she likes dark meat."

The neatly dressed black couple sitting next to Mindell looked at each other, rose, and left the building.

"I expect she's just some rich college-kid Communist freedom rider," one of the women said and diligently rubbed at a stain on her white plastic purse.

"Come to smoke marijuana and make trouble," her companion replied, her eyes fixed angrily on Mindell.

Mindell took Michael's letter out of her pocket and reread it. He would meet her bus, he promised, but in an emergency, she could call a phone number in Neshoba and ask for Kemala Jackson. Kemala—Michael's special friend whose name had produced a sudden, tense silence in Leah Goldfeder's home.

"Leah does not like Kemala?" Mindell had asked Aaron's wife, Lydia.

"She doesn't know Kemala very well. But she doesn't think she can make Michael happy," Lydia replied carefully. She watched her own children at play in the sunny family room. The baby chortled in the crib that Aaron had painted fire-engine red; black-haired Paulette built a block house with small redheaded David, whose efforts sent the uneasy structure tumbling down. David laughed, Paulette frowned, and Lydia smiled, amused at her own involvement in their game. Her desk was littered with urgent messages from her laboratory, yet she continued to watch her children.

Mindell admired the way Lydia balanced her life. She had spent an afternoon on the campus of the state university with Lydia and watched her at work in her laboratory, teaching her seminar. Mindell had been fascinated by Lydia's discussion of a sonogram designed to trace the movement of a fetus within a pregnant woman's womb.

"How long before we can have such an apparatus in Israel?" Mindell asked excitedly.

"It will be a long time before it's perfected," Lydia replied. "In any case my Israeli colleagues are much more interested in the work we are doing on radar evasion techniques."

"I know," Mindell said regretfully. Israel's next war would be fought in the skies of the Middle East; only a sophisticated radar system would ensure Israel's survival.

Lydia frowned and studied a computer printout on her desk. Absorbed in her work, she almost forgot Mindell's presence.

But at home Lydia's attention was riveted to her family. Her children's lives, their happiness absorbed her. She watched as they played, as though she were the audience at a rare and wonderful performance. She was at once amused and concerned, and always vigilant. Paulette threw a block at David, and the small boy cried. Lydia scolded her daughter, gathered her son up into her arms; she soothed him, speaking softly, cradling him gently. The child was calmed and bounded off to rejoin the game.

"Play nicely," Lydia cautioned.

It was, after all, simple to comfort a small child, to issue gentle admonitions. But Leah could not comfort Michael with gentle words, reassuring caresses. She could not call warnings after her son who was a grown man. "Be careful. Love wisely." Mothers did not say such things aloud. Lydia pitied Leah for her impotence, Michael for his vulnerability. She turned back to Mindell, who had not forgotten her question.

"Why not?" Mindell had persisted.

"Their backgrounds are very different."

"Like you and Aaron."

"Kemala is not Jewish. And she is black. And she is very bitter, very angry." Lydia thought back to the few evenings she and Aaron had shared with Michael and Kemala. Always, they had ended in barbed argument, in uneasy, stilted rhetoric. *I, too, have suffered,* Lydia wanted to scream at Kemala. Losses littered her life. The dead drifted through her dreams. Kemala Jackson had not cornered the market on injustice, on human misery. But she said nothing, of course. Their connection to Michael had to be protected.

"If I were a black in this country, I would be bitter and angry also," Mindell had said. She had traveled through Harlem and seen the decaying tenements. She had worked on the pediatric ward that week. A small black girl had been admitted. An emergency case. Lead poisoning.

"They eat the paint from the walls," Jeremy had explained.

A boy had been admitted, suffering from malnutrition. His distended stomach protruded like an inflated basketball.

"Have you ever seen anything like that?" Jeremy asked.

"Yes. But not in Israel."

Her own small stomach had been similarly bloated when she had at last been liberated from the camp. But starvation had been the norm in Auschwitz. This was America.

"Things are changing." Lydia's answer had been quiet, restrained. "I used to think that the whole world could change overnight, Mindell. Now I know that everything takes time, a lot of time." Lydia had hummed a melody then which Mindell recognized—it was a song sung by the Hungarian immigrants who had come to Sha'arei ha-Negev after the revolution.

"I know that," Mindell had replied. "But I want to do my share in that changing."

She had asked no more questions about Kemala Jackson, but she remained curious about her. All right. If Michael did not arrive within the next hour, she would call Kemala. She checked her watch. He was a half hour late. Meanwhile, she smiled pleasantly at the two fat women, who turned hastily away. Finally the door to the bus station was thrust open and Michael burst into the room.

"Mindell! I'm really sorry. The damn car overheated again and I had to wait for a hitch to get some water. My God—I can hardly recognize you. Stand up."

He pulled her to her feet, and she blushed as he studied her approvingly.

She knew she was pretty. Her blond hair was thick and curly, and she wore it gathered in bunches about her ears. Her creamy skin turned rose gold in the summer, and her amber eyes were long-lashed and starkly angular. In Israel tourists had often asked if they might photograph her.

"A real Sabra," they would say admiringly. "You see what it is to be born in a land of sunlight and milk and honey." She never told them that she had been born in Poland and that she had spent such a long time hidden in darkness, eating scraps and drinking dregs, that her first glimpse of the sun had frightened and blinded her and her first taste of whole milk had produced a violent vomiting attack.

"You're certainly not a little girl anymore," Michael said. "Jeremy wrote me about you, but I thought he was exaggerating." (*Mindell is a dream to look at,* Jeremy had written, but he had said little more about her, although he had worked hard at arranging the fellowship for her.)

"You also look different than I remember," she said shyly.

He was thinner than she remembered. His faded jeans and paint-spattered T-shirt hung loosely on his slender frame. His thick dark hair was too long and unevenly cut.

"I suppose I am different," he said. "A great deal has happened to me." Kemala had happened to him. And Mississippi. He had been in search of meaning, and he had found it. Or thought he had found it. Strange how the clarity he had perceived that night in Golden Gate Park, that afternoon when his students had so exuberantly read the word "Freedom," was now shadowed, obscured. *What am I doing here?* he had wondered one afternoon that summer when only two students had shown up for his afternoon tutorial. But then Kemala had come the next day, and again his doubts had abated, but not his memory of them.

"Do you like it here in Mississippi?" Mindell asked as they walked out into the glaring sunlight.

" 'Like' is not a word that I'd couple with Mississippi," he said. "But yes. There is a lot about it I like." *The pink glow of the rows of cotton plants at twilight, the sweet singing of the mockingbirds, the intense concentration on Rodney Mason's upturned face as he grasped a new concept, the scent of Mrs. Mason's corn bread drifting through the half-light of dawn. Kemala.*

"Why were those people in the waiting room staring so angrily at me?"

"You sat down on a bench that's reserved for the blacks. This is Mississippi. Whites and blacks don't sit on the same benches, drink from the same water fountain, go to the same schools. It's called segregation. You've heard about it."

"Oh, I've heard about it. But I never saw it. There were no blacks on the bus coming south."

"You came at an hour when working people don't travel, and most blacks are working people."

"I see." Her voice was very quiet, her amber eyes shadowed.

"It's strange to you."

"No." She got into the car, a battered convertible, its New York license plates caked with mud. In Israel they were wary of mud-caked license plates. Such vehicles were often driven by terrorists who hoped to avoid identification. She looked at Michael curiously. "It's all too familiar to me. Almost a déjà vu. The Nuremberg Laws were also laws of segregation. Jews weren't allowed to go to the same schools as Gentiles, to work together—later they couldn't even ride the same buses. Of course, the Germans called it the 'Laws of Racial Purity,' but it was segregation. My parents were its victims. For whites only. For Aryans only. It amounts to the same thing."

"There are signs in the South," Michael said, "that say 'No Dogs or Negroes Allowed.' "

"There were signs in Germany that said 'No Jews or Dogs Allowed.' "

"A curious parallel."

"Perhaps that is why so many Jews are involved in the civil rights movement—because they remember," she said.

"Most of the Jews I know in the movement don't think much about their Jewishness," he observed.

"It's not what they think, it's what they feel." Mindell's voice was vague, as though she were sifting her own feelings. "Do you have many friends here, Michael?"

"Well, it is my third summer in Mississippi, so I know a lot of people." His third summer of sleeping in a back room in the Masons' tiny house, of seeing Kemala at her whim, of teaching his strange assortment of students in the sweltering classroom, which he had slowly improved each year. He had added bulletin boards and bookshelves, sanded the floors, and painted the walls. This summer he would add a small room to serve as a library. Books were being solicited in the North. And things had slowly happened. Four of his students had passed the literacy test and would vote this fall. Elementary school students were opting for academic courses in high school. That spring James Meredith, whom Michael had met at a party, had been accepted as the first black student at the University of Mississippi, and he was scheduled to enroll in the fall. Of course, Governor Ross Barnett had vowed to keep him out, but there was little doubt that he would be registered. Robert Kennedy had said as much, and this wasn't even an election year.

Michael no longer berated himself for the schizophrenic quality of his life—summers teaching the students of the Delta, whose lives were bounded by poverty and desperation, and the rest of the year teaching at Hutchinson College, where his students were born to privilege and wealth. The Hutchinson coeds' gleaming teeth had been straightened by expensive orthodontists, their skin tended by armies of dermatologists, their gentle minds cultivated in wide-windowed rooms by soft-voiced teachers, comforting mentors who encouraged them to read Dickinson and Hesse. They were kind girls. The Hutchinson Student Council had underwritten the library he was building at the Troy schoolhouse. The family of a Hutchinson girl would underwrite a scholarship for a Delta child at a progressive northern preparatory school. In certain ways Michael's separate experiences merged.

In Mississippi he slept in the rear of the Masons' house and avoided the cars of the White Citizens Council members, who routinely cruised the roads. In New York he lived in the Eldridge Street apartment with Jeremy and Les. He went to parties with them and danced with beautiful young women with long, clean hair who did research for *American Heritage,* answered letters for *Newsweek*, worked as teachers and social workers. Occasionally he went to bed with a girl whose name he could not remember the next week. In

Mississippi he waited stoically for Kemala to appear in the doorway, for a scavenged hour, a stolen afternoon or evening.

He had inured himself to his family's unarticulated disapproval of his life.

"Mama's not happy about your going back to Mississippi," Aaron had told him just before he left for the South. Across the room Lydia worked a jigsaw puzzle with Paulette and looked at Aaron warningly. Small David toddled about the room pulling a wooden toy crafted by one of Michael's Hutchinson students.

"I'm sorry about that," he had replied. "Was she happy when you crossed the border and went to Canada to enlist? When Rebecca went to Israel? When you went to Hungary? Did her unhappiness stop either of you?" His voice was bitter, accusatory. Was the cause he had found less worthy than those that had claimed his sister and brother? Was his work less important?

"That was different." Aaron's voice was tense, controlled.

"Was it? How?" Michael was skillful with the Socratic technique of the classroom—a question answered with a question, improbable parallels suggested, surprising balances revealed.

"Never mind." Wearily, Aaron accepted defeat. He had no appetite for intricate argument, for harsh dissent. He had, at last, found peace and happiness, and he would not endanger it. Always, when he entered his home, he was newly surprised by the sounds of his children's laughter, by Lydia's soft voice. The fragrance of his garden in the spring, of meat cooking on his barbecue, moved him to tears.

He wanted his brother and sister to share his contentment, his ease. But Rebecca's letters were redolent with melancholy. She had lived for so long at the edge of danger. The death of Yehuda's son, Noam, whom she had raised to young manhood, had stricken her with a fear so oppressive that she thought it might crush her. "We miss Noam terribly," she wrote to her family in America, and Aaron, who had always understood his younger sister so well, knew that Noam's death haunted her as past and portent. She and Yehuda had two young sons of their own, Yaakov and Amnon. They, too, would be soldiers in Israel's army. They, too, would court death. And Michael, whose life they had thought would be so calm, so safe, was caught up in the civil rights movement, vaulting closer to danger each year. There would soon be an end to songs and prayer vigils. Freedom riders were being beaten, but there would soon be deaths. Aaron wondered still if Michael would be as drawn to the South if Kemala were not there, but he did not raise the question. The uneasy peace between the brothers was built on a bridge of silence, and he would not jeopardize its fragile suspension.

"Be careful, Mikey," he had said, although it had been years since he had used the affectionate nickname. And when Mindell left to join him, Lydia prepared a food package for her to take south.

"Michael has a weakness for my stuffed cabbage," Lydia had said, and Mindell had not objected, although the food parcel was heavier than her knapsack.

"Lydia sent you a feast," she told Michael now, pointing to the box that he had placed between them in the car.

"Good," he said, smiling. "We'll have a party tonight. Lydia's cabbages and my mother's gefilte fish will make for a change in the diet down here. I'll call Neshoba and some of the kids'll come along. You'll like them, Mindell."

"I'm sure I will," she said.

He smiled. He thought her accent charming, and he was oddly proud of her beauty.

MICHAEL'S FRIENDS from Neshoba and from other neighboring towns gathered in the Troy schoolhouse that night, and Michael introduced Mindell to them. She smiled shyly at beautiful Kemala and shook hands with Matt Williams, who stared hard at her. She blushed beneath his arrogant, open appraisal and turned her eyes away.

"What's the matter?" he asked. "You seem uncomfortable."

"In my country men do not stare at women like that," she replied.

"In your country. Ah yes, in the land of the Jews," he said. His melodic West Indian accent was not without a discernible hardness. "I am told that in your country women do army service."

"That's true."

"And did you do army service?"

"Before my medical studies." She did not like to discuss her army service. She had disliked the regimentation, the discipline, and she had never been able to overcome her aversion to uniforms. She had spent her childhood hiding from uniformed men and women. Even in Israel the presence of uniformed soldiers made her uncomfortable, and she had to remind herself that Jewish stars, not swastikas, adorned the epaulets of the military garb worn by the soldiers she saw on the streets of Tel Aviv and Jerusalem. Uniforms meant war, and war meant death. Even her own uniform repelled her. The other girls in her unit adjusted their maroon berets to a jaunty angle, smoothed their collars, but Mindell never looked in the mirror. Once she had caught sight of her own reflection in a shop window on Dizingoff Street, and the image of her uniformed self caused her palms to sweat, her throat to go dry.

"Did you learn self-defense?" Matt Williams persisted.

"Yes."

"Can you shoot a rifle?"

"And a handgun," she said harshly. She turned her back on him and joined a group of volunteers who were discussing the summer program.

"We have to reach as many people as we can," a girl wearing a Radcliffe sweatshirt said. "This is the last year of groundwork before we begin our real campaign. I wish we could do some basic medical training. Nutrition. First aid. That sort of thing. We'll need it when a full-scale freedom school program gets under way."

"King and Rustin are talking about a march on Washington next year. They think they can get almost a hundred thousand people to demonstrate," said a tall blond youth who wore his long hair in a ponytail.

"It will never happen." Kemala walked to the window and lifted the black shade that they had carefully pulled down. A car cruised the lonely road, slowing perceptibly as it passed the Troy schoolhouse. "We can't even have a party in a black township with just a couple of blacks and whites without pulling down the shades and shivering whenever a car goes by. Do you think in a year's time we're going to be ready and able to march on Washington?"

"I think so," the Radcliffe girl said quietly.

She picked up a guitar and began to sing in a piercingly sweet voice. Other voices joined her and, in soft chorus, they finished the gentle, weary song and looked at one another, smiling sadly. The song exposed their hope and their uncertainty, and they had traveled so far to sing it together in this tiny schoolhouse. They had journeyed from Massachusetts and California, from Maine and Texas. They had confronted their parents' fears and disappointments, the cynical derisiveness of their peers. They had been frightened and ashamed of their fear. The Radcliffe girl slept always in a fetal position, training herself for the day of passive resistance when she would curl up to protect herself from police truncheons. The tall blond boy, a premed student at Swarthmore, had spent three days in a Delta prison because the registration of his car had somehow been questionable. He had spoken to no one for a week after his release, and a strange glaze had settled over his blue eyes. Yet he had stayed in Mississippi and had pledged to return again.

"A great song," Michael said when the room was quiet again.

"Well, you know what the Republicans said about the Spanish Civil War?" Matt Williams's sardonic voice shattered the mood. "They used to say, 'How come the Fascists won the war when we had the best songs?' " He laughed, and the hollow sound of his bitter mirth echoed against their embarrassed silence.

"Come on, Kemala," he said, and Mindell was surprised at how docilely Kemala put down her glass, pushed away her half-finished plate of food, and followed him out, pausing only for a moment to whisper something to Michael.

"They have to drive to Fayette," Michael said, as though an explanation were necessary, but Mindell did not reply. She had seen the hurt in Michael's eyes as Kemala hurried after Matt.

That night, she told Michael that she had decided to give up her cross-country trip and stay in Mississippi for the summer.

"But why?" he asked, although he felt a rush of pleasure.

"I'm not sure myself. Let me try to explain, though. In the camp, at night, the women used to whisper. 'Why can't *they* help? Why don't *they* do something?' Sometimes the whispers were moans. *They. They. They.* I used to wonder who *they* were. I knew only the prisoners and the guards. Later I realized, of course, that *they* were all those not in the camps—those who had freedom, the power to help, to protest. Tonight when I listened to your friends, I realized that now I am part of that mysterious *they*. It's a trick of history. Now I have freedom and I have some power. My medical training. I can do something. I can help set up the clinic, the nutrition program. I'll call Jeremy. He can get me supplies—he might even come down and help me organize. I think it will be a better way to see and understand America than riding a Greyhound bus from one national park to another." She smiled. There was no doubt in her decision, only a tinge of wonder that she had arrived at it with such clarity.

"What will Rebecca say?" Michael asked. His sister had wanted Mindell's stay in America to be careless and carefree, a respite from the danger and stress that had haunted her life.

"Rebecca's not my mother," she replied shortly. "Hitler gave me my independence. I don't need anyone's permission or approval."

He walked her to the village store then and watched from the counter as she called Jeremy in New York. Her voice was soft and her cheeks were very pink. She laughed twice and held the phone very close to her face, as he did when he spoke to Kemala.

"I'll be careful," he heard her say.

"Me too," he heard her whisper.

He turned away.

"Jeremy's a wonderful person," he said as they walked back to the Masons' house through the honeysuckle-scented darkness.

"Oh yes," she said. "I came to know him well when he visited Israel. He's so warm, so giving."

Michael wondered, as he held her arm so that she would not trip over the exposed root of a yucca plant, why her swift acquiescence to his own observation annoyed him.

THE POST arrived at Sha'arei ha-Negev after lunch, but it was not sorted until the late afternoon. Rebecca collected the Arnon family's mail after she had finished working at her studio. She read Mindell's letter as early-evening shadows slatted the sand crater. A hawk lazily circled the twin Christ's-thorn trees, and she shivered and reread the letter, struggling against an inexplicable sense of apprehension.

She passed the letter to Yehuda, who smiled at her. She was working on a skyscape, and her black hair was speckled with the same azulene blue that streaked her smock. A small carmine smudge on her cheek gave her the look of a small girl. His Becca. His long-legged, paint-spattered wife.

"Do you think Mindell is doing the right thing?" Rebecca asked worriedly. She had missed the softness in Yehuda's eyes, the stretch of his hand toward her. "It's dangerous in Mississippi." She read between the lines of Michael's letters, and she was victim to the transplanted American's addiction to the international edition of *Time*.

"Rivka—we can't hide from danger," Yehuda said tiredly. "You step off a curb on a London street, a motorcycle comes too fast, and you're in danger. You swim in the ocean and there is a sudden wave, an undertow." He shrugged, held his hands open in stoic acceptance. Slowly, he had reconciled himself to Noam's death. Noam had died wearing a uniform, but uncertainty and hazard hovered everywhere. There was no sanctuary from the dark forces of chance, the teasing vagaries of fortune. Soldiers returned from wars unscathed; a child chased after a ball on a quiet street and was crushed to death by a speeding car.

"But Mindell is so vulnerable, so trusting," Rebecca said. "Still, it is her life. And she is so excited, so enthusiastic." *I feel my work in Mississippi can make a difference,* Mindell had written. Rebecca had written a similar letter to her mother when she had decided to stay on in Israel and help with the illegal immigration, so many years ago. Leah had not protested then. Rebecca would not protest now.

"I'll tell you what, Rivka," Yehuda said. "I will be in the States this summer. There is a conference in Washington on terrorism. I'll go down to Mississippi again to see our Mindell. Does that make you feel better?"

She nodded and turned away so that he would not see the hurt in her eyes. He had not mentioned this trip to America before, nor had he asked her to join him. He bent to kiss the carmine smudge on her cheek, but she averted her head.

She wrote cheerful letters to Michael and Mindell that night, enclosing sketches of the kibbutz—the children on the swings in their desert playground, the shadowed peace of the avocado grove at dusk.

MATT was standing at the window when Kemala entered, a glass of ice water in his hand. They kept a supply of beer in the battered refrigerator, but Matt Williams drank only water, filling glass after glass from the discolored plastic jug that squatted amid the disorder of his desk.

"Beer's a luxury," he'd said wryly once. "When I don't have to be in control of my thoughts twenty-four hours a day, I'll indulge."

"What's happening?" Kemala asked now. She was sensitive to the atmosphere in the office and knew that something had happened during her absence.

She had been in Troy all afternoon, helping Mindell in the clinic while Michael tutored Rodney Mason for the Stevens School scholarship examination. She spent more and more time with Mindell during her visits to Troy. A natural rapport existed between Kemala and the young Israeli woman. They were both orphaned survivors of hatred. They recognized the dangers that confronted them and their own vulnerability, yet they did not retreat to safety. Shortly after Mindell's arrival they had walked down Neshoba's Main Street together, aware of the leering stares of the young men who lingered on the corner during the lazy, hot afternoons. Contempt and desire mingled in damp eyes; harsh laughter and graphic gesture trailed them. They did not break their pace, nor did they look back.

"Are you frightened?" Mindell had asked Kemala.

"Of course."

They had laughed in acknowledgment of both their fear and their power. They held their heads erect, but their hands trembled.

Often, during recent weeks, they had talked about their childhoods with intense intimacy. They had traded sweet memories, secret dreams. Mindell told Kemala how she had once imagined herself in love with a Swedish volunteer who had spent a winter on the kibbutz. Kemala confided that she had once written long letters that she never sent to a distinguished Berkeley professor. She had even hidden behind a tree near his home and had caught a glimpse of his wife, who was surprisingly unattractive.

"She wore space shoes," Kemala told Mindell, and they laughed with the pride of young women who encase their narrow feet in slender strapped sandals.

But they never spoke of Michael Goldfeder, not even that afternoon as his gentle voice hummed patiently through the wall that separated the clinic and the schoolroom.

"Did you see Michael?" Matt asked her now. Matt had no trepidation about discussing Michael. Increasingly that summer, he had prodded Kemala to talk about him and about the Goldfeder family. He teased her with a controlled bitterness about her visits to Troy. Seldom now did he offer to drive her.

"Only briefly. I helped Mindell in the clinic. But I asked you what was going on here."

She had sensed a grimness as soon as she entered the office. The two organizers in the rear of the room were speaking in soft, desperate tones, and Danny Green, the Harvard law student who served as their legal adviser, was on the phone.

"You must show cause," Danny was saying. "This is still the United States of America. You cannot make an arbitrary arrest." He listened and then said again, "The law is clear. You must show cause." His voice was weary, and he wiped his forehead with a red calico handkerchief. Kemala wondered why all the legal volunteers were addicted to those handkerchiefs. Perhaps it made them feel more authentic, more indigenous to the scene on which they had descended. Still, it was a harmless enough affectation, and Danny Green worked very hard and weathered Matt's sarcasm with relative ease.

"They pulled over a car on the Fayette road. Arrested three of our kids and smacked them around pretty badly," Matt said. "Three nice black Tougaloo boys. One of them was beaten senseless."

Kemala sat down and braced herself against a wave of nausea. The summer's casualties were mounting. Two freedom riders had been pulled off a bus the previous week and pistol-whipped. A small boy had been beaten by a gang of white teenagers for distributing voter-registration materials. He was still in a coma in the Bolivar County Hospital. She touched Matt's hand. His face was a mask of grief.

"I'm so sorry," she said.

"We're all sorry. We've got to stop being sorry and start doing something." His fists clenched and unclenched, and she thought that this was how he must have looked when he learned about the fire that took his parents' lives.

One by one the others left the office, speaking softly, as though they were withdrawing from a house of mourning.

"I don't know what we can do unless Kennedy sends some federal marshals down. It would help if those arrests and beatings got some coverage. Nothing seems to happen in this country unless there's a media blitz," Danny Green said as he left. He was only a law student, but already he had lost faith in the law.

"Well, we're going to do something," Matt said. "Goddamn it, I recruited two of those kids myself."

"What are you going to do, Matt?" Kemala asked when they were alone.

"We're going to make sure that the next time an arrest is made, the kids who are arrested are white. And important enough so that the news of their arrests gets out of this state and hits a couple of wire services and national networks."

She shivered suddenly, although the evening was warm. She reached for her light blue cashmere cardigan and draped it over her shoulders. Her fingers caressed the soft wool, played with the tiny pearl buttons.

"There are assignments that your friend Michael Goldfeder could undertake for us," Matt continued. "This is his third summer in Mississippi. It's time he got out of the schoolroom and onto the highway. Didn't you tell me that he wanted to be a hero like his lawyer brother? We'll do him a favor, Kemala. We'll give him his chance."

"I can't let you do that." Her voice was a whisper.

"Listen to me, Kemala." He whirled her about so that she faced him. The light blue sweater, Michael's gift, fell to the floor. Matt's fingers cut into her shoulders, and she saw the lines of pain etched across his face, the shadow of sorrow in his eyes. "We cannot go on playing games. You are not a little girl, balancing on a seesaw, deciding to go up one minute and down another. You have to make a decision, demonstrate a commitment. Where do you belong? Are you with me, or are you going to continue playing house with Dr. Michael Goldfeder, who lends us two months of his life each summer?"

"You don't understand," she said, but she heard the uncertainty in her protest. As always she swayed beneath the relentless fury of Matt's argument. As always she perceived the pain that engendered his desperate anger.

"Do you understand yourself?" he retorted and slammed out of the office.

She watched from the window as he strode down the street. She saw how thin he had become. In recent weeks he had developed a slight facial tic. Often, in the night, he cried out in subdued anguish. The others saw his strength, felt his power, but Kemala felt his sorrow and understood the source of his zealous intensity. His moods became Kemala's own. His needs hypnotized her.

She bent and picked the sweater up, brushed away the specks of dirt that clung to it. Michael had chosen it carefully. He cared for her, protected her, but her struggle in the end was not his struggle. Leah, his mother, had said as much that distant Thanksgiving day. "*My* people . . . *your* people . . ." Leah Goldfeder had seen the separations between them, the borders they could neither erase nor cross.

And Michael did not need her as Matt did. Michael had his career, his family. Matt had only his cause and Kemala herself. He was right. The time of choice had come. She stood at the crossroads she had so often dreamed about and she knew, with absolute certainty, which path she would choose.

MINDELL." Michael's voice was very soft. He did not want to wake the two Mason girls who slept beside her in the tiny room. She did not stir, and he touched her shoulder. She blinked resistantly into the predawn darkness and smiled, caught still in a lingering dream. He shook her lightly, and she awakened at last and stared up at him. He waited until the recognition and understanding of wakefulness overtook her, lifted his finger to his lips, and tiptoed out of the room.

Of course. She remembered now that they had agreed with Matt Williams that it would be safer and cooler to start out before daylight. Swiftly, silently, she dressed and washed. Jeans and a T-shirt. An extra pair of underpants, her toothbrush, and a small tube of toothpaste ("The prison size, we call it," Kemala had said, giving it to her) in her bag just in case of arrest. There was no real danger, of course. She and Michael were simply driving from Troy to Meridian to pick up a shipment of books for the new district Freedom Library. Still, Mindell's weeks in Mississippi had taught her that there were no simple excursions. Only last week two Brandeis students had been arrested for driving two miles over the speed limit in Madison. They had been held for seventy-two hours and released after the movement office had paid a hundred-dollar fine. The girl had left the state the next day, her face bloated with grief. Some said that she had been raped by a guard. Others said she had merely been threatened, terrorized. Mindell wanted to tell them that a very thin line separated terror from realization and that in some cases the terror was worse. *Let them kill me. I'm so tired of being afraid,* a woman had screamed into the darkness of the barracks.

The Brandeis boy had developed a facial tic. He could not walk down the road without twisting his head in an involuntary spastic gesture.

"Nerves," Mindell had said brusquely when he came to the clinic to see her. She had given him a sedative, advised him to sleep more.

"I'm afraid to sleep," he said fiercely. In the night specters of his own fear visited him, controlled him. Huge roaches had crept across his body in the Madison jail. He had been placed in a cell with a half-crazed felon who had threatened him. "I'll get you, you nigger lover. I'll cut your balls off, you bastard. Go home before we send you home in a crate." The man had spat at him, urinated on him, and now the smell of sour breath and rancid wastes permeated his dreams.

Remembering him now, Mindell put a small box of raisins in her bag and added a chocolate bar. A survival hint from Rebecca, who had also moved covertly through the darkness in Palestine during illegal immigration operations. It occurred to her that a childhood spent in Auschwitz and Mandate Palestine was not bad training for Mississippi in the sixties. She took up her medical bag and tiptoed out of the room, closing the door softly against the throaty whisper of fourteen-year-old Dora Lee Mason, who often talked and sang in her sleep.

Michael checked the car carefully before they started out. Water. Gas tank full. Spare tire and repair kit neatly in place. He moved methodically, talking to himself as he checked off each chore. Rebecca had the same habit, Mindell remembered. Leah's children were so different from each other, yet in so many ways, in so many small habits, they were eerily alike.

Michael checked the jerry can in which he carried extra gasoline. They could not risk running out of fuel on a lonely Delta road where a New York license plate meant an enemy vehicle. Mindell understood now why Michael obscured his plates with mud.

"Do you need that?" he asked, pointing to her medical bag.

"Jeremy said never to travel without it," she replied.

He did not answer, and she wondered vaguely why he never asked her about Jeremy, who was, after all, his closest friend, his roommate. It was curious, she thought, that Jeremy, who had been raised in a household so bereft of Jewishness, should have become so involved in Judaism. But perhaps people searched for that which had been denied them—perhaps that was what had brought Michael to Mississippi. His own instinctive fairness and humanity coupled with a desire to break free of the net of security that had entrapped him from birth. That and Kemala.

"Look!" she cried, pointing skyward. "The morning star."

A phosphoreal taper of light ignited the darkness; moody Venus flirted with sleepbound Earth.

A fortunate omen, she decided, and sat back and tried to relax as Michael drove down the road, slowly because he did not want to be stopped for speeding, but not too slowly because civil rights workers had been arrested for driving below a requisite speed. They were diligent students of a lexicon of fear and caution. Keep your eyes on the speedometer. Don't stop for gas. If you must stop, speak as little as possible. Accents were revealing. Never pick up hitchhikers, black or white. Too often, hitchhikers were planted by the sheriff and made accusations of molestation, a charge that was almost impossible to disprove.

They drove westward and watched the darkness lift languorously; layer by layer it drifted from an ever-lightening mist into a dazzling lucency. The meadowlands were blanketed with white and yellow dwarf dandelions, black-eyed susans, and purple wood violets. Droplets of dew hovered tenuously on the fragile flowers, and hooded warblers sang teasingly to one another from clusters of mountain laurel. Their days in Mississippi were so consumed by work and meetings, so preoccupied with feelings of fear and desperation, courage and hope, that there was no time to notice the beauty of the countryside. Mindell remembered suddenly the day of her liberation from the camp. As she was carried out of the barracks, she had stared at a rosebush that grew just outside the stark and terrible building. The guards had passed the flowers as they entered and left the building, but the beauty and fragrance of the blossoms had not softened them. Once a brave prisoner had covertly plucked a flower, and it had been given to the children hidden in the tunnel. They had passed it from hand to hand, and small Shlomo, who had been with her when she entered Palestine, had wept when it wilted and faded. Shlomo now lived in a moshav, a small collective, on the Lebanese border, and many rosebushes grew in his garden. His flowers won prizes in the Israel Horticultural Competition, but none of them, he complained to Mindell, were as beautiful as the flower of freedom they had caressed in the darkness of their hiding place. The roses of Auschwitz had been pink, she remembered, with golden tendrils at their hearts; red and white roses of a rare fullness and fragrance grew in the meadow where Michael eventually stopped for breakfast.

"I've never seen roses like these before," she said.

"Cherokee roses." He handed her a hard-boiled egg and a slice of the corn bread that Mrs. Mason baked late each night. Kemala had taught him the names of the blossoms. The women of her father's family had crushed the petals, dried them, and used them for sachet bags.

"They're beautiful," Mindell said. She had the desert dweller's reverence for flowers.

He plucked one from a laden bush and handed it to her. The bramble tore his skin. She threaded it through her hair, and he saw that its redness blended with the blush that rose slowly from her neck and crested at her cheeks.

"You're bleeding," she said, looking at his finger.

"It's nothing."

But she took his hand in her own, studied the small cut, and reached for her medical bag. Gently, she dabbed at it with peroxide and affixed a small Band-Aid to it. Her fingers were deft and flew across his skin lightly, easily. The tiniest ribbon of blood escaped the Band-Aid, and she licked it away.

"Your blood tastes terrible," she said.

"Your tongue feels good," he replied, and at once they both averted their eyes, as though they had strayed past an invisible boundary.

"Are you glad you stayed in Mississippi, Mindell?" he asked.

The question broke the silence that had grown between them.

She leaned back and considered.

"Not glad. Not sorry. I know only that I could not have left. You know, when I was a small girl, I used to make a list of all the people who had died. My parents. My sister and brother. Cousins. Friends. My list went on forever. Then I would think: if they all died and I was saved, perhaps there was a reason for it. Maybe I was spared for some purpose. And then it developed that I had a gift for healing. I was ten, and Danielle and I shared a kid—a small black-and-white speckled goat. It broke its leg, and the veterinarian was in Beersheba. I set it myself and it mended, and everyone was surprised because the animal walked almost without a limp. I thought then: ah, I was saved to help the goat. Once in medical school I drew the night shift. A little girl went into cardiac arrest, a Bedouin child with a congenital defect. I was on the pediatric ward and there wasn't a minute to spare. I slit the thoracic cavity, exposed the heart, and massaged it back into life. I thought again: ah, I was saved to help this child. Very egocentric, I know, but I was young and I had invested a lot of emotional energy into making up those lists. After my second year on the wards I stopped thinking like that. I wouldn't let myself. That first day in Neshoba, at the bus station, I felt that I was being pushed back in time. I wasn't in Mississippi, in the United States. I was in Auschwitz, in Poland. And that night at the party when Andrea, the girl from Radcliffe, spoke about the need for a clinic, the thought came back for the first time in years: I was saved to help with this clinic. Kemala told me that she's in Mississippi, working with Matt, because of her father. I think I'm really here because of my parents. Because you can't walk away from hatred, from any kind of hatred. If you do, you become an accessory to it. I don't want to become part of the *they* who never saw the smoke from the chimneys or smelled the burning flesh or who skipped over the Reuters reports on the 'actions' against Jews. I don't want to be part of the *they* who sat in waiting rooms and read signs that said 'No Jews or Dogs Allowed.' I had to stay. Perhaps I didn't accomplish much, but I was here, I did something. My being saved mattered."

She thought back now to the work she had done during her brief weeks in Troy. She had opened the clinic and treated a stream of civil rights workers for diarrhea and depression. ("What drugs do you need?" Jeremy had asked in their initial conversation. "Pepto-Bismol and Valium," she had told him. He had sent them in equal quantities, and she had dispensed them in equal quantities.) She had held workshops in nutrition and first aid for the black community.

She had announced that she would conduct a well-baby clinic on consecutive Mondays.

The first week, only one fifteen-year-old girl had wandered in, carrying an infant who cried incessantly.

"I reckon he's got the colic," the girl, who was no more than a child herself, had said.

Mindell had taken the child's fever, studied his inflamed throat, and administered an antibiotic that Jeremy had luckily included. Two days later the baby was chortling happily, the fever broken, the throat normal. The next week ten women appeared at the well-baby clinic with their children, and the third week there was a line when she arrived.

She had stitched up the split forehead of a Harvard senior who had been attacked as he walked home through the darkened streets after distributing voter-registration pamphlets. He had never seen his attackers, only heard their strident voices.

"Go home, nigger lover."

"Hey, commie, tell Meredith this is what's waiting for him the day he tries to register at Ole Miss."

She had sewn eleven stitches, working carefully, but the youth would always carry a scar to remind him of his nocturnal walk through Troy. What would happen to James Meredith, the first black student to be admitted to the University of Mississippi, when he tried to register that fall? she wondered.

Throughout those weeks she had watched Michael Goldfeder. She had watched his eyes light up when Kemala Jackson came to Troy, and she had seen his eyes darken when Kemala left.

"I'm so tired," Kemala had said to Mindell one heat-bound afternoon and Mindell had understood that Kemala was complaining not of ordinary fatigue but of a deep inner exhaustion. She was like a swimmer battling the undertow of the past, the inexorable waves of the future, unable to float on the brief calm of the present. Matt and Michael each called to her, and she grew weary of trying to please and placate. Soon, Mindell knew, Kemala would make a choice. Soon, Michael would have to recognize what had for so long been apparent.

Her heart turned for Michael, who was so caring, so good. She watched him teach his classes, watched him teach the serious-eyed boy from Sebastopol who wrote poetry but could not spell, watched him teach Dora Lee Mason how to do long division, his fingers guiding hers because she had never learned to hold a pencil properly.

Michael was a born teacher. Even when he played softball with the small black children in the evening cool, he taught. "Toss it a little higher, a little wider. Bend those knees when you run. Come on Timmy, Rodney! Make believe you've got wings on those sneakers." Always, she would remember Michael teaching the children of Troy how to hold a bat, how to leap for a fly ball. Always, she would remember Michael, lithe and fleet-footed, flashing past the white-washed base marks he had painted into the dry red earth.

"Yes, I'm glad I stayed," she said, answering his question at last.

"I'm glad you did also," he said quietly. How careful and caring Mindell was. And how brave. She had volunteered at once to take this trip with him when Matt Williams discussed it.

"It's a simple enough operation," Matt had said. "We want to move these books from Meridian to Neshoba, and you've got a car available, Michael. The school can spare you for a day, I think." Always, when Matt spoke to him, Michael sensed the West Indian's parched contempt, his thinly veiled condescension.

"I imagine so," he said, trying to match the dryness of Matt's tone.

"We'd like someone to go with you. Not that we anticipate any problem, but we like our people to travel in teams. Just in case."

He did not specify the possibilities, but they had been in Mississippi long enough to predict them. *Just in case you are arrested and beaten. Just in case one of you is hurt. Just in case of an accident, an incident, a disappearance.*

Michael's eyes had found Kemala's. She stared back at him and turned back to the mysterious lists she was forever compiling on yellow legal pads. Lists of professors who could be solicited to endorse national advertisements urging Ross Barnett not to violate academic freedom and to peaceably admit James Meredith to Ole Miss; lists of registered voters in various townships; lists of editors of local newspapers and the key advertisers in those newspapers.

"Kemala's too busy," Matt Williams said. "We're drafting a petition asking Burke Marshall to give us more federal assistance. Let the FBI stop trying to find out if Martin Luther sleeps with someone besides Coretta and use that talent on freedom-rider protection."

"Are you too busy, Kemala?" Michael asked.

"I'm too busy." Her voice was throaty, very low.

"Maybe the lady doctor," Matt suggested.

"Of course, I'll go with you, Michael." Mindell's assent had been immediate, and she surprised herself. It was the first assignment she had undertaken outside the clinic, but she had seen the hurt in Michael's eyes when Kemala spoke.

"Good. That's settled, then." Matt had given them maps, instructions, directions. For the first time, he was almost pleasant; he shed his cynical veneer and allowed them to see his humor, the genuineness of his involvement. It had occurred to Mindell that the books could be shipped, but she had said nothing. They had their reasons, she supposed, and besides, she had begun to look forward to the respite from clinic chores, to the excursion with Michael. And her anticipation had not been misplaced. There was a holiday quality to the day—their shared picnic breakfast, the brightly hued Cherokee rose, which she pinned more firmly now into the golden coil of her braid.

They had no trouble finding the address in Meridian. The boxes of books filled the trunk, and they piled the remaining cartons onto the back seat and the floor of the car. Somehow their bulk reassured Mindell. They had not been shipped because the cost of shipping would have been prohibitive. Books overflowed the corrugated carton containers. She smiled at the titles. A full set of the Oz books. She had not known that there were others besides the story of the Wizard that she had read in Hebrew. The children of the kibbutz had once put on a play based on the Oz story. Perhaps the other volumes had not been translated into Hebrew. *Huckleberry Finn*. Yehuda Arnon's son, Noam, had loved Huckleberry Finn and his confederate, Tom Sawyer. Noam and his best friend, Yair, had played at being Huck and Tom, even building a raft, which they pretended to sail on the sands of the Negev. But Noam was dead and Yair limped badly as a result of a wound sustained during the same attack that had taken his friend's life. The innocence of their boyhood had been betrayed by the terrible reality of their young manhood. Mindell stood on the Mississippi road and grieved anew for the fallen soldier who had been like a brother to her.

Abruptly, she banished her grief and asked the Meridian volunteer for some rope. She and Michael tied together the loose volumes of the Childcraft encyclopedia (donated by the children of Hastings, New York, to the children of Troy, Mississippi), so that they would not slide about. There were ten paperback copies of the United States Constitution and twenty more of the constitution of the state of Mississippi. These were needed, she knew, because the Troy registrar administered an examination on a section of the state constitution to prospective voters.

"Goddamn it, we'll get our people to memorize them if we have to," Michael had exploded angrily when a black woman whom he had coached for the third summer failed yet again. The copies of the constitution had headed the list of books he had requested.

They ate lunch with the Meridian volunteers, who were scrupulous about pulling down the shades and moving the table away from the windows.

"Someone fired at the window for no damn reason, just last week," Amos, a black lawyer from Chicago, said wearily. "I guess they're all in training for September, getting their target practice in. The word is that Ross Barnett has called on every Mississippian to do battle to preserve the honor of their schools. They're planning a big 'Save Our Schools' rally sometime soon. Drive carefully on your way back."

"I'm not worried," Michael replied. "I'm an American citizen traveling at the correct speed limit in an inspected, licensed vehicle filled with copies of *Huckleberry Finn* and the Constitution of these United States."

"Oh, you'd be safe all right if you were in the United States," Amos said. "But you're in Mississippi. We had a volunteer arrested here two summers ago for walking down the street. 'Parading without a permit,' the charge read. I had to keep from busting out laughing in the middle of my argument. 'Parading without a permit.' "

They all laughed, but Mindell noticed that the Meridian team stayed inside when she and Michael left. Real fear concealed itself beneath their laughter.

The full heat of the afternoon hit them as they drove back. Mindell's cotton T-shirt clung to her body, and Michael's blue chambray shirt was stained with dark patches of sweat. They took a different route now and passed no meadowlands blanketed with wildflowers.

"Not too much longer," Michael said as they passed the Okatibee Reservation. His eyes were glazed and red-rimmed.

"Do you want me to drive?" she asked.

"No, I'm fine." His voice was weary but firm, and she was relieved. A torpid drowsiness had been trailing her, and she submitted to it now and allowed herself to doze off. Her head rested on Michael's shoulder, and she thought she felt his hand gently stroke her hair, rest lightly on the red rose, wilted now but still bravely fragrant. The rose of Auschwitz had also kept is fragrance long after its petals had wilted and faded. She slept then, rocked by the motion of the car; she surrendered herself to the vagrant, brief dreams of the sleeping traveler. They drifted in sequential tableau.

She was a child dashing across the sandy dunes of Sha'arei ha-Negev. She was chasing after Noam, but he was too swift for her. He wore his summer scout uniform with a pale blue ascot knotted at his neck. He tossed the ascot to her, and she used it to wipe her tears. Why was she crying? "Noam!" she called, but he did not turn, and she understood that she wept because Noam was dead.

She was a young woman standing beside a cypress tree on a Jerusalem hillside. She wore her white medical jacket over her reservist uniform. Why was she dressed in such a manner? Did she need a uniform to protect her from the beauty of the evening, from the urgent entreaty of the young soldier who stood beside her? Yair. Noam's friend. Poor crippled Yair, who had loved her from childhood. He had wanted to marry her. He had not wanted her to leave Israel. He pulled her to him, and the khaki fabric of his shirt was harsh against her cheek. "I'm sorry, Yair."

Uniforms trailed her everywhere, haunted her. A man strode through the mists of her dream, a stern-featured man, red-faced, wearing a gray uniform, carrying a black leather truncheon. The insignia of the death's head glinted at his epaulets. His voice was harsh, terrible. He would make small Shlomo cry. But he was not speaking German. He was speaking English. A strange and slow and terrible English that she struggled to comprehend.

Her eyes opened. He did not belong to the dream. He belonged to reality—to the reality of the unremitting heat, the cracked red earth, the total silence and desolation of the Delta landscape. And the reality, too, of Michael's hand, gentle on her shoulder (as it had been gentle that morning when he awakened her, and gentle on her hair as she drifted into the odd, dreamlike sleep). Michael's voice was controlled, although she saw the tremor in his fingers, the rim of sweat that mustached his mouth. Her own heart beat rapidly, arrhythmically, and her throat was dry. A knot of nausea was entangled at the pit of her stomach.

"Come on, Mindell. Let's get out. It will be all right. We haven't done anything."

Neither had the Harvard senior, she thought. Neither had the boy and girl from Brandeis. Neither, she thought irrelevantly, had her parents. It was not necessary to have done anything, she knew. But she nodded and followed him out of the car into the seething heat, the dazzling daylight.

"Up against the car!"

The orders were issued by one officer, but three others were waiting as they emerged from the car—three red-faced men, sweating freely in the oppressive heat, the dark pants of their uniforms clinging to their thick thighs, their pale stomachs spilling out of white shirts buttoned to the neck. Their neat black ties, too, were firmly in place, but their leather shoulder holsters were empty. They held their service revolvers cocked and aimed at Michael and Mindell. Their eyes glinted with hatred.

"What y'got there, girl?"

Instinctively, she had seized her black leather bag.

"My medical bag. I'm a doctor." She held it tighter.

"Yeah. And I'm president of the Yew-Nited States." His club smashed down on her wrist. She screamed with pain and dropped the bag.

"Hey!" Michael lurched forward, but two of the men grabbed him and held him back, twisting his arms behind his back.

"I'm all right, Michael," she said. The pain was searing, but no bones were broken. She moved her wrist, flexed her fingers, and wondered that she did not cry.

"Are you armed, boy?"

They were both pressed up against the car now, and the officers' hands were prowling their bodies, probing at fabric and skin. They removed Michael's driver's license but did not open it. He was relieved that his identity was still unknown.

Mindell felt the officer's fingers against her breasts, beneath her arms. An animal's paws against her body's vulnerable softness. ("Always I think of them as animals, not as humans," a woman prisoner in the camp had said. "An animal cannot insult me, humiliate me.") The Mississippi officer was an animal, and thus she felt neither violated nor repelled. As though sensing her indifference, he thrust her aside. Beads of saliva foamed at the corners of his mouth. He searched the car now, overturning the carefully packed cartons. A child's picture book flew open. Cinderella in her chariot. His booted foot came down on the golden coach. He spat, and a gob of green phlegm spread across the bright jacket of *The Wizard of Oz*.

"You're under arrest," he said.

"On what charge?" Michael, the American, demanded his rights. Mindell, the child of Auschwitz, had forgotten she had any.

"Title ninety-seven of the Mississippi Code of Law. Transporting obscene literature across the state."

"Cinderella. The Wizard of Oz. The Constitution of the United States—obscene literature?" Michael asked. Honest amusement light-

ened his tone. He invited them to smile with him, to see how ridiculous the charge was.

"Shut up, Jewboy!"

The bull club slammed down across his kidneys. Once. Again. Waves of pain washed over him. Again. He had screamed, he knew, because his throat was raw, but the soft weeping he heard, he acknowledged with relief, was not his own but Mindell's.

"Don't touch her."

He thought his voice could only emerge as a whisper, but it was strong, almost imperious, and he was briefly proud of his own courage. Their reply was immediate, spontaneous. A fist crashed down on his mouth. He tasted his own blood, moved his tongue about, relieved that his teeth were still in place. Someone else struck him on the forehead, just missing his eye. Mindell was crying, sobbing.

"I'm all right, Mindy," he whispered and slid to the ground. "Call Aaron." Had he said the words or only thought them?

The red earth was strangely soft and yielding. He wondered, as his mind slipped into darkness, how they had known he was Jewish when they had not even opened his driver's license.

YEHUDA ARNON sat on the patio that Aaron and Lydia had recently added to their home and gratefully sipped a tall tomato juice.

"Was it as hot as this in Washington?" Lydia asked and removed the pale blue sweatband from her forehead. She and Aaron still wore their tennis whites although they had abandoned their game after playing a single set. It was, they decided, the hottest day of a very hot summer.

"I'd say so. In every way," Yehuda replied. He shifted uncomfortably in the white wrought-iron chair. The air conditioning on the Eastern shuttle had stopped operating as they soared over Philadelphia, and his seersucker suit was drenched. He would finish his drink, place a call to Rebecca, shower, and change. "Some of the congressional advisers lost their perspective during the discussion."

"Still refusing to acknowledge the threat of internal terrorism?" Aaron asked shrewdly.

"Still clinging to the 'it can't happen here' theory of history. They're ready to accept the fact that civilian terrorism is on the rise all over the world. They know all about Algeria and Argentina, bombs on Jerusalem buses, explosions in Dublin factories. But the United States is presumed to be invulnerable to that kind of violence. They tell me that the Ku Klux Klan is a lunatic fringe group and doesn't amount to much on a national scale. And they do not believe me when I tell them that in the next decade terrorism and mob violence are going to increase dangerously."

"The balance has shifted in the South," Aaron said. "Martin Luther King's people are not going to be frightened away by hooded terrorists. There's bound to be a forceful reaction from southern extremists. We're beginning to see it already—the White Citizens Council, self-appointed vigilante groups. They say that in Mississippi it's not simply a question of law enforcement authorities turning a blind eye to harassment—it's more an established fact that sheriffs and their deputies are cooperating openly with the extremists."

He sighed and watched his children at play. Paulette, wearing a bright green sundress that Leah had designed and sewn for her, valiantly tried to teach David to play ring-around-a-rosie. Again and again the child tumbled over at the wrong time until Paulette, haughty with the righteous impatience of the older child, flounced away.

Yehuda, too, watched the children. It was night in Israel now, and his own sons were asleep in the children's house. He knew that at some point during the night, Rebecca would tiptoe through the darkness and stand silently beside their beds, as she had almost every night since Noam's death. What reassurance did that brief nocturnal vigil offer her? he wondered, but he had never asked her about it. It occurred to him now that the number of things that he and Rebecca did not speak of accrued dangerously with each passing year.

"The question is, Yehuda, can anything be done about that kind of civilian violence?" Lydia asked. She plucked a leaf out of Paulette's hair and showed the child how it exactly matched her dress.

"I think so. We've made some progress in Israel. There can be infiltration of such groups. Your FBI has been successful in infiltrating other organizations. Why not do the same with the White Citizens Council, the Klan, Ross Barnett's 'Save Our Schools' movement, black extremist groups if they arise? The federal government ought to be a visible presence in the South—teams of marshals, National Guardsmen. There should be an education program for southern judges and police officers. In Israel we have learned that there must be a policy of no compromise with terror, and the same can apply here. I tried to make this clear to Burke Marshall's people, but I don't think they were impressed. They probably labeled me a paranoid 'Jewboy.' " He shrugged. "I'll have a clearer picture after I visit Mindell and Michael in Troy."

He smiled down at Seth, the baby, who crawled toward him

across the patio. The baby's fingers gripped at his ankles, and Yehuda picked him up. Seth's tousled black curls filled him with a painful yearning for Rebecca and his own children. He decided suddenly that he would not return to Washington to report on his observations in Mississippi. He would send a report and leave for Israel.

The phone rang, and Lydia and Aaron looked at each other apprehensively.

"Damn," Aaron said. "You take it, Lydia. If it's the office, tell them I'm off on a three-day hike. Same thing if it's the university asking for my fall semester reading list."

"Take it yourself," Lydia retorted. "If it's the lab, tell them that all the children have chicken pox and I've run away from home."

The second ring came as David fell and scraped his knee. Lydia picked the child up, and Aaron strode toward the phone, catching it on the third insistent ring. The patio door was open and they heard him clearly, saw him automatically grope for a pad and pencil.

"Hello. Yes." Annoyance tinged his greeting, but Lydia saw his face blanch. "I'll accept the charges. Please. You must speak more slowly." His grip on the receiver was so tight that his knuckles whitened. "Where? Give me the exact address."

Lydia held Paulette closely. Only once before had she heard Aaron use that same tone and ask questions so warily. Although the August evening was warm, she felt a chill and was grateful for the pressure of Paulette's small body against her own.

"What was the charge exactly?" 'Aaron asked. She heard the fear in his voice and moved to his side.

"I'll be there as soon as I can," Aaron said. "You take care of yourself."

Slowly, he replaced the receiver. Paulette whimpered softly, and Lydia passed a soothing hand across the child, comforting her automatically, although she felt the stirring of a deep, remembered fear.

"What is it, Aaron?" Yehuda asked.

He motioned warningly toward the children.

"Paulette, take David upstairs and build a block house," Lydia said.

The children, who had been quarreling only moments before, scurried out of the room, hand in hand, as though relieved to escape the sudden tension. But Seth chortled happily and flailed a chubby arm into the air as a monarch butterfly fluttered lazily past him.

"It's Michael," Aaron said. "He's been arrested in Mississippi. A trumped-up charge. Something about endangering the morals of the children of the state. Transporting obscene literature. He's in jail. We've got to get down there as soon as we can, Yehuda."

"And Mindell?" Yehuda asked, his throat dry. He had remembered Mindell's fear of closed places, of uniforms and violence.

"It was Mindell who called. They let her go, at least. Saw her Israeli passport, I suppose, and decided that they didn't need an international incident. The racist bastards. Lydia, get on the phone and find out the quickest way for us to get to a town in Mississippi called Peachtree. I'm driving over to my mother's house. I don't want her to hear about this from a wire service." Aaron's voice was clipped, decisive.

"Aaron, you can't tell them. Leah won't be able to bear it." Lydia hugged Seth to her, kissed the pink shell of his ear, rested her cheek on his jet-colored ringlets.

"My mother will be all right," he replied curtly. "And Boris has heard worse."

He was right, of course, she realized. Boris had borne the loss of his family in Russia, the struggles of the remnant of Jewry that had survived. He had been jailed and knew the reality of prison. And Leah Goldfeder was a woman whose life had been shadowed by danger, riddled with loss. Still, she had struggled always, fought and survived. She would grow pale, her hands would tremble, but Leah's voice would be crisp, her actions determined. Lydia imagined her mother-in-law placing phone calls to Joshua Ellenberg, to friends in Washington, speaking softly, urgently, marshaling her forces. Weighted anew by her own fear, Lydia envied Leah her tenacity, her courage. She prayed then, in her native tongue, that Paulette, David, and Seth would inherit their grandmother Leah's unremitting strength. Tears stung her eyes, and Yehuda moved toward her and placed a comforting arm about her shoulder.

"He will be all right, Lydia," he said. He understood that she could not bear to confront another loss. She touched his hand lightly, grateful for the rapport that flashed between them. She remembered how brightly the sun had shone as they sipped their coffee on the isle of Rhodes.

"Yes. He will be all right." She reached for the phone, and as she dialed, she thought, *This is America, not Hungary, not Germany. We are safe here. This is America.* Perhaps, if she repeated the words often enough, she would at last begin to believe them.

THE COURTHOUSE in the town of Peachtree, Mississippi, was a small white building that was newly painted each spring and properly landscaped each fall. The encroaching kudzu vines were cut away, and the branches of the twin magnolia trees that flanked its approach were carefully pruned. The American flag, furling and unfurling in a gentle breeze, was hoisted on a glistening white flagpole. A plaque next to it listed the names of the young men of Peachtree who had fallen in service to their country. Aaron had noticed a similar plaque in front of the black Baptist church. Even in death the people of Peachtree were neatly segregated.

"It's a pity that the town of Peachtree doesn't give the American Constitution the same respect it gives the flag," Aaron said loudly to Les Anderson and Yehuda Arnon as they entered the building together. A police officer who overheard him stared sourly and spat onto the pavement, narrowly missing Aaron's shoe.

"Not a bad quote. Can I use it?" Les asked.

"You can use anything I say," Aaron replied. "And if you think of anything I should have said and didn't, let me know and I'll probably okay that, too."

"I might just do that. We're thinking in terms of a possible cover story. There's a twin angle here—censorship and violation of civil rights. If it works out—and I think it will, coming just before the Ole Miss brouhaha—I'll need every piece of material I can get." It was Les's instinct for the "twin angle" that had led to his rapid ascendancy at *Metro* magazine, where he was now features editor as well as a sometime field reporter.

Les's involvement did not surprise Aaron. He had known that his brother's friend and roommate would be both concerned about Michael and see the news value of the situation. And he had been a lawyer long enough to know how the media could influence a trial, even how they could quash an indictment. He would never forget how he and Katie had triumphed against the McCarthy committee—a carefully prepared press packet had resulted in a summary adjournment of the hearing.

Les had already filed his first story, an interview with Yehuda Arnon, international authority on terrorism. It had appeared in dozens of syndicated columns that morning.

"Mr. Arnon, how can you equate the arrest of Michael Goldfeder by law enforcement officers with what you call the phenomenon of terrorism?"

"There is a very fine line between harassment and terrorism."

"But the arresting officers were duly licensed by their state."

"As were the arresting officers who incarcerated Jews and Catholics and liberals in Germany in the thirties. Those arrests were also 'legitimate.' "

The interview had already caused some controversy, Aaron knew. Yehuda and Les had both chosen their words carefully and aimed them well.

Mindell waited for Aaron at the courthouse doorway. She wore the pale blue, long-sleeved dress and the carefully polished white sandals that Lydia had packed for her.

"Judges give different credence to the testimony of a girl in jeans and that of a young woman doctor in a neatly pressed dress and very clean shoes," Aaron had told her. "Same girl. Same facts. A different reaction. A stupid game, I know, but we have to play it."

"Uniforms," Mindell had said obliquely. "It all comes down to uniforms."

A small red-and-white rose was pinned to her collar, and he smiled at the courage of the gesture. A Cherokee rose. Katie had loved them. It was strange how he thought of Katie now with only lingering sadness, melancholy affection. She was a spectral memory, and he wondered sometimes if she had really existed, if he had really loved and married her. Lydia had so completely overtaken and filled his life. Lydia and his children, Paulette, David, and the baby, Seth. The recognition of his own good fortune strengthened his resolve to get his brother out of this mess.

"Are you all right?" Yehuda asked Mindell in Hebrew.

She nodded. "I'm fine. But they won't let me see Michael."

Yehuda looked at her closely. He discerned the desperate worry in her voice, the anguish in her eyes. Her voice had trembled when she said his name.

"It's Mississippi law," Aaron explained patiently. "They can hold a prisoner for seventy-two hours without bringing charges or admitting visitors. But you're not to worry, Mindell. I've seen him and we're going to get him out."

An officer stopped them at the courtroom door.

"I'm Aaron Goldfeder, attorney for Michael Goldfeder," Aaron said pleasantly. "And this is Yehuda Arnon. Mr. Arnon is an international observer."

Yehuda produced the documents hastily obtained that morning

from the United Nations Commission on International Terrorism. The officer frowned, turned to Les.

"Les Anderson. *Metro* magazine. And assorted other places, if you read your morning paper." Les grinned and flashed his battered press card. "Real hot, ain't it? How high do you suppose it'll go today?" His southern background did not desert him; he slipped like a chameleon into the skin of a "good ole boy."

The functionary was flustered. Yehuda's documents frightened him; Les's accent disarmed him. He stared at Aaron, Yehuda, and Mindell. He had been told to limit attendance at the arraignment, but he knew what the consequences could be if he barred a member of the press. Those damn northerners. Why didn't they stir up trouble in their own part of the country? Send their Jew volunteers into Harlem? Les Anderson was the fourth newsman to present his credentials. Stringers from *Time* and *Newsweek* and the two big networks were already there. At least this Anderson guy was a southerner. He might bury his background but not his accent.

"All right, go on in," he said sourly.

"And Dr. Krasnow is an affiant," Aaron said smoothly.

"Sure she is. Okay. Don't block the doorway."

They went into the oak-paneled courtroom, where two propeller fans stirred the heat-heavy air and hummed like huge malevolent flies. Michael stood waiting for them at the witness table. Aaron's heart turned. Michael's lips were swollen, and an ugly purple welt covered his forehead. Dark shadows rimmed his eyes, and his clothing hung loosely from his gaunt frame. Aaron had seen him only briefly in a darkened room and had not seen the full extent of the bruises. Still Michael smiled, and his handshake was firm.

"Thanks, Aaron," he said. "I'm glad you're here, Yehuda."

"Anything for the little brother," Aaron replied. "We'd better get you cleaned up before Mama sees you. You look as bad as Josh used to look when the Irish gang on Pitt Street was through with him."

"How is Mama? Was she upset?" Michael asked.

Aaron shrugged. "You know Mama."

Leah had been upset. Upset but in control. It had been Leah who tracked Les Anderson down and Leah who called Josh Ellenberg, who always kept a large sum of cash on hand in his Great Neck home. ("Josh needs to see money to remind him that he has it—that he isn't poor and hungry anymore," she had told Aaron once when he spoke derisively about Josh's practice. "He remembers enough about the old country to know that you never can tell." And now

Josh's vigilance had worked for them.) Leah had been very tired, very pale. Twice Boris had handed her pills. But her voice had remained firm and her eyes were dry. Always, Aaron had thought, remembering back through the years, in a crisis situation his mother's voice was firm and her eyes were dry.

"All rise." The bailiff's command was almost genial, the voice of a barker anticipating an amusing show but keeping a wise eye on an unpredictable audience.

Aaron watched the judge enter: an older man, his silver hair paper-thin and pressed into place across his freckled scalp. His considerable girth was enveloped in the well-pressed judicial robes. Aaron found the judge's age and his weight to be oddly reassuring. They were ordered to sit. The court clerk conferred with the judge, who examined the docket folder, tracing each line he perused with a pointer. He was a careful man, then, and perhaps a fair man. Aaron had noticed that the two qualities went together in jurists. He motioned to the bailiff and requested permission to approach the bench. When the judge nodded, he made his way forward.

"Your Honor, I am a member of the bar of the state of New York. Inasmuch as the defendant, Michael Goldfeder, who is to appear before you this morning, is my brother, I should like to represent him in this court. I respectfully request permission to be admitted *pro hac vice* for this purpose." His throat was dry. He had asked the judge to permit him to practice in the state of Mississippi "for this time only"—a judicial courtesy that could be arbitrarily denied. If it was granted, Judge Archibald Merrill would reveal himself as a fair-minded man.

Judge Merrill rustled the paper. He looked from the tall, dark-haired defendant to the attorney whose fiery hair was streaked with gray. He, too, had a younger brother in a distant state who resembled him not at all. It showed decent family feeling for the man to travel so far and so swiftly on his brother's behalf. But then the Goldfeders were Jews, and the Jews, he had heard, had strong feeling for their kinfolk. That much, at least, they shared with Christian Mississippians. And the *pro hac vice* courtesy carried with it an unwritten reciprocity. If he denied it, a New York judge might deny it in turn to a Mississippi attorney.

"Permission to be admitted to the bar of Mississippi *pro hac vice* granted," he said in a gravelly voice, but he did not look up at Aaron, who nodded appreciatively and returned to his seat.

"A preliminary hearing in the case of the People of Mississippi against Michael Goldfeder," the bailiff read out importantly.

The arresting officer, Sergeant Carey, was called. He was a burly, overweight man whose neck bulged within the confines of his starched collar; his fingers fidgeted nervously with the tight knot of his narrow black tie. The prosecutor spoke to him in the low, reassuring tones of a sympathetic colleague.

"You just tell us all what happened that led you to make this here arrest, Sergeant Carey," he instructed the officer companionably.

"We were just patrolling the road routine-like when we saw this beat-up car with New York license plates speeding along. We asked the driver to pull over, and when we looked inside the car we seen all these cartons of stuff spilling all over the place. We opened them, and they were mostly books and such—magazines, pamphlets. Now, we got a special memorandum from Jackson to be on the watch for people bringing obscene literature into the state, so we put two and two together and impounded the books and arrested the driver of the car. That's him sitting over there." He thrust a fleshy finger at Michael who noticed a Band-Aid on the officer's knuckle. He was pleased at the thought that the sergeant might have sustained a bruise from hitting him in the mouth.

"What was your aim in making this arrest?" the prosecutor asked.

"My aim was to protect the children of Mississippi from obscene literature according to . . . uh . . . title ninety-seven, chapters twenty-nine through thirty-nine, of the Mississippi Code of Law." He read carefully from a worn index card. He had clearly been well prepared.

"Your Honor, the people move to submit this sample carton of books in evidence as People's Exhibit A."

The judge nodded.

"Did you recognize any of the books?" the prosecutor proceeded.

"Wasn't one of them I got in my house," the officer replied. "And my wife is a regular at the Tuesday Afternoon Book Circle."

There was muted, appreciative laughter in the courtroom. The judge allowed a thin smile to crease his lips.

"Your witness, Mr. Goldfeder."

Aaron rose and stared hard at the officer. He studied the notes he had made during the man's testimony, frowned, and cleared his throat.

"You said that 'this beat-up car with New York license plates was speeding down the road.' Is that correct?"

"That's correct," Sergeant Carey replied complacently.

"I see. What is the speed limit on that road?"

"Thirty miles an hour."

"And how fast was this beat-up car with New York license plates traveling?"

"I didn't clock him."

"That's interesting. You didn't clock him. I see. How fast, then, do you estimate that he was traveling? More than thirty miles an hour?"

"No." The sergeant shifted in his chair. The bailiff brought him a glass of water, which he sipped appreciatively.

"Less?"

"Probably less." Water dribbled from the corner of his mouth.

"How can you be so sure?"

"Well, I didn't have to put on any speed to follow him, and I don't go faster than twenty-five on that bayou road—it's got a tricky curve."

"And yet you said he was speeding."

"I didn't mean going over the limit. Down here, when we say 'speed along,' we mean moving at an even clip. I said 'speeding along.' I didn't say nothing about exceeding the speed limit."

"I see. Then this beat-up car with New York plates was traveling at the lawful limit or, indeed, below it?"

"That's right. We didn't arrest him for speeding, did we? We didn't have to trump up no charge."

"What made you pull the car over?"

"We got a phone tip that there was going to be some action on the bayou road that afternoon. Some northern agitators transporting trouble like they do. Kids from New York. This car had New York plates and it wasn't in great shape."

"But you saw at once that it had its proper inspection stickers, and the license of the driver and the registration were in order?"

"Well, after we pulled him over, we saw that, but how would we know unless we'd done that?"

"And yet despite the lack of irregularity, you proceeded to search the car?"

"We'd've been remiss in our official duties if we'd done different. We got all sorts of people coming into this state these days. They call themselves freedom riders or civil rights workers, but some of them are selling marijuana and worse. We don't want no northern drugs in Mississippi. Governor Barnett sent a directive to our chief to be extra careful. And then, like I said, we had this phone tip about a New York car coming down that road at about that hour. I did the right thing." Sergeant Carey leaned back in his chair in the attitude of a man well satisfied by his performance.

Michael turned his head and saw that Matt Williams and Kemala had slipped into seats at the rear of the courtroom. He was grateful to them for coming to Peachtree, yet something in the glance they exchanged disturbed him. He turned quickly away so that Kemala would not see his bruises. He did not want her to be upset.

"When you searched the vehicle driven by the defendant, did you find any marijuana?"

"No."

"Did you find any controlled substance—that is, drugs—of any kind?"

"I know what a controlled substance is," the sergeant replied in a surly voice.

"Of course you do. And did you find any?"

"No."

"What did you find?"

"You got it all written down in that paper. And I already said it." The officer was irritable. His shortness of temper did not displease Aaron.

"Your Honor, please direct the witness to answer the question."

"Answer the question, officer." The judge was curt. He had recognized one of the television journalists as a newsman whom his wife watched regularly every Wednesday evening. The man was taking rapid notes. And the newsman scribbling down almost every word was Les Anderson, whose picture appeared next to his weekly column in *Metro*. What the hell were all these big shots doing in Peachtree on this penny-ante case? He remembered now where he had seen Aaron Goldfeder's name. He had argued an immigration case before the Supreme Court. Argued it and won. There had been an article on it in one of the law journals. Judge Merrill leaned forward in his seat with the interest of a professional watching the performance of a talented colleague.

"We found all these here seditious and obscene books. They weren't no private reading matter. Boxes and boxes of books and pamphlets and magazines. Not what ordinary law-abiding citizens would be carrying in their cars."

Aaron walked leisurely over to the evidence display and plucked a book from the carton that had been admitted as state's evidence.

"With Your Honor's permission, I read from material offered in evidence by the people."

"Permission granted," the judge said gruffly.

" 'We, the People of the United States, in order to form a more perfect union, establish justice, insure domestic tranquility, provide for the common defence, promote the general welfare, and secure the blessings of liberty . . .' et cetera, et cetera. Do you recognize these words, Sergeant Carey?"

"Sound familiar." The sergeant furrowed his brow. *Blessings of liberty . . . we the people*—the kind of commie language those commie bastard nigger lovers used. *Establish justice.* That meant, he supposed, niggers and whites using the same toilets, the same drinking fountains. Uppity James Meredith registering at Ole Miss. They oughta say "establish jewstice." His own pun amused him. He couldn't wait to repeat it to his wife after this road show was over. His lips curled in a smile.

"I should think it would sound familiar. You're an educated man. You uphold the Constitution of the United States, don't you?"

"I got a Distinguished Service Cross," the officer replied proudly.

"Then of course you uphold the Constitution. And what I just read was the preamble to the Constitution. That's not seditious, is it?"

"I guess not."

"You *guess* not?"

"No, it's not seditious."

"There were twenty-five copies of the Constitution of the United States and twenty-five copies of the constitution of the state of Mississippi in the cartons which you impounded. I might add that they were being transported to a library in the town of Troy for the purpose of teaching the people of Troy knowledge of the law and respect for it."

"There was a lot of other books in them boxes also. Fiction books that had spit to do with the law."

Aaron reached into the carton and removed another book. This one was clearly not a law book. It had a brightly colored jacket featuring a drawing of a golden-haired woman wearing a white dress that exposed her arms and shoulders. Aaron looked at it and frowned, as though he had blundered, miscalculated.

Michael grew tense. Aaron's maneuver had paid off the first time around, but it might not work again, and he could not face the thought of spending yet another night in a Peachtree prison cell. The stench of the bucket in his cell that served as a toilet, the thin, dirty mattress, through which bedbugs crawled in desultory procession, the mournful graffiti scratched on the walls, and the verbal abuse of the jailers who thrust the spoiled food he could barely swallow through the judas hole—the memory of all that would cling to him forever. *Ain't you got enough trouble in the North, Jewboy?* they had snarled at him. *We'll really nail you if you ever come through here again.* Michael shivered, and Mindell's hand reached out and covered his.

Aaron replaced the book, and the officer smiled complacently.

"You have a fine library here in Peachtree, do you not?" Aaron asked.

"Yes. We do." Sergeant Carey regained his confidence. *Jewstice.* The ball was coming into his court at last. He had only been doing his job, following orders. What the hell?

"I visited the Peachtree Library this morning, and I was much impressed. I made a list of the members of the acquisition committee. Are you by chance related to Adelaide Carey?"

"Sure am. She's my wife."

"Yes. You mentioned before that she was interested in literature. An afternoon reading group. Surely Mrs. Carey would not approve of having any obscene literature in the Peachtree Library."

"Of course not."

"And yet this book"—Aaron lifted the volume that he had set aside—"which you impounded from the defendant's car, *Ozma of Oz* by Frank Baum, is in the Peachtree Library. And so is this book, *Huckleberry Finn*. And so is this book, *Illustrated Tales from the Bible*. In fact, officer, every book involved in this case is in the Peachtree Library, which you yourself testify is innocent of distributing seditious or obscene literature. It would follow, then, that the books impounded are neither obscene nor seditious. Would you agree with me?"

"I suppose so," the sergeant muttered. Despite the fact that he sat directly beneath the propeller fan, streaks of sweat glistened on his neck.

"No further questions," Aaron said quietly. "The witness may step down. If it please Your Honor, I think that it is now abundantly clear to this court and to my learned colleague who represents the people that there was no justifiable cause to stop the vehicle in which the defendant was traveling. The arresting officer had no warrants that would justify either the search of the defendant or the vehicle, yet he violated constitutional rights and proceeded with such a search.

The materials found in the car were in no way obscene, and the charge preferred, therefore, is frivolous at best, malicious at worst. I move for its dismissal.

"The world is watching Mississippi now. This beautiful state is much in the news. There are those who say that Mississippi will not respect the laws of the land, the Constitution of this great country of ours. I, for one, do not believe that. I have seen courtesy and honesty in this courtroom this morning. The officers of this court surely respect the law of the United States and the rights of all its citizens—even those who were born beyond the Mason-Dixon line and who drive beat-up cars." (The journalists, taking down every word, glanced at one another and smiled. That kind of statement made a "quote of the day," a filler at the end of a column. Aaron ignored them, although Judge Merrill, shifting his weight, did not.) "I therefore respectfully request that all charges against Michael Goldfeder be summarily dismissed."

"Motion sustained. All charges are dropped. The defendant is free to leave, and his property will be restored to him."

The judge rose, and everyone else also stood. In the rear of the room Matt Williams half leaned against the bench, a satisfied smile gliding across his lips.

THEY celebrated that night with a party at the Troy schoolhouse. Mrs. Mason prepared an enormous platter of fried chicken. Norma Anne contributed freshly baked rolls, and Lizzie, who had not come to classes that summer, appeared with a basket of sautéed frogstools, the tender bayou mushrooms for which Michael had developed a special fondness during his summers in Mississippi. There were pitchers of iced tea and strawberry Kool-Aid, and Aaron hauled in a case of beer, which they could not get cold enough. The atmosphere reminded Yehuda of a kibbutz celebration after the completion of a project. He remembered suddenly the platters of golden fried chicken Rebecca had prepared after the new dining hall had been completed.

They laughed and told jokes and imitated the judge and the bailiff and Sergeant Carey. Matt Williams improvised a scenario in which the sergeant confronted his wife at home and asked her why she allowed "them dirty books" in the Peachtree Library. Les Anderson phoned his story into *Metro* and insisted on reading the lead to them.

"Today in a Peachtree courtroom, Judge Archibald Merrill proved that the lyrics of the state song of Mississippi ring true—'Go, Mississippi, continue to roll—Grow, Mississippi, the top is the goal.'

When charges against Michael Goldfeder were dismissed, this southern state acknowledged that it would continue to grow and to expand the democratic process and would eventually reach the goal set forth by the United States Supreme Court when it ruled against segregation. . . ."

"Don't you think you're going a little overboard on that, Anderson?" Matt Williams asked. "After all, we didn't witness the Second Coming today."

"No, I don't think so, Williams. Think you could do better? Give it a try." Les Anderson was one of the few whites who were not disconcerted by Matt Williams's biting sarcasm. "It's my southern upbringing," he said jokingly. "I'm used to bigots in all sizes, shapes and colors."

"Are you all right, Michael?" Kemala asked. She touched his bruised lip, and he flinched. It was Mindell who prepared a poultice of Burow's solution and placed it on the ugly swelling. Kemala remained at Michael's side and moodily watched Mindell as she worked.

Slowly, the party wound down. They linked hands and sang "We Shall Overcome," and then, reluctant to lose the moment, they sang "Blowin' in the Wind." Aaron and Yehuda did not join the circle. They remained in a corner of the room, speaking softly to each other. Michael, who stood between Kemala and Mindell, was angered because they had separated themselves out at this moment of sharing. Why should his family isolate themselves from this course that he had chosen, from these people whose cause had become his own? It was not enough for Leah to write checks, for Aaron to sweep down and make brilliant arguments in a southern courtroom, for Yehuda to offer abstract generalizations about the dangers of terrorism. He wanted his brother and his brother-in-law to share his sense of involvement, his commitment, to lift their voices with his. But none of them except Mindell had done so, and Mindell was not of his family.

He looked at her now and heard her charmingly accented voice rise in the sweet song of hope. Jeremy was lucky to have her friendship, her love. Michael had recognized the softness in her voice when she spoke Jeremy's name, the pleasure in her face when she received a letter from him.

He moved out of the circle, and Mindell's rose-gold hand encased Kemala's dusky palm. She was so beautiful, so brave. He would have to tell Kemala about it when they were alone. It was strange that he and Kemala had not managed any time alone together throughout the entire afternoon, the evening. But perhaps when the others left, she would stay and they would walk to the meadow and watch the cottonwood tree silhouetted in the moonlight.

Gradually, people drifted out, everyone stopping to shake hands with Michael, to murmur appreciation to Aaron. At last only Matt Williams, Kemala, Mindell, Michael, and Aaron remained in the schoolroom amid the happy debris of the party. Yehuda sat apart from them, his eyes half-closed

"Nice work, counselor," Matt Williams said.

"Thank you. Nice work on your part too," Aaron replied evenly.

"What do you mean?" Matt's eyes narrowed. Feline glints of gold sparked, and he leaned back and reached for the last full beer can.

"Didn't the scenario play out exactly as you planned? You set it up, didn't you? Two white civil rights workers on a lonely bayou road, driving a beat-up car. New York plates. The back seat loaded with suspicious-looking cartons. You don't drive a car with New York plates, Williams, and if you did, you know damn well you wouldn't drive it down that road at that hour. Michael tells me that you told him to leave before dawn. Safer and cooler, you said. Safest and coolest to leave at night and travel back before dawn. My brother-in-law, Yehuda, comes from Israel, which has a very hot climate. He saw that at once. But those weren't your instructions. And then there's the mysterious phone tip the Peachtree cops received. A beat-up car with New York plates coming down the road at precisely that hour. Who could have known that? Who could have phoned that tip in? It's just too neat. You set Michael up, and it's pure luck that he didn't get killed. Am I on target, Williams? Did I leave anything out, get anything wrong?" Aaron's voice was dangerously low, and his fists were clenched with anger. Yehuda rose and moved closer to him. He knew about Aaron's temper. He remembered Budapest.

Matt Williams sipped his beer and smiled.

"Oh, you're on target, but let me draw a couple of things in. Let me ask a couple of questions. Supposing I had been arrested and the girl in the car had been Kemala and not our altruistic doctor friend from Israel. Would you have left your posh, air-conditioned office and been on a plane south in just a couple of hours? Would your mama and the great industrialist Joshua Ellenberg have given you a pocketful of cash for my bail?"

"Probably not," Aaron said.

"And if two blacks had been arrested in Mississippi, would Les Anderson of *Metro* magazine, the TV networks, and the *Time* and *Newsweek* stringers have scurried south sniffing after a big story, a juicy human-interest story? Bullshit they would. Kemala and I would have rotted in that jail. Black-and-blue marks don't show so good on black skin, so even if we were beaten, and I guarantee you we would have been, it wouldn't have come out terrific in color shots—nothing like your little brother's black eye and bruised lip. Believe me, I know. I've been held in a lot of jails in this great state, which today demonstrated its commitment to justice. We wouldn't have had a color shot in *Metro,* and we wouldn't have had our fifty-four seconds on national news. You get the picture?" Matt tossed the beer can across the room.

"I had the picture," Aaron replied. "I only needed you to put the finishing touches on it."

"Maybe you think I'm going to apologize," Matt said. "I'm not going to apologize. I'd do it again. You Jews aren't doing us any big favor by being down here. You're having a joyride on our misery. Michael Goldfeder's here to prove he's as brave as his big brother who fought the Nazis and his big sister who fought the Arabs. He found himself a cause. He's fighting Mississippi whites. The other Jews from Harvard, the Quakers from Swarthmore, the Haverford do-gooders—they're here because they feel guilty, because their fancy educations are paid for by black dollars. You know what James Baldwin said—or maybe your Scarsdale book club didn't get to Baldwin yet, maybe you're still on Wright? Anyway, James Baldwin says that the Jew is playing the role assigned to him by Christians long ago—he's doing the dirty work, like the court Jews, the tax agents, the rent collectors. You did it for the whites; why not for the blacks? You owe us more. When they burned the crosses on our lawns, they left yours alone!" His voice was harsh. The veneer of sarcasm was gone, and the raw, splintered anger was exposed.

Mindell shivered under the stream of invective. She shivered and drew closer to Yehuda. Michael put his head in his hands. He flinched from Matt Williams's words as from a physical blow. He had told only Kemala of his feelings about Aaron and Rebecca. He remembered the night of their first meeting. They had sat in the starlit darkness of Golden Gate Park, and he had told her about Aaron and Rebecca. He had spoken of them as she lay in his arms beneath the magnolia trees. He had wanted no secrets from her. He had shared her griefs and exposed his own, and she had taken his tender revelations and offered them to Matt Williams.

"It didn't bother you that you risked Mindell's life?" Aaron asked coldly.

"She was the cookie topper," Matt answered. "A doctor. She told me herself that she had been in the Israeli army, that she knew self-defense techniques."

"There's a lot she didn't tell you," Yehuda said. "Not that knowing would bother you." Matt would have behaved no differently if he had known of Mindell's terror of enclosed places, of uniforms, of the heritage of her grim and terrible childhood. Matt was at war, and he used whatever weapon came to hand.

"You knew about this, didn't you, Kemala?" Michael asked.

She nodded but did not look up. He would never see her golden eyes again, he knew, and he was surprised at how little he cared. There had been a slow withering of all that had been between them, but he had willed himself to ignore it. She had changed and he had changed, but they had never been together long enough to assess the changes. Winters apart. Furtive summer visits. Snatched hours. She had used him, in the end, as a pawn in an intricate and dangerous game, but he would not have forgone all that she had offered him. He remembered, with detached melancholy, the interstices of sunlight and shadow on her dusky skin, the glossy coil of her hair about his wrist, the lingering sadness in her voice when she spoke of her father. He wanted to touch her, but he did not. Their time of closeness had passed.

"It doesn't matter," he said.

What mattered was that he had come to Troy and met the Mason family, and now Rodney Mason would come to New York and prepare for a university. Because of Kemala he had taught brave Norma Anne and Lizzie and the boy from Sebastopol whose poetry would be published that year in a respected journal. He had, after all, made a difference. Matt Williams's invective did not alter all that he had done. He felt suddenly the power of his contribution, the potency of his participation. He was a teacher and he had taught. He had opened minds and liberated talents. He was bruised, exhausted, betrayed, but suffused with an emotion he had not known before. He sat in the quiet schoolroom, resonant with accusation and counteraccusation, with disappointment and betrayal, and he felt a simple yet powerful pride.

"You're playing with fire, Matt," he said quietly, a new authority in his voice. "Don't you know what the real danger is? The real danger is that we'll be set up against each other—Jews against black—and the white elite will sit back and enjoy it. Is that really what you want?"

The West Indian did not answer. Michael, Mindell, Yehuda, and Aaron left the room. Briefly, they stood outside the schoolhouse, looked up at the star-spattered sky, and sniffed the cool evening air, fragrant with the scent of Cherokee roses and cinnamon fern. In the distance a mockingbird sang plaintively into the lonely darkness, but there was no answer to its sweet song.

THE WEEKS after the arrest and trial passed swiftly. On his last day in Troy, Michael looked with satisfaction at the neatly arranged bookshelves and lettered a small placard: THE TROY FREEDOM LIBRARY. Rodney Mason nailed it into place. Mindell had reserved a shelf for the books and pamphlets she had collected on nutrition and child care, medical home advice, and first aid. The collection seemed meager to her, and she looked at it sadly.

"Is this all we're leaving?" she asked.

"No," Michael replied. "We're leaving much more than that."

Mrs. Mason wept when they left. She stood beside them in the dim light of dawn and enfolded each of them in strong embrace.

"You come back. You hear? You come back." Her love-born command was fierce, intense.

The Mason children pressed close to them. Dora Lee wept, and Rodney hugged both Michael and Mindell. Michael remembered how they had been too shy to talk to him when he first arrived three years ago. But now the barriers of color had broken down. They were at last sharing, caring friends.

The family waved as they drove away, and Mindell turned toward them until they disappeared into the distance. By midafternoon they had crossed the Mississippi border, and they stopped to rest and eat on the banks of Pickwick Lake in Tennessee. Michael stretched out beneath a wide-branched persimmon tree and watched two painted buntings skitter playfully from branch to branch. The birds cooed flirtatiously to each other, and their rainbow-colored wings flashed as they chased each other through the thick, dark foliage. Mindell sat beside him and plaited a wreath of wildflowers, a skill she had been taught by Leah on a distant afternoon in a distant land. Deftly, she interwove black-eyed susans with trillium and columbine.

"No Cherokee roses," he said.

"No Cherokee roses."

"What will you do now, Mindell?"

"Go back to the hospital. Finish my research project. And then . . . I don't know. And you, Michael?"

"My contract at Hutchinson extends for another year. After that, I don't know. Teaching, of course. Research, perhaps. But how and where, I don't know." Oddly, this indecision no longer troubled him. He knew who he was and of what he was capable.

"What about Mississippi?"

"That's over, " he said sadly. "Oh, I'll go on with my work for civil rights. It's part of me, part of my life. But I can't go back to Mississippi."

She did not ask why. Kemala was in Mississippi. A letter from Kemala had been delivered to the Mason home, and Mindell had brought it to Michael at the schoolhouse. She had seen him stare at the envelope and slowly rip it into shreds without opening it. Days later, she had met Kemala on the street in Neshoba.

"You're angry with me, but I did what I had to do," Kemala had said fiercely. "Matt explained it to me. What we're fighting for is more important than anything else. And he was right. The coverage of Michael's trial focused attention on what's happening in Mississippi. Matt knows these things. He knows how to do things, accomplish things. He doesn't get lost in philosophy, false codes of morality." He was not like her father, who had read *On Liberty*, believed in the goodness and reasonableness of his fellow man, and died of gunshot wounds in a North Carolina woodland. "You understand, don't you, Mindell?"

Kemala clutched her wrist, and Mindell saw how thin her arm was, the veins of her neck strained bluely against her dusky skin. She felt a new sympathy for the tormented young woman whom Michael had cared for so deeply.

"I understand in a way," she said.

"I knew you would."

Unexpectedly Kemala kissed her on the cheek and hurried away. Mindell looked after her. They shared a bond, she and Kemala. Suffering and persecution united them. They had both lived in fear, had recoiled from the hatred and contempt in the eyes of uniformed men. But a strange thing had happened to Mindell that day on the bayou road when their car had been surrounded by officers. She had lost her fear of uniformed men and their cruel and terrible authority. She had been struck and had sustained pain, but the pain had neither threatened nor subdued her. Inexplicably, she had been cut free of terror. Now, in her dreams, she walked a sunlit lane through a dark and threatening forest. Mississippi had liberated her from Auschwitz.

Beside her now, Michael turned, moving closer into a ribbon of shade.

"You'll be working with Jeremy?" he asked.

He offered her his friend's name tentatively, although he anticipated her revelation. Les had prepared him for it.

"We'll have to look for someone else to share the apartment," Les had said. "Jeremy's in love. He wants to get married. He's only waiting for her to get back."

Her. Mindell, of course. They had been close during Jeremy's visit to Israel. It had been Jeremy who had arranged for her fellowship to the United States and Jeremy who had met her on arrival, guided her through her first weeks in the country. Mindell's conversation was peppered with quotes from Jeremy. "Jeremy thinks . . . Jeremy says . . ." As once he had searched for any excuse to mention Kemala's name. Kemala. The thought of her saddened him now but caused him no pain. They had separated from each other, he realized now, long before that night in the Troy schoolhouse. He had known, he thought, since the night of the Makeba concert and perhaps even before then, that they would never be together. And perhaps, too, he acknowledged now as he watched Mindell's fingers weave the flowers into a colorful pattern, he had stopped caring but had been unwilling to relinquish the dream. How lovely Mindell's hands were, how gentle. How graceful were her arms. She wore a lemon-yellow sundress that matched her hair, and he noticed, for the first time, the small dimples that blossomed at her golden shoulders. Lucky Jeremy, damn him. An anomalous sadness stole over him.

"Jeremy wants to go to Israel for a while. He's interested in the Hadassah family-care clinic concept."

"That will make it very easy for you, then," he said. A heaviness settled on his heart, and his sadness was no longer nameless. He had lost her. Without knowing that he had wanted her, blind and stupid, he had lost her.

"For me?" She looked at him quizzically, plucked up a sprig of larkspur, and wove it in with the trillium. "What has it to do with me? It's between Jeremy and Melanie."

"Jeremy and Melanie?"

"Yes. Didn't Les tell you? They're going to be married."

"I didn't know." His heart soared. The painted buntings flew skyward in tandem, rainbow-winged arrows aimed straight for the sun. "I thought . . . all summer I thought it was you and Jeremy."

"No, Michael," she said gently. "All summer, for me, it was you and me. But there was Kemala."

"Yes. There was Kemala. I'm sorry." He looked at her. "You and me. Michael and Mindell."

"Michael and Mindell," she repeated.

"For forever after?"

"For forever after." Her answer came in a whisper. The floral crown, completed, rested on her palms.

He took the wreath of flowers from her and placed it on her inclined head in gentle coronation.

"My noonday princess," he said. "My forever-after love."

His lips touched the dimples on her golden shoulders, traced the veins of sunlight on her arms, the dappled shadows of her face, and settled, at last, against the full, sweet softness of her mouth.

They drove north through the late afternoon, into the lingering haze of twilight. Mindell's head rested lightly on Michael's shoulder. She was asleep. He touched her hair and drove slowly, moved and soothed by the long, mysterious shadows of evening that carpeted the narrow highway.

KIBBUTZ SHA'AREI HA-NEGEV

1966

THE SETTLERS' HOMES on Kibbutz Sha'arei ha-Negev stood at the base of a martello-shaped sand crater that glowed rose-gold in the harsh light of the desert morning, turned topaz in the late afternoon, and was, at last, rilled by gliding shadows as the sun slowly surrendered into evening darkness. The children of the kibbutz called the crater *malchat ha-midbar*, the desert queen, and told stories of a mysterious romantic regent garrisoned in the fortress of sand. The small white bungalows were built in a straight line, equidistant from one other and from the natural bastion that dominated them. Rebecca, during the planning period of the kibbutz, had worried over the landscaping and argued for scattering the houses. One could be built in the shade of the acacia tree, others near the grove of date palms, and still others in the small natural circle formed where a terebinth stole the sunlight from the crouching Sodom apple tree.

It would be more interesting, more aesthetic, she had insisted, and the other members had patiently agreed with her and even more patiently explained that there was the problem of security compounded by the kibbutz philosophy of egalitarianism. They explained very carefully, because she was an American and an artist, and they understood that their ways were new to her. Houses built in a line were more easily defended, and if all the houses were alike and similarly situated, there could be no lingering feelings of resentment and inequality.

"Equal doesn't have to mean the same," Rebecca had murmured to Yehuda, but she had been new to the group then and unwilling to threaten its harmony by persisting in her argument. In those early days she had been compliant, acquiescent. Nothing in the world had been as important to her as her love for Yehuda.

Now, almost two decades later, she conceded that the others had, after all, been right. She walked toward her bungalow, after a long afternoon at her studio, and was pleased at the way the small homes, newly whitewashed, gleamed in the receding light; their symmetry in the desert wilderness had a reassuring geometric beauty. A dwarf palm had been planted in front of each house, and a luxuriant garden bloomed on the common lawn. Rebecca's life on the kibbutz was marked by the garden's plantings. The beds of lavender marked the birth of her son Yaakov, and on the day of Amnon's circumcision, she and Yehuda had embedded iris bulbs deep into the unyielding earth. Always, the flowers bloomed with seasonal certainty in time for her younger son's birthday. When Yehuda returned from the Sinai Campaign, he carried with him cuttings of Egyptian savignia, and now the tiny lilac flowers were deeply rooted and marked the weeks of danger, the hour of return.

All the houses shared a view of the twin Christ's-thorn trees; their beadlike orange fruit glittered among the cruel, serrated leaves. A family of warblers nestled in the branches, and their sweet and tender songs pierced morning silence, evening quiet. Always, Rebecca looked forward to that quiet at day's end when she could listen to the birds and watch the leaves of the thorn tree cast their wild shadows across the patterned sand. But today there would be no quiet hour, she remembered suddenly, with a mingling of annoyance and regret. Amnon waited for her at the bungalow in imperious stance, his short legs apart, his hands plunged into the pockets of his shorts. He stared at her with the aggrieved indignation of a child whose urgent pleasure has been irrationally thwarted by adult indifference.

Rebecca smiled at him. Newly showered, with drops of water still clinging to his extraordinarily long eyelashes, he glowed with health and cleanliness; his fresh white shirt and shorts sharply contrasted with his sun-burnished skin. Both her sons, Amnon and Yaakov, had inherited her topaz complexion and dark hair (fretted with silver now) and Yehuda's lucent gray eyes. But now Amnon's eyes were smoky with wrath (as Yehuda's were so often these days, she thought with sinking heart), and he tapped his sandaled foot impatiently.

"*Ima*, aren't you ready? You are coming to the wedding, aren't you?"

"I'm very tired, Amnon. I worked so late this afternoon that I just managed to pick up the mail before Sara closed the office. The wedding procession will pass by the bungalow. I'll watch it from the window." She fingered the letters in her pocket, impatient suddenly to read them. The crisp white envelope was from Charles Ferguson, embossed with the imprint of his art gallery, and the air letter was from Mindell. Sweet Mindell, who had been daughter and friend to her and was now her brother's wife.

"But I want to go," Amnon said petulantly. "I want to be in the wedding with the others."

"Of course you do, and of course you'll go," Rebecca said, struggling against the irritation in her voice. It occurred to her, disloyally, that her brother Aaron's children did not seem to be as nagging and insistent as Amnon. It would be a sociological irony if her kibbutz-bred son turned out to be more spoiled than his Scarsdale cousins. "You'll go with your brother and sister." She pointed to Danielle and Yaakov, who crossed the lawn and walked toward them, moving very slowly because Yair Ben Dor accompanied them. Yair, still in uniform, propelled himself awkwardly forward on the prosthetic leg that had been recently fitted for him at the Tel ha-Shomer hospital.

Danielle looked especially beautiful, in a yellow cotton dress that matched her flowing hair and hugged her narrow waist. She spent so much time with Yair now, Rebecca thought uneasily, and wondered if that was because Yair had been with Noam on the day of his death. Odd, how they always spoke of Noam's death, yet never said that he had died. The noun, *death*, was somehow more passive, more acceptable than the harsh verb, *died*. When Rebecca thought of strong, young Noam, she visualized him streaking across the fields of the kibbutz. He had worked on the irrigation system, and his days had been spent monitoring the veinwork of pipe and spigots that guaranteed the survival of their desert crops; he had checked for breakages and pressure, his long body hugging the earth he nurtured so carefully, so jealously. She saw him, too, in memory, tossing a ball to Yaakov and Amnon or galloping up to their bungalow on the black stallion, the legacy of a group of marauding fedayeen who had been routed before they could mount their steeds. Their kibbutz neighbors had been annoyed by that; the horses' hooves had mangled the pampas grass that the new immigrants from Argentina had planted so laboriously. It had always amused Rebecca that the kibbutz members were as house-proud as the Westchester homeowners of her childhood. She had apologized and promised that it would not happen again. And it had not, because a week later Noam was dead. She had been sketching the horse in charcoal on the day of his death. She had finished the drawing, tears streaming down her cheeks, and then she had crushed the stick of charcoal between her palms.

"When did death come to him?" Yehuda had asked the army

officer who was too young to be assigned his sad task. He wiped Rebecca's hands with his handkerchief as he waited for the answer. A father had the right to know when death had come to his son. The old died, as was natural, but death came to the young in pursuit, swooped down upon them and captured them in the vulnerability of their youth. Death had come to Noam Arnon, it was reported, as afternoon melded into evening, and often, as daylight faded, thoughts of him crowded their minds.

"Aren't you coming to the wedding?" Danielle asked.

"You take Amnon. Perhaps I'll come later, when your father comes home." She took the two envelopes from her pocket. "I have letters I haven't had time to read yet."

"But I want you to come," Amnon protested peevishly.

"Later," Rebecca said firmly, fighting the wave of fury that swept over her. Damn it, she was so tired of doing what other people wanted her to do, of going to meetings when she wanted to be in her studio, of taking her turn in the kitchen when she needed every scrap of energy for the large landscape, of playing dominoes with Yaakov and Amnon when she wanted to read a book or write a letter. Now, shamed by the inexplicable irrationality of her mood, she smiled with a penitence she did not feel.

"Save us seats at the meal and have a good time," she said.

Danielle lingered as the others walked on.

"Are you all right, Rivka?" she asked gently, and Rebecca remembered when Yehuda's daughter had stopped calling her *Ima*. Danielle, wearing the same yellow dress, her hair brushed loose, had returned from a party in Eilat and Yehuda had stared at her in astonishment, seeing her for the first time perhaps, as a young woman. "You look exactly like your mother," he had said, his voice muted by pain and memory, "exactly like Miriam. Mia."

Resentment had stabbed Rebecca then. She had spent the two decades of her marriage striving against the ghost of her husband's first wife. She had mothered her children and competed with the myth and memory of the courageous golden-haired woman, the loving companion of Yehuda's youth, who had died in a forest in Czechoslovakia, blocking a bullet that had been meant for her husband. Brave, beautiful Miriam. Rebecca could never vanquish that memory. She had told Aaron as much, years ago in a London restaurant.

She was "Rivka" to Danielle now. The ghost of Miriam had triumphed.

"I'm fine, Danielle," she said firmly. "I just need a little time alone."

"I know." Danielle touched Rebecca's cheek lightly with her fingers, a private gesture of comfort, and hurried to catch up to the others.

What did she know? Rebecca wondered wearily. Had Danielle sensed the constraint and uneasiness between Rebecca and Yehuda? She had noticed surely that her father was moody and irritable, obsessed by worries that he could not share with his family. He answered Rebecca's questions with monosyllabic replies, and his lovemaking was too swift and oddly violent. He was en route from Jerusalem now—the third time that month that he had been summoned to the capital for urgent meetings. Always, he returned fatigued and dispirited, swaddled in anger and silence.

"I thought we had bought ourselves at least two decades of peace," he had muttered angrily after his last journey.

"Well, there is an arithmetic progression of sorts," Rebecca had rejoined. "Eight years between the War for Independence and the Sinai Campaign, and now we've had almost ten years of relative peace. Nineteen fifty-six through nineteen sixty-six. An improvement." She had laughed wryly, as all Israelis did when they discussed war and peace.

She searched Yehuda's face for a good-humored response to her feeble attempt at humor. There had been a time when she could coax him into reluctant laughter, no matter how bitter his mood. Then, she would watch his lean, bronzed face crease into riant lines and his silken gray eyes flood with warmth; she would stir with pride at her own power over this man whose strength had thrilled her from the moment of their meeting. But that power had been eroded, and now he clenched his fists as he spoke to her so that the muscles of his sun-stained arms rippled with anger. She felt herself subdued by his fury and bitterness as once she had been subdued by his earnestness and his love.

The force of Yehuda's conviction had always exerted a strange, inexplicable magnetism over her. She had soared on the whirling vortex of his fierce belief. He had enticed her into the wider world of his vision. She had become his accomplice in illegal immigration, his comrade in the war for Israel's independence. He had dreamed of founding a new kibbutz in the Negev, and she had never doubted that his reverie would become their shared reality. His moods, febrile, incandescent, ignited her own. She reveled, then, in his power over history. Yehuda Arnon—her fiery lover, her tender husband—had fought wars, saved lives, and would reclaim a desert, yet his lips were gentle on her own, and she in turn could cause him to laugh and to weep. But now, suddenly, all that was altered.

"You can't call this peace," he had retorted harshly, and she had turned away in mute acknowledgment that great changes had overtaken them. Noam's death had affected them both, and their moods were subject to the ebb and flow of their grief. Rebecca had willed herself to struggle against her sorrow. Determinedly, she had absorbed herself in her painting. She spent long hours in her studio, and she took long hikes, carrying her sketch pad and her pastels. The diurnal victories over grief and fear were obviated by the apprehension that overtook her in the stillness of the night. Planes flew overhead, and she reached for Yehuda. All their lives in this land were vulnerable. There was no certainty. She had expected to dance at Noam's wedding; instead she had wept at his funeral.

It was then, when the nocturnal terrors consumed her, that she stole from her bed and visited the children's house, where her sons slept.

"They will be all right," she assured herself as she stared down at their dream-bound faces. And some nights she even believed that it would be so.

Yehuda's moods were as erratic as her own. He had overcome his desperate sorrow, his fierce anger, but he could not subdue the tension that ruled his days, poisoned his nights. Sometimes it seemed to her that all humor had deserted him, even the bitter wit of his countrymen. Anxiety and uncertainty had fatigued him, etched deep lines in his face, shadowed his eyes. His earth-colored hair was dusted with gray now. Mortality stalked him, even as he had stalked danger in the forests of Europe, on the wild waves of an angry sea, on desert battlefields. He feared now that his luck would abandon him. He worried that peace would never come. His eldest son had been killed, and still he sat in the councils of his nation's leaders and pondered new lines of defense, new methods of *konenut*, preparedness, and acknowledged that there would be new deaths. He woke in the night writhing with stomach cramps, his head swelled with aching. In dream he lurched from danger to danger. Once on a hot night, when a thunderbolt ripped across the desert sky in a swift electric storm, he screamed in his sleep. "Mia! Mia!"

Rebecca lay beside him, rigid, her mouth sour. His arms sought her, and he held her close in dream-bound embrace. Did he dream of Mia as he held her? Rebecca wondered, and she did not sleep until the pale light of dawn streaked the sky.

Since Noam's death, Yehuda's face darkened when he read the papers. Daily, the front page featured a smiling swarthy Nasser, greeting Soviet diplomats, acknowledging a new shipment of arms. Like small boys boasting of their toys, the Egyptians and Russians displayed their lethal playthings—antipersonnel mines, long-range cannons, sleek and shining missiles. Always the Russian was glum—the reluctant guest, the recalcitrant child who has been told that he *must* give, he *must* share, he *must* ingratiate himself. Always Nasser was the happy host accepting his gifts, greed glittering in his eyes, his lips moist, expectant. And daily, the Fatah increased its attacks on Israel's northern borders. Mortar rained down from the Golan Heights. Rockets exploded in Kiryat Shmoneh, Nahariya, Metulla.

"We're losing the balance," Yehuda muttered. "We've had nothing substantial since Kennedy sold us the Hawk anti-aircraft missiles." But Kennedy was three years dead, and a forest had been planted in his memory in the Jerusalem corridor, dominated by a great sculpture of a tree severed at the trunk before it could reach full growth. As Kennedy's life had been severed. As Noam's life had been severed, Rebecca had thought when she saw it. She planted a small rose garden in memory of Noam, near the kibbutz children's house, but Yehuda planted a tree for his son in the Kennedy forest. He had noticed that many trees were planted in the Kennedy forest, for young soldiers. There was, he supposed, a fellowship of mourning for those who died before they reached the fullness of their years.

Yehuda's lips pursed in bitter retort as he listened to the radio newscasts. De Gaulle could not be trusted. Harold Wilson was too damn ambivalent. Despite Suez, it would take a long time for Britain to forgive Israel for the Mandate years. The new American president, Lyndon Johnson, was obsessed by Vietnam and ignored the Soviet courtship of the Arabs. And that prince of bastards, U Thant, smiled obsequiously while Ahmed Shukairy held news conferences in Damascus boasting of an escalation of border raids.

"We will force Israel to retaliate," the Palestinian leader promised. His new uniforms made him brave, and he waved a Palestinian flag and pointed to a map of Israel. Circles were drawn with grease pen around Tel Aviv, Haifa, Beersheba. "When the Palestinians have an air force, no Jewish city will be safe," he warned.

But currently Shukairy was content to launch attacks on settlements, singling out children's houses for grenades lobbed through open windows. It was because of such an attack, on a moshav near Metulla, that Yehuda had traveled to Jerusalem.

"Another ineffectual conference," he had told Rebecca as he drove off. "Eshkol thinks solutions can be found in committee meetings."

Still, he had promised to be home early that day because of the wedding. The bridegroom was the son of an old friend. The bride's mother had been Miriam's classmate.

Everywhere, Rebecca thought, there were connections to Yehuda's first wife, to the childhood that he and Miriam had shared even before their marriage. She chided herself for resenting these constant reminders of his past. She herself had so few relations in Israel. Her mother's brother and his family lived on Beth ha-Cochav, a northern kibbutz, and a few distant cousins were scattered through the country. The lack of roots oppressed her. In all of Israel, there was no one who had known Rebecca Arnon as a child, no one who remembered her black ringlets, her childhood penchant for sweets, the small griefs and joys of her girlhood. No one in Israel ever said to her, in the dreamy voice of reminiscence, "Do you remember when . . . ?" She had arrived in the country as a woman, and almost immediately she had been caught up in Yehuda's life. Often, it seemed as though she had surrendered her past to him, and her American existence had been all illusion. Crazily, it occurred to her that perhaps she had never been Leah's daughter, sister to Michael and Aaron. In Israel, she was as a driven leaf, weighted only by Yehuda and the life they had built together. Yet now, after all their years together, that anchor had slipped. She was oppressed by a sense of aloneness. Yehuda called to another woman in the darkness as she lay rigidly beside him. They coped separately, divergently, with the loss they had suffered together.

She sighed and sank down into the canvas chair that Yehuda had so carefully placed in the square of shade cast by the dwarf palm tree. She took up her two letters and opened the cream-colored heavy envelope from the Ferguson Gallery first. Her mother's teacher and devoted friend, Charles Ferguson, ran a prestigious Madison Avenue gallery, and through the years he had represented Rebecca, selling her work to major collectors. He wrote that he wanted to mount a retrospective. His patrons would lend him her earlier works for exhibit, and he would also hang her newer canvases. It would be a showcase for kibbutz painters as well, and he wondered if Rebecca could arrange to come to New York for the opening. Her presence would certainly enhance the show and give American critics a chance to meet her.

She frowned, acknowledging both her pleasure and her fear at his suggestion. She folded the letter carefully and set it aside. Her fingers shook as she opened Mindell's letter, but as she read, a smile lit her face.

"Wonderful," she murmured aloud. "Wonderful."

Yehuda Arnon, hurrying across the lawn, paused when he saw her. It had been months since he had seen Rebecca smile, heard her laugh. How beautiful she was, he thought. The sun stole through the palm fronds and splayed her face with leaves of gold; her green eyes shone with a mysterious, wondrous warmth. She had a joyous secret, he knew, and he wanted to share it. They seemed to share little enough these days. His fault, perhaps, but he was so preoccupied, so harried by the constant meetings and briefings. Still, she had known about his work when they married, had even shared in it during the days of illegal immigration and the War for Independence. He wondered, sometimes, if she wanted to recant the bargain she had made so many years ago, and he cursed himself for his curtness, his fatigue, for the terrible fear that had weighted him since Noam's death. He had been unfair to her, his darling Rivka, his wonderful wife. Yet he himself needed time alone now—time to sort out his grief and his memories, time to overcome his despair. And Rebecca, too, he knew, sought an evasive solitude. He saw it in her eyes, sensed it in her recent work, her sketch of the shadow cast by a dwarfed olive tree on a deserted road, her pen-and-ink drawing of a lone hawk soaring darkly through a cloudless summer sky. How talented she was, his Rebecca, his wonderful Rebecca. He wanted desperately to be fair to her. He spoke her name in the soft, tender voice of an uncertain lover. She turned to him and smiled.

"Such good news, Yehuda. A letter from Mindell. She's pregnant."

"Wonderful," he said, but he did not reach for the letter, and she did not offer it to him. She wanted to reread the paragraph in which Mindell asked her, with strange and restive urgency, to come to the States for the birth if she possibly could. A double summons then, doubling also her longing and her uncertainty.

"Am I too late for the wedding?" Yehuda asked.

"No. They're just coming now," Rebecca said. "Look."

She pointed across the lawn, and he saw the small crowd surging joyously forward, heard the singing voices of the kibbutz children and the vibrant strains of Mordechai Meiri's accordion.

The children, all dressed in white, danced their way across the lawn. Garlands of flowers were looped about their necks: blood-red desert anemones, pale blue cactus flowers, fragile-petaled roses of Sharon, newly plucked from the bushes that Rebecca had planted in Noam's memory—*shoshanot Noam*, Noam's roses, the kibbutz children called them, and Rebecca smiled sadly when she heard them. The children pulled the kibbutz tractor, which was gaily decorated with flowers, laced with branches and vines. The very young bride sat on the driver's seat beneath a flowered canopy. She smiled shyly and clutched her bouquet of pink and white meadow saffron threaded with clusters of the delicate pale star-of-Bethlehem. Her name was Ronit, and she had, from childhood, been a plain girl who wore her light brown hair pulled back in a careless ponytail, always moving awkwardly in heavy, earth-caked boots. But today she claimed her bridal legacy and radiated a fragile, luminous beauty. She had added a blue satin sash to the simple white dress, traditionally worn by all the kibbutz brides. Her hair was brushed into silken folds and crowned with a coronet of pale blue cornflowers.

Oren, her bridegroom, stood proudly beside her, wearing the newly pressed khaki dress uniform of the paratrooper. His recently earned insignia gleamed on his epaulets. A white skullcap was balanced uneasily on his bright red curls, and he raised a freckled hand from time to time, to make certain that it was still in place. Friends from his brigade danced behind him in a vigorous line hora, their arms linked, their khaki shirts blotted with sweat. Buoyantly,with irreverent joy, they sang the ancient wedding hymn, the biblical nuptial choruses.

"Joy to the bride, happiness to the groom. . . . Rejoice, O Jerusalem, in the joy of their hearts!"

One soldier danced alone, his rifle held in both hands stretched before him, an obedient metallic partner. Sweat beaded his brow, trickled down his face.

How young they were, Rebecca thought—they were Noam's generation, in their late teens, early twenties. Many of them, she knew, would also marry in the next few months. Always, in Israel, apprehension of war brought an increase in marriages, just as the aftermath of war brought an increase in pregnancies and births. Danger beckoned love, the seizing of the day; death encouraged life, survival.

Tears filled her eyes. She did not want her sons to marry because they feared death. It was zest for life and love that had brought her and Yehuda together. They had plunged into their marriage, into the miracle of their lives together with eagerness and joy. The war was behind them. The time of danger and desolation was over. They had stood quietly on a Galilean hillside bathed in the golden warmth of a new peace. She could not bear to believe that they had been deceived, that new wars, new dangers and desolation had eroded the foundation of that hopeful love, that daring commitment. She had loved Yehuda then. *Then.*

Yehuda's hand rested on her shoulder. He sensed her mood, she knew, and she prayed that he had not perceived her fear.

"Let's watch the wedding, Rebecca," he said softly.

Together they walked to the grassy area in front of the dining room.

The bridal couple stood beneath a blue velvet wedding canopy that matched the desert sky. It was held up by four pitchforks at each corner, tightly clutched by kibbutz youngsters. Yaakov Arnon, who held one of the pitchforks, noticed his parents' entry, smiled, and concentrated again on his task. It was a kibbutz legend, repeated often in the children's house, that a boy had once dropped a pitchfork and the marriage had ended in divorce. But Yaakov's grasp was firm. He had inherited Yehuda's power of concentration, his dedication to the task at hand.

The guests sat on the benches that had been carried out of the dining hall. Later they would move the benches to the tables that had been set up across the lawn and spread with bright linen cloths. Rebecca and Yehuda found a place in the rear and listened as Oren made his pledge to Ronit.

"Behold you are consecrated unto me with this ring according to the laws of Moses and of Israel."

Yehuda's finger moved across Rebecca's narrow gold wedding band, worn thin over the years. The paratrooper's booted foot shattered the wineglass and shouts of *"Mazal tov!"* filled the air.

"Bridegrooms shouldn't be married in uniform," Rebecca said suddenly. Uniforms were symbolic of war; they did not belong beneath the tabernacle of love.

"But I was married in a uniform," Yehuda recalled absently.

"No." She withdrew her hand from his, inched away from him imperceptibly. At their wedding he had worn an open-necked white shirt and khaki trousers. It was his marriage to Miriam that he had so carelessly recalled; Rebecca had seen that wedding photo with Yehuda in his Haganah uniform, Miriam in a simple white dress not unlike Ronit's.

"I'm sorry," he said softly.

"It's all right," she replied, but her voice was muted.

"Is it?" he asked.

"No," she said in a flat, dead tone.

Yet even her bitter reply encouraged him. It was, at least, an improvement on the silence that sometimes stretched so tautly between them.

"What else did Mindell say?" he asked.

"She sounded a little frightened. She asked if I could come to New York for the birth."

"And I noticed another letter."

"Yes. From Charles Ferguson. He's mounting an exhibit of my work. A retrospective."

"And does he also want you to come to New York?"

"Yes. But it's impossible, of course."

"Why impossible?" he asked. His tone was light, and its casualness wounded her. She had anticipated fierce protest; he had responded with an almost indifferent query. She turned away and did not see how his gray eyes darkened or how he clenched his thin lips, as though willing himself to silence.

He wants me to go, she thought, with sudden frightening clarity. He wants me to leave him. Everything is changed between us. It's not only Noam's death, the tension in the country. It's everything. She almost spoke the words aloud, as though articulation would challenge their credibility, but instead they ricocheted through her mind and hurtled against her heart. She remained seated as the other guests hurried toward the tables, laden now with cold meats and salads, with bowls of fruit and pitchers of wine.

"Come on, *Ima*," Amnon called, pulling her up. "We're hungry. We want to eat."

She followed him to the table where Danielle sat beside Yair, and watched Yaakov as he clowned for his friends, wearing a maroon beret borrowed from a paratrooper. Sara Meiri, Rebecca's closest friend, stared at Yaakov. Her eldest son had also worn the paratrooper's beret. He had been killed during the Sinai Campaign. Her face was wreathed in sadness, and Rebecca's heart turned.

"Take that off," Rebecca said harshly to Yaakov, and they all turned and stared at her in surprise. Abruptly, she rose from the table and ran back to her bungalow, where she threw herself across the bed and waited for the tears that did not come.

She realized as she lay there, grieved but dry-eyed, her heart pounding in arrhythmic beat, that she doubted everything about her life in Israel. Her husband's love, her commitment to the kibbutz, and, above all, the future she wanted for her sons, all were shadowed by her own sudden uncertainty. She knew that she did not want her sons to be wounded in a war and sit as Yair sat, maimed and disabled, while other men whirled in a raucous hora. She did not want death to come to them, as it had come to Noam, as it might yet come to the redheaded bridegroom and to the soldier friends who had escorted him in song and dance to the marriage canopy. She was not as brave as Sara Meiri, who had lost her son, or as Miriam—the Mia of Yehuda's dream and memory—who had lost her life. She closed her eyes and allowed the tumescent sleep of emotional exhaustion to engulf her.

When she awakened, Yehuda was sitting in the chair beside the bed, slowly turning the pages of *ha-Aretz*.

"What time is it?" she asked.

"Not late. You slept for about an hour and a half. The entertainment is still going on."

She heard the strains of Mordechai Meiri's accordion. Soon it would be time for the bridal couple to steal away, and then the guests would dance again, forming wide circles for a hora, weaving across the field in elegant debkas until the younger people urgently called for Western music—frenetic twists, slow fox trots, and the intricate rhumbas and sambas that the Argentine immigrants had introduced. It was simple enough to entertain the young people of Israel, Rebecca thought. It was more difficult to protect them.

"Do you want to go back?" she asked.

"No. I want to talk to you," he said. "Rebecca, I am going to be away from the kibbutz a great deal."

"You are always away from the kibbutz a great deal," she replied. The bitterness of her answer soured her mouth. What was happening to them that they spewed spite at each other? And why, after almost twenty years in the country, was she suddenly so gripped by uncertainty, so entangled in a net of apprehension?

"You knew when we were married that I had special obligations."

"That was almost twenty years ago. Don't these special obligations ever come to an end? Doesn't another generation inherit them?"

Her voice was harsh. Yehuda had fought for the British in Europe, and then he had fought against them, at war's end, as a Mosad agent smuggling illegal immigrants into the country. He had been wounded in the War for Independence, and he had done battle during the Sinai Campaign. And always there had been clandestine trips out of the country—secret meetings in Larnaca and Athens, unexplained journeys to England and America. Surely, it was someone else's turn to take up that "special obligation."

"I must go," he repeated.

"Why you? Always you?"

"Others are also going."

"Where?"

"I cannot tell you."

She was silent. She could not argue against his secrets. The postcards would arrive, casual scrawls with colorful stamps that the children claimed noisily, clamoring for the stamp with the portrait of Idi Amin, Queen Sophia, the French tricolor. He would be scavenging arms and allies again, she knew, courting danger in European airports, African hotels, spacious homes in American suburbs. And she would be alone with her fear and uncertainty and her irrational jealousy of a woman long dead who surely would have been neither frightened nor uncertain. Miriam, Mia, whose name her husband sometimes whispered in his sleep.

"I think you should go to America while I am away," he continued. "You'll be with Mindell when she needs you. You'll be in New York for your exhibit."

"But the kibbutz, the boys," she protested. "How can I leave them?"

"The kibbutz is well staffed. We're flooded with volunteers just now, all keen to see a war. And the boys will be well taken care of in the children's house. Danielle is here. And you haven't been back to America for any length of time since we were married."

"Do you think I ought to check and see if there's something I might have missed?" she asked lightly.

"Perhaps. I would think it strange if you had not wondered from time to time what your life might have been like if you had stayed in America." He would not allow her forced flippancy to deceive them both. "I do know that it will do you good to get away. You've been so tense lately, so irritable."

"We have both been tense and irritable," she said. She would not allow him to exonerate himself. "There is something wrong between us." Their last refuge, she acknowledged now, was honesty.

"You must never be afraid to say what you feel," her father had once cautioned her gently. She had summoned her courage and spoken.

The words she had feared to utter had slipped out, and she waited for him to refute them. She wanted him to embrace her, to look at her and murmur, "No, there is nothing wrong. You are my Rivka, my darling Rivka." His silken-gray eyes would be soft upon her face, as they had been so many years ago in the Jerusalem hospital where she had tended his wounds and claimed his love. But he said nothing and continued to stare out the window at the evening shadows that cast violet streaks across the sand crater.

He was quiet then, as though drained of words. She struggled to assess his silence, to coax forth explanations, to understand the pain she read in his eyes. But she understood that she could not invade his struggle. They had reached a crossroads, and now, for a time, they would take separate paths. Still, briefly, she persisted.

"How can I leave the country when there is danger of war?"

"I do not think there will be war this year. Only saber rattling. Algeria inspired Shukairy. Why fight a real war when terror is so potent?"

She rose and stood beside him at the window, her head resting on his shoulder. Stars spangled the desert sky, and the wedding music drifted toward them.

"It will not be easy," she said, "but I think that you are right."

"Sometimes it is necessary to go away only so that one may come home again. Really home. At last."

How gentle his voice was. She stood revealed before him, she knew. He recognized her love and her longing, her courage and her fear. His large hand covered her head; his fingers fondled the thick tendrils of her coarse black curls.

"It will be all right," she said, but he did not answer. He held her even closer because soon they would be apart and alone.

REBECCA

1966–1967

MINDELL AND MICHAEL GOLDFEDER pressed their faces against the glass window of the observation tower and watched as the El Al jumbo jet tipped its blue-starred wings and taxied to a halt on the rain-streaked runway at Kennedy International Airport. Stairwells were swiftly slipped into place at the plane's exits, and slowly, warily, the passengers disembarked and peered toward the wide-windowed arrivals building, as though even from the distance they might discern a relation, a friend. Two bearded men in black caftans and wide-rimmed fur hats carefully picked their way down the metallic steps and waited as their bewigged wives trailed after them. A lanky youngster wearing jeans and a Hebrew University sweatshirt descended, awkwardly balancing his guitar. Michael would not be surprised to see him, in a few weeks' time, sprawled in the student lounge at Hutchinson College, playing mournful songs about the Galilee at twilight to wide-eyed, long-haired coeds.

Harried couples, managing too many bags and supervising too many children, barely looked up, but the slender woman whose dark hair was winged with silver peered above the head of the small blond child she carried and smiled as droplets of rain fell on her upturned face.

"There she is," Mindell said, and she waved frantically, although she knew that Rebecca could not see her.

"Yes. I see her." Michael felt ashamed because the child in his sister's arms had deceived him and he had stared past her without recognition. It would be like Rebecca to assist another passenger. Leah's children had been well taught. He himself often found himself holding a stranger's baby in airports or carrying shopping bags for the elderly men and women who lived on his street. "We are all connected to each other," their father had told them again and again. "It is the smallest kindness that counts," Leah had reminded them. Leah and David, during their journey from Russia to the States, during their early years of poverty and struggle, had so often depended on the kindness of others.

"Rebecca looks tired," Michael said.

"But beautiful."

Mindell was reminded now of the first time she had seen Rebecca, as she descended the stairwell to the cellar hiding place in Bari. Mindell had been taken there after her release from Auschwitz, and she remembered still how frightened she had been when she glimpsed her own reflection in the mirror. A small ghostly face, framed with lank strands of pale gold hair, had stared back at her. She had stared in wonder then at Rebecca, who had been recruited by Yehuda to escort that group of children to Palestine. She had marveled at the young American woman's high color, at her thick black hair and full figure. There was verve in her voice and vibrance in her laughter. When she spoke, the frightened children began to believe in the possibilities of freedom and joy.

Rebecca had married Yehuda, and as the years passed, the desert sun had burnished her skin and the youthful softness of her features had been honed into the chiseled profile that intrigued Israel's leading portrait photographers. Mindell kept a copy of *Ariel*, Israel's cultural journal, which featured a photo essay entitled "Rebecca Arnon—Kibbutz Artist," on the small coffee table in their Eldridge Street apartment.

Often, she studied the photograph of Rebecca reading to Yaakov and Amnon and the accompanying shot of Rebecca and Yehuda carefully pruning a rosebush they had planted in the garden in memory of Noam. She especially loved the portrait of Rebecca at work, her full lips pressed closed in concentration, her fingers gripping the paintbrush with such intensity that the furl of skin where the flesh tensed about the wood was perceptible.

The essay that accompanied the photographs included an interview with Rebecca. Did the artist regret her decision to settle in Israel? "No. I have found satisfaction here." "But surely," the interviewer had persisted, "in America there would have been more opportunity to study, to meet with other artists, to mount exhibitions that would attract international recognition." "Such opportunities are more than balanced by what I found in Israel," Rebecca had replied.

Mindell wondered whether Rebecca's answers would be the same now if similar questions were asked. She had visited Israel twice since her marriage to Michael, and on each visit she had been conscious of new tensions between Rebecca and Yehuda. A controlled courtesy had replaced the spontaneity that had characterized their early years together. They spoke little and seemed to measure their words carefully.

They remained leaders of the kibbutz. In open meetings they radiated authority; their opinions were listened to with respect and consideration. Always their voices were firm and rang with conviction. Younger members came to Rebecca with their problems, sought her advice. Yehuda sat on important committees. Rebecca sat in for him occasionally, because he was so often out of the country, and there was general agreement that she spoke with his voice, reflected his feelings. Yet, when they were alone together, they sometimes spoke with the controlled courtesy of estranged friends who wish, at all costs, to avoid a confrontation. Too often, Yehuda averted his eyes from her intense gaze; too often, Rebecca ignored his outstretched hand. They seemed then, despite their energy and strength, oddly vulnerable, and Mindell, who observed them with love, was troubled.

"Is there something wrong between Rebecca and Yehuda?" Mindell had asked Danielle during her last visit. Yehuda's blond daughter had nodded.

"It's been that way since Noam's death. Sometimes I think it's because my father is away so often—more now than ever before. And sometimes Rebecca does not even know if he's in the country or abroad. Once Yaakov became ill and ran a high fever, and we could not locate him. At first she was frightened and then she was angry. She needed him, and she was alone. It was not easy. It is not easy."

Danielle blamed neither her father nor Rebecca. There was no culpability. That was the way life was in Israel. They never discussed her father's work, but it was assumed that he was involved in intelligence operations.

Mindell thought about the secrecy of Yehuda's work and the restrictions it imposed on his marriage. She and Michael had long conversations each evening about their jobs—his students, her patients. What would their marriage be like, she wondered, if they had to conceal such important aspects of their lives from each other?

"And, since Noam's death, I think Rebecca has been frightened," Danielle added hesitantly. "Not for herself. Never for herself. But for the children—for Yaakov and Amnon."

Fear was a stigma in Israel, where clouds of danger threatened the brightness of each day. Every border was hostile, and acts of terror plagued the cities and towns, haunted the settlements. Daily the papers carried stories of bombs discovered beneath sand pails on the beaches, explosives concealed in supermarket shopping carts, Fatah members apprehended at the Lebanese border. But fear was the greatest enemy because it threatened any semblance of normality and validated the philosophy of terror.

"I don't blame Rebecca for being frightened," Danielle continued. "We were born into the danger. It came to us as a fact of life, a challenge. When I was very little, the children's house on our kibbutz was burned by the Mufti's gang, the Black Hand. I remember still the woman who carried us to safety through the flames, kept on cautioning us not be frightened. 'You must be brave, children,' she kept saying. We were scared, of course. Our faces were black with soot, our eyes smarted, and we did not know where our parents were. Still, we sang a song proclaiming our bravery, even though our voices cracked as we sang. 'We will never leave the land. We are proud and we are brave.' " Danielle hummed softly. "But Rebecca did not grow up here. The danger, the responsibility, was thrust upon her. I don't think her life in America prepared her for it. Still, everyone remembers her courage during illegal immigration. Always she is the last to descend to the shelter."

"Michael told me that her parents, Leah and David, called her their princess. All they wanted was to see her happy, to hear her laugh," Mindell acknowledged. There was no danger on the tree-lined streets of Scarsdale village, no terror and threat in the rolling hills of Vermont where young Rebecca Goldfeder had studied art. "But still she did come to Israel. And she loved—loves—your father. She chose this life—she loves this land."

Mindell remembered walking with Rebecca through the fields of Sha'arei ha-Negev on a distant summer dawn. The air had been cool and threaded with the thin rays of pale gold that preceded the brilliant radiance of the desert morning. They had paused at a newly planted tract where the pale green ovoids of young melons swelled on thick-leafed vines.

"Look, Mindell. And they were sure nothing would grow here," Rebecca had said, triumph and pride in her voice. She had knelt and touched the earth, and Mindell had seen tears glinting in her eyes. Danielle was right. Yehuda had led her to the dream, perhaps even imposed it upon her, but it had, with the passing years, become her own. Chance had magically drifted into choice.

Yet Mindell did not share this memory with Danielle. There was no need to offer a defense of Rebecca—strong, brave Rebecca who required no advocate.

Danielle smiled sadly.

"Perhaps she didn't recognize then what her choice involved. The loneliness, with all her family in America. The secrets. The danger. She could not have known what it would be like to be the mother of sons in Israel. I watched her at Noam's funeral. She held Yaakov's hand so tightly that he had to pull it away. She never took her eyes off Amnon. I saw then that Rebecca's grief for Noam was mingled with fear for her own sons. And I understood that fear."

"How do you know all this, Danielle?" Mindell asked. Danielle's perceptions awed and mystified her. She and Danielle had grown up together, as sisterly friends, inseparable companions, and always, it had seemed to her, Danielle had been possessed of an intuitive wisdom. Even as a child she perceived the source of another child's misery, sensed and soothed night terrors. Often, her sweetly singing voice had calmed the frightened youngsters as they huddled in the shelter. Motherless Danielle had known how to mother others.

"I don't know," she replied. "I only suppose. Maybe because now I acknowledge my own fear. Sometimes I think that I will marry Yair partly because I love him and partly because he is crippled and he will never have to go to war again. I will never have to fear for him, I will never have to be afraid that he will be killed before our children are grown. Can you understand that?"

"Yes, of course I can." Mindell had leaned forward and stretched her hand out to Danielle. "It's nothing to be ashamed of."

"I am not ashamed," Danielle had replied.

Would Rebecca be ashamed, Mindell wondered now, to acknowledge her fear, to confront her loneliness? It was strange how roles were reversed. Throughout their childhoods, Rebecca had mothered Danielle and Mindell. Now it was they who worried over her and sought to shield and protect her.

"Come, Mindell. They are passing through customs."

Michael took her arm, and they hurried down from the observation tower. By the time they reached the main floor, Rebecca Arnon was making her way through passport control. She moved slowly, weighted by a weariness induced by more than the long journey. Her face was veiled in a sadness Mindell had not seen before. Then suddenly she looked up and saw Michael and Mindell waving excitedly at her from behind the glass partition. She smiled brilliantly and stood erect, recalling to Mindell's mind that bright-faced, strong young American woman who had stood before the frightened children in the concealed basement of the Bari house so many years ago.

"Rebecca!" she shouted joyously, and Rebecca Arnon waved in return, with the relieved exuberance of a traveler who has safely returned from a long and treacherous journey.

SHERRY ELLENBERG surveyed her brightly lit living room approvingly, flushed with the anticipation of the evening ahead. She had always loved giving parties. As a small girl, growing up in a shabby council flat in Bournemouth, she had improvised parties to celebrate her friends' birthdays, her relatives' anniversaries. Later, during the war years when she had worked as a nurse at a military hospital, she had tossed streamers of colored paper through her ward and served pastries begged from neighboring tearooms to mark one patient's leaving, another's birthday. Joshua Ellenberg, a patient in that hospital, had fallen in love with Sherry as she led a group of convalescents in a rousing chorus of "Happy Birthday." He had forgotten about his right hand mangled during a battle along the banks of the Rhine; he had forgotten also about Rebecca Goldfeder, whom he had thought he loved but who did not love him.

"Sing!" Sherry had urged, and suddenly he had heard his own voice, sounding surprisingly strong and carefree, joining in the song. He had realized then that he was alive and having fun and that his life would be filled with tomorrows. When he proposed to Sherry, in a quiet London pub where a lone drunk mournfully sang "The White Cliffs of Dover," he had promised her that their life together would be a wonderful partnership full of joy and excitement.

"One day we'll have a wonderful house," he pledged. "Cars, vacations." There would be trips to England to visit her family, the best of everything for their children. The certainty of his own success pulsed through Joshua's veins, throbbed in his voice. The postwar years would be boom times, and he would be ready for them.

"And parties?" Sherry had asked teasingly.

"And parties," he had promised.

He had kept his promise. They had hosted small parties in their first apartment to celebrate the success of Joshua's first year as an independent manufacturer, Aaron Goldfeder's first marriage, the birth of the twins, Scott and Lisa; there had been larger gatherings and barbecues in their first tract house in Levittown and then, as Ellenberg Industries expanded and the two younger children, Joanna and Stevie, were born, the famous open houses on their Great Neck estate.

Sherry's floral arrangements were unique—pussywillows and orchids to celebrate Aaron Goldfeder's appointment to a judgeship, rainbow-colored gladioli for the twins' high school graduation party, russet chrysanthemums for Stevie's bar mitzvah, and scarlet roses in nests of baby's breath for Joanne's sweet-sixteen. But always Sherry's most spectacular party was given on New Year's Eve—a dual celebration of the twins' birthday and the year's end. And this year, because the party was also in honor of Rebecca Arnon's first extended visit to the United States, Sherry had worked doubly hard.

Joshua had told her that Rebecca loved yellow roses, and though they were out of season and outrageously expensive, she had ordered masses of them. The long-stemmed flowers filled the tall crystal vases that stood on every table and were gracefully arranged in the copper planters that banked the marble fireplace. The dancing flames tossed topaz shadows across the delicate petals, and their fragrance filled the room with the scent of summer. Lemon-colored cloths covered the small tables that the caterer had arranged, and on each table a bud vase contained a single tall sunshine-colored blossom.

"Doesn't the room look beautiful?" Sherry asked Lisa, who had wandered in.

Lisa shrugged and a frown furrowed her high forehead. She had inherited her mother's auburn hair, which fell in silken folds about her shoulders. Her black turtleneck sweater emphasized the pallor of her skin. She seemed so thin in her faded, ink-stained jeans, Sherry thought, and she looked away from the lines of fatigue that webbed her daughter's eyes. As always, Lisa was working too hard, studying too intensely.

"It should look beautiful," Lisa replied. "It cost enough. We probably could have bought a mimeograph machine for the Coalition office for what you paid for those flowers."

Sherry did not answer. She did not fully understand her daughter's affiliation with the Coalition to End the War in Vietnam, but she accepted it as she accepted all things that engrossed her children. Always Lisa's involvements had been intense, passionate.

She had been a grave-eyed child who had wept inconsolably over the death of a small dog, struck by a speeding car on their street. Tearfully she had gathered up the broken forms of fledgling robins and buried them in a corner of the garden. When she walked past Bloomingdale's, she held coins in readiness for the palsied man who hawked comic books in front of the emporium. She averted her eyes as she dropped the money into his outstretched cup. Death and cruelty, deprivation and suffering, bewildered and saddened her. She could not reconcile the prosperity of her home, the protected and protective ambience of her childhood, with the misery and hazards of the world around her. Her parents exhorted her to be happy, and, obediently, Lisa went to parties, took horseback riding lessons, skied in the winter and sailed in the summer. Her father demanded her laughter, and she turned away so that he would not see the pain in her eyes as they drove through the streets of St. Albans on their way to Great Neck. Something had to be done to make the world different, better. There had to be something, anything, that she, Lisa Ellenberg, could do.

When a young physician from the Coalition showed explicit and terrifying films of the aftermath of a village bombing in Vietnam, during Lisa's freshman year at Hutchinson College, she had wept openly, written a check that consumed her entire monthly allowance, and returned to her dormitory. There, she lay awake in the darkness and saw, again and again in her mind's eye, the scarred bodies of small children seared by napalm, the frightened eyes of aged montagnards who had been forced to leave their mountain villages. When she slept at last, she dreamed that she stood alone on a sloping sand dune while graceful yellow-skinned men and women paraded past her and walked mindlessly into a sea of blood. The next morning she cut all her classes, boarded a train for New York, and signed up as a volunteer at the Coalition.

Her work and her studies absorbed her, and she was increasingly impatient with her family, with the opulence of the Great Neck home, her twin brother's determined academic ambition, and the frivolity of the younger children. Scott, an economics major at Harvard, had known since his first day as a freshman that he would go on to do graduate work at the Wharton School of Business.

"Don't you give a damn about the world around you?" Lisa had asked him contemptuously.

"I give a damn. I just happen to think more change can be effected by having enlightened people in the seats of power than by having a bunch of screaming Yippies who dropped out in their freshman year making scenes in the street."

"The people in the Coalition are not Yippies," Lisa had retorted. "And they're not flunking out. At least I'm not."

She was, in fact, compulsive about school and made the dean's list consistently each semester. It was a mystery to Sherry how Lisa managed to work so many hours for the Coalition and still keep her grades high. She had mentioned this to Michael Goldfeder, who taught Lisa's sociology seminar, and he had laughed indulgently.

"She's Joshua's daughter. She has his energy. A couple of hours of sleep, a quick shower, and she's back in business. She's one of the sharpest gals in that class, Sherry. Not to worry."

And Sherry had noticed that although Lisa often arrived home dull-eyed and listless, within a few hours she would emerge from her room as though recharged, moving almost hyperkinetically, her green eyes glittering, her color high. She looked exhausted now, but by the time the guests began arriving, she would be aglow with the wonderful incandescence that caused Joshua to look at her with proud satisfaction. His children's happiness and beauty validated his own success, and he would hug his elder daughter and never notice that her hands trembled and her eyes were dangerously bright.

"I'll change now," Lisa said wearily.

Sherry kissed her daughter on the cheek.

"Happy birthday, darling," she said. "I asked the Goldfeders to come a bit early for a birthday toast, so you don't have all that much time."

"I'll be ready," Lisa promised. She loved and admired the Goldfeders, who had been an ancillary family to her all her life. And because she felt a vague disloyalty when she compared her own mother to the Goldfeder women, she hugged her with special warmth and hurried upstairs.

LIKE a latecomer to the theater, Rebecca paused hesitantly at the entry of the Ellenberg living room and studied the scene in progress before her. She stared at Sherry Ellenberg, resplendent in a turquoise taffeta dress, and wondered if her own simple white wool dress was too austere. Sherry moved among her guests, talking softly, smiling and motioning almost imperceptibly now and again to a uniformed maid who hurried over to offer a glass of champagne or remove an empty plate.

A richly patterned Oriental rug covered the polished floor, and the guests moved soundlessly across it, to greet and embrace one another. The trill of laughter and the hum of earnest conversation filled the room, growing louder as glasses were refilled and more guests arrived. Jakie Hart kissed Rebecca and introduced her to his third wife. She smelled the scent of martini on his breath and remembered how, as a small boy, newly arrived from Europe, he had seemed always to smell of onions. Her cousin Jakie had come a long way.

Aaron and Lydia sat on the deep-gold velvet love seat, their hands linked, and listened to Scott Ellenberg's analysis of Lyndon Johnson's domestic policy. The president was naive, Scott asserted with the absolute and impenetrable certainty of the young. A great society could not be legislated into existence. It had to evolve gradually and systematically.

Lisa Ellenberg listened to her brother and said nothing, although her lips curled with impatience and she toyed nervously with her long strand of amber beads.

Mindell and Michael stood before the fire with Leah and Boris. The dancing flames ignited Mindell's fair skin, turned her fair hair the color of honey. She laughed at something Michael said and turned to Leah, who nodded and smiled. Leah looked happy, Rebecca thought, and she watched as Sherry joined the group and led Boris and Leah to seats near the fire. Joshua joined them, carrying a glass of white wine for Leah, a snifter of brandy for Boris. Sherry rearranged the short-stemmed yellow roses that filled a polished copper bowl. She selected two buds and deftly placed one in Boris's lapel and the other in Joshua's. The men smiled their approval. Joshua kissed her, and Leah leaned forward and patted Shery's upswept auburn curls. Her marriage to Boris had reinvigorated Leah. Joy and companionship, purpose and fulfillment had been restored to her. Her studio was littered with new projects, and she kept a sketch pad in her purse.

Sherry smiled and moved on to another group, Joshua beside her. A bittersweet jealousy stole over Rebecca. She recognized, with detached clarity, that she was looking at the life that might have been hers. Sherry's spontaneous gesture might have been her own. Even the yellow roses, displayed in such profusion, would have been the flowers of her own choice. She remembered a distant summer when she and Joshua, childhood companions, had wandered away from the Catskill colony where their two families shared a bungalow. They had found a rosebush growing wild and untended in the garden of an abandoned farmhouse. The profusion of sun-colored flowers had fascinated the tenement children; they had plucked them with wild abandon, pricking their fingers with thorns and scratching their thin arms with the spiky tendrils of their fragrant burdens.

"When we grow up, I'll bring you yellow roses every week," Joshua had promised her. "We'll live in a big house, and I'll fill it with flowers."

But with the passing years reality had betrayed fantasy. Rebecca had stood beside Joshua in a Vermont meadow and renounced his dream. She remembered still the sad and awkward bulge the ring she had rejected made when he thrust the blue velvet case back into his pocket. Their lives had been severed then, and they had followed separate paths, each finding a new togetherness—Joshua with Sherry, Rebecca with Yehuda. Still, Joshua had not entirely abandoned his dream. He had built a big house and filled it with flowers, and Rebecca came as a guest into the room where she might have stood as a welcoming hostess.

The thought frightened her, filled her with an unfamiliar and bewildering guilt.

I don't regret it, she told herself fiercely. She had not loved Joshua. She had never loved Joshua. It was Yehuda, with his silken-gray eyes and his earth-colored hair, who had caused her hands to tremble and her heart to turn. He had wrenched her free of the life she had known. Like a seductive sorcerer, he had drawn her into the enchanted circle of his dream and spirited her away to live in the whitewashed bungalow at the base of a sand crater in Israel's southland.

His voice had been vibrant as he described the life that could be theirs, the exciting horizons that stretched before them. He had held her in his arms, and she had felt herself infused with the energy that drove him. Her body weakened beneath the impact of his certain strength and, in the quiet aftermath of their love, she touched his eyes, the thickness of his ocher hair, the milk-white scar that cleft his high forehead. He had mesmerized her with the intensity of his dream, with the sweet power of his smile, and with the knowing tenderness of his touch.

She had, of course, been a willing and eager subject. Yehuda's dream had fired her enthusiasm, ignited her own creative energy. And she loved the country. Its landscapes sprang to life beneath her brush. Her fingers quivered as she sketched. She dreamed in pastels, in vibrant, layered oils. Its history became her own. She and her children, she and Yehuda, were part of a great experiment—they were creating a new nation, a new society. She escorted American visitors through Sha'arei ha-Negev and could not restrain the pride in her voice as she told them that when she and Yehuda had first settled there the kibbutz had been a barren waste and for the first two years they had lived in a trailer. Now the kibbutz fields were lush with burgeoning crops, and neat white bungalows formed a crescent in front of the sand crater.

She did not tell the visitors that many of the early settlers had left the kibbutz. Even native-born sons and daughters of Israel had found life in the desert too difficult. But she, Rebecca Arnon, who had played tennis on the lawn courts of Scarsdale and walked the shaded meadows of Bennington, had never contemplated leaving. Yehuda's world, during that time, had become her own.

It was only in recent years that she had begun to fret over the basic inequity in the love bargain she had struck. It was she who had left home and family. It was she who had had to learn a new language and who dreamed in a tongue unlike the one she spoke. She returned to America and felt herself a visitor and a stranger in her native land. Her children and her brother's children were strangers to one another. The list of debits shamed her, and she acknowledged, too, the assets, the gains, that settling in Israel had brought her. Still, she could not balance the ledger. Perhaps now, on this journey home, she would reach a justified accounting.

Rebecca watched Lisa Ellenberg walk across the room. She had been only a few years older than Lisa when she left for Palestine. She heard Lisa laugh and saw her dance away in the arms of a long-haired young man, and she thought that someone should warn Joshua's daughter to tread carefully because the decisions of young girls became the lives of women.

"Are you all right, Rebecca?" Leah asked as Rebecca approached her. Rebecca's eyes were too bright, and her color was dangerously high, almost febrile.

"I'm fine," Rebecca assured her and went off to join Michael and Mindell, but Leah watched her with worried gaze. Boris pressed her hand.

"She will find her way," he said softly, and Leah sighed, acknowledging that her children had, of course, crossed the borders of her protection and were independent journeyers. And Rebecca, she knew, had the tenacity and strength to endure the most treacherous odyssey.

"Time for the toast," Joshua called, and they gathered in front of the fireplace.

The Ellenbergs lifted their glasses. Lisa's head rested lightly on her father's shoulder, and Scott stood tall beside him. Sherry, flushed with excitement and happiness, held the hands of the younger children, ignoring Stevie's impatience, Joanna's giggling.

What were Yaakov and Amnon doing now? Rebecca wondered. She watched Joshua and Sherry with their children and experienced an almost visceral yearning for her sons. She imagined them asleep on their narrow cots in the kibbutz children's house, Amnon's long lashes sweeping across the rise of his cheekbones, Yaakov smiling at a mysterious, happy dream. How beautiful her sons were and how soft their fingers against her upturned palms. What was she doing so far away from them? She would call the kibbutz that night and discuss a speedy return to Israel. She had seen her mother and her brothers, her American friends and relations, and the retrospective did not require her presence. Her life was in another country. The new determination lightened her mood, excused the bitter thoughts of moments before. She leaned against the mantel and listened to Joshua.

"Tonight," he said, "Scott and Lisa celebrate their twentieth birthdays. We wish them joy to match the joy they have given us. We wish them long life and happiness. To our son and daughter. To Scott. To Lisa." His voice trembled. He embraced his wife and beamed at his children. His toast was not wish but edict. His success would guarantee their happiness.

"To Scott. To Lisa."

Their voices rang with gladness, and they saluted the twins with brimming glasses. Scott touched his father's goblet with his own, and the other guests imitated the gesture. The gentle crystal tympany that filled the room was shattered suddenly by the sound of breaking glass. Lisa's goblet had slipped from her fingers, and the polished floor was covered with glittering shards.

"Never mind. Never mind. It will be taken care of." Sherry moved swiftly forward and a maid armed with brush and dust pan hurried over. But Lisa knelt and, like a sleepwalker, touched a sliver of glass. A tear-shaped drop of blood formed at her fingertip, and she stared at it until Joshua pressed his handerchief against it.

"Another toast." Aaron's voice diverted their attention, restored their mood, and they turned gratefully to him.

"To the new year of 1967. To peace and freedom."

"To peace. To freedom." Again they lifted their glasses, but this time their voices were resonant with solemnity.

They drank to peace, although they daily inhaled the sour breath of war. Uniformed youths marched across their television screens as they watched the war each night, heavy-hearted with sorrow, glassy-eyed with disbelief. They leaned forward to study the incineration of a mountain village and averted their eyes from the footage of moaning men, writhing with pain as they were carried to helicopters.

They flicked their sets off when weeping children trailed across the screen. Jakie Hart's oldest son was a combat soldier in Vietnam. A youngster Michael had tutored in Troy had been wounded in the Tet offensive; Jared Parks, his Berkeley student, had been killed. Michael lifted his glass, but he did not drink. He could not drink to peace when war haunted his thoughts. He looked at Rebecca, who shivered, although the fire was hot against her back.

"To peace!" Aaron had said, but Rebecca remembered the last radio broadcast she had listened to in Israel—Nasser's bellicose voice and the thunderous response of his people. "What are they saying?" she had asked Yehuda, whose Arabic was fluent. His reply had been flat. "We want war. Kill the Jews." He had invited her then, perhaps, to understand why he had to continue what he called his "special obligation," but she had not responded. She understood all too well. Her comprehension lay heavy on her heart, formed a ganglion of doubt and fear that she fought daily.

They drank to freedom and thought of the fires that had blazed that past summer in the ghettos of Cleveland and Chicago, of the civil rights workers who had been terrorized and beaten in the hamlets and on the highways of the South.

The champagne left a bitter taste in Les Anderson's mouth, but he downed it because he was determined to get drunk. He was exhausted after his work on an in-depth essay on James Meredith's march from Memphis to Jackson. He wondered if he should tell Michael that he had interviewed Kemala. She had married Matt Williams, but it was rumored that the marriage was not a happy one. Her replies to his questions had been laced with bitterness.

"Meredith's just lucky that the bullet that stopped him didn't kill him. Time is running out for nonviolence."

She had not asked about Michael, and she had stared contemptuously at Les as he copied her comment into his notebook. He had used it as the closing quotation for his article. A stupid summation, he decided, and allowed the maid to refill his glass.

"To freedom," he said, but his voice was flat, deadened. He hoped his essay would not win any journalistic prizes. He did not want to write any more civil rights stories. He would ask for an assignment overseas and cover a real war in which armed men fought one another openly. He was sick to death of bombs concealed in the basements of southern Baptist churches where blacks came to worship, of sniper bullets whizzing across highways and rooftops, of volleys of hatred fired aross the airwaves. He would go to Vietnam, perhaps, or to the Middle East, or even to Biafra. One thing was certain about the new year of 1967—he would be offered a varied choice of wars.

The doorbell rang again and again and more and more guests arrived. Men and women in evening dress smiled benevolently at younger guests in jeans and open shirts, in brightly colored mini-dresses and loose-fitting dresses of African design. They talked and laughed, flushed with the cold and with drinks consumed at other parties. A light snow fell, and Rebecca tasted the melting flakes as she dutifully kissed the cheeks of the relatives and old friends who pressed forward to greet her.

"So wonderful to have you back, dear. Isn't it wonderful to be home again? Your mother is so pleased."

But I'm not home, she wanted to reply. *Or at least, I don't think I am. In fact, for the first time in almost twenty years I'm not sure where home is.*

Instead she smiled and nodded and pretended not to hear their murmuring voices as they walked away. (*She's still so pretty, our Rebecca. But she looks so tired. . . . Perhaps it's just that white dress. Leah should have found her something more colorful. . . . You know how those Israeli women are, not at all interested in clothing—so idealistic. . . .*)

Rebecca studied the crowd, searching out familiar faces, trying to match husbands with their wives, to remember the bits of gossip about friends and relations that had filtered down to her through the years. She recognized the Levensons, who had been their neighbors in Brooklyn, and the buxom woman whose hair was dyed bright red was Pearlie, who had boarded with them during those early years in Eldridge Street. But who was the tall man with iron-gray hair who was talking so earnestly to Charles Ferguson? His craggy, uenven features were teasingly familiar, but she could not place him. An old friend of Charles's, she supposed. She turned to greet her uncle, Seymour Hart, grown so frail now that she could not match him with her memory of the buoyant man who had tossed her into the air each evening of her childhood, delighting her with scraps of fabric, empty bobbins, and bits of sticky penny candy.

"You're well, Becca?" the old man asked her. "Everything is all right by you?"

"Yes, Uncle. Why do you ask?" His question and the knowing worry in his eyes aroused her defenses.

"*Nu?* You think I don't know what it's like to be born and grow up in one country and then to live in another? You think in one language and you speak in another. When I first came to America I used to dream every night about the meadows and forests of Russia. Still I can remember the smell of the pines and the feel of grass and leaves beneath my feet. That I remember. That I didn't forget."

He forgot so many other things. His grandchildren's names eluded him, and when he went for a walk he counted the blocks carefully because once he had lost his way and it had taken him hours to find his house. His wife, Mollie, Leah's sister, had died years ago, but still in the darkness of the night he talked to her, even quarreled with her. But he never forgot the woodlands of his Russian boyhood or those early years in America.

He studied his niece with his shrewd, old man's eyes.

"Still, I don't worry about you, Becca. You're your mother's daughter. You know how to fight, how to survive. Like Leah knew."

He looked at Leah, who stood before the fire, laughing at something Boris said. Seymour Hart's own mirth was thin and hesitant, but Leah, who was of his generation, laughed as young women did, with zest and eagerness. There was no need to be concerned about the daughter of such a woman. Rebecca's struggles, like Leah's, would be arduous, but in the end, her laughter, too, would ring with vibrancy and she, too, would move from strength to strength. Seymour Hart sighed, impatient with himself because he was an old man who knew too much yet remembered too little.

"Rebecca! You look marvelous." Charles Ferguson made his way across the room to her. He was full of news about her retrospective. Every major critic had accepted his invitation to the opening, and it was certain that *Art News* would do an interview. Just today he had had an inquiry from public television about a possible feature. "Isn't it exciting?" he said and rushed away before she could tell him that she was thinking of returning to Israel before the opening.

A trio of youthful musicians set up their instruments near the window, and couples danced to the mellow commingling of piano, flute, and guitar. The music was slow and dreamy. Rebecca swayed to the rhythm of the slow fox trot of the *Carousel* theme. She remembered dancing to it during her Bennington days, barefoot and wearing jeans and her father's oversized white shirt, her black hair clustered in bunches at her ears. She had been Joe Stevenson's girl then. Joe had been her sculpture teacher, her first lover and now her friend. He and his Danish wife, Inga, had been invited to this party, she knew, but Sherry had told her that they had called earlier in the evening. The fog was thick above Nantucket Island where they lived. They would see Rebecca at the opening of her show.

The pianist played alone now. "Strangers in the Night." She moved to the music, so lost in her mood that she did not notice the man with iron-gray hair and craggy features until he opened his arms. Obediently, she danced into the circle of his embrace and allowed him to lead her out to the improvised dance floor. His hand held hers lightly, gently, but his arm against her back was controlling as he danced her around the room. He did not release her when the song ended but held her until the musicians struck up "The Tennessee Waltz."

Now they whirled about the room, and she surrendered to the ease and grace of the dance. They sang the first verse softly together, as though they had long been partners and this was an established custom between them.

They laughed because the next line eluded them and instead they hummed softly. Their voices joined again as the words rushed at them in a sudden spurt of memory.

The music stopped and they stood looking at each other, song and laughter still on their lips. Each waited for the other to speak, but their silence was oddly comfortable and unstrained.

"Excuse me." Joanna Ellenberg stood beside her. "My mother said to tell you there's a call for you. You can take it in the den. I'll show you."

Rebecca's heart beat more rapidly. Names rushed into her mind and her throat grew dry with fear. Yehuda. Yaakov. Amnon.

"Excuse me."

"Of course."

She felt his eyes follow her as she hurried after Joanna, but she could think only of the phone call. It would not be bad news, she decided. Any bad news would have been communicated to her brothers. Surely, the call was from Yehuda. He was calling to wish her a happy new year, to apologize for the few hastily scrawled letters he had sent her since her departure, to tell her that he loved her and that he wanted her to return soon—soonest. *Rivka, my Rivka.* The sound of his voice was reverberant in her memory. "Yehuda, my Yehuda," she whispered. She smiled at Joanna, closed the oaken door of Joshua's den, and picked up the receiver.

But it was Danielle's voice, crackling with excitement, that greeted her, magically strong as it traversed continents and oceans.

"Rivka—happy new year! Don't be worried. Everything is all right. But I wanted you to be the first to know."

"To know what, Danielle?" She felt dizzy, caught on the mixed currents of relief and disappointment. *Everything was all right, but it was not Yehuda who had called.*

"Yair and I have decided to be married. Just today we came to the decision."

"I'm glad, Danielle." She had always liked Yair, and she admired the way he coped with his disability. He was neither bitter nor dispirited. And he would never have to go to war again. Danielle, whose mother had been killed by a German officer and whose brother had been murdered by an Arab terrorist, would not be widowed by war. That was something. That was a great deal.

"Yaakov and Amnon are here in the office with me," Danielle said. "Do you want to talk to them?"

"Yes, of course. I want to speak to everyone, but let me speak to your father—to Yehuda—first."

There was silence, and Rebecca feared that their connection had been lost, but then Danielle was speaking again, her voice more subdued, more distant.

"I'm sorry. He's not here. He's traveling about and told us that we might not hear from him for a while. We're not even sure that he's in the country. Hasn't he written you?"

"Yes. Of course." Yehuda's few letters had been posted from Israel, but that meant nothing, she knew. Often, before he left for a mission, he prepared letters in advance, which were mailed periodically to the children so that they would not be anxious. Almost always she had known when he would be out of the country. But this time she did not know. He had been vague about dates, destinations. He had thrust her further out of his life, out of his confidence. Damn his "special obligation." Anger flashed and replaced disappointment.

But her voice was controlled as she spoke to her sons. Yaakov sounded treacherously mature as he assured her that he watched over Amnon and complained that Amnon did not always mind him. Amnon's voice quivered. He struggled against tears, she knew.

"Are you coming home soon, *Ima*?" he asked.

"In a while," she replied and realized that she, too, struggled against tears.

And then Yair was on the phone, his voice bursting with his triumph, with his love.

"I'm going to make Danielle very happy," he promised.

"I know," she assured him. "Yair, is everything all right in the country?"

"Yes. I think so. The attacks on the northern border are all for show—something to keep Kosygin happy. We have to worry about the Arabs when they stop shooting." He laughed, the mocking, defiant laughter of the native-born Israeli.

She passed the phone to Mindell, who had burst into the room and was shouting her congratulations into the receiver until the operator interrupted and the connection was severed.

They went back to the party then. Crowds milled through the dining room, and Rebecca filled a plate with the delicacies of Sherry's ample buffet. She looked at it with lack of interest and set it down. The large television set had been switched on, and the older guests were looking at their watches, counting the minutes before midnight. The musicians had abandoned their corner, and instead the amplified voice of Sandie Shaw shrilled from the stereo unit. "I'm Only a Puppet on a String"—the singer mourned the lyrics sweetly, sadly.

"As I have been," Rebecca thought suddenly. For too long she had been controlled by the dreams and desires of others. Since the day she had met Yehuda in Italy (how bright the sun had been on the piazza as they sat over their plates of gem-colored ices), she had danced to the rhythm of his destiny. It was time now for her to make new assessments, new evaluations. It was time for her to find her own music. She felt a surge of strength, a new determination.

Someone turned the television louder. The announcer counted the final seconds of 1966. Guy Lombardo led his band in "Auld Lang Syne." Mindell pressed her cheek against Michael's. Aaron held Lydia close. Leah and Boris stood side by side and watched as Sherry and Joshua Ellenberg danced slowly, dreamily, crossing the border from one year into another.

Rebecca drifted from one crowded room to the other. Jakie Hart gave her a glass of champagne.

"Looking for someone?" he asked.

She acknowledged, then, that she had been looking for the tall, craggy-featured man with iron-gray hair whose name she did not know. But he had left the party. She stood at the window, sipped her champagne, and studied the lightly falling snow, as though she might discover an important secret in the swirling flakes.

IT SNOWED on the afternoon Rebecca's retrospective opened. It was the first heavy snow of the season, and the hurrying shoppers on Madison Avenue slowed their steps and lifted their faces to the thickly falling flakes. Their fingers stiffened with the cold, and frost glazed their clothing and their hair, but the snow promised excitement and adventure, sparked memory and longing. Charles Ferguson hired an extra doorman to stand in front of the gallery to hold a sheltering umbrella over his guests as they emerged from their cars and taxis. A uniformed maid stood in readiness in the vestibule to relieve them of their wraps and guide them into the brightly lit gallery, where a blazing fire welcomed them.

Exhilarated by the cold, soothed by the light and warmth, they accepted glasses of mulled wine from the smiling young art students who considered it a privilege to assist at a Ferguson opening. The snow continued to streak the huge plate-glass windows, but they moved through the white-walled room and studied canvases that irradiated brilliant sunlight, moonswept desert, and verdant mountain land. They nodded and murmured softly to each other, glancing from catalogue to painting, stepping back to study one work and moving forward to admire another. Their slow pace pleased Charles Ferguson. The elderly art dealer knew that a viewer who paused before a large canvas and then returned to study it yet again was a potential purchaser. He would wait for the right moment to sidle up to such a patron and talk softly to him about Rebecca Arnon's work, the power of a particular painting.

Rebecca herself walked slowly from canvas to canvas and studied her work as though each canvas were new and unfamiliar to her. She had, in fact, not seen some of them for many years. She had routinely sent the completed canvases she wished to sell to the New York gallery. Charles Ferguson had kept a careful record of her sales, and he had gone to great efforts to borrow back her early works for this exhibit.

She stood before a display of the Jerusalem cityscapes she had done during her first year in the country, and she remembered how long it had taken her to blend the oils that captured the rhodochrosite hue of a Jerusalem sunset. She had painted the emptiness of city streets at the evening hour, the loneliness of the Judaean Hills as shadows fell. She and Yehuda had been separated then too—he had been involved in illegal immigration, smuggling the concentration camp survivors into Palestine, and she had been a student at the

Bezalel art school—the mood of her aloneness, she saw now, permeated that early work.

Then there were the paintings of their first happy years in the Galilee. They had married, certain of their love and certain, too, that each could triumph over the other's past. The purposefulness of the life he offered her would compensate for the separation from her family and the life she had known in America. Her love for him would soothe the grief and loss he had felt since the death of his first wife during a World War II intelligence mission. She had worked feverishly during those early years, fired by the happiness of their life together. There were her pastels of the children dancing at the festival of the first fruits, her complex gouache of the kibbutz members celebrating a communal seder. She had sketched Danielle and Mindell fondling a small goat, but she had used vibrant oils to paint Noam as a boy, burdened with sheaves of wheat that matched the golden radiance of his skin. *Noam*. She closed her eyes now and tried not to remember his body in the plain pine coffin that the military ambulance had delivered to Sha'arei ha-Negev. The burial society had washed the body carefully, but the charred flesh remained the color of ashes.

"Who is that boy, Rebecca?"

Lisa Ellenberg, wearing the inevitable uniform of jeans and black turtleneck sweater, stood beside her and studied Noam's portrait with an intense gaze. Joshua's tall, bright-haired daughter looked pale and tired. She had spent the afternoon at the Coalition offices, sorting through photographs from Vietnam. It was almost certain that Martin Luther King would announce plans for a Vietnam summer, and the Coalition wanted to be ready with a massive photographic display that could be shipped from city to city as demonstrations were launched.

Lisa's eyes had grown bloodshot and weary, looking at pictures of weeping, displaced youngsters, of mothers stupefied by grief, staring down at the bodies of their dead children. Staring at the black-and-white prints of maimed adolescents who smiled shyly, trustingly, at the camera and displayed the stump of a mutilated arm, a clumsily bandaged foot, she had longed to hurry back to her room at Hutchinson College, to the solace of the small white pills that calmed her and the gem-colored capsules that revitalized her. But she had promised that she would make an appearance at Rebecca's opening, and Lisa always kept her promises. She was a good girl who always met her deadlines, produced good grades, and smiled brightly at her father because she knew that Joshua Ellenberg could not sustain the burden of her sadness.

"That is—was—Noam, my stepson, as a boy," Rebecca replied. "He was killed three years ago in a border incident." The calm of her own voice as she spoke of Noam surprised her. Had she lived for so long at the edge of death that she had become inured to it? No. Of course not. She grieved for Noam every day, felt his loss, the sad waste of his young life. Even as Lydia, who approached them now, grieved for Paul.

They were bereft but not defeated. Lydia had survived her losses and created a new life for herself. She approached them now with a purposeful gait, her face bright with pride. Rebecca's paintings caught the spirit of Israel. She kissed Rebecca and smiled at Lisa, with whom she felt a special affinity. Like Lisa, she, too, had once thought to change the world. She strained to hear Lisa's words. The girl's voice was very quiet.

"War," Lisa said. "Goddamn war. So insane for anyone to go to war."

"But sometimes necessary," Lydia interjected gently.

"Never," Lisa protested. "War is of our choosing. If we said no—one mighty no—if we all worked for peace, there would be an end to it."

"And what if we are not given the choice?" Rebecca persisted. "Noam, you know, was not given a choice." Nor would her own sons have a choice—gentle Yaakov and willful Amnon. Like Noam, they were sons of a land bordered by war, shadowed by death. They would have no choice unless she offered it to them, snatched them from danger. Again the idea invaded, adhered, teased. She could take her sons away. They could grow up, like their American cousins, on peaceful suburban streets where leaves rustled gently in autumn winds and snow fell silently, softly, through wintry days and nights. She looked at the falling snow, and it occurred to her that she had never painted a landscape of winter. She imagined working with a tube of titanium white, blending it lightly with English pink, to capture the tone of a drift at sunset. A line from the poet Zalenko teased her, but she could not recall it. Zalenko wrote the kind of winter odes that she yearned, quite suddenly, to paint.

"Everyone has a choice," Lisa said, and her voice rang with the certainty of the young. She thought of the Cornell sophomore who had visited the Coalition office that afternoon to borrow money for bus fare to Canada. His number in the draft lottery had been dangerously low, and he had vowed that he would never fight in a war.

"I've made my choice," he had said calmly when the weary psychologist who served as a volunteer counselor at the Coalition asked if he had considered everything.

"I wish you were right, Lisa," Lydia said wistfully. She wanted to use her knowledge for peaceful purposes, but instead her energy was concentrated on a project designed to protect nations at war. On Rhodes, Yehuda had stressed the importance of radar evasion techniques, and he had been proved right. They were racing against time, and there were no choices.

"I think I am." Lisa's voice was heavy. Her fingers toyed nervously with the silver peace emblem she wore on a leather thong that hung about her neck. She was tired, so very tired. She was sorry now that she had not refilled the vial of pills in her purse. Still, with a bit of luck, she could catch the 5:49, reach her Hutchinson dormitory by 6:30, swallow an upper, and be ready to tackle the French paper that was due the next day. Her French teacher was fond of Lisa and expected great things of her. Lisa did not want to disappoint him. She did not want to disappoint anyone. She turned to Rebecca.

"I'm glad I saw your paintings, Rebecca. They're wonderful. When my parents come, would you tell them I just couldn't wait to see them? Too much work. A French paper due tomorrow." She smiled engagingly, but Rebecca recognized the weariness in her voice, the dullness in her eyes.

"I'll tell them, Lisa. Thank you for coming."

She watched Lisa shrug into her duffle coat and elbow her way out of the room. The gallery was crowded now, and Rebecca felt a secret pleasure because no one had recognized her. She had preserved her anonymity in this room full of people who were examining her work, studying her deepest perceptions. Her photograph appeared in the catalogue, but it had been taken years ago, just after Amnon's birth. The photographer had captured her as she worked on a landscape, wearing cotton slacks and a smock, her hair loose and falling in wavelets of dark curls about her shoulders, her face set in lines of intense concentration. She had worked well then, she remembered. She had been absorbed in her work, happy with her young sons, content in Yehuda's enveloping love, the affection of Danielle and Noam. They had known then that their desert kibbutz would succeed, and she remembered how, at day's end, she and Yehuda had rushed toward each other, trembling with the joy of their life and their love. But that had been before they had been worn down by the constant threat of war, grief-weighted by Noam's death, Yehuda's constant absences, and her own troubling doubts. But she would work that way again, she decided defiantly. She smiled at a woman who stared vaguely back. The young woman in the photograph bore little resemblance to this new Rebecca in a dress of peacock-blue silk, whose silver-streaked dark hair was coiled into a neat chignon.

Fragments of conversation drifted toward Rebecca as she moved slowly from picture to picture.

"I think I like her earlier work better. It's so much more optimistic."

"But these desertscapes are wonderful. Melancholy, but so romantic."

"They say that Ferguson is donating a percentage of his commission to the Coalition for Peace in Vietnam."

"Wouldn't it be more appropriate to donate it toward peace in the Middle East?"

They laughed bitterly, because they had so many wars to choose from and because their dry cynicism and clever humor briefly banished their fear.

The students whispered knowingly to each other as they offered glasses of white wine to the patrons. Hilton Kramer of the *Times* was here, and Harold Rosenberg from the *New Yorker*. Someone had recognized Les Anderson, who just written that in-depth piece on James Meredith's march for *Metro*. Joe Stevenson, the sculptor, was expected, and the tall silver-haired woman in the dramatic magenta velvet suit was Leah Goldfeder, the designer and painter. She was Rebecca Arnon's mother, someone said, and they stole covert looks at the two women, and saw the resemblance.

The students inhaled the fragrance of rich perfumes, studied the well-tailored suits, the elegant gem-colored dresses. Briefly, they forgot their barren downtown studios, their walk-up flats on the Upper West Side, the canvases on which they worked despairingly and the doubts that awakened them inexplicably. Those were the worst times, when they lay inert in the darkness and wondered if they were good enough, if they would ever be good enough. Openings like this one renewed them. One day, their paintings, too, might hang in a white-walled, wide-windowed gallery, drawing subtle criticism, sweet praise. Rebecca Arnon had been lucky, and her good fortune offered them rekindled hope.

Rebecca paused before the largest canvas she had ever undertaken and studied it with a disapproving eye. She had used oils to paint the great sand crater at the twilight hour when deep and varicolored shadows moved slowly across its multitextured surface, concealing the secrets of sand and stone. The crater, like a massive breast, a nurturing fortress, rose from the desert floor, and always, Rebecca had perceived it as a symbol of mingled strength and desolation. It was a vigilant natural formation that would survive and endure. Those who lived in its shadow were transient—they would struggle with the desert, do battle with the drifting sands, with only their hope for guarantee. But the crater would remain in place forever, beautiful and unyielding, simultaneously sheltering and threatening. She had worked too hard, she thought. The painting lacked the subtlety she had hoped to achieve.

"Odd that she didn't choose to do this on a smaller scale," a man's voice said musingly to her. "Chalk would have been natural for it. Yes, chalk."

Rebecca was startled. His words plundered her thoughts. *Chalk*, she had been thinking. *And a smaller surface, much smaller*.

She looked up. The man with iron-gray hair and craggy features, with whom she had danced at the Ellenberg's party, stood beside her. Again memory nagged and eluded her. He had seemed familiar then and seemed familiar now, yet she could not place him.

"The subject is quite massive," she replied cautiously.

"Yes. But in her other work she juxtaposed scope and subject. She used a large, stark canvas for the landscape of the Judaean hill-side—the one with the dwarfed olive trees—and she did the gouache of Mount Carmel on a smaller treated sheet. She lost her nerve on this one. Still, the colors are dramatic—the mauve shadows sweeping across that ocher expanse . . ." There was grudging admiration in his tone. "She's not consistent, but she's a hell of a lot better than most of the Israeli artists."

"You don't like Israeli artists?" She kept her tone light and noticed that the leather patch on his worn tweed jacket was loose and his shirt collar frayed. Either lack of money or lack of a woman's care, she thought, and decided in favor of the latter. The jacket was very expensive and the V-necked tan sweater he wore was fashioned of the finest cashmere. Her observation amused her. How swiftly she had fallen back into her girlhood pattern of judging; she never noticed such things in Israel, never thought about them.

"I don't like most Israeli artists," he acknowledged, and she felt herself bridle defensively. "They're too blatantly ethnic, most of them. Moshe Gat's earlocked Yemenites and Reuveni's Hasidic rabbis. They hit you over the head with their subjects. I like Anna Ticho very much, and the early Schatz was good, but then he got too self-conscious—he painted the Zionist message the way Chagall keeps on painting the fantasy of the rootless Jew. I can't relate to too many Hasidim dancing on rooftops—fiddlers or no."

"Chagall will be desolated to hear that," she said sarcastically, although secretly she agreed with him. Chagall's whimsical figures seemed too facile and stereotyped to her.

"Now, this Arnon woman could develop if she expanded her horizons, gave herself full scope. There's too much timidity, too much constraint. She's not at peace with her landscapes. Don't you think we'd see some really interesting work if she loosened up, experimented?"

He turned then from his study of the painting and looked directly at her. Recognition flashed in his eyes.

"But we know each other, don't we? Didn't we dance together at some party at Great Neck on New Year's Eve? You wore a white dress."

She was oddly pleased that he remembered that. "Yes. At the Ellenbergs'," she replied. She would tell him now that she was Rebecca Arnon and avoid further embarrassment, but he gave her no chance.

"I remember. You were called away to the phone, and the friends whom I was supposed to meet there never arrived. I left just before midnight."

"Don't people usually stay until midnight on New Year's Eve?" she asked. "That's the magic hour, the reason for coming." It was dangerous to be alone, at the midnight hour of a dying year when past and future converged in mysterious nexus.

"Not for me. Not this year," he replied. "This year midnight was my reason for leaving." The vigor drained from his voice, and his tone was dull, almost despairing.

"I'm sorry," she said, offering him her hesitant compassion for the sorrow that masked his face, quite suddenly. She held her hand out, intent now upon telling him her name and learning his, but he had turned away.

"Rebecca!"

She experienced a thrill of nervous pleasure as Joe Stevenson advanced toward her. Joe had been her teacher at Bennington, and it was he who had awakened her to the joys of art and to the wondrous closeness of love. The world had been in flames during her student years; all of Europe had been a battlefield, and too many gold stars hung in the windows of modest Vermont homes. Her own brother, Aaron, had been missing in action, and she had sought refuge from war and loss in Joe Stevenson's arms. Eager for certainty, she had thought then that they would be together always. But Joe had been older and wiser, and he had recognized that they belonged to separate worlds. She had felt herself abandoned and alone when he wrote, from his European army base, to tell her that he would not return to her. But with the passing years she had fallen in love again. She had married Yehuda Arnon and forged a new life in the newborn state of Israel. And Joe had achieved an international reputation as a sculptor and married a beautiful Danish ceramicist. She and Joe had written to each other infrequently but with affection through the years and always they had exchanged gifts on their birthdays. Joe and Inga had visited Israel. Yehuda and Joe had been comfortable and at ease with each other. Rebecca had liked Inga, and she had visited the Stevensons at their Nantucket Island home on one of her hasty visits to the States. It pleased her that the love that she and Joe had shared had mellowed into a sweet and loving friendship.

She was delighted to see them now, but it was the man who stood beside her who hurried up to them. He kissed Inga and enveloped Joe in a bear hug of affection.

Joe beamed with delight.

"Benjamin. You look wonderful. And Rebecca. Of course you found each other. It was inevitable." His square chestnut-colored beard was laced with snow; the droplets melted on Rebecca's cheek when he kissed her.

It was Inga who saw the bewilderment in Rebecca's eyes and noticed the sudden awkwardness, the constrained silence.

"You have met?" she asked gently.

Rebecca shook her head.

"We've met, but we haven't been introduced," she said faintly.

"Then I will introduce you. Rebecca Arnon, our dear and good friend, please meet our dear and good friend, Benjamin Nadler. Surely, you've read Benjamin's work, Rebecca? His essays are often in *Art World*, and I think we sent you his *Study of Modern Landscape Art* for your birthday."

"Yes. Of course you did." She knew now why Benjamin Nadler had seemed so familiar to her. His photograph appeared on the jacket of the important and insightful volume, which she had read and reread all that year. It was a serious, brooding photo—the craggy features taut with concentration, the unruly iron-gray hair brushed into place. The print had been in black and white, so she could not have known that his eyes were amber-colored like the sands of the northern Negev.

"Rebecca Arnon," he repeated in a tight, hard voice. "You are the artist whose work we honor today? I never suspected. I thought we were discussing an Israeli painter. I should have remembered that Joe once said that you had been his student, that you were an American. Still, it was clever of you not to have told me who you are."

"You didn't give me a chance." She was at once angry and apologetic.

"Do you often discuss your work as though it is not yours at all?" he continued, and she saw that his lips curled contemptuously.

"Oh, come on, Benjamin," Joe protested. "That's not Rebecca's style at all. It's all a misunderstanding—right, Rebecca?"

"Of course," she said, anxious for the incident to be over. She extended her hand. "I'm glad to meet you, Professor Nadler."

He hesitated for a moment and then took her hand. Their fingers touched briefly, and he excused himself and joined a group at the opposite end of the gallery.

"Stupid situation," Joe said uncomfortably. "He shouldn't have reacted that way, but he's not himself just now."

"His wife died only a year ago," Inga added. "Very tragically. It changed him a great deal."

"I'm sorry. It doesn't really matter," Rebecca assured them.

"How is Yehuda?" Joe asked.

"He's well," she replied. "He's in Europe just now." Only that morning she had received a postcard from him, postmarked Paris. He was well, working hard. He was thinking of going to Cherbourg for a rest. She had smiled bitterly. Yehuda would go to Cherbourg, but not for a rest. He would go there to look at the new French submarine assembly plant, to study the waterfront, to make contact with de Gaulle's friends and with de Gaulle's enemies. She had torn the postcard into long strips, and then she had pieced it together again and pressed it to her lips.

"Rebecca, I love the new paintings. But it's time you tried your hand at winter. Come to the island and visit us. We'll sketch together."

"I'd like that," Rebecca said.

She smiled at the Stevensons, but her eyes followed Benjamin Nadler, who continued his study of her work. He stood before each painting, holding a pad and pencil; he made copious notes, but he never once glanced in her direction.

Charles Ferguson introduced her to Alan Zalenko, the talented young poet who had just been awarded both the Hobart Prize and an Endowment for the Arts fellowship. Rebecca knew many of his poems by heart, and she was impressed by the sad-eyed man who held her hand gently in his own, turning their brief introduction into a silent rapport.

"I admire your landscapes very much," the poet told her. "You pierce nature's secrets and share them with your viewers."

"As you do with your poems," she rejoined.

"We work in different forms, yet our work is not dissimilar," he acknowledged thoughtfully. "Perhaps one day we might interpret each other's work."

"I should like that."

They smiled at each other, and the poet returned to her painting of the dwarfed olive trees and stood for a long time, studying it with hooded gaze.

Latecomers arrived, and small blue-and-red stickers appeared beside several canvases, indicating that they were either sold or were under consideration for sale. Critics and admirers pressed forward to offer Rebecca their congratulations, to ask questions.

"Do you have a yearning to paint outside of Israel?"

"I suppose I do. Of course the landscape of Israel is very varied. But it seldom snows there. I should like to capture scenes of winter."

Alan Zalenko hovered at the edge of the crowd but said nothing.

"Do you miss America?" one of the students asked her.

"Of course. When I am in Israel I miss America, and when I am in America I miss Israel."

Her eyes met Benjamin Nadler's, and then he turned away and she saw him leave the gallery, pausing in the doorway to pull up the collar of his coat. She noticed, with an almost detached sadness, that although the snow was still falling heavily, he wore neither boots nor overshoes.

Her family surrounded her. Their joy in her achievement was palpable, overwhelming.

Leah's eyes were bright with pride. In the Russian village of her birth it was said that children offered their parents a second chance—they fulfilled the dream. Leah's own creative life had always been divided. She had been torn between painting and design, and often economic exigency had determined her choice. She had begun her work late, and Charles Ferguson's settlement-house studio had given her her only training. But Rebecca's career had combined gift with opportunity, and she had used both well.

"It is a wonderful show," Mindell said. Her silk honey-colored maternity dress matched her hair. She stood close to Lydia, whose black braids formed a coronet threaded with satin ribbons of the same hue as her simple skirt and blouse.

"Our ladies of the rainbow," Michael said to Aaron.

"Your ladies of the rainbow—our daughters from afar," Boris added, and they looked at one another, reminded of the improbabilities of chance and choice that had brought Leah and Rebecca, Mindell and Lydia, together in this wide-windowed Madison Avenue gallery.

"It was a wonderful show," Mindell said.

"Just think—our sister is an artist of international esteem," Aaron said to Michael, quoting the announcement of the show that had appeared in the *Times* that morning. The brothers smiled with pleasure at the recognition accorded their sibling.

"What a successful opening." Charles Ferguson was flushed with excitement. "The *Times* is planning an in-depth review for the Sunday edition. And *Art News* is planning a center spread. Alan Zalenko told me he plans to come back tomorrow."

"Benjamin Nadler left early," Joe Stevenson observed.

"Yes. But he did tell me that he plans to do a long piece for next week's issue of *The Metropolitan*."

Rebecca turned away. The excitement of the afternoon was dimmed and overlaid with an unhappy apprehension. She was suffused with a hot anger at Benjamin Nadler, who had read her thoughts and shadowed her day.

She wrote Yehuda a long letter that night, filling the pale blue airletter with the questions she had not dared to ask him. But in the morning she tore the letter up and wrote him a precise account of the opening. "When the reviews and articles appear, I will send them to you," she wrote, and her heart beat too rapidly at the thought of Benjamin Nadler's critique.

YEHUDA ARNON did not have to wait for Rebecca to send him the reviews of the retrospective. He was in Paris as part of an unofficial delegation of Israelis who were meeting quietly with members of Premier Georges Pompidou's staff to arrange for the shipment of military supplies to Israel. Yehuda Arnon's presence had been specifically requested by the premier. He had worked with Yehuda after the war when Yehuda had organized Bericha rescue operations and he had been manager of the Rothschild Banking House in Paris. He had not forgotten the calm, deliberate manner Yehuda maintained in the face of a crisis. He remembered still the courage and ingenuity that Yehuda had exhibited during those tragic years.

"My people will speak to Arnon," he had said in a curt dispatch to Jerusalem.

Yehuda read an in-depth analysis of Rebecca's work in the international edition of the *Tribune* as he drank his morning coffee and ate a croissant at the Café des Deux Magots. An ashen wintry light streaked the broad windows of the famous café. The chairs and tables that filled its terrace during the warmer months were stacked in awkward pyramids and shrouded with black rubber sheeting against the snow that would surely envelop Paris before the day was over. The only other patrons were a middle-aged couple who sat in a dimly lit corner, huddled in their winter coats. The man lit one Gauloise after another, carefully placing the burnt-out stubs in the limp blue-and-white packet. The woman sat very still, her gloved hands encircling her coffee cup as she wept with an odd, controlled steadiness. Her face was not contorted and her movements were contained, yet tears streaked her cheeks, and her companion made no move to comfort her.

Yehuda read the critique carefully. The writer had recognized Rebecca's strengths and appreciated the subtlety of her work. "The tenderness Arnon feels for her landscapes," he wrote, "is apparent. Her brush caresses the canvas . . . one imagines how her pen must have danced across her pad as she sketched the shivering cypresses of Jerusalem, the crouching olive trees of Judaea. And yet an almost overwhelming sense of loneliness, of isolation, adds to the complexity of the artist's achievement."

Yehuda reread that paragraph and then folded the newspaper and slipped it into the pocket of his duffle coat. The review had been reprinted from the New York edition, and he supposed that Rebecca had already seen it. He hoped that the critic's insight would not wound her. She was so easily hurt, his Rebecca, his Rivka. He was, he acknowledged, all too familiar with the signs of pain that flashed across her face— the rapid blanching of her skin, the lines of sadness that etched their way into her smooth forehead, the shadow of sorrow that blurred the brightness of her sea-colored eyes.

He wanted, at such moments, to pass his hand across her face and banish the sadness with his touch, to hold her in his arms and soothe and reassure her. But in the years since Noam's death his own uncompromising grief had restrained and weighted him. He could not comfort his wife when he could not comfort himself. He had surrendered instead to a whirlwind of activity, to urgent journeys and clandestine missions. Fatigue subdued sorrow, obscured anguish. He understood his wife's pain, her uncertainty, but he could not assuage it. He acknowledged that they were drifting apart, but he was powerless to draw closer, and his own impotence frightened him. He absorbed himself instead in the needs of his country. There was one constant in his life, he told himself—Israel's vulnerability, Israel's need. He had been a young man when he had first met with Georges Pompidou in Guy de Rothschild's oak-paneled office and pleaded for funds to spirit the remnant of child survivors out of Europe. Years had passed, and now he met in a conference room of the Ministry of Defense and pleaded for Mystères and for spare parts to be used by these same children, who were soldiers of Israel now and might soon have to fight for their lives.

Rebecca both understood and resented his work. Occasionally, when he was back on the kibbutz for a brief respite, he had awakened in the night and had known instinctively that Rebecca was gone from their bed. She wandered through the starlit desert night, a bright shawl flung over her thin white nightdress. Slowly she made her way to the children's house, where she looked down at her sleeping sons. She was frightened, he knew, but he was too mired in his own inner struggle to offer her strength. Instead, he watched from the window as she completed her lone nocturnal mission.

He had reassured himself then that she had a need for solitude. They were lonely acrobats, he and Rebecca, each precariously balanced on a shared tightrope of sorrow. They would have to traverse it alone, he knew, and he went back to bed and pretended to be asleep when she returned to their room.

He had not withdrawn from her out of indifference. Sometimes it seemed to him that besides Israel the only certainty in his life was his love for Rebecca. That love was as intrinsic to his being as the beat of his heart, the intake of his breath. Even through the grief-shadowed years since Noam's death, that love had remained a steady beacon, beckoning him back, a clear and luminescent flame. He did not want it to be clouded by fear and regret; he did not want its glow to become artificial and harsh. If their marriage was to endure, it would have to be because they loved each other and understood the exigencies of that love.

He did not want her to remain with him because she was restrained by loyalty, bound by duty. He had never been a man to settle for half measures. He had recognized the risk he took on the evening of the kibbutz wedding, when stars spangled the sky and the music of gaiety invaded their sadness. He had urged her then to leave him so that she might gather perspective, understanding. He had known then, and he knew it still, that he would rather hazard the loss of her love than live with the knowledge that it had been reduced to a simulation, to a sad and stagnant charade.

He was not unaware of the dangers of his daring gamble. Rebecca would return to the beneficent world of her girlhood, to the protection of her brothers and of Leah, her mother and her friend. In Israel, on the kibbutz, she lived at a remove from the world of her profession (the perceptive critic had written of her "sense of loneliness, of isolation"), but New York was the center of the art world. She would meet painters and sculptors, visit museums and galleries.

He knew, too, that men would be drawn to her, attracted by her warmth and beauty, her talent and charm. It was not difficult for an attachment to form unbidden, for mysterious desire to stir. Solitude engendered strange and sweet aberrations, and Rebecca would be alone. He remembered still, half with shame and half with wonder, how he had been dangerously drawn to Lydia that distant afternoon in Rhodes. Loneliness made men and women dangerously vulnerable, caused them to respond with strange intensity to the magic of a fleeting moment.

Only the previous evening, he had attended a diplomatic reception on the Rue Faubourg. A young French woman in a silver sheath that matched the metallic shadow on her eyelids had laughed with throaty excitement at a small joke he had told. He had been pleased and flattered. He had escorted her home, and in the darkness of the hallway, she had lifted her face to his and smiled teasingly. He had touched her hair, brushed his lips against her shimmering eyelids, and thought how easy it would be to follow her into the darkened flat, to assuage both his loneliness and his desire. Abruptly, he had made his apologies and left, hurrying back to his hotel room, where he had stared long and hard at the photo of Rebecca that he carried in his wallet.

He understood that he had undertaken dangerous odds. Rebecca might not return to him. But he knew that, win or lose, he owed Rebecca the opportunity to make her choice. He had married a young girl in a dangerous and exciting time. He had swayed her to his destiny, ensnared her in a web of dreams and love. But now she was a woman, and she would make a woman's choice. No muted regret, no unarticulated fear, would shadow their lives.

He drained the last of his coffee, grown cold and bitter now, and called for his check. It was time for his meeting with Pompidou's first assistant, for a discussion of how to circumvent de Gaulle's reluctance to send spare parts for the Mystères from France to Israel. It had occurred to Yehuda that they might be shipped from Holland. In war, too, direct routes were not always possible. He smiled wryly at the strange parallel.

As he paid his bill, the couple who had occupied the shadowed corner edged their way out of the café. The woman was pale, and she had not ceased to weep. Yehuda envied her those freely streaming tears. His own heart was weighted with a tumescent sorrow, which he knew would not soon be relieved.

A CURIOUS DEPRESSION adhered to Rebecca during the days that followed the opening of the retrospective. She experienced a vague sense of aimlessness, a detachment, as though she were a theatergoer observing the interplay of other people's lives but not involved in them.

She visited Aaron and Lydia. Their Scarsdale household was suffused with calm. Their three children played amiably, quarreled harmlessly. Lydia's work schedule was intensely accelerated. Even at home she reworked calculations, studied reports. Her desk was studded with envelopes from the Technion, the Weizmann Institute, the Royal Research Centre in London.

"Can't you relax?" Rebecca asked.

"This is a crucial time for radar scientists—we're racing against history," Lydia replied.

Rebecca understood. The *New York Times* lay open on Aaron's chair, its ominous headlines clearly visible. The air war in Vietnam was intensifying. Russia had announced the renewed sale of planes to Egypt and Syria.

"My wife is of the opinion that the future of the free world is in her hands," Aaron said. "And I suppose, to a degree, it is." He stroked Lydia's hair and smiled at his sister.

Aaron was a judge now, but he continued to teach at the law

school. Still, Rebecca had noticed that despite the demands on their time, Aaron and Lydia almost always managed to have dinner with the family, and they seldom missed a Friday night meal at Leah's. They talked easily, casually. Aaron had heard an interesting case; Lydia was working on a grant proposal. Paulette told three consecutive "knock, knock" jokes, and David explained them patiently to Rebecca. They did not listen to the news every hour. They did not stir uneasily when a plane flew too low. They anticipated peace and togetherness, just as Rebecca anticipated war and separation.

She had dinner with Mindell and Michael at the Eldridge Street apartment—the same apartment where her parents had lived as poor, newly arrived immigrants. The little room that she and Aaron had shared would be a nursery for Mindell's child. Already, brightly patterned curtains hung at the window and a gleaming white rocking chair stood in the corner where the small Rebecca had created dolls from the clothespins and fabric scraps that Joshua had scavenged from the pushcarts of neighborhood peddlers.

"Rebecca, could you paint a mural—something with flowers and a smiling sun?" Mindell asked. Mindell's own childhood had been spent in hiding, and she was determined to guarantee sunlight and happiness to her unborn infant.

"Of course." Rebecca smiled. She envied Mindell her excitement, her certainty that she could control her life, her love. She, too, had felt that certainty in the early years of her marriage, but it had vanished with the passing years, with the compounding of sorrow and loss, with Noam's death and Yehuda's repeated absences, his necessary silences. ("How was your day?" Lydia asked Aaron casually. It was not a question Rebecca asked Yehuda.)

She visited Hutchinson College and studied the work of the art students. They listened to her with intense concentration, asked urgent questions. Her present might be their future. A girl whose long black hair fell to her waist asked Rebecca if she felt any conflict between her role as a mother and her role as an artist. Rebecca explained that the unique quality of life on a kibbutz made it possible for her to combine both lives.

"My children are cared for. I have a studio and a budget for supplies. In return, the proceeds of my work belong to the kibbutz."

They nodded. They knew about communes. They clutched their tattered paperback copies of *The Feminine Mystique* and fingered their shiny metal buttons variously stamped with the dove symbol of the peace movement, the black and white clasped hands of civil rights solidarity, the feminist insignia of the National Organization for Women. Their beliefs were pinned to their sweaters, their faces were pale with exhaustion, but their eyes were bright with hope. Theirs was the generation that would make a difference.

Lisa Ellenberg, wearing an army fatigue jacket (the khaki fabric of war now gaily decorated with the blue-and-white satin decals of the peace movement), listened carefully. She wished that she had brought her tape recorder; she was just too damn tired to take notes. She had stayed too late at the Coalition office the previous evening and had missed the last train back to campus. Still, she would make it through the day. A premed student at the Columbia dorm where she had slept had given her a handful of bright green capsules.

"They kept me awake through organic chemistry—they'll keep you awake through anything," he had told her.

Their color reassured her, reminded her of the emerald necklace her father had given her mother for their anniversary—her father, the giver of gifts, who believed that happiness could be bought and paid for, like emeralds and yellow roses purchased out of season. Lisa stared at Rebecca Arnon and wondered if it was true, as family rumor had it, that her father had once imagined himself in love with her. She yearned suddenly to tell Rebecca how tired she was, to ask her how a life could be organized and molded.

"Your children may be physically well cared for in a children's house. But don't they need mothering? For instance, who takes care of them when you are traveling?" asked a blond girl wearing a matching navy-blue cashmere sweater set and a strand of pearls. Hutchinson had been a mistake for her—she would soon transfer to Finch College.

"This trip is very rare for me," Rebecca answered carefully. "It is the first time I have ever been away for so long. When I am on the kibbutz, I think my children do not lack for affection. It is the quality of the time that one spends with children, not the quantity, that counts."

There was a brief spate of applause. She had given the Hutchinson girls the answer they wanted, but she thought of her distant sons and wondered if she believed it.

That night she dreamed of a weeping Yaakov and a shivering Amnon. Barefoot, they scrambled across the surface of the sand crater, calling her name in sleep-strangled voices. "I'm coming," she replied and she struggled toward them through billowing clouds of sand, as white as newly fallen snow. But they did not hear her and renewed their cries. She awakened and trembled in the darkness of her girlhood room. *What was she doing here when her sons were in another country?*

She tried to call the kibbutz the next day, without success. "All circuits are busy," the bored overseas operator told her. "I will keep trying your number."

But when the phone rang at last, it was Charles Ferguson. His voice trembled with excitement. Pelican Press planned to publish an extravagant edition of Alan Zalenko's poems, and he had asked Rebecca to illustrate them.

"He says he has an instinctive feeling that you understand his work," Charles told her.

Rebecca thought of Zalenko's poems. He was obsessed by loneliness. He wrote of the desolate skyscapes of winter, of snow-swept coastal villages and frosted windowpanes glittering in the early darkness. Illustrations for such a volume would take months.

"But you did plan to stay on for a few more weeks," Charles said reasonably. "This is January. You would be through easily by April, May at the latest."

"I'll have been away for six months," she protested.

"But think of what you'll have to show for it."

The book would be a classic, she knew, as all Pelican editions were—a limited-edition collector's item. She had always wanted to work on such a project. Already an idea for a single illustration flowed through her mind—a micaceous reef patterned with winter-stiffened seaweed.

"I'll think about it," she promised.

She replaced the receiver and almost at once, the phone rang again. Miraculously, it was Yehuda. His voice was strong, soaring across the enormity of the distance that separated them. Her spirits lifted. He was calling to tell her how he missed her, that he wanted her home. He was calling to absolve her of choice.

"You're back in Israel," she said with relief.

"Of course." She was unprepared for the insouciance of his tone. He did not say where he had been or whether he would be leaving again. He did not say that he had missed her. They were separated by more than distance. An abyss of silence and secrets, of shadow and fear, yawned between them.

She heard herself telling him about the success of the exhibition opening, the Zalenko poems. Her voice was too bright, her words too swift.

"Do you want to do these illustrations?" he asked.

"Do you think I should?"

"You must do what you think right." His voice was even, noncommittal. "And a book endures." She recognized his generosity and was grateful for it.

"But what about Yaakov and Amnon?" she asked weakly. (*And what about you?* she thought. *Don't you miss me—need me? What has happened between us?*)

"It's only a few extra months. The boys miss you, of course, but Danielle manages wonderfully with them. They will understand, I think. Take as much time as you need."

She sensed a hesitancy and waited for him to continue, but he said nothing.

"I'll think about it, then. I'll let you know."

She remembered the decision she had made New Year's Eve—that she would carve out her own destiny. Yehuda was giving her license to do so. *All right, then, all right*, she thought.

"You must do what you yourself want to do." She looked out the window.

"It's snowing here."

"This morning we saw the first almond blossoms."

She was bounded by winter, while he looked out at the promise of spring.

"Shalom."

"Shalom."

The click of silence sounded. The connection was severed, and no word of love or longing had passed between them.

"Yehuda." She said his name aloud, in pledge and affirmation.

REBECCA went into New York that afternoon. She would pick up a copy of the Zalenko manuscript at the gallery and at least read the poems very carefully before coming to a decision. The snow fell in light flurries when she left Scarsdale, but by the time she reached the city a fierce storm was in progress. The huge flakes descended with blinding thickness through mists of fog. Cars moved slowly, tentatively, plowing their way through the streets like clumsy wounded animals. Pedestrians pressed close to the facades of buildings, seeking the brief protection of the brightly lit store windows.

The gallery was deserted except for an elderly couple. Elegantly dressed, white-haired and soft-skinned, they walked from painting to painting with the leisurely gait of the old who have no need to hurry; their decisions have been made and their achievements recorded. Rebecca envied them their calm. They paused before her painting of the youthful Noam. The woman put a white handkerchief to her eyes, and Rebecca wondered if she, too, had known a golden-skinned boy whose flesh had been seared by the fires of war.

Charles Ferguson was out, but he had left a copy of the Zalenko poems and an advance tearsheet of Benjamin Nadler's essay as it would appear in *The Metropolitan*. She clutched the thin sheets with icy fingers and read slowly.

> Rebecca Arnon, an American-born artist who has lived in Israel for almost two decades, startled the art world with her versatility. The retrospective exhibition, mounted at Charles Ferguson's prestigious gallery, revealed a depth of perception and a mastery of subject unmatched by other Israeli artists. . . .

He went on to describe her work and technique in intricate detail. She braced herself to read his critique of her rendition of the sand crater. It was mild enough, she decided with relief. "An unfortunate choice of medium for a dramatic and demanding subject," he had written. "Arnon has yet to take that daring step which will topple her from mere competence to authoritative artistry." But it was his concluding sentence that she read and reread.

> The viewer feels Rebecca Arnon's pain and struggle—the loneliness of the outsider who lives on the periphery of a landscape and a life that is at once beautiful and exciting but not quite her own. Still, there is the sense that this accomplished artist will have the strength to confront and surmount her own ambivalence.

Rebecca reeled at the accuracy of his perception. She felt revealed and betrayed. Who was Benjamin Nadler to know so much about her without knowing her at all? The tears she had been fighting since Yehuda's phone call stung bitterly, and she snatched up the packet of printed matter and hurried out onto the street.

The fog was even thicker now, and a strong wind caught the snowflakes and tossed them through the air in whirling gusts. Their cold touch on her face mingled with the heat of her tears as Benjamin Nadler's words ricocheted through her mind. She recognized the truth of his insights. She had arrived at a time of choice. She could not straddle both her worlds; somehow she would have to bridge them.

The hurrying urban crowd pressed against her; auto horns screeched angrily, importantly. A group of schoolboys in brightly colored anoraks hurtled down the street tossing snowballs at one another. One of them shoved a friend, who slid toward Rebecca. She darted away to avoid him, half blinded by the snow and her tears. She did not see the curbside, lost her footing, and fell into the street. A car rushed toward her, its glaring lights almost level with her eyes. Desperately she tried to crawl out of its path, but her wet clothing weighted her down. Brakes shrieked and a woman screamed. Rebecca smelled the burning rubber and wondered if her face was moist with tears or snow or blood. Perhaps the car had struck her, yet she had felt no impact, endured no pain. Then someone picked her up; she was cradled in strong arms.

"Here's her purse. Her package." Concerned voices, kindly passers by.

"Goddamn it. How could I see her? I didn't see her." She opened her eyes and saw the driver, a small man in an oversized coat. He stood beside his car, trembling with the knowledge that he had almost killed her.

"It wasn't his fault," she said to the man who had carried her to the other side of the street and who stood her on her feet now, with great gentleness. "Someone pushed me."

"I know," he said. "I saw the boys."

She recognized his voice and looked up, into Benjamin Nadler's amber-colored eyes.

An hour later she sat opposite him in the small bright yellow kitchen of his apartment. She had allowed him to lead her there, nodding acquiescently when he explained that it was only a few blocks away.

"We'll get you dry, make you a cup of hot tea," he had said soothingly, and, wordlessly, she had placed herself in his charge. She had followed him up to the second-floor apartment in the narrow brownstone on East Sixty-seventh Street, allowed him to remove her sodden winter coat, accepted the pale blue robe he gave her, and obediently disappeared into his bathroom.

She slipped out of her wet clothing, spread the garments out on the radiator, and then stared at herself in the mirror. Streaks of dirt slashed her face and clumps of slush nestled in her hair. She peeled off her stockings and saw that her knees were bruised where she had fallen. Her entire body ached. She had thought only to remove her wet clothing, but now she turned on the shower and stepped beneath the hot water. The strong, steady spray cleansed and soothed her. She washed her hair, and to her own surprise she began to sing softly, pausing when she heard the bathroom door open and then close again. When she emerged from the shower, she saw that he had placed two thick white bath towels on the vanity. The small attention pleased her. She felt safe, cared for.

She combed her hair, but as always, when it was wet, it nestled into recalcitrant clusters of dark curls spattered with silver. She slipped on the blue silk robe—a woman's garment, almost new. She thrust her hand into the pocket and found a neatly folded batiste handkerchief embroidered with the initials E.N. Its scent was the lavender fragrance she herself favored.

She followed the aroma of freshly brewed coffee and warming croissants into the kitchen, where Benjamin Nadler sat reading a manuscript.

"You look like a little girl," he said and set his work aside.

"I feel like a little girl—skinned knees and all," she replied, smiling. "I suppose now is the time to say thank you."

"You are a well-brought-up little girl." He poured coffee for both of them and spread lavish smiles of butter across the croissants. "And I think I must be just as well brought up and apologize for my behavior at the opening."

"A misunderstanding." She kept her tone light. "And thank you for the review as well."

"I went back to the gallery, you know. Several times. I hope I understood you."

"I think you did. Especially your remarks about the loneliness. I fool myself into thinking that I can conceal it, and yet you saw it." She shared the secret of her solitude with him now, as though it were a gift, a reward for all his ministrations of that afternoon. "How did you discern it?"

"I recognized it. I learned a great deal about loneliness this year."

She reached into the pocket of the robe and placed the neatly folded handkerchief on the table.

"Ellen's," he said and pressed it to his cheek.

She waited and slowly, softly, he began to speak, his voice strained at first and then sonorous with reverie.

He and Ellen had met as students at a huge midwestern university, drawn to each other by a shared interest in the arts, a gentle capacity for silence and irreverent laughter. They had been youthful friends before they became lovers.

"We were almost like brother and sister, people thought," Benjamin said musingly, stirring his coffee, looking hard at Rebecca.

She nodded. It was said that Yehuda, her husband, and Miriam, his first wife, had also been almost like brother and sister. How wonderful it must be, she thought, to marry a man who knows all the secrets of one's childhood, who understands the mysterious network of family connections. The terrain of her childhood was foreign to her husband, and she did not know the words to the songs he had sung as a boy.

They had married as graduate students, Benjamin continued. He had been twenty-two and she twenty-one. Life rippled out before them. They would earn their degrees, find teaching jobs on a rural campus, buy a large old house, and fill it with many books, many children. And they had earned their degrees and they had traveled to Europe. Their blueprint was operable. They found jobs at a new experimental college in the Blue Ridge Mountains, and they found a large white shingled house girdled by a sprawling porch. Ellen became pregnant and then miscarried. There were two other miscarriages, and at last she carried a child to term. The delivery was long and hard, and the child, a boy, was stillborn. Benjamin, beside her in the delivery room, prevailed upon the doctor to allow him to hold the tiny corpse. He caressed the dead body of his infant son, felt the moisture of the birth waters on the pale, bluing skin, and promised his weeping wife that it would not happen again.

They abandoned the dream of the rural campus, the large house, and moved to New York, choosing the apartment where he and Rebecca now sat, because it was only blocks away from a huge teaching hospital with the most advanced neonatal center in the world. She taught literature at Barnard. He conducted seminars, wrote his articles, his books. Ironically, their move to New York catapulted them into a kind of academic fame. Art dealers sought his opinion; collectors invited him to offer his evaluations.

They were a much-sought-after, much-admired and -invited couple, but in the night, Ellen lay rigidly beside him and wept. She was a very small woman with sandy-colored hair that she wore always in a boyish bob. Sometimes when he took her into his arms, he thought that it was a little grieving girl he held. But at last she became pregnant again, and the very distinguished obstetrician they consulted, the chairman of the department at the large teaching hospital, assured them that it was a strong pregnancy. No problems. No complications.

She laughed and played records and gave parties and decorated a nursery. Bluebirds winged their way across its ceiling and the floor was painted with grass and flowers. All the artists of their acquaintance shared their happiness and wanted to add to it.

The child was due at the year's end, and when she went into labor on New Year's Eve, they saw it as a happy sign. The labor was swift, and she was delivered of a small, beautiful girl-child. They called her Felice, seeing her as their happy fortune, and they carried their beautifully formed, wonderfully healthy child home to the room where birds sang and painted flowers blossomed.

Three weeks later, Ellen, singing softly, had entered the nursery and found Felice curled into a tiny, still bundle of death.

Inexplicable, the doctors said, but unfortunately not unusual. With professional facility they quoted statistics, made learned, irrelevant guesses. And again, Benjamin Nadler held a lifeless child in his arms and wondered at the near-weightlessness of the tiny corpse.

Now there was no reclaiming his wife. Ellen feared another pregnancy, and he dared not press her; they abandoned their love to silence. And then, only a year ago, she felt a strange pain in her abdomen, was frightened by a new fullness, sudden bleeding. She went to a doctor, and he told them that nodules of death grew where life should have been nourished. Cancer. The dread word was uttered gravely, but the doctor's voice was reassuring. The growth was confined to the reproductive system. They could operate, remove it. Ellen listened as though in a daze. She thought of the invading carcinoma as an ill-fated child, another death force that would be expelled from her womb. She delayed the surgery, and they did not press her. The cancer was contained. They gave her the names of psychiatrists, therapists. She nodded and promised that she would call but instead she talked sadly to herself, wept as she prepared dinner, graded papers.

"Tomorrow I'll make an appointment," she promised Benjamin Nadler.

"Next week," she assured him.

"After the new year," she said.

He feared to press her. He was advised to be patient. It was late December. They could wait another week, the grave-voiced doctor assured them. He prescribed painkillers and tranquilizers and sleeping pills. The rainbow-colored capsules jeweled her bedside table, and he was comforted because she smiled in her sleep and no longer cried as she stood at the sink.

On New Year's Eve he returned home late in the afternoon, carrying a bottle of champagne. They would have a quiet toast together because Ellen had declined all invitations. The apartment was spotless. A newly lit fire blazed, and the radio, tuned to WQXR, played Purcell. His heart soared with hope. She was getting better—she would recover.

He went into their bedroom, dark except for the needle of light cast by the bedside lamp. She wore her best nightgown, a lavender batiste that he had bought her when Felice was born. Her sandy hair was newly washed and capped her small head like a child's helmet. Her knees were curled to her stomach, and he knew, without touching her, and before he saw the empty pill bottle and the tall glass to which only drops of water clung, that she was dead. New Year's Eve, their daughter's birthday, had become her death-day.

"I'm sorry," Rebecca said.

He nodded, accepting now the compassion that she had offered him that afternoon in the gallery, when she had perceived his sorrow without comprehending it.

"What I don't understand," he said, "is how we drifted. I try to look back, to chart the hour that we first stopped talking. Did I withdraw from her, or did she close me off? How was it that once we shared everything and then suddenly we shared nothing?"

"It happens. I know."

And then she told him about her own marriage, about Yehuda and the joys and adventures of their early years together and the mysterious rifts that now scarred the carapace of their marriage.

"I used to think that it began with Noam's death, but I realize now that the strain between us had been building for many years. Our lives before we met were so very different. Always his first marriage was a shadow between us. And then, of course, his work meant so many absences, so many silences. He could not tell me where he had been, what he was doing. I understood, of course, but it created barriers. Sometimes I needed him because a child was ill and I didn't even know where he was. And then, with Noam's death, we felt the cumulation of all those years. At first we were both stunned with grief. We sank beneath it and surfaced separately, differently. We had lost the habit of sharing. I could not tell Yehuda that Noam's death made me fear for Yaakov and Amnon. I thought that perhaps he would see that fear as a betrayal.

"He threw himself into his work. Always, there was a trip, a meeting. He would do what he could to prevent other deaths. He would keep himself so busy that there would not be time to remember that his son was dead—his son had been killed." Her voice trembled with sadness. She pitied herself and she pitied Yehuda and she pitied the youth who had died on a Galilean hillside.

"With Ellen, during those last months, I didn't know what I wanted. Do you know, Rebecca?" Benjamin asked, and she understood that he offered her the secret of his marriage as clue to the mystery of her own.

"I'm not sure," she said. "Sometimes I think that I'm just not strong enough for him. Perhaps I'm not strong enough for life in Israel." Her own words startled her. She had, after all, been strong enough for life in Israel for two decades.

"But he loves you?" Benjamin Nadler asked.

"Perhaps." She did not tell him that Yehuda sometimes whispered his first wife's name in his sleep. Mia. The name was a verbal caress that pierced her with sadness, filled her with shame. She was jealous of a woman long dead, a woman whom she had never known.

They had dinner together in a small Italian restaurant. They spoke with the intimacy of old friends and were not surprised to discover that they liked the same artists, the same music. A reproduction of Soutine's *Woman in Blue* hung over his desk. She had framed that same reproduction for her kibbutz studio. They talked about Joe and Inga Stevenson and the beauty of Nantucket Island, and they conjectured about the young couple who sat in a corner of the restaurant and did not exchange a word throughout the meal.

"Perhaps they're mutes," Rebecca said wickedly.

"No. They've been married too long and can no longer discuss the wedding and the presents."

They looked hard at each other then, acknowledging the aching sadness of marital silence.

He walked her to Grand Central. The snow had stopped, but huge drifts lined the sidewalks and an overlay of ice glistened brilliantly. He took her arm to steady her and did not release it even when they reached the interior of the cavernous terminal. The train to Scarsdale was delayed, and they stood at the gate, joining the weary commuters and the discontented women shoppers who had stayed in the city too long and too late. Gently, he touched her face. His fingers traveled to her eyes, followed the lines of her cheeks, the curve of her lips. And then her own hand reached up and she traced the soft, dark slashes of brow that crowned his amber-colored eyes.

When she boarded the train at last, she was suffused with the languorous warmth that often overtook her in the afterglow of love. She sat quite still, her eyes closed, until the Scarsdale station was called.

Benjamin Nadler phoned the next morning. He was scheduled to give a series of lectures at Bennington College. He would be speaking on Modigliani, Utrillo, and Soutine—artists for whom she had a special affinity. Could she join him?

Rebecca took the call in the breakfast room, and as she spoke she watched her mother and Boris, who lingered over second cups of coffee. Leah's face was radiant against the pale wintry light. Her marriage to Boris had infused her with new strength, renewed energy. She and Boris seized each day with concentrated enthusiasm. Against all odds, they had each been granted another chance, and they raced against time. They traveled. They chaired committees. They had made the cause of Russian Jews their own. Boris addressed crowds of students on college campuses, stood vigil in front of the gates of the Russian consulate in New York, the Soviet embassy in Washington. He bore witness. His life was testimony. Leah's poster—letters of flame rising from snow-covered hillocks: "Let My People Go"—had won an international graphics competition.

"I almost decided against doing it," Leah had confided to Rebecca, "but I suppose I've learned that the only thing one regrets are the opportunities missed—the chances that were not taken."

Rebecca remembered her mother's words now. She held the phone tightly and experienced an unfamiliar eagerness, as though she, too, were racing against time.

"I'd like to come," she said. "You know, I was a student at Bennington, a lifetime ago." She was eager suddenly to travel back in time. Rebecca Arnon, the woman, would visit the landscapes that had been so dear and familiar to Becca Goldfeder, the girl.

The campus was little changed. She walked with Benjamin Nadler down the tree-lined paths she had followed during her college days and showed him the building where she had studied French literature, the auditorium where Martha Graham and Hanya Holm had danced, the wide-windowed studio where she had studied with Joe Stevenson.

The girls who hurried past them on the campus reminded her of her own classmates. They, too, wore long batik skirts and heavy homespun sweaters, and their small waists were circled by wide leather belts. They circulated petitions to end the war in Vietnam, jangled canisters on behalf of the children of Biafra, sold buttons for CORE and the Southern Christian Leadership Conference. All causes for the good were their own, and they believed fervently, with the enchanted optimism of the young, that the signatures on their petitions and the quarters dropped in their canisters made a difference.

Rebecca smiled at them. Her own classmates had collected money for the refugee children of Europe, for the victims of Hiroshima. Their petitions had called for the creation of an international organization, a United Nations. The Bennington chorus had sung the United Nations Hymn with sweet strength. Rebecca had recalled the words to the song that morning, with rare bitterness, as U Thant's visage drifted across the television screen and he acknowledged, to an unsmiling Arthur Goldberg, that an Arab guerrilla attack on an Israeli civilian intercity bus was "deplorable." The chorus of Bennington girls had sung of a different United Nations, but that song was twenty years old now, and hardly anyone remembered the words.

In the lecture hall where, as a freshman, she had heard white-haired Robert Frost read his own poetry, she listened to Benjamin Nadler relate the tragedy of Modigliani's life to his paintings. In the dining room of the Bennington Inn, she argued with him about the essence of an artist's solitude. And later, in the wood-paneled bedroom where a great fire leaped and blazed in the half darkness, mocking the whirling wind and the leafless branches that scratched the windows, she lay still as Benjamin Nadler's hands traced the contours of her body, his lips searched out the secret sources of her tenderness. Gentleness restrained his passion and ignited her own. She surged toward him, and they came together at last, weeping and laughing, each whispering the other's name. In that firelit room, they subdued their sorrow and banished their loneliness.

They stayed in Bennington for three days, and when they returned to New York she sent a cable to Yehuda telling him that she had decided to do the Zalenko book.

"Are you sure it's wise to stay away that long?" Leah asked.

Rebecca spun around.

"Didn't you go to the fashion shows in Europe when I was a girl? And from there to Russia? And that was before air travel was so common. I can be in Israel within hours if there is an emergency—you couldn't have done that."

"You know that I had special reasons for going," Leah replied. She had traveled to Europe in 1937 to try to persuade her parents to leave Russia. She had not succeeded, and now she lit a memorial candle for her parents on the eve of each Day of Atonement because she had never been able to determine either the dates of their deaths or the concentration camps where they had been killed.

Sadness dimmed Leah's eyes; anguish veiled her face. Rebecca turned away. She had been unfair, she knew, to counter her mother's concern with accusations, to create a false scale on which past experiences were weighed with present demands. She knew, with instinctive certainty, that she was right to stay, even as her mother had been right to go to Europe so many years ago.

Still, her decision was tempered with tension, unease. She had dreamed about her sons again. Yaakov and Amnon had stood with Yehuda at the edge of a yawning chasm, and she had called to them from the opposite side. Amnon had tried to bridge the distance. He had lifted his arms and hovered dangerously close to the precipice. She heard his shriek of terror and answered it with her own monitory scream. She had awakened, her body soaked with sweat, her face dampened with tears, her throat aching. Had Leah, too, known such dreams? she wondered.

"I'm sorry." Rebecca put her hand on Leah's shoulders. "You went to Europe then because you had to. And I, too, think that I am doing what I must do. It is not easy."

"I know," Leah said. Rebecca stood at a crossroads, and no one could help her choose direction.

Boris listened to them without comment. He had learned to be the silent observer, the listener, in the battles of love Leah fought with her passionate children. He turned back to the letter he was writing to a congressman asking for more direct intervention on behalf of Russian Jews. His head ached and his eyes burned, but he continued to write. He had been lucky. He had found Leah and thus a new life. He could not abandon those who did not share his good fortune.

BENJAMIN NADLER came to the Scarsdale house for dinner. He studied Leah's paintings, discussed the glories of the Hermitage collection with Boris. He had visited Moscow twice and planned to go again. Leah and Boris liked him, Rebecca knew, and perversely, she resented that liking. It would have been simpler to counter their open disapproval.

"He's a very fine man, your Benjamin Nadler," Leah said, when he left.

"He's not *my* Benjamin Nadler," she retorted sharply and turned away from the worry in her mother's eyes.

She read the Zalenko poems carefully, etching them into her thoughts and feelings, and made her first tentative sketches. Increasingly she worked at Benjamin Nadler's apartment, and his book-lined study became her studio. Rebecca's easel was placed where Ellen Nadler's desk had stood. Ellen's books were packed into cartons to make room for Rebecca's supplies and for the books of photographs and reproductions she was studying. One afternoon she brought a framed photograph of her sons and placed it on a shelf above the window seat. She remembered then that Benjamin had told her how he had often found Ellen seated at the window watching the children play in the courtyard below. She removed the picture and took it home with her. She began to leave clothes at the apartment and called Scarsdale often to tell her mother that she had decided to stay in the city.

"All right," Leah said wearily. She never asked Rebecca where she was staying. Her daughter was a grown woman now, a mother herself. But still my child, Leah thought worriedly. Still my wandering child.

REBECCA ARNON, who had grown up in New York City and Benjamin Nadler, who had lived there for years, explored the city as though they were tourists. They visited Madison Avenue galleries where subtly placed track lighting illuminated paintings and sculptures; they climbed narrow staircases to lofts where canvases were piled against peeling walls and young painters watched them nervously as they looked at oils and etchings, lithographs and sketches. They went to the Beekman Towers and watched the city speed by below them. Cars jumped lights, pedestrians hurried—only they were suspended in time.

One twilit evening, they walked the length of the city to the Eldridge Street apartment, where they shared a Chinese dinner with Michael and Mindell. Mindell, in her last trimester of pregnancy, was radiant, optimistic. The nursery was fully decorated now. Rebecca had painted a smiling sun beaming down on a sheltering tree, just above the small white crib. Benjamin Nadler averted his eyes when he saw it and Rebecca knew that he was thinking of another nursery and of his infant daughter Felice, who had not been protected by whimsical beauty.

Mindell discussed possible names. It was foolish, she knew, but she did not want to name her children for her parents, who had died in Auschwitz. Their lives had been so vulnerable, their deaths so tragic. She wanted a different life for her child—she wanted her child to be protected, shielded.

"Children in this country are safe, cared for," Rebecca said, and she was surprised at the bitterness in her voice. Her son's lives were not protected. They would wear uniforms and go to war. She felt, suddenly, a visceral longing for them. She wanted to hold Amnon in her arms, to tousle Yaakov's thick hair. She had been away for only two months, yet in the snapshot that they had included in their last letter, Amnon looked taller, more vulnerable, and Yaakov's mouth was set in a firmer, more mature line. Yehuda's letters assured her that they were fine, that they missed her but were pleased that she was doing work that was meaningful, important. "As I am," he had added. He was on the kibbutz now, but he did not know how long he would stay. He could not tell her where he might be going. He did write that he had seen a wide-winged Bonelli's eagle soar across the sand crater. Once, Rebecca and Yehuda had looked up during a twilight walk and watched the rarely seen bird shadow the ocher sands. They had held hands very tightly then, awed by the primeval beauty they had witnessed. She understood that Yehuda was reminding her of that moment, of all that they had shared.

"I'm afraid you are both wrong, Rebecca, Mindell," Michael said, turning from his sister to his wife. "There is simply no way a parent can shield and protect a child—anywhere."

The civil rights workers he had known in the South had come from sheltering homes and had swarmed to danger and even to death. His Hutchinson students left their peaceful, protected campus and flocked to the cities, to demonstrations and rallies. They sang of peace and were stalked by death. Only last week a pretty blond sophomore had been beaten at a rally in Union Square. It was only a question of time before a student protester was killed by a nervous police officer, a frightened National Guardsman. He had seen Lisa Ellenberg that afternoon. Her eyes were circled with fatigue; her hands trembled as she spoke to him. Her father had built an industrial empire; an elaborate alarm system protected his Great Neck mansion, but he could not protect his daughter from the impact of her own times. Poor Lisa. Poor Joshua. Michael decided that he would set up an appointment with Lisa. He fumbled to phrase the warnings he would offer her. *Lisa, you are too intense. You care too much and work too hard.* Useless words, he knew. He could neither mitigate nor dilute her intensity, her caring.

"Still, there is more of a chance for a safe life here," Benjamin interposed.

He had read a story in that morning's *Times* about mine throwers used in an attack from Lebanon against Israeli settlements. He had clipped the item to show to Rebecca, but in the end he had decided against it. It would be an unfair tactic, he knew, to use against his unknown and absent adversary. He acknowledged that he was in a struggle against Yehuda Arnon, against her life on Kibbutz Sha'arei ha-Negev. He knew that she feared for her sons and felt an aching distance from her husband. He knew, too, that she struggled against her feeling for him, yet she wept in joyful submission when his strength conquered and subdued her. There was hope for them. He loved Rebecca Arnon—vibrant, talented Rebecca, who had drawn him away from the precipice of his grief and thrust him back into caring and sharing. He wanted her to stay with him always.

They made love that night with swift desperation, as though they were caught up in a race and had no time to spare. They fell asleep with their arms knotted, their bodies close upon each other, as though the smallest space between them might admit doubt and memory, threaten the fragile balance of their togetherness.

"What shall we do?" she asked. Her voice was loud and clear in the night silence, but when he looked down at her he saw that she had spoken in her sleep, and his answer died on his lips. They would go away, he decided. They needed distance and time alone together.

THE AIR on Nantucket Island smelled of salt and snow. A thin sheet of frost was stretched across the undulating beach, and as Rebecca and Benjamin walked, they heard it crackle. The winter clothing they had brought from New York was not adequate against the cold. Rebecca wore Inga's down-filled red parka and pulled the hood tight so that it covered her cheeks. Benjamin went into town and bought a blue woolen cap and a long bright green muffler, which he wrapped and rewrapped about his neck. The Stevensons had warned them about the cold when they offered them the use of the house. They themselves were off to Mexico.

"Like any sensible artist," Joe had said. "Nantucket in the winter is hardly a haven."

Still, Rebecca was glad they had come. She loved the wintry

solitude of the island, the blanched majesty of the snow-crowned dunes, the glittering, icy expanse of the beach, and the gray reefs spackled with mica that glinted in the pale sunlight. The rhythm of the waves breaking against the shore soothed her as she sketched. Her easel was mounted on the beachhead, and when she heard the wild shrieks of the gulls, she lifted her eyes and watched the winged convoy soar in graceful formation.

There were few trees on the island, but a great elm grew in the Stevensons' yard, and small sparrows, as gray as the wintry skies, perched on the barren branches and chirped mournfully to each other. At night the wind whistled a secret and wild song, and she moved closer to Benjamin in the darkness and smiled at the warmth of his breath against her neck. They had found safe haven in this winter solitude. They were strangers here, and the islanders, jealous of their own privacy, would not invade theirs. Here they were protected from curious glance and worried gaze, from her mother's unarticulated questions, her brothers' concerned uneasiness, their wives' muted sympathy. She had seen the wary glances Mindell and Lydia exchanged when Rebecca spoke of Benjamin or entered a room with him.

Like Rebecca, they understood the anguish of uprootedness. Lydia and Mindell loved their husbands and their new lives, but they dreamed of the lands of their girlhoods. A decade had passed since Lydia's flight from Budapest, but she remembered still the taste of the cream pastries sold in her favorite café on Béla Bartók Boulevard, the flaming slash of light across the Buda woods at sunrise. Mindell walked with Michael along the broad avenues of his city and longed for Jerusalem's narrow streets; he brought her hothouse roses in winter, and she thought of the anemones in the Galilee, the lavender that inexplicably and briefly carpeted the Negev sands. Still, their choices had been simple: Rebecca walked a dangerous tightrope.

"Rebecca will do what's right," Rebecca had overheard Michael assure Aaron.

"But what is right?" Aaron the judge was uncertain.

Rebecca loved her brothers for their fairness, for their caring and unconditional love. She could not offer them any reassurance, any answers. Like Aaron, she did not know what was right.

She had written to Yehuda and told him that she had a new friend. An art critic, she said carefully. A man who understood her work, who understood her. Benjamin Nadler. She felt relief, vindication, because she had revealed her lover's name to her husband.

But Yehuda made no mention of it in his reply. He told her only that it was likely that he would have to leave the country again. There was great unease. There was civil unrest in Syria, and as always Israel was blamed. Egypt was moving its troops northward. Unlike most of his colleagues and countrymen, Yehuda did not think there would be war, but still intelligence had to be clarified, Israel's position reinforced.

Rebecca imagined Yehuda at secret meetings on Cyprus and in Athens. He would meet purveyors of arms in Constitution Square, handsome young men who wore suits tailored on Savile Row and ties of Liberty silk. He would meet informants in the cafés of Larnaca. Her husband was concerned with a nation's destiny. He could not spare time for hers or for his own. She crumbled the letter and quickly smoothed it out again, her fingers trembling as they moved across the thin pale green paper so closely covered with Yehuda's cramped script.

Yehuda's letters did not follow her to Nantucket Island. Nor did the daily newspapers. She was absorbed in her work. In pen and ink, in charcoal and chalk, Zalenko's words were translated into picture images. The poet wrote of spiritual desolation, and she drew the deserted beachscape of winter—frozen lichen clinging to bleached driftwood, snow soaring across sand. He wrote of desperate yearning, and her airbrush flew to capture a gull in lonely flight. "Thus wintry day drifts and fades into darkest night," he wrote and she used pastels, for the first time in years, to capture the delicate pinks and violets of the melancholy March sunset.

Benjamin Nadler sat with her beside the fire and studied her work.

"You understand Zalenko," he said. "You understand his landscapes of loneliness."

She sighed and looked out the window. A strong wind blew, and the branches of the elm tree quivered. Beyond the darkened beach, waves crashed furiously to shore. Pearl-gray clouds, shaped like spectral flowers, drifted menacingly through the night sky. In the distance the lamp of the Nantucket lighthouse blinked, warning sailors of the brewing storm.

"It must be beautiful outside," she said.

"Come."

They put on their heavy coats; she pulled the hood tight and he wrapped the bright green muffler about his neck. They went up to the second floor of the house where a french door opened onto the widow's walk—the narrow railed balcony that girdled many of the sensible white clapboard houses of Nantucket. Here, in years gone by, the wives of sailors had stood, anxiously watching the sea for the sight of their husband's sailing ships. Rebecca shivered, as though brushed by the ghostly shadow of their worry. She felt herself sister to those vanished women. Her husband, too, confronted hazard, courted danger. She, too, feared that he might not return to safe harbor. How was it possible, she wondered with bitter irony, to worry about her husband as she stood beside her lover? Her life and her loves were severed, and she despaired of ever making them whole again.

Now the waves rose to a threatening height as they rocketed shoreward. They crashed against the great boulders, battled the weather-worn reef, and broke at last against the frost-laced beachhead. The wind whined like a lost and wounded creature and swept the snow and sand in its wake.

The violence and desolation of the scene frightened Rebecca. Still, she knew that in a few months, the beach would again radiate warmth, reflect sunlight; the storm-tossed skies would be serene and the air calm. But when would her own life regain its serenity? When would she be free of the buffeting clouds of uncertainty? As though he read her thoughts, Benjamin Nadler drew her closer. He wrapped the end of his muffler about her neck, and they stood as one as the snow began to fall.

"Stay with me," he said. "Stay with me always. Don't go back to Israel." The plea he had restrained for so many weeks exploded with sudden force. "Always!" His voice rose to compete with the roar of the wind.

"How can I?" Her voice was strangled. "My children—Yaakov and Amnon . . ." Her eyes closed. Newly fallen snowflakes rested on her eyelids, jeweled her long lashes. He kissed them away and tasted her tears. *And Yehuda.* His name filled her mind, her heart, but she dared not utter it.

"We'll bring them here. They'll be safe. I'll take care of them. They will be the children I never had. . . ."

His voice broke, and she silenced him by pressing her mouth against his. She could not bear his grief; she could barely sustain her own. The wild wind died and silent snow fell steadily, blanketing them in layers of white.

That night, she lay awake beside him in the darkness.

What shall I do? she thought. Surely, there was a path that she must take, but snow and sorrow had obscured it. Exhausted, she fell asleep at last, as the pale mauve light of dawn stole across the wintry sky.

"MAY I come in, Rebecca?"

Leah hesitated in the doorway and watched Rebecca, who stood at the window of her girlhood room, her hair loose about her shoulders, staring at the maple tree. Although winter winds still blew, furled leaves of tender green had formed on the graceful branches. There was a new softness in the air, and the first shoots of crocus and hyacinth moved tentatively upward through earth still lightly sheathed in snow.

"Yes. Of course. Please."

Rebecca's voice was very low, and Leah was reminded of her daughter as a young girl, standing at this same window, caught up in the inexplicable and anomalous misery of adolescence. Now, as then, she placed her hand on Rebecca's shoulder and stood beside her at the window.

Boris, walking through the garden, looked up and saw the two women standing side by side, wearing the purple velvet robes that Joshua Ellenberg had recently given them. They were of an equal height, and their strong, even features were so similar that strangers knew at once that they were mother and daughter. Leah's hair had turned completely silver now, and her face had settled at last into the peaceful lines of accepting age. Streaks of that same silver glinted in the thick dark curls that hung loosely about Rebecca's shoulders. Her face was contemplative, and Boris was reminded of Leah's expression when she struggled with a decision and cautiously weighed each alternative. They were not careless women, Leah and Rebecca. They did not deny their passion, but they were not ruled by it.

"Let me think about it," Leah had said when Boris first proposed that they marry. "Give me time."

He imagined that Leah had made a similar plea to Eli Feinstein, whom she had loved during the days of her young womanhood. Always her life had been intertwined with those of so many others; she could not and would not deny her obligations. As Rebecca could not and would not.

A weaker woman might take an emotional plunge—abandon the tensions of a marriage grown sad and complex for a leap into a new beginning. But Rebecca Arnon was not a weak woman. She was

Leah's daughter, and she would struggle from uncertainty to conviction. She had been in the throes of that struggle since her arrival home from Nantucket Island, Boris knew. He had seen it in her face, heard it in her voice. He watched now as the two women turned from the window, a single ray of sunlight casting a lucent stole about their regal robes.

"Can you tell me about it, Rebecca?" Leah asked gently as she felt Rebecca's shoulders quiver beneath her touch.

They sat side by side on Rebecca's bed, their hands pressed tightly together.

"I don't know what to do," Rebecca said at last. "Sometimes I feel as though I've spent twenty years living in a dream and I am only just awakening. And then I feel that I want that dream to continue—I want to believe as I believed when Yehuda and I were first married—that peace was possible, that each day was a new beginning. It's strange; during all those years in Israel I was never frightened for myself. I still don't fear for myself. But since Noam's death I am desperately afraid for Yaakov and Amnon. I want to keep them safe. I must keep them safe."

There was a new and frightening fierceness in her voice. A picture of her sons stood on her bedside table, and she lifted it, looked down at their smiling faces, and pressed the framed photo hard against her breast; she shielded their likenesses as she would never be able to shield their lives. Tears glinted in her eyes, settled like moist brilliants on her lashes.

"Rebecca, do you love Yehuda?" Leah asked.

Rebecca was silent. Her long fingers played with the ruffled edge of the coverlet that was spread across her girlhood bed. She remembered now that Leah had bought it to soothe some youthful disappointment, to dispel a melancholy mood. But she was a woman now, and ruffles and laces provided no relief, offered no appeasement. When she spoke at last, her voice was very low.

"I don't know if you will understand this—or even if I can explain it properly. I don't understand it myself. I care for Yehuda. I'm obsessed with worry for him. My heart turns when he calls. He told me last night that he had to go north, to the Lebanese border, and I lay awake worrying because now they are using mine throwers on that border. Still, at the same time, I am angry with him and frightened for him and hurt by him. I think that if there is so much anger and so much hurt and so much fear, then there must be love. And yet there is Benjamin Nadler and what I feel for him."

"And what do you feel for him?" Leah asked. The question had seared her mind since Rebecca had first introduced her to the art critic, but she had not dared ask it until now.

"I feel so safe with him, so protected. We are calm together—at least when we are not thinking about the future. We share our work, our thoughts. There are no secrets between us, only tenderness and need. He has been lonely. He wants to make me happy, to take care of my sons. Yaakov and Amnon would be safe if I raised them here." Her voice grew vague, troubled, and she turned away from her mother.

"There are no guarantees of safety," Leah said, more harshly than she had intended. She had fled Russia as a young woman, searching for a safe haven in the United States, yet Aaron had fought in World War II and had been taken prisoner, Rebecca had risked her life in Israel's War for Independence, and Michael had confronted danger on the highways of Mississippi.

"Perhaps you're right. But you must admit that the odds are better here," Rebecca said without rancor.

"Yes. The odds are better. Not certain, but better."

Rebecca's fingers still fretted the ruffle.

"Mama." Her voice trembled as it had when she was a small girl asking a serious question. "Do you think it's possible to love two men at once? It's a crazy question, I know, but I feel a little crazy."

"I don't think it's a crazy question," Leah answered carefully. "I have thought about it, and sometimes, it seems to me, that our lives are divided into seasons, and there are different loves for different seasons."

She paused and allowed herself to dream back across the years; memories surged forward, and she struggled to sort out the seasons of her own life. Her first husband, Yaakov, Aaron's father, who had been killed during a pogrom on an Odessa street, had been the love of her halcyon days, of the summer season of her girlhood. In the burgeoning springtime of her young womanhood, there had been Eli Feinstein, the labor organizer, her lover, who had died in the terrible Rosenblatt fire. Grief had paralyzed her again, but David Goldfeder had pierced that grief with the force of his love, and she had shared the gentle autumnal years of child-rearing, of life-building, with him. And now, in the winter of her life, Boris Zaslovsky stood beside her in tranquil companionship. Too neat a formula, perhaps, but all she could offer her daughter now were her own secret joys and desperate losses—the legacy of remembrance.

"Rebecca, you know the name Eli Feinstein?"

"Yes. He was the labor leader, the man you worked with who died in the Rosenblatt fire. You dedicated a painting to him—*Lost in Flames.*"

"I worked with him and I loved him. That, of course, you could not have known. Your father and I had reached a time of separateness, aloneness. He was in medical school, absorbed in his studies, and I was caught up in my factory and union work. Both of us were exhausted, worried always about lack of time, lack of money. Eli and I worked together. We shared the same ideas, and we were drawn together. First as friends and colleagues. Then as lovers. We could not help ourselves. As perhaps you and Benjamin Nadler cannot help yourselves."

"I never knew," Rebecca said woodenly. She looked at Leah, feeling strangely betrayed, but there was neither apology nor regret in Leah's eyes, only the wistful glaze of memory.

"Of course you didn't know. You were a little girl then. You went off to the mountains that summer with your aunt Mollie—you and Aaron and Joshua and his mother. And I stayed in New York—with David, my husband, and with Eli, my lover. And I wondered then, as you do now, how it was possible to care so deeply for two men at once."

"What happened?" Rebecca asked.

"Life intervened. There was the fire. Eli was killed. I mourned him." Remembered grief thickened her voice, and her fingers flew to her white hair. Black, it had been, in the days of her grief, and she had hacked it off with blunt scissors, weeping without restraint. Time had faded her sorrow but had not erased it. She thought of Eli's death and the life she and David had shared. It occurred to her, with a sudden flash of insight, that if she had not cared for Eli, she might never have learned to love David. Love, like seasons, melded. So it might be for Rebecca.

"And if there had been no fire?" Rebecca asked.

Leah smiled sadly. It was a question she had often asked herself.

"How can we reconcile all the *if*s of our lives, Becca? What *if* you had not gone to Israel in forty-seven? What *if* you had not been in Jerusalem when Yehuda was wounded? What *if* Benjamin Nadler had been lecturing in the Midwest during your visit to New York? The backward trail is endless; all our lives are a series of accidents and chance."

"I know," Rebecca said.

She leaned over and kissed her mother's cheek, grateful for all that Leah had shared with her. They sat together for a moment longer, mother and daughter in their purple velvet robes, encircled in sunlight—Leah looking back across the past, Rebecca straining bravely, arduously, toward the future.

ON the first day of spring warmth, a long letter from Yehuda arrived. Rebecca read it leaning against the maple tree, so that the shadows of the young leaves dappled its pages. She reflected on how the quality of his correspondence had changed during the months of her absence. At first he had written brief notes, cursory and curt postcards. But more recently he talked to her in his letters, shared his thoughts and feelings. It was, she thought, almost as though her journey away from him had released his restraint.

Dearest Rebecca, he wrote in the tight English script he had learned at a Mandate school,

It hardly seems possible that almost five months have passed since you left. A long time for us to be without you, but we are glad that you have had this opportunity to be with Mindell and with the rest of your family after all these years. I was glad to see the sketches for the Zalenko book which you enclosed in your last letter. I showed them to Danielle and Yair, who were somewhat bewildered by them. I realized then that my daughter and her fiancé are, after all, children of sunlight and desert and cannot easily understand the landscapes of snowbound beach and winter-weary cities. "How lonely these pictures are," Yair said, and Danielle nodded in agreement. It is difficult for our young lovers to understand that love does not conquer solitude, does not obviate separateness.

Yaakov and Amnon are fine, although they miss you and talk about you a great deal. Last night Amnon was particularly moody and I asked him why he was so sad.

"I miss Ima *and I want to be with her," he said. "Wherever she is, I want to be with her."*

"Soon," I promised. "Soon you will be with her, wherever she is."

I, too, have missed you greatly, but I think that it was important for you to have had this time to step back into the life you left behind when we married. Loss can be assimilated—there is no arguing with the finality of death. But regret lingers, teases, poisons. I would not have you haunted by regret, my dearest Rivka. I know that it has not been easy for you since Noam's death, and I cannot promise that it will be easier in the years to come. But I can tell you that I will try to share more with you. If *that is what you want, after this time apart.*

I went north last week. The anemones are in bloom. Do you remember

their brightness, their sweetness? Do you remember how we walked together so many years ago, through flower-spangled fields?

He had signed the letter simply, *Your Yehuda*, and enclosed a few blossoms in the envelope. The brittle petals fell, like scarlet teardrops, onto her palm. She held them and they crumbled, but their fragrance clung to her skin.

The phone rang in the house, but Rebecca made no move to answer it. She folded Yehuda's letter and thought of how he must have looked as he wrote it—his silken-gray eyes hooded, his full lips tightly compressed. He had searched deeply and offered her acknowledgment but not false promises. He recognized doubt and uncertainty. He had told Amnon that he would be with Rebecca, *wherever she is*. He countered the danger that he perceived only with memory and the fragile scarlet flowers of the Galilee.

Her mother answered the phone. The french doors that led to the garden were open, and Rebecca heard Leah's voice rise with excitement. Still, she did not stir, but read her husband's letter again. Gentle, generous Yehuda. Strong and vulnerable Yehuda. Her heart broke for him and for herself. He should have written earlier, spoken sooner.

"Rebecca!"

Leah rushed toward her and seized her wrists, her face radiant.

"Mindell's had a girl. A beautiful baby, born this morning. A girl. Michael has a daughter."

"And we have a new granddaughter." Boris Zaslovsky beamed. His own children had been killed at Babi Yar by the Germans, and he had never thought to know joy again. But he had learned, with the passing years, that each new life avenged a death and that the laughter of living children vanquished the fearful whimpers of the dying. Leah's grandchildren were his own. He visited Lydia and Aaron's children and crafted small wooden animals for Seth, the youngest. He told Paulette and David tales of the Russian steppes, of the wicked Siberian snow wizard and the brave prince of the Khazars. He studied the framed photographs of Amnon and Yaakov. One day he would travel to Israel and meet Rebecca's children.

"I'm so glad," Rebecca said. She went to the phone at once, but as was often the case, all lines to Israel were busy. Instead she sent Yehuda a cable. It was Yehuda who had taken Mindell's hand, so many years ago, and led her from fear and hiding into courage and freedom.

Rebecca visited a radiant Mindell at the hospital and stood beside Michael at the nursery window, entranced by the newborn infant. She marveled at her new niece's perfectly formed tiny pink limbs, the aureole of soft pale hair, and the long lashes that swept across tear-dampened cheeks.

"She's beautiful," she said. "What will you call her?"

"Shlomit," Michael replied. "It means 'peace,' you know."

There was a hint of whimsical defiance in Michael's voice. He would name his daughter for peace, although she had been born in a time of war. The war in Vietnam had escalated and angry mobs had besieged Hubert Humphrey in Paris. Michael's students at Hutchinson College wore black armbands on their brightly colored sweaters. Young people stood vigil at the White House and chanted, "Hey, hey, LBJ, how many kids did you kill today?" Each night the honor roll of death flickered across their television screen. "Killed in Vietnam today were the following area residents . . ." Mindell's labor had begun as the nightly tabulation concluded. War hovered over the Middle East. An air battle over the Sea of Galilee had destroyed six Syrian MIGs. Egyptian troops moved closer to Israel's frontier. There was talk of closing the Straits of Tiran, and Nasser spoke vigorously of expelling the United Nations Emergency Force. U Thant posed for photographers with his hands lifted helplessly, his enigmatic smile betraying his impotency.

That afternoon Michael had graded Lisa Ellenberg's ambitious paper on "The Etiology of War." He had, with regret, given the paper a B minus, which would disappoint Lisa, who strove for perfection. But he had named his daughter Shlomit because he shared Lisa's dream of peace, and that would please her.

"I know what Shlomit means," Rebecca said. "I lived in Israel, after all. It's a beautiful name."

Michael noted, with sinking heart, Rebecca's use of the past tense, but he did not comment on it.

"We will keep her in peace, then," he said. Shlomit's unseeing eyes opened, her tiny feet and arms flailed, and she began to cry.

"We will try," Rebecca said, but she was thinking of how hard it was to keep a child in peace. An Israeli lieutenant had been killed the previous week as he patrolled below the Golan Heights. He had been twenty years old, the son of Bergen-Belsen survivors. His mother had wept at his graveside and repeated again and again, "We only wanted to keep him in peace." The newspaper report noted that she had said the same words in Yiddish, Polish, and Hebrew.

"Shlomit," Rebecca whispered, and smiled at her brother's newborn daughter. If only names were talismans, guarantors of protection.

"Amnon. Yaakov," she added softly, invoking the names of her own sons in unarticulated prayer.

She met Benjamin Nadler for dinner that night at a small East Side restaurant. The first daffodils of spring stood in a blue vase on their table. They smiled at each other across the butter-colored flowers and lifted their glasses in toast to Shlomit. There was a new buoyancy in Benjamin's voice, and he filled his glass and her own again.

"Another toast," he said.

She smiled. The evening had a holiday quality. With wine and laughter, at their leisure, they fended off the future. Her work for the Zalenko book was almost completed, and he was working well ahead of his deadline on a critique of the Impressionists. Briefly, they were freed of pressure.

"What shall we drink to?" she asked.

"To this."

He passed an envelope across the table to her. She held it tentatively, fearfully, in her hand. It was heavy, containing more than one sheet of linen-weighted paper. It would tip the scales, she knew.

She removed it from the envelope. Three sheets closely typed, the cream-colored stationery embossed with the emblem of a California university. Benjamin Nadler was invited to assume the deanship of the school of fine arts. Attractive terms were set forth, including a large residence, to which the previous dean, a painter, had added a glass-enclosed skylit wing. There was a generous travel allowance to cover international seminars and lectures. The university participated in exchange programs with major universities, and the dean's duties would include visits to campuses in France, Spain, Italy, and Israel.

Rebecca read slowly. She imagined herself coming to Israel as a visitor, as the wife of a visiting academic dignitary. She smiled bitterly.

"What do you think?" Eagerness lit Benjamin Nadler's craggy features. She saw, for the first time, a gold cast in his amber eyes. "A house large enough for children. Wonderful country for youngsters. A marvelous studio." He tallied advantages, envisioned a life. Her sons would sleep in wood-paneled rooms. She would paint in a glass-enclosed studio.

The waiter brought their meal—a holiday repast, chosen for lovers. Leaf-shaped *morelles* floating on spinach pasta. A salad of russet-fringed lettuce, slender celery wands, ebony olives. Neither of them lifted a fork.

"They want an answer soon," he said.

"So I see." She handed the letter back to him.

"Will you come with me?" His voice was very low.

She did not answer.

"Will you marry me and come with me?" Now his tone was firm and his eyes commanded a reply.

"I don't know."

Her hands cupped her wineglass. She stared at the yellow daffodils. She lifted the glass to her lips, but her fingers trembled and tear-shaped droplets of wine trickled onto the snow-white cloth. She looked at them and thought of the dried petals of the anemones that Yehuda had picked in the Galilee and that had crumbled in her hand.

MICHAEL GOLDFEDER, flushed with the joy of new fatherhood, stopped at the Barton's candy shop in Grand Central Terminal and bought two large boxes of chocolate-covered mints, which he distributed to the students who attended his seminar on "The Sociology of Politics" that afternoon. He also bought a can of Almond Kisses because he knew that the chocolate-covered nuts were Lisa Ellenberg's favorites. But Lisa cut his seminar that day, although she was due to give an oral report. He asked the smiling girls, who flocked teasingly about his desk to accept his chocolates and offer their shy congratulations, if they knew the reason for her absence.

"Spring is here," someone suggested pertly.

"That's not like Lisa," Michael said, and frowned.

"I saw her last night," a tall blond girl who lived in Lisa's dormitory volunteered. "She was at some sort of teach-in at Columbia and almost missed the last train. She said she had a Lit paper due and would probably work all night. She's probably at the dorm sleeping it off."

"All night?" Michael was vaguely disturbed. Lisa was pushing herself too hard, he thought. She had looked too tired recently to sacrifice a night's sleep. But then he recalled his own student days at Princeton and at Berkeley. He, too, had often stayed up all night working on an assignment. A dramatic excitement accompanied those nocturnal work sessions. He remembered the secret satisfaction of working through the night in a building where everyone else was asleep while the light of his student lamp cast its cornucopia of brightness across the completed pages. Lisa was only doing what students had always done. Kids that age could afford sleepless nights, he assured himself.

Still, he wanted to tell her of Shlomit's birth. He called her dormitory and left a message asking her to call him during his office hours later in the day. He taught his second seminar and held conferences with two tutorial students. The department secretary handed him a sheaf of messages, but none of them were from Lisa. He frowned and tried her dormitory again.

"Her room doesn't answer, Professor Goldfeder," the girl on phone duty said. "And I know she has a Lit class this hour."

His next scheduled appointment was canceled, and he glanced at his watch and decided that he would catch an earlier train and manage another visit with Mindell and Shlomit. As he packed his attaché case, he noticed the can of Almond Kisses, still unopened. He had time to drop them off at Lisa's room and still make his train.

Briskly, he walked across campus. Tiny buds had formed on the dogwood trees in the library meadow, and star-shaped yellow blossoms sprouted on the forsythia hedges that rimmed the dormitory compound. He was pleased that his daughter had been born in the season of sweet blooming. A child of spring named for peace. The student at the reception desk in Lisa's dormitory looked up from the poster she was working on and smiled at him in recognition. She had covered a large sheet of oak tag with a rainbow and scrawled the word *peace* in different languages. *Pace. Pax. Paix. Salaam.* A Japanese student had painted the word in the graceful characters of her own language.

"Can you think of any other languages, Dr. Goldfeder?" she asked flirtatiously.

Michael selected a purple Magic Marker and penned his daughter's name in Hebrew.

"Shlomit," he said, and wondered if the utterance of her name would always give him such pleasure.

"Thanks." She smiled at him. She was a pretty girl who was overtly conscious of her charms.

"Is Lisa Ellenberg in?" he asked.

"Gee, I haven't seen Lisa today, although she was supposed to work on these posters with me. I just came on duty, though. She's probably up in her room. Go on up. I'll sign you in."

He hesitated and glanced at his watch. If he left the candy and a message at the reception desk, he would be in no danger of missing his train. But he intended to call Joshua and Sherry that night, and he wanted to tell them that he had seen Lisa. They worried about her, he knew. He bounded up the stairs, taking the steps two at a time, hurrying past open doors. In one room he glimpsed a group of coeds in plaid robes, seated on the floor in a semicircle, notebooks and texts open in front of them.

"Rimbaud was a visionary," one said.

"Rimbaud was a romantic. Romantics are not automatically visionaries," another protested.

The chorus of "The Impossible Dream" drifted from another room and mingled with the strains of a student flautist practicing trilling scales. He looked at the girl and thought of his infant daughter. Smilingly, he considered the miracle of the passing years. One day she, too, would spend a spring afternoon analyzing Rimbaud, practicing the flute, drawing rainbows on sheets of cardboard.

He tapped on Lisa's door. There was no reply, and he knocked loudly now, insistently. The door across the hall opened and a Chinese girl in a red kimono looked at him worriedly. He recognized her. Sue Li. A good friend of Lisa's.

"Professor Goldfeder. I'm glad you're here. Lisa hasn't been out of her room all day, and her door is locked." Sue's voice was very soft, almost frightened.

"Why didn't you call someone?" he asked with a harshness born of the commingling of worry and irritation. His palms were very damp and his heart thumped with rapid beat.

"I didn't know what to do," she said. "When I left this morning she was still sleeping, I thought. I knocked when I came back, and when she didn't answer I thought she had gone out. But when I picked up my mail and messages, I saw that hers were still there, so I asked around and it turned out that she didn't go to any of her classes—not even her Lit course, although she worked all night so that she could hand in her paper on time today. Then I began to worry, but I didn't want to cause any trouble. . . ." Her voice trailed off, but Michael was no longer listening.

He pounded harder.

"Lisa!" he shouted insistently. "Lisa, you must open the door."

Girls streamed out of the open doorways and gathered in the corridor. They clutched their books to their chests like shields, and their faces were pale and wreathed with worry. Someone switched off the phonograph, and the flautist no longer played. They stared at one another apprehensively in the sudden, unnerving silence.

"Nancy went to find the resident adviser. She has a master key," someone said, but Michael knew that he could not wait for the resident adviser.

He stepped back, braced himself, and rammed his shoulder against the door. The weak lock yielded almost at once and the door flew open.

"Oh no," Sue Li whispered. "Please no."

Lisa, wearing her perennial jeans and black turtleneck sweater, lay on the floor, her bright hair fanned out about her pale face. Her skin was the color of palest parchment, and the black stylus pen whose ink stained her fingers was caught in a fiery tendril. Her bare feet were very white, and irrelevantly, Michael thought of Shlomit's tiny pink toes clenching and relaxing. Tiny emerald-colored capsules that almost matched her open, staring eyes were scattered beside her.

He rushed forward and knelt beside her. He lifted her wrist. It was ice-cold and slowly stiffening. He pressed his mouth against hers and breathed hard, rhythmically, but her mouth was fetid and dry. He knew, and had known, from the moment he saw her, that he would find no pulse, coax forth no life.

Grief weighted him, slowed his movements, but now there was no urgency. Slowly, he disentangled the pen from her hair; he pulled the translucent lids down over her eyes while tears ran down his own cheeks.

"Why?" Sue Li asked sorrowfully, but no one offered her an answer.

The girls parted to allow Michael to pass, and he went to the phone, briefly bewildered as to whom he should call. At last he dialed his mother's number. Leah would know what to do. As he waited for her to answer, he thought of the linkage of life and loss. Always, the celebration of his daughter's birth would be commingled with memories of Lisa's death. Behind him Sue Li sobbed with piteous softness.

THE ELLENBERGS held a private graveside service for Lisa. They could not bear the thought of a chapel. Walls could not contain their grief. Sherry and Joshua stood close together, each fearful for the other. Joshua searched his wife's face; she knotted his silk scarf, although the day was mild. Their children stood protectively beside them. Joanna touched Sherry's sleeve, smoothed her hair as though to remind her that she still had a daughter—she, Joanna, was alive; her tear-streaked face was swollen with grief and love. Scott and Stevie stood side by side. Scott's eyes were red-rimmed, his face blotched. Lisa had been his twin. Their lives had been linked. Her death left him strangely maimed, bereft of self. Resistance, incredulity, tempered the family's sorrow; they wore the new mourners' masks of bewildered and unaccepting grief.

"How could it have happened?" Joshua had asked again and again as Michael and Aaron sat with him through the long night of watching beside Lisa's coffin.

Again and again, they repeated what the doctors had told them, what Lisa's autopsy had revealed. She had been taking amphetamines, and her heart had not been strong enough to sustain the stimulant. She had not committed suicide. There was no question of suicide. That much comfort they could offer her father, but they knew that it was no comfort at all. Joshua Ellenberg had drifted into old age that night, and the friends of his boyhood could not soothe his sorrow.

"What did we ask of her? What did we want of her? Only that she should be happy. That was all. Everything I would have given her. Everything I would have given for her."

Joshua rocked back and forth in the ancient rhythm of mourning. Again and again, in broken voice, he assured himself and his friends that there was nothing he would have denied Lisa. Always he had worked for his children, protected them. Station wagons had awaited them after school, after club meetings. An electrically controlled fence ringed the Great Neck estate. As a child, Lisa had suffered from frequent colds, and Joshua had sent her to Florida each winter and installed sun lamps in the house. Always, he had met her train at the station and insisted that she take cabs in the city because the subways were uncertain, unsafe. And then, on a spring evening, she had swallowed a glittering emerald-colored capsule that matched her eyes, and all his vigilant efforts were defeated, his precautions mocked. His beautiful firstborn daughter was dead, and he would never again be able to keep her safe, to keep her happy.

"Lisa. Lisa."

Joshua wept and Aaron embraced him as he asked, yet again, "Why did it happen? How could it happen?"

Aaron had flown to Israel when Noam Arnon was killed, and he had stood beside Yehuda during the nocturnal vigil when Jews guard the bodies of their dead before committing them for burial. Yehuda, the veteran soldier, the agent who had crossed dangerous borders and fought in too many wars, had asked the same question during that long night of watching.

"Why did it happen? How did it happen?"

He pitied Joshua now, as he had pitied Yehuda then, as he pitied himself and all other parents—for their helplessness, their impuissance. They were powerless to shield their children from grief and disappointment; they could not vouchsafe their happiness or even, in the end, guarantee their survival.

Rebecca slept fitfully the night before the funeral. Again and again, fragmented dreams jerked her into melancholy wakefulness. Yaakov and Amnon ran barefoot through thickly falling snow, plunging into pristine drifts. She chased them, clutching winter garments, calling their names, but they ignored her pleas. Joshua held Lisa close, but she writhed away from his embrace and floated away, waving a spectral arm. Rebecca sat upright in bed and shivered, although the room was warm. She could not protect her sons from hazard, just as Joshua had been unable to protect his daughter.

She slept again, and now Yehuda spoke to her from a distance, and she moved closer yet could not bridge the space between them. Benjamin Nadler glided toward her through mistbound shadow. She could not discern Yehuda's words, and Benjamin vanished before he reached her. She awakened alone, her arms outstretched, embracing emptiness.

She drove to the cemetery with Leah and Boris. Leah sat tall, her eyes dry but her face pale. She had loved Lisa as she loved her own grandchildren, but she could not, would not, succumb to grief. On a day such as this, the old, experienced in death and grief, loss and finality, gave strength to the young. In the car Rebecca wept, suddenly and violently.

"It is so terrible," she said, as though her tears required explanation, "when parents bury their children." She knew. She lived in a country where parents, too often, buried their soldier sons. She had stood beside Yehuda at Noam's grave. She wept now for Lisa and for Joshua, for Noam and for Yehuda, and for herself. At last her tears ceased, and she understood exactly what she had to do.

Leah touched her daughter's hand—a light monitory touch of recognition, understanding.

"It is terrible," Boris agreed. "But one recovers even from such a sorrow." His children had died, but he had learned to live again. He had not forgotten their tears and suffering, but he had relearned the secret of laughter, reclaimed his wonder at the beauty of a soaring bird, an infant's tiny hand. Eventually all griefs were absorbed. They ached but they did not fester.

"I know," Rebecca said softly. She thought of Sara Meiri, her closest friend on the kibbutz. Sara had been inconsolable after the death of her son in the Sinai Campaign. She was a flautist, but she had abandoned her music. Yet each week her husband polished her silver flute, and finally, one quiet afternoon, Sara had lifted it to her lips and played a gentle lullaby. The kibbutz members had bowed their heads as they listened. Two older women, bonded because each had lost a son in the War for Independence, looked at each other and nodded. They had known that although Sara could never vanquish her sorrow, her long period of mourning was over.

Rebecca realized now, with sudden clarity, that Yehuda, too, would cease his mourning, abandon his anger, just as she now surrendered her fear. Noam was dead and would not be forgotten, but the laughter of Amnon and Yaakov rang clear; Danielle would soon be a bride, and Mindell had become a mother. Life, after all, outbalanced and outweighed death. Yehuda might call the name of his first wife in the darkness, but he slept beside Rebecca, and she recognized, as she stood beside the newly dug grave, that she would not have had him forget the bride whom he had married in his youth.

Sherry Ellenberg emitted a desperate, denying moan. Joshua, grayfaced, his own hands trembling, steadied her, whispered softly into her ear. Their Great Neck home was shrouded in mourning now, Rebecca knew. She and Leah had draped sheets over the mirrors and arranged for the low stools of sorrow to be placed on the carpeted floor. But Sherry and Joshua would slowly recover. They would give parties again, and their house would be filled with laughter and music. Lovers would dance into each other's arms and walk together through a garden lit by fairy lights. Summer would come to Nantucket's snowbound beach. All losses were finally assimilated, all griefs arbitrated, and life progressed.

Benjamin Nadler came to the funeral with Charles Ferguson. He did not move toward Rebecca, although his eyes never left her face.

A light rain began to fall, and the mourners lifted their faces to the gentle spray as the rabbi spoke. He was a tall, white-haired man who had known Lisa from childhood. He had stood beside her at her bat mitzvah, and her death had shattered him. His grief and confusion comforted and soothed those to whom he spoke. He offered no explanation, no rationalization. There were those things which were inexplicable, which defied reason. It would help, he said, speaking so softly that they strained to hear him, if they who had loved Lisa could think of her brief life as a gift, a sweet loan too swiftly terminated. It was true that they had lost Lisa, but they would not rescind the memory of her golden days, her light laughter, and her youthful idealism.

"Always in our memories she will be young and full of hope and convinced that her life can make a difference."

Those who had loved her nodded and clutched at the fragile strand of comfort he offered them. Lisa would never know the inequities of age, the dimming of hope, the sadness of disillusionment. The mourners touched one another's hands, moved closer together. Sue Li sobbed, and Joshua moved toward her, drew her into the circle of the family. Joanna took her hand. Lydia's head rested on Aaron's shoulder. Mindell's fingers pressed hard against Michael's palm. Rebecca looked at Benjamin Nadler and saw that tears coursed down his craggy cheeks. He had not cried for Ellen, his wife, he had told her, but he wept now. He had been warmed and stirred to life. His thick hair was rain-spackled. She went to stand beside him.

The plain pine coffin was lowered into the newly dug grave. Joshua and Sherry moved forward. They each dropped a clump of moist spring earth onto the pale, rough wood. Their lips moved soundlessly (as Yehuda's lips had moved at Noam's funeral, Rebecca remembered now). The soil streaked Sherry's hand, and Joshua wiped it with his tear-dampened white handkerchief. Scott wept openly as he dropped a smooth stone onto his twin's coffin. He held Stevie's hand and spoke gently to his younger brother until Stevie at last released the patch of turf he had dug up in their garden that morning. Tendrils of green threaded the soft earth, and Rebecca thought of how the tender grass would yellow in the darkness of the grave. Joanna scattered violet crocus petals onto the wood because Lisa had loved the first flower of spring. The men took up the shovels, and the women stooped to gather up stones and soil. Together, they blanketed the coffin with a dark, moist coverlet of earth. And then Joshua intoned the mourner's Kaddish; the others repeated the final response in unison.

"May God, Who establishes peace in the heavens, grant peace unto us and unto all Israel. . . ."

Rebecca's voice was vibrant. It was Lisa's own prayer. She had dreamed of peace and worked for it. They would not abandon her dream, her prayer.

"Amen." Benjamin Nadler's voice was sonorous, and when she looked up at him she saw that again his eyes were moist with tears.

CHARLES FERGUSON waited until the Ellenbergs' week of mourning was over before issuing invitations to a private exhibit of Rebecca's illustrations for the Pelican Press edition of Alan Zalenko's poems. Again, Rebecca walked the deeply carpeted corridors and watched strangers study her work. Again, she stood before her drawings, and Benjamin Nadler stood at her side. She watched his pen fly across the pages of his pad, making swift, cryptic notes, although he knew these pictures well, had watched them come into being.

The managing director of the Pelican Press hurried up to her. The drawings were wonderful. The book would be a great success, a classic. Would she be available to undertake other projects?

"Mrs. Arnon's future plans are uncertain," Benjamin Nadler said politely.

Rebecca held her vellum-bound copy of the book tightly. It was a beautiful volume, and she would have always been haunted by regret if she had not undertaken the drawings. Yehuda had been right to encourage her to stay.

Benjamin made no notes as they stood before the double-folio pen-and-ink sketch of the lonely beach after a snowfall. Rebecca had captured the ambience of loneliness as drifting snow whirled about misshapen dunes and long fingers of glittering ice trembled on the barren branches of beach-plum bushes. Low horizontal clouds streaked the sky and cast ominous shadows across the beachhead, yet a pale crescent of sun would not be obscured. It formed a coronet of hope above the wintry desolation.

"You did that on the day after the storm." He remembered.

She nodded and thought of how he had held her close on the widow's walk and wrapped his bright green muffler about her neck.

They left the gallery and, once outside, blinked against the sudden brightness of the spring sunlight. Young women in light-colored linen suits hurried down the street, and men set down their attaché cases, loosened their ties, and purchased bunches of flowers from the vendors who stood on every corner.

"How far away Nantucket seems," Benjamin said.

"Our winter island." Rebecca's voice was wistful but not regretful.

Like invalids, they had withdrawn to that seabound, snow-glazed landscape that so exactly matched their own winter of despair. There, isolated and alone, they had ministered to each other's loneliness. They had defied storm and cold and wakened each other to warmth and caring. They had confronted encroaching darkness and risen to canescent dawns. They had gathered strength and reassured each other, and now, standing in a patch of sunlight in front of a gleaming plate-glass window that mirrored their upturned faces, they acknowledged their separate recoveries.

"You're going back to Israel—back to Yehuda?" He had known since Lisa's funeral that she would leave him.

She nodded.

"I must. I want to."

"I know."

"You'll have a good life in California."

"I hope so," he said cautiously, and she smiled. They were too wise for certainty.

Again, he walked her to Grand Central station, and in the familiar dimness of the terminal, he kissed her gently. She took his hand and held it, and then, briefly, pressed his fingers to her lips.

"Goodbye."

"God bless."

The roaring train muted their farewells.

WHENEVER Yehuda Arnon remained at Kibbutz Sha'arei ha-Negev for any length of time, he asked to be assigned to the avocado grove. He loved to work among the tall trees, checking them for dead or withered branches, allowing the pale green leaves to brush his face. Even after all the years he had lived on kibbutz, he retained a fascination for the mystery of growing things, and he watched with wonder as the small flower, devoid of petals, evolved into the ripe, slender-necked, pear-shaped fruit. The work in the grove was difficult. In addition to the pruning, he checked the irrigation and the fertilizer and studied the tender bark for insect pests and fungus diseases. He was usually weary by the end of the working day, but it was the pleasant fatigue that comes with a physical task competently accomplished. He preferred it to the terrible weariness that swept over him at day's end in hotel rooms in foreign capitals or in the conference rooms of the Defense Ministry in Jerusalem.

He had worked late that May afternoon, trying to pinpoint a leak in one of the underground feeder pipes, and he was exhausted when he returned to his bungalow. He showered and listened to the news, his face darkening. He switched the radio off and went to the window. The peaceful scene gave lie to the newscaster's ominous report. Surely, he was not looking at a community poised on the brink of war.

Small children laughed and chattered as they played on the lawn. Two older men played chess beneath an acacia tree, intently observed by a group of boys. A girl hung a bright yellow blouse out to dry on the rail of her porch. The desert heat would dry it within the hour, Yehuda knew, and he thought of how Rebecca loved to wear such a garment, newly dried and smelling of sunlight. He leaned forward and listened as women called to one another from their windows.

"Aliza, please bring me grapes from the dining hall when you go."

"Chava, can I borrow a cup of milk?"

The tiny two-burner gas stoves hissed and kettles and pots clattered as the women busied themselves importantly with the light predinner snack. Rebecca had never been able to understand the Eastern European custom of having a hot drink at this hour, in the desert heat. Always, she had kept a pitcher of iced tea in their small fridge, with sprigs of fresh mint floating in the amber liquid. There was nothing in the fridge now except a bottle of Maccabee beer and the tins of fruit juice he kept on hand for Yaakov and Amnon, who were off to the Galilee on their school trip. The curriculum planners had not waited for the traditional outing at the end of the semester. They read the headlines carefully. Examinations were coordinated with Egyptian troop movements; class excursions to the north depended on Syrian maneuvers.

A group of young people sat beneath a dwarf palm tree and sang softly as a bearded volunteer from Germany strummed his guitar. They sang the words from Ecclesiastes in Hebrew, in German, in English.

"To every thing, there is a season, and a time to every purpose . . ."

Their voices, fluid with sadness and hope, mingled with the sweet, clear mellifluence of Sara Meiri's flute.

A newly married couple lived in the bungalow adjacent to his own, and Yehuda could discern their lovers' laughter, their murmurs and sighs of pleasure. An almost corporeal loneliness suffused him. Always, at this hour, he missed Rebecca most keenly. The small sitting room was permeated with her presence. Her paintings hung on the whitewashed walls, the woven fabrics of her own design covered the cushions on the narrow beige sofa. Her art books were ranged on the low coffee table. He glanced at their titles. Gombrich's *Social History of Art*, a biography of Modigliani, *A Study of Modern Landscape Art* by Benjamin Nadler. He turned away from the portrait of the author on the jacket and went outside.

Two men kicked a soccer ball to their young sons. Sweat darkened their fresh white T-shirts, and they moved with long-legged, easy grace, laughing as the chubby youngsters lurched after the black-and-white ball. One of the men waved to Yehuda.

"Anything on the news?" he asked.

Yehuda shrugged.

"The same. Hussein is off to visit Nasser in Cairo. The mobilization continues. Eban's done with de Gaulle and Wilson and is on his way to Washington. He'll have as much luck there as he had in Paris and London." Everything was in abeyance while diplomats and heads of state flew from capital to capital, their diplomatic smiles frozen into grimaces, their hearts pounding. He was relieved that he had not been asked to accompany Eban on this trip. Younger men would feed him the intelligence he needed. Rebecca was right. It was time for him to step back, to work in the avocado grove and play with his growing sons.

The men nodded and returned to their game. Their uniforms were clean and ready, their kit bags packed. They listened at the appointed hours for their reserve call-up. But while Hussein was in Cairo and Eban was in Washington, there would be no fighting. Not yet. Impatiently they shouted at their sons to keep their eyes on the ball, to straighten their knees. Their voices were too intense. Each game might be their last; the hours of peace and play were numbered.

Yehuda recalled how he had assured Rebecca that it was safe for her to leave the country, that there would be no war that year. His predictions had been honest, but they had been wrong. The war clouds had darkened and lengthened during the months of her absence. The idle speculations had become fierce and certain storm warnings. They no longer spoke of "if" war came—now they talked of "when." They had not abandoned their efforts for peace, but preparation was being made for war. They were calling in all their chips, mobilizing all their resources. Yehuda had sighed with relief when he had received a cryptic letter from Lydia Goldfeder.

"The project we discussed on Rhodes is now completed," she had written.

Soundlessly he thanked Aaron's wife and reflected that his mission to Budapest was, at last, accomplished.

"It has been good to have Rebecca with us," Lydia had added. "Now, after all these years, we have come to know each other and we are friends."

He had been right, he knew then, to insist that Rebecca journey back to the States, that she reestablish contact with her family and with herself. It had been a calculated risk, but he and Rebecca had never shied away from dangerous odds.

They had needed the time apart. He had sensed her restlessness, the wistful regret in her voice when she spoke of family and friends, of the New York art world. It was only right that she know what it was to live the life she had once abandoned. He traced her mood in part to his own desperate weariness. He had been numbed by mourning and fatigue. He had reacted to Noam's death by undertaking too many assignments, keeping himself so busy that he would not have time to sink into the bitter depression that threatened him. He had withdrawn from Rebecca then, he knew, because he had felt himself unable to reassure her and sustain her.

They had hovered at the edge of a dangerous precipice, each claimed by a separate past, trapped by disparate fears and memories. They struggled with oddly matched bits of grief and yearning. In the heat of the desert night they lay rigid beside each other, haunted by thoughts of what might have been. She thought of autumn walks through a Vermont forest, and he remembered a clearing in Czechoslovakian woodland. More than once he saw her study Leah's painting of the maple tree that stood sentinel in the garden of her girlhood.

There had been no alternative to her leaving. He had gambled and so had she. He prayed now that the war would not come before their cards were called, their dice revealed.

The newly married couple emerged from their bungalow and smiled at him with the benign kindness that lovers bestow on those who are alone. The young bride's fair hair was damp and her skin was bright, polished by touch and caress. Her husband licked at his smile, struggled to subdue his joy. He did not want to offend Yehuda Arnon, whose wife had been in America these many months. He would never let his own wife travel so far for so long. Yehuda hurried away before they could invite him to join them for coffee.

He turned and walked to the sand crater, slatted now by the shadows of dusk. Once, he and Rebecca had slept beneath the natural fortress and watched the light of dawn turn its ocher crest the color of fading firelight. Once they had climbed to its summit and surveyed the small kingdom of their settlement. The twin Christ's-thorn trees had seemed joined from such a height, their branches ensnared and entangled. They had imagined the trees as clinging lovers who would not be parted, and they, in turn, had clung close to each other on their sandy parapet.

He stood in the protection of the crater's shade now and watched as two egrets in search of a nesting place circled its crown. Briefly they rested and then soared northward toward the Dead Sea, their white wings flashing in twinned sweep through the vinous sky. He watched them and thought it wondrous that they should move as one. He remembered the days when he had moved as one with his young American bride.

"Rebecca. Rivka," he said softly, and his heart turned with longing.

"Rebecca. Rivka," he repeated in a stronger voice that resounded in the silent twilight. He trembled with loneliness. He stood alone now, on a desert plain, yet once, in this same springtime season, he had walked with her through the fields of the Galilee and anemones had blazed in scarlet fires at their feet.

"Rivka." He whispered again because her name comforted him.

"Yehuda."

He did not turn. Surely, he had imagined her answering call, the tremulous softness of her voice. He had heard that solitude and loneliness played such cruel tricks.

"Yehuda." His name again, and then the sound of footsteps running lightly across the desert floor. Fearfully, yet not without hope, he turned, saw her moving toward him, and knew that he was not deceived. How beautiful she was, her silver-streaked black hair falling to her shoulders, her deeply inset green eyes like jewels against her topaz skin. Her arms were outstretched, and he rushed into them and encircled her in the strength of his embrace, in the fullness of his love.

"You're home," he said. "You've come home."

"Home," she repeated, and her tears seared his shoulder.

A Kfir plane, flying very low, streaked through the sky, but they did not look up. They stood as one in the shadow of the sand crater until the first stars of evening, like vagrant silver shards, lit the desert sky.

JOURNEY'S END

Sha'arei ha-Negev, 1978

SUMMER ends slowly, languorously, in Israel. Gradually, the feral heat diminishes, and often, in late afternoon, the sky darkens and a sudden rain cools the air, pelting it with rapidly falling lucent droplets. Children skip through the downpour with the fierce gaiety born of the knowledge that the season of carefree days, of hot golden hours and warm starlit evenings, will soon be over. Adults lift their faces to the falling rain and do not brush away the drops that moisten their cheeks, jewel their lashes. The old stand at their windows and watch the lovers who hover in doorways or sprint laughingly through the glittering showers.

In the countryside the grain is stacked in shining sheaves, and baled blocks of hay border the fields that lie fallow, resting and waiting. The cattle nibble at the stubbled gleanings, and flocks of terns and egrets wing their way southward to their nesting places along the Red Sea. They perch briefly on trees long since stripped of their bright fruit and sing the mournful melodies of their flight. It is the Hebrew month of Elul, when the Book of Life is inscribed, when atonement is made and accounts are closed. It is the season of solemn ending and hopeful beginning.

The tall silver-haired woman paused in her walk across the desert hillside to pull her bright blue shawl tighter about her shoulders and to shift the basket of golden dates she carried from one hand to the other.

"Are you tired, Grandma?" the dark-haired girl who walked beside her asked.

"A little." Leah smiled down at her granddaughter Shlomit. "But then an old woman has the right to get tired."

"You're not old!" Shlomit was indignant. She knew about old people. She often accompanied her mother when Mindell attended the clinic. Shlomit had seen the elderly as they sat quietly in the Golden Age room at the Ellenberg Center, unread magazines on their laps, their voices low, their faded eyes filling suddenly and inexplicably with tears. Her grandmother Leah was not like them. She was always busy, completing one project and formulating plans for another, although Shlomit had noticed that often, as now, she paused abruptly, as though to gather new strength. But still her eyes were bright, her hands quick and skillful, her laughter strong.

Old people were submissive, Shlomit knew. They moved their magazines aside and followed the aides to the lunchroom. They obediently produced color snapshots of their children and their grandchildren. Leah carried no snapshots. She needed no celluloid reminders of her children; their lives were part of her own. Shlomit's family and her aunt Lydia and uncle Aaron and their children gathered each Friday evening at Leah's Scarsdale home. She had refused to move when Grandfather Boris died. (Shlomit mourned him still. She had loved him for his wonderful stories and his sad eyes, and she had been glad that his death had been gentle. He had gone to sleep one night and had not awakened again. "I want to die like that," Shlomit had told her mother, and she had been angry when Mindell held her too tightly and would not let her go.)

"Of course I will not move," Leah had said angrily when Uncle Aaron suggested she move in with him.

And it was Leah who made the arrangements for the journey the family made together each year to Sha'arei ha-Negev. Her voice was vigorous as she arranged for tickets, assigned tasks. She was not like the old people who touched Shlomit with quivering fingers as she passed them.

"All right. So I'm not old," Leah said agreeably, and she smiled at Michael's daughter. It was not right, she knew, to have a favorite granddaughter, and yet there was something special about Shlomit. The child's eyes sparkled with warmth and she ran with a litheness and grace that reminded Leah of her sister Mollie as a young girl. Shlomit's laughter was swift and bell-like, yet often she would sit quietly, lost in a world of fantasy. Always, she had sung softly to herself—a sweet-voiced, black-haired child named for peace, a dreamer, shy and fragile.

Leah looked up. A single, smoke-colored cloud drifted across the azure sky and shadowed the sand crater. The rain, when it came, lasted only minutes, long enough to dislodge a porcupine from its sunbaked rock. The indignant animal scurried between them and they laughed. Leah's mirth lit her lined face, and Shlomit's laughter rang with startled joy.

Leah's children and grandchildren sat on the covered patio and watched them, and she, in turn, lifted her eyes as she approached Rebecca's cottage. She saw Yehuda touch Rebecca's cheek, heard Lydia laugh softly. Aaron stood between Mindell and Michael, his hands resting lightly on their shoulders. The grandchildren were clustered about the Monopoly board, Shlomit's young brothers perched on the laps of their older cousins. The sun that had so swiftly followed the rapid shower wrapped them in a circlet of light.

Leah smiled. Her children were friends to one another, and their children, in turn, laughed and played together. David would have been pleased. David. They would go together to his grave that evening—she and her children and grandchildren. But now she felt the familiar sweet fatigue that overcame her, with increasing frequency, each afternoon.

"Are you tired, Mother?" Rebecca went to meet her, frowning slightly.

"A little," Leah acknowledged. "I think I will go to the bungalow and lie down."

"You look tired also, Shlomit," Mindell said worriedly. Shlomit was recently recovered from the late summer cold that attacked her each year at the onset of school.

"Come, Shlomit. Keep your grandmother company," Leah said cajolingly as the child drifted over to the Monopoly board.

"We'll start a new game with you later," Seth promised his cousin. He shook his flame-colored curls and winked conspiratorially.

Shlomit smiled. She loved her cousin Seth. She wondered if Uncle Aaron had looked like him when he was younger. She wondered if it was all right for first cousins to marry each other.

"All right," she said.

She was tired, and it would be cool in the small room across the hall from her grandmother. The desert air conditioning moistened the air, and her mother always closed the shutters.

She took her grandmother's hand, and together they walked across the compound to the guest bungalow.

"Have a good rest, Shlomit," Leah said, and the child smiled sleepily.

Minutes later, when Leah entered the room, Shlomit lay asleep on the bed, one sandal on and one sandal off. Gently she removed the sand-caked shoe. She left the door open and returned to her own room. Afternoon naps, she thought gratefully. The luxury of the very young and the very old.

She glanced at the luminous green dial of her bedside clock and closed her eyes in sweet surrender to the kaleidoscopic dreams that teased the light sleep of daylight. She was a young girl again, dancing in the tall grass of the Russian woodlands, her dark hair garlanded with the crimson flower they had called the Blood of Russia. Yet suddenly she wept and hurried toward the shelter of a lombardy tree. The tree's trunk opened and became a ship. Sea spray kissed her face, its saline moisture matching the tears that filled her eyes. "Leah." David called her name in a voice so gentle it broke her heart. "Mama." The baby Aaron clutched her skirt. Children's laughter. Rebecca the girl, Michael the child, hurtling toward her across a sun-dappled lawn. "My Leah." A man's voice, tense with anguish, with desire. Eli. Her long-ago lover lost in flames. How they had licked toward her that long ago Friday, a city day of desert heat.

She writhed in her sleep.

She remembered those flames, those fiery golden tongues, the smoke that darkened and poisoned the air, searing her throat, weighting her limbs. She screamed but no sound came—a dream-bound cry that thrust her into wakefulness.

She struggled to open her eyes—why did they burn and smart so?—to look at the bright green numerals of her clock. She jerked forward. She could not see them. They were obscured by the spiraling smoke that filled her small room.

"Grandma!" Shlomit's voice, trembling with terror, pierced the wall. "Help me, Grandma."

"I'm coming." Her voice rasping, unfamiliar.

She struggled through the smoke and flung open the door. Flames danced in the narrow corridor that separated the two rooms. Rivulets of fire flowed into a great incandescent wave. She plunged through it, felt the fire singe her hair, smelled her own charred flesh. Still she rushed to the child's bed, wrapped her in the blanket.

"It's all right, Shlomit. I'm here."

The small girl was heavy in her arms, her sweet-singing grandchild named for peace. Again she passed through that rush of flame, staggering beneath the child's weight, her head down, her eyes closed lest the bright scarlet and golden wavelets blind her. The door to the guesthouse was open; she glimpsed the clear air outside and labored toward it. Her breath and strength ebbed. The child sobbed; her hot tears seared Leah's cheeks. There were inches to go, but she saw them as miles; each small step exhausted her. Somewhere an alarm sounded and screams pierced the air.

"Mama!" Rebecca's voice strident with terror.

"Shlomit!" Michael calling with desperation to his daughter.

Once before she had been imprisoned by gates of flame. Memory surged forth, memory mined from dream.

"Jump, Leah!" Eli had shouted at her. "Jump!" He had kissed her on the lips and thrust her forward. Now, as if in a trance, she kissed Shlomit on the lips and thrust her toward that open door, toward that clear air.

"I have her!"

Michael lurched forward and Leah saw with joy that he held his daughter. Shlomit was safe.

Painfully now, she edged forward, fighting the great heaviness that had settled on her. Pain and fatigue slowed her steps and each breath was a labored effort. It would be so easy, she thought, to lean back. Perhaps the columns of flame would support her. Their phosphorescent light teased and beckoned. Still, she resisted and struggled on. One more step. Two. She gained the doorway and paused. She wondered why it was that Rebecca clung to Yehuda—why Aaron and Lydia wept as they rushed toward her.

"It's all right," she said. *Aaron. Rebecca. Michael.* Soundlessly her lips formed their names. "It's all right."

Slowly then, she stepped out of the embrasure of flames, swayed and fell onto the soft and fragrant grass. They knelt beside her—Rebecca's cheek upon her own, Michael's face against her hair, Aaron's hand upon her wrist.

"Mama." Aaron's voice caressed the word; but a last, gentle smile played upon her lips and her children knew that she would not answer them again. She had, at last, reached journey's end.

More Bestselling Books From Jove!

___ **YEARS** 08489-1/$3.95
LaVyrle Spencer

___ **PASSIONS** 08103-5/$3.50
Lillian Africano

___ **COMPROMISING POSITIONS** 08552-9/$3.95
Susan Isaacs

___ **MEMORIES AND ASHES** 08325-9/$3.95
Kathryn Davis

___ **NOT SO WILD A DREAM** 07982-0/$3.95
Francine Rivers

___ **SABLE** 08125-5/$3.95
Ellen Tanner Marsh

___ **FLAWLESS** 08246-5/$3.95
Burt Hirschfeld

___ **THE WOMEN'S ROOM** 08488-3/$4.95
Marilyn French

___ **LEAH'S CHILDREN** 08584-7/$3.95
Gloria Goldreich

___ **SEDUCTIONS** 08576-6/$3.95
Georgia Hampton

___ **LIVING WITH THE KENNEDYS: The Joan Kennedy Story** 08699-1/$3.95
Marcia Chellis

Available at your local bookstore or return this form to:

JOVE
THE BERKLEY PUBLISHING GROUP, Dept. B
390 Murray Hill Parkway, East Rutherford, NJ 07073

Please send me the titles checked above. I enclose ______. Include $1.00 for postage and handling if one book is ordered; 25¢ per book for two or more not to exceed $1.75. California, Illinois, New Jersey and Tennessee residents please add sales tax. Prices subject to change without notice and may be higher in Canada.

NAME ______________________________

ADDRESS ______________________________

CITY ______________ STATE/ZIP ______________

(Allow six weeks for delivery.)